THE SAPPHIRE SOUL

ELDRITCH HEART BOOK 3

MATTHEW S. COX

DIVISION ZERO PRESS

ISBN (ebook): 978-1-950738-28-1

ISBN (paperback): 978-1-950738-29-8

CONTENTS

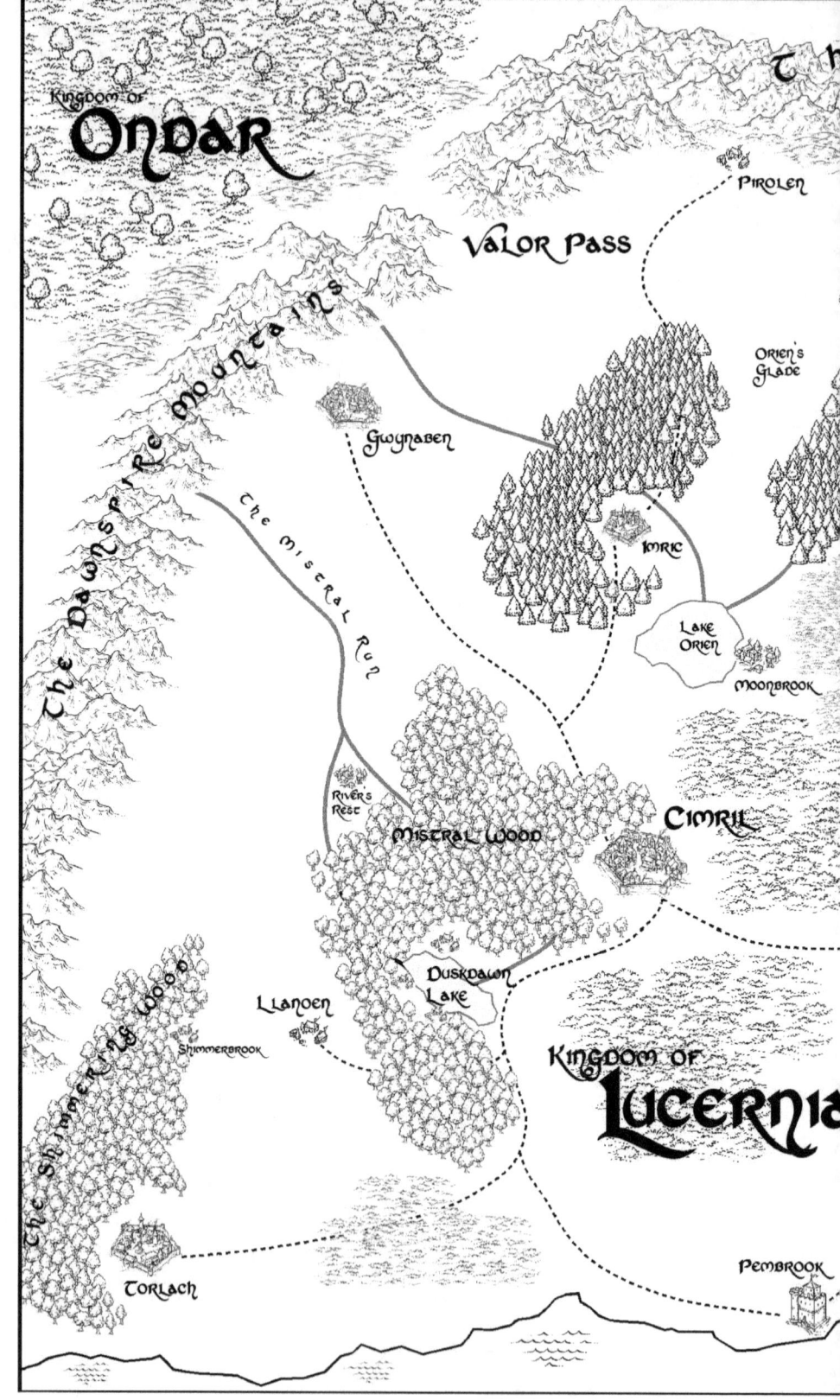

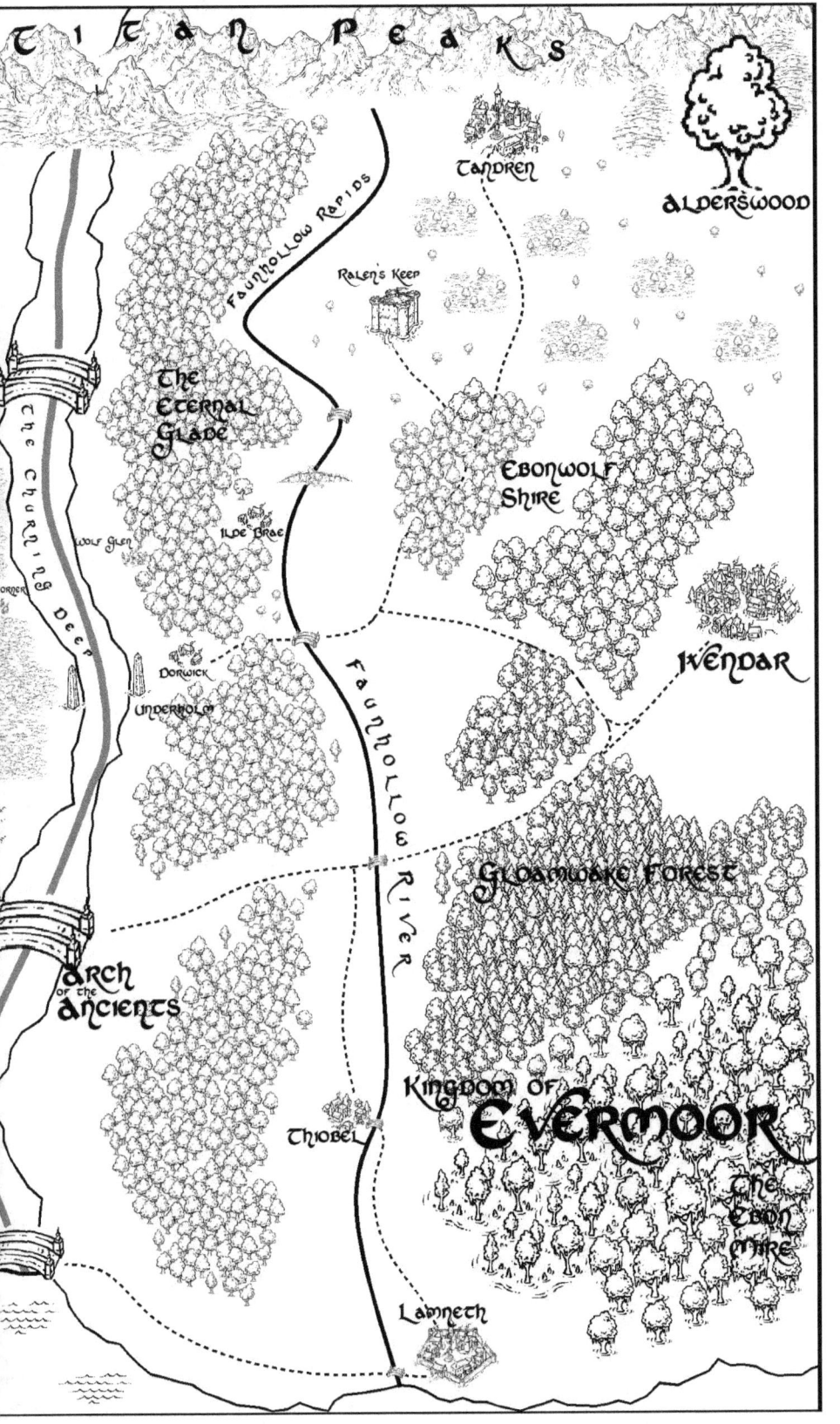

THE HUNT FOR FAERIES

OONA

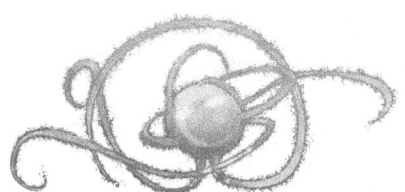

*P*eaceful moments occurred far less often than Oona would have liked, despite the war being over.

The days no longer brought one distressing report after another, made worse by the ever-present fear of assassins. War and all its intolerable misery receded from reality to the ceaseless discussions of scholars trying to understand how it happened. The same elders who for so long believed beyond doubt Oona would lead an army to destroy the neighboring kingdom of Evermoor now quibbled about 'meanings.' How had they all come to misunderstand The Foretelling so wildly? What did it mean the former king and high priest of Lucen—the god of purity and truth—lied for so long without divine consequence?

They kept asking *why* so many people had to suffer and die before it all stopped. Where had the gods been and why hadn't they intervened?

Learning about Evermoor opened Oona's mind to an uncomfortable truth. The four gods of Lucernia she once regarded as the only powers in the entire world did not possess limitless authority. Evermoor's people revered nature spirits and manifestations of animal aspects—not demons as she'd been told most of her life. Citizens of Ondar worshiped an entirely different pantheon. Lucen, Navissa, Orien, and Tenebrea *were* gods, but as with all deities, they could do only so much.

Whether the betrayal by the former king weakened Lucen, sent him into a state of sadness, or angered him enough to let the war grind on, Oona didn't know. She dared not ask the gods why they chose to do, or not do, anything. As much as it pained her to look into the faces of all the orphans and all the people who had lost husbands, wives, sons, and daughters, she had to trust in the gods' wisdom.

For reasons she couldn't begin to understand—nor did she question—the gods had taken particular notice of her. She'd always enjoyed a kinship of sorts with Tenebrea, the Goddess of Death, youngest child of Lucen and Navissa. People tended to shun her, averting their eyes from any statues or temples of her, refusing to speak her name, not wanting others to believe they acted too comfortable around her. While no members of any temple specifically stated so, Oona suspected the young goddess felt like an outcast. Depictions of her varied, showing her as a young woman anywhere from fourteen to sixteen years of age despite being centuries old.

Oona, being sixteen, knew how she must feel... as much as any mortal might know the mind of a deity. Only, she hadn't possessed the courage to admit to society *why* they would shun her, pretending to be like everyone else. Lucen's priesthood had, for many decades, taught that love between two women or two men was impure. None ever really justified exactly what made it impure, merely claimed it so. She'd spent years keeping her secret love for Kitlyn to herself, terrified of being ostracized, attacked, or even killed as a heretic.

King Aodh Talomir had many flaws, but in spite of them, he defied the temple, issuing a brazen challenge to Lucen himself to speak if he disapproved of their love.

Remembering the moment made Oona blush. It had been a shock to hear him talk in such a manner. Whether or not he'd ever considered love between two women wrong, she didn't know. He might have, only changing his mind upon realizing his daughter had such love—then challenging tradition to ask the gods themselves for an answer. He didn't challenge Lucen as much as asked him to send a message. However, after twenty years of ignoring Lucen's teachings, he had little chance of being heard.

But Tenebrea sent a message.

Perhaps due to a clear sign of approval from the Goddess of Death, the citizenry of Lucernia had largely kept their disapproval of two young women marrying confined to the occasional disdainful glare from afar. However, the reaction proved far less harsh than expected. After so much war, the people viewed Oona and Kitlyn as heroes. They'd not only made peace with Evermoor, but Kitlyn had openly defied her father, exposing his treachery.

Neither wanted to be queen, but the kingdom needed them.

Orien, the god of life and strength, also saw fit to bless Oona with a healing gift in a moment most dire. She still sometimes saw Kitlyn bleeding from the neck in her dreams, at the edge of death. Each time, she'd wake up to find her alive and safe in bed beside her.

Having both Lucen and Orien gift her their magic, plus Tenebrea's close attention, humbled her.

On most days she didn't need to be at the castle, she'd visit the Orien temple assisting the healers or helping summon food for the needy. Average citizens adored how she walked among them without excessive pageantry or even caring if anyone noticed her. The nobility largely considered her the 'peasant queen' in whispers, aghast she'd be seen in public in 'ordinary' garments.

Even in peace time, the life of a queen turned out to be far busier than she'd ever expected. Granted, the former king, the man she'd spent most of her life thinking of as her father, rarely left the castle. He might have been fearful, knowing Lucen's magic abandoned him for his treachery, or merely arrogant, lazy, and elitist. Whatever the reason he hid from the people, it no longer mattered. She would not be a distant ruler who ignored the people. If fate decreed she and Kitlyn would be queens, they would do so as best they could.

But every so often, Oona needed a day like today.

Summer would soon give way to autumn, so she wanted to feel the grass upon her bare feet before the days became too cold. She lay in the castle garden beside Kitlyn, gazing up past green-shrouded tree branches at the sky. A pleasant breeze carried the scent of flowers, changing leaves, and the dampness of mossy earth.

One thought intruded on her solace, threatening the joy the garden brought her. History spoke grim tidings of the Talomir line. Except for one person, Lady Avalina, no descendant of the family lived into old age. Many suspected she only survived to eighty-six due to refusing the crown upon the death of her older brother. Fear the same curse would claim Kitlyn's life often came out of nowhere.

Oona didn't make requests of the gods lightly, but she prayed to Tenebrea at least once a week to either protect Kitlyn or welcome them both into her realm at the same time. Thus far, the only answer she received had been a momentary feeling of reassurance. Given the fear would invariably creep back into her mind at a later time, she suspected the brief reprieve from dread meant the goddess wanted her to be patient and would help when needed.

Working feverishly to help the people in Cimril kept her mind occupied and away from worry on most days. The castle city, capital of Lucernia, already showed signs of a more prosperous future. A few traders from Evermoor had already risked the journey, unsure how the citizens of a nation they'd warred with for two decades would receive them.

Thankfully, almost everyone in both kingdoms laid the blame on the former king. However, his guilt and duplicity made a handful of citizens, especially the nobles, worry his daughter couldn't be trusted. The wealthy viewed Kitlyn with unease for the same reason the majority of citizens adored her—she'd grown up ostensibly poor, without the attitude, expectations, or mannerisms of a royal daughter.

Oona had all of those, having unknowingly played a decoy princess. Out of guilt from dangling her as bait for assassins, King Aodh spoiled her. However, her roots came from a poor family in a small farming village. People viewed them both as queens in touch with the ordinary citizen. A few nobles occasionally referred even to Kitlyn as a 'peasant queen' in spite of her bloodline being legitimate. To protect his daughter from the enemy, the king made her live as the lowliest of servants, not even telling her who she really was.

A scowl curled Oona's lip at the thought. It vexed her to think of him as it unfurled a complicated mess of emotions. She'd loved him like a father, yet he'd been responsible for *so* much suffering. Gradually, she'd come to accept his death had likely been for the best, even if she still missed him.

"What are you thinking?" asked Oona, eager to shift her mind to happier topics.

Kitlyn stretched her arms out over her head. "Wondering what the birds are saying to each other."

They lay in silence, listening to tweets and trills for a moment. Birdsong filled the air, but none of the little creatures showed themselves.

"Do you think they speak like we do?" She gazed around at the branches.

"Hmm." Kitlyn shifted closer, resting her head on Oona's shoulder. "I am still attempting to figure it out."

Oona laughed.

Kitlyn reached over to trace a finger across her chin.

"It's so peaceful here." Oona, her eyes half-lidded, leaned into a gentle kiss.

The instant their lips met, a burst of warmth spread over Oona's chest, forcing out the bad thoughts and worries. Her wife's gentle touch created an entirely different emotion than what welled up within Oona behind closed doors. Here, out in the garden, she basked in an overwhelming sense of love and serenity. Simply being with Kitlyn made her want time to stop in place and never move forward.

Alas, the kiss ended far too soon, but Kitlyn's dark emerald green eyes inches from hers soothed her disappointment.

Kitlyn teased at her hair. "What are you thinking now?"

"I don't remember ever being this happy ever before." Oona whistled back at the birds.

An impish smile formed on her wife's face. "Happier now than when you saw me upon Omun's back riding toward you?"

Oona stared straight up at the sky, giving a pretend-annoyed huff. "Much different. I'd thought you dead. This is... peaceful. I want to stay here with you for days, would that no one disturbs us."

"Fauhurst certainly won't," deadpanned Kitlyn.

"True." Oona pointed straight up, struggling to contain a laugh. As cruel as the man had been to Kitlyn, finding humor or pleasure at his spending the rest of his life in prison seemed wrong, even if he did try to kill them. "I do not wish to waste any more of my life thinking of him."

Kitlyn brushed a hand at Oona's hair. "Then we shan't."

"I'm sorry."

"For?"

"I was such a fool, not telling you how I felt for so long."

Kitlyn swished her feet back and forth. "I'm guilty of the same. We've forgiven each other, but if you wish to torment yourself over an unchangeable past... don't. Instead, imagine the nobility finding us laying here on the ground in such common attire."

Oona snickered. They both wore a similar sort of basic dress without frill, looking much like a pair of merchants' daughters. The nobility would most assuredly gasp in shock, not only for the queens in such *ordinary* clothes, but also sprawled out on the grass.

She couldn't bring herself to care what they thought of her anymore.

Kitlyn smoothed her hands down the lush green fabric covering her stomach. "I am quite fond of this material. Fonder still of being able to breathe in it."

"I know, my love."

"Perhaps I shall wear this one to court."

Oona pretended to clutch her chest and have a spell, emitting the same stuttering gasp Lady Parrington did the first time she noticed Kitlyn not wearing shoes while on the throne.

Once their laughter ebbed, Kitlyn fussed at Oona's hair. "It's so long. Do you still want me to let mine grow again?"

"It is your hair, so do whatever you like. But I do miss seeing you with it long."

"You don't think it will make me look like a child?"

Oona squeezed her hands in vexation at how Kitlyn had been forced to work as a castle servant from age twelve. She'd cut her hair to shoulder length, so it didn't get in the way. As poorly as she'd been treated, no amount of anger could change the past. *I am no longer a spoiled little princess.* She rested her head on Kitlyn's shoulder and let her anger melt away. "No. I think you will look beautiful. But you'd look beautiful no matter the length of your hair. You'd look beautiful covered in mud."

Kitlyn laughed loud and sudden, a noise like a startled chicken quieting the birds. "No one is beautiful covered in mud."

"You would be."

"I suspect you would as well."

Oona raised an eyebrow. "Suspect?"

Kitlyn playfully bit her lip.

"We could conduct an experiment. For scientific purposes, of course." She pointed off to the right. "The pond has mud."

"I don't want to ruin this dress. It's comfortable."

Oona examined her fingernails. "Who said anything about wearing a dress at the time?"

"In the castle garden?" whispered Kitlyn. "Dare we?"

"It isn't as if Fauhurst will catch us."

Kitlyn's face reddened, though she appeared to be considering the idea.

"It would be more a scandal if we held court in these plain dresses than if someone caught us in the lake. Though, I suppose it would depend on what exactly we were doing when caught. They wouldn't care if we'd simply gone for a swim."

"I am thinking we might dare to—" High-pitched giggling came from the dense bushes to the left along the garden path. Kitlyn feigned a frustrated grimace. "Do nothing at this time."

"Hah!" Oona covered her mouth to hold in laughter.

Evie and Pim appeared at a bend in the path, the children racing around a fat, rounded bush almost twice their height. Oona's six-year-old sister held her pink dress up so she could sprint, her long, blonde hair streaming behind her like a cape. Pim, the head cook's eight-year-old son, ran beside her, neither lagging behind nor pulling ahead. His well-worn brown tunic made the difference in station to his new friend visually obvious, though neither child cared.

Exactly like us at the same age. Oona smiled wistfully.

"Nothing in Lucernia has as much energy as a child released from their tutor," said Kitlyn.

The kids scrambled over and flopped on the grass nearby, Evie all but jumping on top of Oona. While she burst into rapid chatter about what she learned today, Pim sat patiently, smudging at a jelly stain on his tunic.

Kitlyn spent a little while entertaining the kids, using her magic to levitate small rocks into the shapes of various animals both real and imaginary, like dragons. Oona made a bird out of blue light—a little trick she'd been practicing but never did in front of the children before—earning a squeal of delight from Evie and awestruck silence from Pim.

"We're going to look for faeries today," chirped Evie. "Pim says he saw one last night."

"I did." The boy thrust his arms out to either side. "In the yard where you used ta wash clothes."

"Oh, you did, hmm?" Kitlyn folded her arms, making the same suspicious face at him she used whenever one of the nobles complained about something—though with much more of a smile.

Pim pointed to the side. "Honest. She flew into the garden."

Oona blinked at him, astonished the boy spoke truth. Lucen's gift revealed when someone lied—however, only to the veracity of the person speaking. The boy truly believed he'd seen a faerie, regardless of what he'd actually observed. Her gift only revealed deliberate lies, lacking the power to draw unknown truths out of thin air. Kitlyn could not claim to definitely be cursed and have Oona reveal the truth of it, since neither of them knew for certain.

"I know they're real." Evie leapt to her feet. "They're in so many books."

Kitlyn chuckled. "Something being written about in a book doesn't mean it's true. Do you think Grengwylf is real?"

Pim bit his lip, suggesting he might. Evie shook her head rapidly while laughing, making her hair whip back and forth.

Oona tried not to blush too much. At Evie's age, she'd believed the faerie tale monster who stole children out of their rooms at night was real. She'd never admit to anyone—except Kitlyn, and only then if asked—but she'd still had nightmares about him as recently as age thirteen. *I feel so foolish now. The whole castle thought me a selfish brat. I really had been an overgrown child.*

"They're real because I saw one." Pim bounced on his toes. "They have'ta be in the garden."

"Can we go look for them?" asked Evie, hands clasped in front of her.

"All right." Oona nodded once at her. "Don't go too close to the pond unless we're there."

"We won't." Evie hugged her.

The kids darted off down the path, soon disappearing into the foliage.

Kitlyn glanced at her.

"He believes he saw one," said Oona.

"Do you think they exist?"

Oona lay back down, gazing up at the branches. "I used to be as convinced as Evie."

"Not anymore?"

"Don't they seem a flight of fancy?"

Kitlyn twirled a lock of black hair around her finger. "More so a flight of fancy than Omun?"

"*You* believe in faeries?" Oona blinked.

"Why not? We're still children." Kitlyn smirked, poking fun at some of the nobility who didn't trust them to run the kingdom. Of course, the same nobility had no complaints about Aodh wearing the crown at age eleven.

Oona covered her mouth to muffle laughter.

"Honestly? I think they probably were real, but aren't around anymore. Like the Anthari." Kitlyn breathed a somber sigh while reclining next to her. "I didn't think the elves existed at all until we went to Evermoor."

"Yes. Difficult to argue after seeing Ivendar." Oona whistled to herself, her thoughts roaming back to the strange architecture.

"Could the faeries have gone away to wherever the Anthari went? They are basically tiny elves."

"With wings."

"Of course. If you're stuck being five inches tall, you'd need wings or it would take a month to walk anywhere."

Kitlyn grinned, rambling about all the ways being so small would make life difficult. Oona countered by pointing out advantages each time. When Kitlyn said they couldn't work doorknobs, Oona mentioned they could slip under the doors. They went back and forth until running out of ideas, then theorized about the possible fate of the Anthari. The castle library didn't contain many books about them, certainly none offering any clue as to what happened, so they made up guesses. At Kitlyn musing about them fleeing a long-ago war, Oona's thoughts turned somber again.

A few wealthy people had wanted assurances any war orphans they took in would not compete with their natural children for inheritance. The arrogance made her frown. She didn't approve of their focus on money, but sensed no desire to mistreat the children, so didn't object. A large number of war orphans had found homes in the preceding months, though many remained at the temple. Thankfully, Orien provided. The priests never needed to worry about feeding anyone.

She smiled, staring at Kitlyn's face while she spun theory after theory about faeries, elves, and other creatures described in books everyone considered made up. Watching her dearest friend turned wife lose herself in such idle flights of fancy brought on an unexpected pang of worry.

Evie and Pim played happily in the distance. Kitlyn smiled, no trace of frustration, anger, or sorrow in her eyes at all. Everything about this moment terrified her for being too perfect.

No sooner did worry about the curse rise like a formless black wraith in the back of her mind, a heavy sense of guilt crashed onto her shoulders. The two of them, and anyone to sit on the throne of Lucernia, deserved to die for what they did.

Oona sat up abruptly, clamping a hand to her chest and gasping.

"Oo?" Kitlyn sat up as well, grasping her shoulder. "What's wrong?"

The bizarre emotion faded fast, escaping on a breath. It no longer felt like they personally deserved a cruel death, but someone else had done something horrible. *The gods are trying to tell me something.*

"Oo?" Kitlyn gave her a light shake.

"I'm…" She grasped Kitlyn's hand. "The strangest sense of guilt came out of nowhere all of a sudden. It felt as if we—I mean the kingdom, not us—is somehow at fault."

"For…?"

"I don't know." Oona leaned against her. "I worried something might happen to you bec—"

"As you always do, love."

Oona hung her head. "As I always do, yes. We're so happy right now, it made me afraid something would ruin it."

"We have to stop thinking such things or we will never be truly happy."

Oona pulled her hair off her face. "I was truly happy for a bit there. It just ended."

Kitlyn stuck out her tongue. "Well, stop being sad."

"I'm not sad. I'm scared." Oona poked her in the side. "There is a difference. And no, this is not me being me."

"A message from the gods because you are so in tune. Or you're so sweet it makes you sad to think about the idea bad things can and do happen."

Oona fake pouted. "I suspect that is part of it. I admit to being sad at the idea you will succumb to the curse."

"This again? Didn't we determine it's rubbish? The previous rulers all did horrible things."

"Branok wore the crown for a single week. He was seventeen," said Oona.

"Might have been a nasty sort of person. There are no records of how he acted. A week is still enough time for a king to cause harm."

"Sadly. I fear the danger may be real."

Kitlyn put an arm around her. "What do we need to do?"

Oona let all her air out, took another breath, and sighed again. "I don't know."

They stared at each other for a few minutes before weak smiles grew to real ones.

"It's so peaceful here," whispered Kitlyn.

"Yes." Oona listened to the birdsong—and lack of children's voices. "Too peaceful."

"How can it be too peaceful?"

Oona scrambled to her feet. "I don't hear Evie and Pim."

"Eep!" Kitlyn jumped upright.

Gripped by panic, Oona ran down the trail in the direction the kids had gone over an hour ago, calling after them. Kitlyn veered left, following a different fork in the trail. Oona searched frantically around among the flower bushes, statues, trees, and shrubs. Minutes later, she still hadn't spotted any sign of the children when Kitlyn emerged from the woods where the footpaths joined. They stood there in worried silence, staring at each other.

A child's whisper came from behind Oona, off the trail on the right. "Do you see any more?"

"Looking," replied Pim.

Tentative relief eased Oona's panic. She spun to face the direction of the voices and cringed somewhat at the thickness of the bushes and trees. The corner of the garden opposite the large pond held a particularly dense copse of trees and old thorn bushes long since dead, resulting in a near impassible tangle of brown wooden vines wrapped around stout, gnarled trees. Not even the groundskeepers bothered trying to hack their way in to clean it up.

"They've gone in there," whispered Oona, a faint bit of remembered worry from childhood making her voice uneasy.

Kitlyn embraced her from behind. "You don't still believe Miss Harper's nasty stories about the wood-witch, do you?"

"Believe? No. Remember? Yes." Oona huffed a determined sigh, again grateful to Kitlyn for insisting on the simpler dresses.

They walked down the footpath, passing in front of the massive tangle of dead bushes. Upon spotting a clear child's footprint in the dirt, Kitlyn lay down on her stomach to peer under the plants. Oona got down beside her, also trying to see into the dead area. One of the larger trees creaked in response to a sudden uptick in the breeze. Expecting the wood-witch, Oona jumped, startled.

Feeling somewhat foolish for being so jumpy, she blushed.

Kitlyn tried to stop herself from smiling, but couldn't quite do it.

A few-inch-high gap under the bushes gave Oona a view of a small area of open dirt in front of a great tree at the deepest part of the dead corner—but no sign of children. It didn't seem possible for a child, even one as small as Evie, to wriggle in there, at least not without losing most of her dress—and some skin—to thorns. In odd defiance of the dead state of the vegetation, a sweet floral smell hung in the air. A few little violet flowers sprouted up from the dirt among the gnarled roots, but certainly not enough to give off such a strong aroma.

Something does not feel natural here.

A giggle came from her left. Oona glanced toward it, spotting Evie and Pim kneeling in the live bushes on the opposite side of the trail from the dead corner. She scrambled to her feet and hurried over to them, Kitlyn trailing after.

They found Evie and Pim kneeling on either side of a patch of dirt, studying it. Tiny leaves and forest detritus decorated their disheveled hair and clung to their clothing. Both children looked as if they'd gone tumbling down a long hill of hedgerows. Oona pushed the bushes aside, the crunch making the kids jump and look back at her.

"Why didn't you answer us?" rasped Oona.

"Answer you?" asked Evie, all innocence.

"We've been shouting for you for some time." Kitlyn walked up beside Oona.

Pim made an 'uh oh' face. "We didn't hear you."

Oona furrowed her brow. Despite the size of the garden, she didn't think it so big a person couldn't hear shouting even from all the way across. Still, neither child lied as far as Lucen's gift told her. Perhaps they'd been so focused on their hunt for faeries, they'd simply not noticed—or something unexplainable had occurred.

Relieved to find them in good health, she decided to forgive them for not responding.

Pim pointed at the ground. "We found a faerie."

"Not really." Evie folded her arms. "Just footprints. Pim says he saw one."

"I did." He beamed.

Oona knelt between them, putting an arm around each child. A row of minuscule footprints traced a line in the patch of dirt between the kids. The tracks started abruptly, took twenty-six steps, and stopped—almost like a tiny flying person landed, walked a short distance and took off again. The direction of the trail went directly toward the impassable dead bramble in the corner.

"Is that?" Kitlyn took a knee. "A rat walking on two legs?"

"No. Is a faerie," said Pim.

"Those don't look like rat tracks." Oona leaned closer, holding her hair back so it didn't fall in the way. The indentations in the dirt resembled slender human feet, only smaller than her thumbprint.

"You saw an actual faerie?" Kitlyn gazed up into the tree. "No one has been back here for a very long time."

"Almost." Pim frowned. "At first, I thought we saw a bird, but it made light. Flew really fast."

Oona looked at Kitlyn, mouth open. "Do you think?"

"You've met Omun... is it terribly strange to consider faeries exist?" Kitlyn smiled.

For one brief moment, Oona felt like a little kid all over again and let off a squeal of delight—that Evie promptly echoed. She gazed around in hopeful awe. *Have they been hiding in this corner?*

"I do so loathe being the adult in the garden," said Kitlyn. "But it shall soon be time for supper. We should return to the castle."

Oona stood with a sigh and took Evie's hand. "Yes. Come along, you both need to clean up before we eat. You're covered in leaves and mess."

The children laughed. Evie shook her hair out to rid it of leaf bits and grass.

2

A VISITOR MOST UNEXPECTED

KITLYN

*C*ertain she dreamed of being in a strange forest, Kitlyn decided to see where the path led.

She saw from the eyes of someone else, a woman with skin the color of tree bark, dressed in a light leather tunic and knee-length skirt. Somehow, the armor felt lighter than it ought to have, and moved like fabric. Barefoot, she stole through the woods, following the sensation of the Stone revealing distant heavy footsteps of clumsy outsiders crushing everything in their path. This woman seemed torn between fighting the invaders or doing what she'd been asked and hurrying to deliver a scroll. She hated the message, infuriated and saddened at the contents… but clung to her duty.

She knew she would never again see her home.

Kitlyn's eyes opened to the richly detailed ceiling of the royal bedchamber in Castle Cimril. Gold patterning decorated burgundy, around the edges of domed squares. A faint honey-floral scent, the soap Oona had used on her hair last night, filled the room.

Bedding covered only her lower half, but Oona's voluminous hair draped across her chest lessened the chill. Her wife snuggled close at her side, content and asleep. Kitlyn lifted her head, peering down at herself. Though she felt thin compared to most people, the dream figure had been more so, moving with such grace among the trees she seemed to be more flying than running. She couldn't have been a faerie as the world around her looked normal in scale.

People in the upper two-thirds of Evermoor had brownish skin as well, but not the same. This dream woman could have stood beside a tree and all but disappeared. Perhaps her coloration came from magic or paint? Kitlyn recognized the way the Stone revealed other people nearby. She possessed the same magic as whoever she'd dreamed about.

She lay awake for a while attempting to make sense of it. Had the Alderswood sent her an old memory or did it all come from her imagination? Eventually, the same discomfort responsible for her being awake forced her to disentangle herself from Oona and slip out of bed. She had, perhaps, consumed too much wine and water with dinner.

After pulling on a nightgown, Kitlyn padded across the royal bedchamber and dragged open the ponderous door. The garderobe sat all the way at the end of the hall, presumably to ensure no unpleasant smells reached the place where the king and queen—or queens—slept. It made for an annoying walk in the middle of the night, especially with such a full bladder.

With the war over, I should no longer need to fear assassins startling the mess straight out of me.

As much as she downplayed Oona's fears about the curse on the Talomir line, she couldn't ignore dread entirely. Lady Avalina avoided it by refusing the crown. Life as a servant girl had been miserable, but despite being the king's true daughter, she hadn't been at risk from the curse then. Of course, she didn't have the same option as Avalina—no younger brother to defer the crown to.

The two of them could have run off as soon as the priests warned her they planned to declare Aodh apostate. However, if they'd abdicated the throne, Lucernia would surely have fallen to chaos at the sudden absence of a ruler so soon after the end of such a devastating war. Kitlyn had no doubts the noble families would have torn each other—and the nation—apart in a struggle for power. Lucernia may well have broken apart into separate tiny kingdoms, divided by the landholdings of the nobles. How many more would have died over border disputes?

Aodh Talomir had subtly taught her the basics of how to govern, mostly by insisting she dust shelves or be present in the war or throne rooms during important discussions, but she still felt woefully unprepared. Perhaps it had been naïve of her to expect Aodh might continue ruling after the war ended, leaving her and Oona to their own devices. A man guilty of such horrid things had to face consequences.

Upon reaching the garderobe, she hurriedly took a seat and buried her face in her hands. There in the quiet privacy of the tiny chamber, she surrendered to a moment of feeling frightened and small. Barely halfway through her sixteenth year and the weight of an entire nation sat on her back. In most respects, citizens of Lucernia would consider a girl her age more or less an adult. However, she doubted any would voluntarily give the crown to someone so young. If not for the rules of hereditary ascension, the people would undoubtedly prefer an older, wiser leader.

She worried her inexperience would lead to an error and hurt people. To go from scrubbing floors to queen in such a short amount of time made it all seem unreal. Any day now, she'd wake up in her little closet of a bedroom to discover all of it had been a dream. Whenever Oona jokingly suggested they run off together into the forest and never return, it tempted her far more than she'd ever admit. The idea of having no cares or worries, merely all day to spend with Oona like they'd enjoyed as children provided a romantic, yet impossible distraction.

If nothing else, she'd inherited her father's stubborn streak and refused to give up. Kitlyn had thus far hidden her doubts and insecurities from everyone, especially Oona. Her wife was so sweet and loving—and at times delicate—she feared what would happen if she didn't appear to be in control, a stone pillar for Oona to cling to.

She's changed.

Kitlyn raked her fingers through her hair, thinking of how different Oona acted after they'd returned from Evermoor. The notion of her screaming at people for leaving the wrong hairbrush out for her to use sounded so ridiculous now, but had been true six months ago. Seeing Oona transform so rapidly from the kind of girl who shrieked at mice and spiders to a young woman capable of staring down a demon also made everything feel dreamlike.

It didn't matter if she liked or disliked being queen, she'd ended up on the throne. If the curse came for her life, so be it. She feared mostly the effect her death would have on Oona as well as the citizens. Many times, it seemed as if only she and Oona stood between the nobility and the people. Tradition—having a monarch—kept their greed at bay. While she wanted to spread power from a total monarchy to something of a council, too much change too fast would destroy tradition and give the nobles an opening they must secretly crave.

They've all given up scorning us far too quickly. What game are they playing?

Perhaps in light of Tenebrea's public acceptance of their love for each other, the nobles feared reprisal. More likely, they knew the end of the war and the unusual wedding had made them something of darlings in the eyes of many. Attacking them for who they loved would seem an obvious, shallow ploy. No, the nobles bided their time, waiting for any small political error they could exploit.

Balancing power between the throne and a council of senators—or some such thing—would make it easier to replace a monarch or continue in the absence of one. Push it further, and the queen or king would become a figurehead rather than a true leader. The more people involved in ruling, the greater the chance of corruption—but also the less likely a *bad* monarch could hurt people. Conversely, a good monarch might face challenge from corrupt senators.

Not now... too soon. The people need stability.

Kitlyn took in a deep breath and stilled her nerves.

I cannot continue to hide anything from Oona. She is my wife. I must confide my fears in her.

Upon exiting the garderobe, Kitlyn stopped short, one foot in the hall, aware of an unusual presence in the air. Half hidden behind the door, she stared down the corridor. Darkness concealed the grey stone walls, hanging tapestries, small tables bearing vases, and...

something else. The marble beneath her left foot chilled her toes while the stone floor inside the garderobe remained warmer — despite the window and hole to the outside.

While the castle could become quite chilly at night, even in summer, it had abruptly become colder in the span of a few minutes. Kitlyn eased herself out into the hall and shut the door behind her, making as little noise as possible. Her breath appeared in puffs of fog. Given the relative calm lately, she'd gotten out of the habit of carrying a sword around all the time in the castle. However, she doubted a blade would be of much use against whatever entity lurked in the darkness ahead.

Nervous, but not quite afraid, Kitlyn proceeded forward. As a child, she'd never been afraid of the dark, but this went beyond a simple lack of light. *Something* had come to Castle Cimril. Her need to rush back to Oona consisted mostly of the desire to protect her, but she also felt much safer in her company.

The idea they both sometimes felt like frightened children running to each other seeking a protector almost made her laugh. It sounded so thoroughly silly for her to be afraid of a creepy energy in the air. Kitlyn's magic could tear the whole castle apart... but it didn't bother demons too much. A flying rock, even one shrouded in magic, was still a physical attack — which creatures from the Pit tended to laugh at.

Step by step, Kitlyn crept along the frigid corridor, alert for anything jumping out at her. She couldn't remember the castle ever being so quiet. Despite wanting to run back to her bedchamber as fast as she could go, she resisted the urge. Surely, as soon as she let her guard down, *it* would strike out at her. She eyed every tapestry wondering if it concealed the strange entity. All the shadows appeared darker, colder, and aware of her staring into them.

Upon hearing faint whispers coming from the door to the library, she stopped short.

Kitlyn clenched her fists, let the rush of fear pass over her, then listened. Rather than the shadows themselves, the whispers belonged to three separate voices. One had a fearful tone, another insistent, a third repeatedly shushing the other two. All three sounded young.

The innocence in the voices lessened the unearthly otherness in the corridor, allowing her to brush the unnerving mood in the corridor aside as a product of her anxious mind.

She eased the library door open, trying not to startle whoever might be inside. Her caution resulted in a suitably spooky creak. Three frightened gasps came from deep within the room. Though she saw no one in immediate view, the supernatural dread no longer gnawed at her. The voices sounded too ordinary and quite alive. She stood in the doorway, surveying the large chamber. Tall bookshelves created something of a maze, offering plenty of spots for people to hide. She and Oona had often exploited them to elude their former governess as well as castle guards on occasion.

No longer anxious, Kitlyn entered the library, intent on finding the source of the whispers. The air held the fragrance of recently extinguished candles, more evidence the 'presence' she felt watching her had likely been quite the opposite of supernatural. A few twisty passages between bookshelves led to the central area where two long tables lay strewn with books—and six still-smoking candles.

A book slipped from a shelf on Kitlyn's left as she brushed past it, falling to the floor with a *slap*. Despite being aware she'd bumped the book, she still jumped at the surprising loudness. Three whimpers came from under the table.

Curious, Kitlyn approached, grinning impishly as she expected to find a trio of young maids. She knocked twice on the table. The whimpering stopped. Kitlyn knocked again.

"Lucen protect us," whispered a voice.

Kitlyn crouched, lifting the tablecloth to peer in at Mary, Laura, and Rowan huddled under the table, clinging to each other, all in nightgowns and slippers. The three twelve-year-olds jumped away from her, falling back sprawled on the floor and screaming.

"What are you three doing in here?" asked Kitlyn.

At the sound of her voice, the girls calmed. Mary's dark brown hair covered her face except for one eye. Laura's flaxen hair puffed up as wild as her stare. Rowan blinked once, then darted forward, grabbing onto her like a frightened child.

Kitlyn brushed a hand over the girl's red hair. "Shh. It's only me. Why are you so frightened?"

"You look just like it," whispered Laura.

"Well, at first." Mary gathered her hair off her face.

"I look like what?" Kitlyn waved for the other two to come out from under the table. The severity of Rowan's trembles put her on edge. Something more than childhood imagination—or a knock on the table—had scared the girls.

Rowan mumbled something into Kitlyn's shoulder.

"The scary lady." Laura crawled out and stood close while staring out at the dark library.

"I'm sorry, highness." Rowan tried to recoil away from her, but Kitlyn held on.

"Shh. It's all right. You are scared."

Rowan relaxed. "We saw a scary lady walk by. When you lifted the cloth, we thought you were her."

"You have black hair and a white dress, too," said Mary.

"The three of you should be in bed at this hour. What are you doing in the library so late?"

"Practicing reading." Laura managed a feeble smile. "We didn't want to disappoint Oona."

"Queen Oona," whispered Mary.

"She doesn't like it when we call her that." Laura bit her lip.

"Only when we're in private. It's not proper." Mary folded her arms.

Rowan gestured at Kitlyn as if to say 'isn't it the same when we're alone with her?'

"She's been teaching the three of you to read for a while now."

The girls nodded.

"Do you normally stay up this late?"

"No." Rowan shook her head. "We were about to go off to bed when the scary lady appeared."

"We've been hiding for a long time." Laura clutched her hands at her chin, peering around at the bookshelves, her entire body shaking.

"There is nothing here," said Kitlyn.

Rowan finally stopped trembling. "She was. You look so much like her, but not as scary."

"The scary lady is taller." Mary fanned herself. "And she looked angry."

"We thought she found us when you lifted the cloth." Rowan exhaled hard. "You feel it, don't you, highness?"

Kitlyn forced herself not to cringe. Not long ago, these girls would've treated her no differently from any other castle servant. Well, perhaps *somewhat* differently. Being new and still quite young, they wouldn't have regarded her with the same contempt as the others when everyone believed she flaunted the rules of status. Even servants had a pecking order. Contempt for those even slightly lower on the social ladder didn't come naturally in children. It had to be taught. Certainly, given a year or so in the castle, they would've come to look down on her, too. Except maybe Rowan. The girl had, after all, brought her food when the whole castle believed her a thief. The redhead had a huge heart, like Oona.

"You don't have to call me 'highness' when we're in private. I'm only four years older than you three, and still remember crawling around on the floor with a brush most of the time."

Mary and Laura tittered nervously.

Rowan clasped her hands in front of herself, holding her chin up. "You and Oona ended the war and saved *so many* lives. You deserve respect."

"Well… as long as it's respect and not worship. Save worship for the gods. I'm not my father." Kitlyn patted her on the shoulder. "Please don't ever feel like you are worth less than me or anyone else. The work you do here is important, too."

"We mostly dust and clean floors," said Laura.

"Sometimes fold linens." Mary yawned.

"Dusting, cleaning floors, folding linens." Kitlyn rolled her eyes. "I've not a clue what it's like to do any of that."

The girls giggled.

"Come, now. Go and sleep. Your mothers will be worried if they wake and find your beds empty."

Kitlyn walked with them into the maze of bookshelves. All three girls clustered close around her, fearful the 'scary lady' would reappear at any moment. Once out of the library, the girls appeared to lose their fear. They bid her good night and scurried off. She watched them go until they reached the stairwell and disappeared from sight around the corner. Her bedchamber—and Oona—waited for her in the opposite direction.

She turned back toward the library to close the door—and froze stock still at the sight of a glowing white blur drifting between shelves. Equal parts frightened and curious, Kitlyn jogged after it. The closer she came to the aisle among the bookshelves, the more the hairs on the back of her neck stood on end. Her toes went numb from the cold floor, an unusual sensation as her Stone magic always kept her comfortable. Wintry chill in the air traced her breaths in clouds of vapor. An inexplicable floral perfume fragrance teased at existing, so subtle it might have only been imaginary.

The cold made Kitlyn rub her hands up and down her arms for warmth.

It's the dead of winter in here.

At the end of the first passage, she paused, peering only her face around the corner—and gasped.

A woman in a glowing white nightdress stood at the next corner, not twenty feet away, her back mostly turned. She had a similar slender build like Kitlyn as well as jet-black hair, only much longer, down to her waist. The woman also seemed taller and a bit older, into her twenties.

Kitlyn opened her mouth to say hello, perhaps ask the woman who she was, but hesitated upon noticing she could see books *through* her. A spirit. Words crashed into a brief, meaningless squeak.

The apparition reacted to the noise, glancing over at her.

Dumbfounded at the sight before her, Kitlyn found herself unable to think of what to say or do. She instantly recognized the ghost's face from the giant painting she so often stared at: Queen Solana, her mother. An assassin murdered her in her bed when Kitlyn had been three years old.

Tears gathered in the corners of Kitlyn's eyes. No wonder the girls mistook her for the 'scary lady.' The apparition looked remarkably like an older version of her. Half wanting to run and embrace her, half dreading the rumors of the woman's supposed coldness, she stepped out from behind the bookshelf into full view of the spirit.

"M-mother?" whispered Kitlyn.

Solana faced her, the emotion radiating from her shifting from dread to melancholy. After a moment, she glided closer in the smooth manner of a candlestick sliding across a table, no motion of feet disturbing the bottom of her nightgown.

Kitlyn stood her ground, neither afraid of the spirit nor deterred by the increasingly severe cold.

"I am proud of you, daughter." Solana's voice sounded as though it came from quite far away even though the spirit stood an arm's length from her. "Despite who you have chosen to spend your life with."

No… Kitlyn clenched her jaw, stuck between fury and heartbreak. *Don't do this.*

3

AN UNCLEAN DEATH

OONA

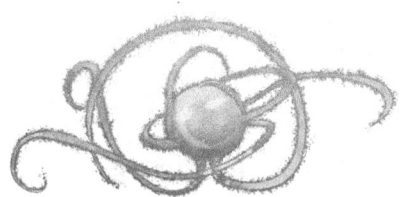

*B*right sunlight bathed the street of an ordinary village Oona didn't recognize.

Citizens strolled by, some in a rush, others meandering. Children darted back and forth at play while a scattering of animals—dogs, chickens, and a cat or two—wandered about. The small town looked familiar in the sense of being within the kingdom of Lucernia, though she couldn't tell exactly where.

Her massive, elaborate gown—the sort of affair it would take a team of handmaidens over an hour to help her into—stood out as obviously as a demon in a temple to Lucen. Some of the children wore simple sack dresses or tunics. Most of the commoners had much nicer clothing than burlap, but all basic linens. Oddly, no one paid any attention to her presence whatsoever.

The best dressed people in sight looked like 'modestly above poor' people from Cimril, on par with the castle servants. Houses, as well as shops, here all appeared to be simple affairs crammed close together, suggesting the center of town lacked cobblestone paving and a true mercantile district.

For no particular reason, Oona walked down the street, smiling and attempting to greet people. She may as well have been a ghost no one could see. This dream—for it certainly could not be reality—made little sense. Even at her most spoiled, she would not have insisted on wearing such an ostentatiously elaborate garment to a remote town. She also would likely have not wanted to travel so far and spent most of the trip complaining about being away from home.

A group of men came out of nowhere, surrounding her. They pushed her back and forth to each other within their circle like a pack of school-aged children teasing her. Oona flailed, trying to yell 'what do you want' at them, but couldn't make a sound. Momentarily helpless, she struggled to escape the hands shoving her around, managing to stay calm until she noticed the audible rips of tearing fabric.

"No!" screamed Oona, attempting futilely to defend her wardrobe.

The bizarre attack stopped as abruptly as it started. Eight men, their faces indistinct and blurry, stood in a ring around her holding the shredded remains of her elaborate gown. About to gasp in mortified horror, Oona stopped short, gawking down at herself in confusion.

She hadn't been left naked—rather in an ordinary, slightly threadbare, pale blue dress. Such a garment would have been normal for her had King Talomir not whisked her off her mother's farm at age three. Thoroughly confused, she stared at the dirt smudged on her arms, much like everyone else here who worked outside in the fields.

Am I being shown what my life would have been like?

Oona looked up. The men who took her gown had vanished. Townspeople now noticed her, giving her strange glances as they passed by. No one gave off an overt sense of hostility, their mildly disdainful expressions making her feel as if she'd stumbled into a place she didn't belong. She instinctively shied away, worried they looked down on her for loving Kitlyn. Though, they didn't feel hateful. Perhaps they simply disapproved of the peasant girl pretending to be a princess.

She kept walking, drawn forward by an urge she couldn't explain.

Other citizens regarded her with surprise, as if astonished to see one of the royals among them without a massive entourage of guards preventing anyone from coming too close. The average Lucernian citizen would be more shocked to see a noble wearing such common clothing than nothing at all. Not to say they wouldn't be aghast at nudity, but it would be easier to socially recover from than being caught in peasant clothing. Even nobles went swimming or sought amorous liaisons in the bushes from time to time. An occasional awkward moment could be explained away as necessary for certain activities. Wearing cheap clothing, on the other hand, had no acceptable excuse.

Oona decided not to care.

She and Kitlyn were queens. They had no obligation to be slaves to trends. As the rulers of Lucernia, they didn't have to obey anything but the common good. Perhaps some nobles would even thank them for pushing fashion toward the practical from the ridiculous.

Despite the odd stares, Oona made her way down the street waving, smiling, and greeting everyone who looked at her. No one said anything back to her, staring in mute shock as though she ran around a funeral singing happy songs.

The uncomfortableness of it got her fidgeting, but she kept trying to be friendly and polite.

Oona had come to agree with Kitlyn. She preferred the lack of a huge procession of guards and attendants. Whenever the former king allowed her into town during the war, it would always become a major event involving thirty or more soldiers, several servants, and a fancy coach. Perhaps he tried to embarrass her on purpose so she'd stay in the castle, but she suspected he adored being king and wanted to remind everyone of his importance, wealth, and power.

Having even ten soldiers following her around made her feel conspicuous and arrogant.

It might not be wise considering she'd become half head of state, but the best security came from ruling in a way where the people liked and respected their leaders. Moments like this, free to walk around like every other citizen, gave her more happiness than any amount of gold or fancy silk could ever provide.

Ignoring the continued strange stares, she followed the compulsion to wander the town, going wherever whim pulled her. Children, for the most part, smiled back at her while the adults continued staring at her like she'd done something wrong. It further made her suspect the dream reflected her worries of the kingdom. Little ones didn't care who loved who until their parents taught them to believe only certain types of love were 'correct.' Except for the children of nobles, little ones also didn't care about social status.

A dream most bizarre. Do I envision my insecurities or see a message from the gods? Oona looked around. *Which town is this?*

At someone walking up close on her left side, she turned to greet them—and froze, gawking at a human skeleton. She assumed it formerly a man due to being only as tall as its chin. It had no clothing, possessions, or anything to suggest an identity or profession. Despite the ghoulishness of a moving skeleton standing beside her, its presence didn't bother her beyond a momentary pause to take in the sight. No one else reacted to the dead person.

I understand. They look at me the way they look at Tenebrea's priestesses.

She held her chin up, refusing to let their apprehension bother her. It unnerved people to hear Oona speak openly about the Goddess of Death, but she considered them wrong for shunning her. Death existed as part of the natural way of things. Tenebrea didn't kill anyone. She didn't even decide when anyone died, merely guided and protected worthy souls when it came time for their inevitable journey.

"Hello," said Oona.

The skeleton nodded.

"You are a messenger."

Again, he nodded, then pointed.

"All right."

The skeleton guided her to an intersection not far from where it appeared, turning left onto a larger street. They passed a blacksmith's stall across from a wainwright's shop, a general store, and several private homes before reaching a T intersection. There, the skeleton stopped and pointed ahead at the house in front of them.

"I understand," said Oona.

The skeleton disappeared into a whorl of pale grey smoke.

She crossed the remainder of the street, entering the little yard in front of the home. Before she could knock, the door opened on its own. It seemed a bit rude to barge into someone's house, but she brushed her hesitation aside. Not only was she in the midst of a dream, a messenger from Tenebrea sent her here.

Murmured voices and the clink of forks led her to a small dining area where a man, a woman, and two children around four years of age ate dinner. Except for the family showing no reaction to her walking in, everything appeared to be normal. Trusting she'd been sent here for a reason, Oona patiently watched them eat.

Both children appeared unusually quiet, the girl refusing to look up from her plate. Her brother occasionally glanced at their father as though the man spoke, despite his lips never moving.

"It's something with him…"

The man snapped his head up, staring at Oona, his eyes having gone completely black. Blood tears ran down his cheeks. Both children and their mother started to scream in terror—but the room fell silent in an instant. All four people vanished. Oona jumped at the sudden change from daylight to darkness. Plates containing half-eaten food remained on the table, though the people had disappeared.

Heavy footsteps came from the left.

The father walked out of a doorway, his tunic spattered with blood. Oona stared in horror at the axe dangling from his right hand. He paused in the middle of the dining room, glanced straight at her, and disappeared.

"Papa, why are you angry?" asked a small child from a short hallway deep in the house.

A shrill scream broke the silence.

Oona rushed into the hall, catching herself on the doorjamb of the closest room. She stared in disgusted horror at two small beds, mercifully empty but covered in blood. Horrified, she cringed away.

Wait… I am dreaming.

A floorboard creaking nearby made her open her eyes.

The skeleton stood in the hall beside her.

"Has this happened?" whispered Oona.

He shook his skull to the negative.

She sucked in a hopeful breath. "Can it be prevented? Oh, forgive me. Such a silly question. Why else would you be showing this to me?"

The skeleton nodded once.

"It cannot be their time if Tenebrea is not yet ready to welcome them. Black-filled eyes… it must be a demon." Oona clenched her hands into fists, narrowing her eyes. "Where… where is this?"

4

A MOTHER'S WARNING

KITLYN

Queen Solana's mournful expression did little to quell the fury rising in Kitlyn.

She'd watched Oona crumble emotionally when her real mother rejected her for being in love with another girl. In the span of hours, she'd learned the truth of her identity, found a mother she thought dead — not to mention an entirely different person — and had her newfound joy scorched to cinders in the fires of hatred.

Oona's mother Ruby had been so filled with rage at learning her daughter loved Kitlyn, they both feared for the safety of her little sister Evie — who didn't understand how love could be wrong. The little one already suffered beatings for minor errors. Only the gods knew what Ruby might have done to her if the child challenged her over hating Oona. Bringing the girl to the castle had been the right decision. Ruby chose money over her daughter. Shameful, but the child would be better off.

Kitlyn, however, knew her mother was dead. Unlike Oona, she no longer had any dreams of finding a long-absent parent and having any sort of future relationship with them, no hope for hate to destroy. Ghosts were ephemeral beings at best. However, the spirit's disapproval still hurt. Most of the older castle staff often spoke of Queen Solana in unfavorable terms. She'd been cruel to the servants, even the younger ones, screaming at them for minor infractions such as making eye contact or daring to speak in her presence.

The spectral woman looking at her had appeared so forlorn, almost innocent, Kitlyn found herself questioning the truth of such stories—until the ghost opened her mouth.

"The man lied," said Kitlyn, trying to maintain a calm tone. "Lucen does not object to my love for Oona."

Solana looked down. "You misunderstand me, daughter. It does not vex me you love a woman. She is from a peasant family."

"Oh..." Kitlyn's fury exploded to numbness. "Are the things they said of you truth?"

"There is some truth." The spirit bowed her head. "I believed in the importance of station. In moments of weakness, the servants bore the brunt of my frustrations—perhaps more than they should have. I did not treat them quite so poorly as they tell. In death, I've come to understand my disdain for the poor was as wrong as the way our society held such disdain and animosity toward anyone who did not love as they deemed 'pure' enough."

Kitlyn reached as if to touch the spirit, sensing a particular note of sorrow in her mother's voice. "You...?"

Solana lifted her gaze from the floor, making eye contact. "Yes. My heart belonged to another who was not your father."

"A woman." Kitlyn's fingers found only cold air where her mother's arm appeared to be.

"Lady Harrington."

"But..." Kitlyn blinked. "She's not so much older than me, three and twenty years."

Solara smiled wistfully. "Not the daughter. Her mother."

"Oh. You and..." Kitlyn exhaled a slow breath, her head spinning both from the gravity of the revelation and the shock such a secret managed to stay quiet. "But... Aodh?"

"Political. I did not mind him as a person, but to say we were in love would offend Lucen. It would be true to say he loved me."

Kitlyn covered her mouth, unable to imagine being married to a man while pining for Oona. "Oh… Mother…"

"Our servants suffered for my unhappiness. Death has granted me clarity of thought I did not possess in life. My anger and frustration at society condemning the love Isolde and I shared became contempt for society itself. I lost my temper on those of lower status because I could do nothing else."

"It must have pained you to watch him make a servant of me."

"I could not bear the sight of you suffering." Solana brushed a hand at Kitlyn's cheek with all the substance of a chilly draft. "He met the end he deserved. I am proud of you for doing what I could not. Forgive me my thoughtless comment. Where Oona came from does not matter."

Choked up, it took Kitlyn a moment to find her voice. "I am sorry you could not be with the woman you held in your heart."

"You are much braver than I. How cowardly of me to remain here like a prisoner."

"He held you against your will?"

"No. Only my fear did." Solana glanced momentarily off to the side as if hearing a noise. "I did not know what he did to the tree."

"He fooled you like he fooled everyone else. I am not angry with you… I know so little of you other than stories passed among servants."

Solana's presence shifted dark, angry. "Yes. The assassin killed me when you were so little. Even my death did not convince Aodh of his error."

"He loved no one as much as he loved power," muttered Kitlyn.

"In his own way, he loved you more than himself."

Kitlyn exhaled. "He might have loved me more than himself, but he loved power more than both—or he would have returned the Heart and ended the war. The threat to my life, the entire reason he made me think myself a servant, was his doing."

"By Lucen's grace, may you never do anything so foolish as he." Solana again traced her fingers down Kitlyn's cheek.

"Mother?"

"Yes?"

Kitlyn hesitated.

"What is it, daughter?"

"Do you know if there is any truth to a curse being on the crown?"

The spirit's wrathful presence shifted to concern. "Yes. It is the reason I am here. Tenebrea has let me journey from her realm to warn you. Your life lays beyond the gates of Isilien."

"Gates of… Isilien," whispered Kitlyn.

"Yes. My time runs short. Many regrets haunted me, but having you was never one of them."

Kitlyn's breath trembled. Unable to force words past the growing tightness in her throat, she could only stare mutely as her mother's ghost faded away. Her mind spun with a hundred different ideas of what life might have been like had Aodh not killed her. It didn't matter his hand never touched the blade; his actions set everything in motion.

My mother loves me… and understands my love for Oona.

Kitlyn sank to kneel on the floor, folded her arms across herself, and wept in silence. Sorrow lasted a few minutes before anger took its place. Depriving her of a loving mother added one more line to an already long list of Aodh's crimes. While she could do nothing more about him, it lessened what little guilt she harbored for not trying to stop him from drinking poison.

The priests would have exiled or imprisoned him. All the people of two kingdoms wanted him dead. Even if he could tolerate the humiliation of being excommunicated, he would not have lived long.

"Tenebrea, thank you for watching over my mother. May she find the serenity in your realm this world denied her."

After a moment of quiet reflection, Kitlyn hurried back to her bedchamber. She *had* to tell Oona about the ghost and confess to her fears. *Not married a whole year yet and I've already failed at it. She's stronger than she looks. I cannot hide my fears from her, even if my intention is to protect her.*

Kitlyn spent the minute or so it took her to reach the bedchamber debating if she should wake Oona up to talk now or wait for morning. A few hours didn't seem worth depriving her love of sleep, so she crept into the room, trying not to make a disturbance. She approached the bed, slipped out of her nightgown, and pulled the covers back to crawl in.

Oona abruptly sat up. "Shimmerbrook!"

"Gah!" yelped Kitlyn, jumping back and clutching her chest.

5

BY LUCEN'S LIGHT

OONA

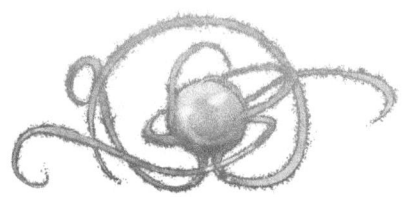

*A*n unexpected yell close to her right made Oona jump and 'eep.'

Kitlyn stood beside the bed, both hands over her heart. They stared at each other for a few seconds, then Kitlyn burst into laughter.

"What?" asked Oona.

"Did you just scare yourself by startling me?"

"I don't understand." Oona held the covers up. "It's chilly."

Kitlyn crawled into bed, snuggling up to her. "I wasn't expecting you to sit up so fast. You startled me, and then yelped at me being startled."

"Oh." Oona exhaled. "Yes. I startled myself then. We have to go to Shimmerbrook right away."

"Why?" asked Kitlyn.

"A message from Tenebrea." Oona explained her dream. "I am certain there is a demon intending to kill an entire family."

Kitlyn curled up, nestled in the soft bedding beside Oona's warm body. "Do you feel it has to be us, or can we send a fast rider to the temple there?"

The vision hadn't made it too clear on that point. While it might be possible the goddess sent the warning to Oona without particular concern to whether or not she acted herself or instructed another to intervene, it would be quite difficult for her to explain in a letter which house the demon intended to attack. Any confusion might lead to tragedy. "It would be best for me to go. There isn't much time and I don't know any names."

"All right then." Kitlyn squeezed her arm. "Must we leave this moment or is morning okay?"

"The man is going to murder his wife and children."

Kitlyn sat up. "Okay."

"Well, a demon. Not the man."

Oona leapt out of bed, gasping at the wash of cold air on her body. She hurriedly dressed in a plain tunic and pants before grabbing her armor from the wardrobe cabinet. Though custom made to fit her, their army's scouts wore the same style of double-stitched leather. Oona hadn't touched it since they'd traipsed across the countryside hunting a lich.

"I need to tell you something." Kitlyn rushed into her clothing and armor beside her.

"Of course. We can talk while we get ready and ride."

"I don't want to say this when we aren't alone."

Oona paused to look over, her armor chest piece halfway out of the cabinet. "Bad?"

"In a way. I haven't been truthful with you."

What? She swallowed. "You..."

"I have not lied. I merely pretended to be braver than I am." Kitlyn bowed her head. "I didn't want you to worry or be frightened. I'm more concerned about the curse than I've admitted. And I'm also afraid of being too young and inexperienced to bear responsibility for an entire kingdom."

Relieved, Oona leaned against her. "Oh, Kit. I knew."

"You knew?"

"Of course. We've been together most of our lives. It's easy for me to tell when something is bothering you. I know you've been keeping it to yourself to avoid worrying me." Oona kissed her on the cheek. "Thank you, but you don't have to."

"If you read me so well, why did we wait so long to tell each other how we felt?" asked Kitlyn in a sad half-whisper.

"No one would call for our execution or exile as blasphemers for saying we're a little nervous about shouldering so much responsibility. I'd been so anxious about everything, I didn't trust myself to really be seeing what I hoped I'd been seeing. I feared you would find me disgusting more than they would kill me for heresy."

"I felt the same, only had you found me abhorrent, I wouldn't so much have minded the execution."

"We agreed to stop apologizing for being chickens." Oona hugged her. "And no more talk of welcoming death."

"You are right… we did agree. Sorry. I… saw my mother in the library."

"They moved the painting?"

Kitlyn shook her head. "No, her spirit visited me. Scared poor Mary, Laura, and Rowan, too."

"Are they all right?" Oona pulled the breastplate on.

"Yes." Kitlyn recounted the conversation she had with her mother while they finished getting into their armor.

Oona gawked. "Queen Solana was in love with Lady Harrington's mother?"

"Apparently, yes."

"Aww." She sighed, heart heavy. "I feel so bad for her… and entirely horrified at my earlier suggestion."

Kitlyn looked up from fastening her sword belt. "Which one?"

"Remember the day out by the garden when I'd been all mopey about responsibility and said we should talk Aodh into finding a new queen?"

"Oh. That." Kitlyn grimaced. "Had we gone through with it, I believe my mother's ghost would have come back much sooner."

Oona covered her mouth to hold in an unexpected laugh despite feeling horrible at the thought. Of course, nobles often did things far more squeamish than marrying the daughter of their wife's lover. At least, she'd heard partial rumors.

"Ready?" asked Kitlyn.

"Yes. Sorry for forcing you out of bed at this awful hour."

"I cannot weigh the inconvenience of a day starting too early with the life of four people, especially two small children." Kitlyn drew her longsword a few inches out to check the blade, then slid it back into the scabbard. "We will have many mornings to sleep... I hope."

Nervous tingles washed over the bottom of Oona's stomach. She didn't really know what to expect in Tenebrea's realm, though it did appear consciousness continued to exist there. On the walk downstairs, she contemplated the oddity of fearing death but not its steward. Perhaps she didn't need to worry so much about it after all. If she and Kitlyn could remain together, even as spirits in some other realm, what did she truly dread?

Too much thinking along those lines worried her, too. Otherwise, why race out of the castle in the middle of the night to save the lives of four people? If the family remained together after death, what did they lose? There had to be *something* unpleasant about the other side, or Tenebrea would not have given her the chance to spare them. Why would Orien grant his priests the ability to heal the injured if death didn't matter? Perhaps life amounted to feasting on cake and ivenberries while after death one merely received porridge.

Is it possible to not fear death while endeavoring to avoid it as long as possible? She shifted her jaw side to side. *Perhaps it is like the nobility. I am not frightened by them, but I'd rather not endure their presence.*

At the base of the grand stair, they paused by two soldiers.

"We must journey to Shimmerbrook," said Kitlyn. "An important matter has come up and it cannot wait. Inform Captain Lorne and Beredwyn."

"Right away, highness." The man saluted and hurried off.

"Shall we wait for an escort?" Kitlyn smiled at her.

"Beredwyn will fuss over us if we do not." Oona let her mind drift momentarily, but felt nothing one way or the other in regard to a minor delay. "We may be able to spare a few minutes."

"We'll give them ten." Kitlyn grinned.

TWO DAYS LATER, OONA, KITLYN, AND EIGHT SOLDIERS RODE across the meadow toward the town of Shimmerbrook.

Oona explained to the eight soldiers accompanying them the reason for the hasty journey. Given her prior brattiness, she initially expected one of them to crack a joke about an 'emergency shopping trip' when they first prepared to leave, but the six men and two women said nothing. Once they understood the actual reason, they all approached the journey with the same urgency she did.

Their horses, Apples and Cloud, appeared to enjoy a chance to stretch their legs, though the white horse kept eyeing the woods, unusually skittish. Cloud had always been something of a chicken, but his unusual nervousness put Oona on edge.

He senses danger humans cannot.

A scattering of small buildings dotted the grass ahead at the edge of the Shimmering Wood, a backdrop of greens, browns, and yellows behind them. Above the forest, a darker blue haze hinted at the outline of the Dawnspire Mountains, many miles farther to the west. The late afternoon sun already started its journey beyond the distant peaks, painting the forest and the town of Shimmerbrook in shadows.

Even from a few miles away, Oona sensed malice. Despite the beautiful early autumn day, she found the scenery anything but relaxing.

Their trip from Cimril southwest along the edge of the Mistral Wood had been uneventful until after passing Duskdawn Lake and entering the forest on the road west to Llanoen. A few men Oona suspected of being bandits had watched them from the trees, though did nothing other than wave greetings. A few hours into the woods, a creature rushed out of the shadows as if to attack them—but upon seeing ten people, eight of whom had metal armor, it ran away screaming.

Oona hadn't seen it as she'd been too engrossed in a conversation with Kitlyn about Isilien in the seconds before it appeared—not to mention struggling to keep from falling off Cloud the moment the supposed creature leapt out into view. The two men up front described a three-foot-tall humanoid being with green skin, big ears, and yellow eyes. It sounded an awful lot like a goblin, but such creatures didn't really exist anywhere but storybooks.

She assumed a child from a tiny village dressed up to scare people—though her horse wouldn't have reared at a human child playing a prank. He wouldn't even have reared at an adult bandit seriously intending harm.

The previous night spent in Llanoen brought restless sleep and heavy thoughts. Oona had been born there, living with her mother Ruby until age three. Had she not accidentally zapped a chicken, she likely would have spent her entire life there, never meeting Kitlyn. Visiting the town where her mother once lived brought the pain of her cruel rejection to mind as well. Fortunately, they wouldn't encounter her. After accepting the coins and leaving Evie in Oona's care, the woman sold her house and disappeared, likely to flee the scorn of people knowing she valued money more than her children.

King Aodh had also essentially 'bought' Oona from her thirteen years ago.

Of course, even if the discovery of another child the same age as his daughter having magic hadn't given the king the idea to use her as a decoy for assassins, she likely would have been whisked off to the temple of Lucen anyway around age twelve. Anyone possessing magic was required to join the temple corresponding to their gift. People like Kitlyn—who had magic not from the gods—tried desperately to conceal it or faced imprisonment, banishment, or in some cases, death if they resisted.

Evermoor didn't punish anyone for having magic nor did they force them to join temples, likely why it seemed so many more people from there had it. Oona suspected an equal number of Lucernians wielded magical abilities—or if not equal, at least far more than anyone knew about—but kept quiet or fled north to the Kingdom of Ondar. She and Kitlyn had already instructed the four high priests and all magistrates to cease dragging children off to the temples. Those truly called to serve one of the gods would find their way.

Oona couldn't help but insist on riding past the house in which her mother once lived. Another family owned it now. Two boys a little younger than her worked in the field with their father while a younger girl fed chickens. She felt little emotion for the place beyond pain over her meeting with the woman who should have loved her unconditionally. Evie didn't seem to miss it, having adjusted to life at the castle. Her little sister also didn't talk about their mother much.

Oona tried her best not to say awful things about the woman. She couldn't even try to soften the truth by claiming their mother thought it would be better for Evie to stay in the castle where she would have everything she needed. The child had been right there and watched the woman choose money over her daughter. Of course, Evie also didn't ask to stay with Ruby, even when Oona said she could keep the money if her little sister preferred to remain with their mother. An overly sweet child who loved everyone choosing to stay at the castle with a sister she'd only just met spoke volumes.

Evie is afraid of her.

The ride out of Llanoen earlier that day passed in a blur of fatigue due to a restless night. If not for having Kitlyn with her, she wouldn't have slept at all. Upon reaching the edge of town, Oona sat up in the saddle.

"What?" asked Kitlyn. "Did you see something?"

"Not yet. Be wary. We face a creature most foul."

Kitlyn raised one eyebrow. "What's a barrister from the mercantile guild doing here?"

"You know I mean demon."

"I do. And at risk of offending the gods, I respect demons more than those men."

Oona gasped.

"Demons at least do not pretend to be anything more than they are." Kitlyn frowned. "What kind of person can, with a straight face, claim securing the interests of commerce is more important than families having homes?"

"I know you do not seriously respect demons, so I won't protest."

Kitlyn exhaled out her nose. "If I granted his request, a dozen families with over thirty children between them would have had nowhere to live... and he said 'they should have considered living arrangements before having so many children.'"

"Truly a wretch." Oona shook her head. "We were right to deny his request."

"The guild is *still* complaining. It's not as if trade is prevented. Their large wagons merely need to take a longer route to reach the guild hall. It is not worth destroying people's homes to make a straight path for oversized traders' wagons."

"Agreed."

"If it bothers them so much, they can build a new guild hall closer to the gates."

Oona glanced sideways at her. "You needn't continue debating. I agree with you."

"Sorry. I'm annoyed all over again thinking about it."

Apples snorted as if to concur.

Quite unlike her dream, the citizens of Shimmerbrook mostly greeted them with happy faces. A few older people scrunched up their noses as if smelling bad eggs. She could practically hear them wondering how she could possibly have 'those feelings' for a girl. Their bafflement, even disgust, didn't bother her as long as it didn't take the form of screaming or threats. Neither she nor Kitlyn wanted everyone to adore them or even change their opinion. They merely wanted to exist without fear. Thankfully, word of the former king's brazen demand of Lucen as well as Tenebrea's response had more or less spread throughout Lucernia. For so long, the people had been told Lucen frowned on women loving women and men loving men — but to receive visible, actual proof from the gods no such disapproval existed had left some people confused.

Lucen *not* smashing Aodh for his audacity as well as Tenebrea's appearance had thus far kept reaction to their union minimal. It also helped to have hundreds of witnesses at their wedding see Lucen grant his blessing. Even High Priest Balais Aldin—formerly of the opinion such pairings were against the gods—had changed his mind.

The people seemed to largely consider the two of them saviors: both from the war as well as Mad King Aodh. That they carried themselves in almost the entirely opposite fashion as him endeared them to the citizenry. The former king would never have ridden on an open horse into a small town near the edge of Lucernia—

especially not wearing the armor of an ordinary scout. Nothing in Lucen's teachings forbade pride, but the former king took it too far. He never attempted to hide how he considered himself above everyone.

Considering their ordinary armor, no crowns, and not having been personally to Shimmerbrook before, it remained unclear if anyone recognized them. The sour faces on the older citizens might have simply been them squinting into the sun. Word had to have spread to the farthest reaches of Lucernia by now. Everyone knew a pair of queens occupied the throne, one blonde, one raven-haired. People meeting them in person often reacted in surprise to their being younger than expected. However, in common soldier's armor, they tended to be overlooked—an aftereffect of the former king's pageantry plus society's preoccupation with status. Many simply refused to believe royalty would be seen out in public wearing garments not worth a small fortune.

"We are searching for a blacksmith across the street from a wainwright's shop." Oona patted Cloud's neck, trying to keep the fidgety horse calm.

They continued into the town, asking directions from the citizens until directed to the main thoroughfare. Once on the larger street, Oona recognized her surroundings from the vision and urged Cloud up to a fast walk. She had the fortune of riding one of the quickest steeds in the land, but also the most cowardly. People began to take notice of them, though perhaps mistook them all for soldiers. A small group of curious townies followed them.

At the T intersection, she spotted the man from the vision inside a leatherworker's shop attached to the right side of the house. He appeared ordinary, a few years short of thirty and far less sinister than he'd been in the dream. Oona didn't trust her eyes, or his pleasant smile of greeting. A hint of sweat on his brow revealed a hidden war going on inside his mind, a war she knew he'd lose in a few hours.

He would have killed them tonight. Oona dismounted and approached the shop.

Cloud scooted back from the building, bumping into a merchant cart of vegetables at the opposite side of the intersection.

The soldiers got down from their horses. One rushed over to grab Cloud's reins before he crushed the produce cart while the others followed her. Nearby citizens dropped everything so they could gather around and watch. Having eight soldiers file into a shop often put people on edge. With the war over, they wouldn't be there to commandeer armor. Doubtful they suspected the man of any crimes bad enough to justify direct intervention from the military. Since no one shouted or reacted in any obvious way, Oona believed no one recognized them. Even if the people realized who they were, she and Kitlyn hadn't been on the throne long enough for the citizenry to know what to expect. A thick veil of nervous curiosity saturated the street from the growing crowd.

One small dog yapped.

Kitlyn entered the shop, glancing around at the various items for sale—mostly boots, belts, saddles, and scabbards. "He doesn't appear unusual."

The man stopped smiling, seeming worried.

"Hello." Oona nodded in greeting. "May I know your name, good sir."

"Bertelis Kol." The man shifted his gaze back and forth between her and Kitlyn, then glanced at the line of soldiers behind them. "What brings the queens' fine soldiers to my humble shop?"

"We are here to aid you, Bertelis." Oona walked closer to him, stopping three paces away.

"Aid me?" He leaned back. "I have no problems worth the attention of the army."

"Da?" called a tiny girl in the doorway connecting the shop to the house.

Drat. Oona gave Kitlyn side eye.

Kitlyn read her intention and shot a look at the nearest soldier. He rushed over, intercepting the four-year-old before she got near Bertelis.

"Da!" yelled, the girl, straining to reach for him as the soldier carried her off into the house.

"Pardon?" Bertelis faced the man rushing his daughter away. "Please put her down."

"In a moment. There is something I must say to you first." Oona raised her hands toward him.

Bertelis started after the soldier holding the girl—but stopped as two more moved in front to block him. "What is going on here?" He glared at Oona. "I've done nothing wrong."

She summoned azure light around her hands. "In the name of Lord Lucen, I banish the dark entity assaulting Bertelis Kol. You have no purchase upon his soul. *Begone.*"

The child's whisper of, "Ooh, pretty!" at the light drowned under an anguished scream from her father. Bertelis grabbed his head in both hands, reeling backward. Blood poured from his nostrils. His skin undulated under his clothing, swollen masses bigger than fists appearing and vanishing in a continuous display of pulsating horror.

Groans of shock and discomfort came from the soldiers—and the people nearest the door who could see inside.

Bertelis collapsed to his knees, bending forward until his head touched the expanding pool of blood leaking from his face. The soldier holding the girl darted into the house, carrying the child away from the frightening scene.

"The light of Lucen cleanses." Oona raised her hands over her head, intensifying her light orb.

Gasps and whispers of awe came from the crowd outside. Many voices called out in praise of Lucen, beseeching his protection. Bertelis flipped up into the air as though a giant had grabbed him by the head and swung him into the wall. Dark vapor gushed from his mouth, rapidly gathering into a solid figure.

The demon took on a generally human shape with backward-bent knees and the clawed feet of a large bird. It lacked a nose, the mouth lipless, exposing a tall oval of exposed silver teeth frozen in a permanent grimace of pain. Long, sinewy arms extended to either side, three-fingered hands sprouting talons as long as daggers. Smoke peeled from its ink-black skin, already burning in the divine light saturating the small store. It leaned forward, screeching at her. The stink of rotting eggs and carrion flooded the room.

Kitlyn and the remaining soldiers all drew their blades, coughing on the foulness in the air.

"Let no vile creature of torment plague the sacred land of Lucen." Oona thrust her arm out, projecting a beam of pure light at the demon's chest.

The demon's body disintegrated, evaporating into a whorl of greasy smoke that burned away in the radiant light. As soon as the last of the vapor dissipated, the sense of malice hanging over the building faded, as well as the stench.

Oona lowered her arms, bowing her head. "By Lucen's grace and Tenebrea's counsel, the demon is no longer."

Quiet murmurs of reverence came from the crowd.

None of the soldiers spoke.

Bertelis emitted a pained wheeze.

Eep! Oona rushed to his side. "Kit… help me roll him."

Kitlyn sheathed her sword and ran over.

They eased the man onto his back, revealing a face covered in claw marks and a slash across the front of his throat.

"By Orien's grace, may your wounds mend." Oona held her hands over him. Orangey-gold light gathered beneath her palms.

Over the course of several minutes, the slashes and bruises lessened to minor scabs and discolorations. Once she sensed the magic Orien gave her could do no more, Oona rested a hand on his forehead and recited an invocation to Lucen asking he be shielded from darkness. After a person suffered an attack of this nature, they remained quite vulnerable to future demonic attack without such a blessing.

Bertelis moaned.

People in the crowd outside whispered amongst themselves, wondering if Queen Kitlyn and Queen Oona had really shown up in their town… with only eight soldiers. Some didn't think they'd be dressed so plainly. A few cited the display of Lucen's power as proof.

Bertelis moaned again and opened his eyes.

"What's happening in there?" called a woman from the joining doorway.

"Annora?" Bertelis attempted to sit up. "Is my wife all right?"

Somewhere behind her, a child wailed.

"Yes." Oona squeezed his hand. "She is fine."

Kitlyn waved at the soldiers. "Let her in. It is all right. The danger has passed."

A dark-haired woman ran over, gasping in horror at her husband laying in a pool of blood. "Bert!"

"He'll be all right." Oona sat back on her heels.

"Oh, thank Lucen," muttered Bertelis. "The children?"

"Frightened but unhurt," said a soldier near the joining doorway.

"Is anyone going to tell me what is happening?" asked Annora.

"A demon attacked your husband." Kitlyn set her hands on her hips. "Oona received a warning in a dream, so we rushed here as fast as we were able."

"Demon?" She blinked. "Why would a demon attack us?"

"I am wondering that as well." Oona patted Bertelis on the arm. "Do you remember where it came from?"

"Yes." Bertelis managed to sit up and take his wife's hand. "I'd been out checking my traps in the woods west of town earlier today. A woman..." He rubbed his forehead. "My memory is not clear. I remember seeing a beautiful woman walking around, but not beautiful like Annora. Evil beautiful."

Kitlyn, Oona, and Annora exchanged glances.

"As soon as I looked at her, she... I lost control of myself. Her voice filled my mind. She didn't like me having a family." Bertelis broke down in tears while describing his losing efforts over the past several days to hold back the urge to harm them.

"The demon is gone. You have nothing to fear." Oona stood. "We should check these woods."

"Didn't you destroy it already?" asked a soldier.

Oona grimaced. "I cannot say for sure. The demon we faced here did not have much power. My concern is a greater one lurks in the woods."

"Pardon, me, highness." Annora bowed her head at Kitlyn. "Did you say you left Cimril to come to Shimmerbrook... for my husband?"

"Yes." Kitlyn nodded.

"For your entire family." Oona smiled, trying not to think about what the demon intended to do here.

Annora glanced down at him.

Oona shook her head. "The darkness did not come from him. He is protected."

"Thank you, highness." Annora bowed deeply. "How can we repay your kindness?"

"You need not do more than live your best life and hold reverent the gods." Oona stood. "Demons have no place here."

"But you... you are the queens. You came in person." Annora blinked.

"I needed to make sure the fiend was stopped before you or your children suffered. It is all right. I am overjoyed to have been fast enough."

Annora looked back and forth between her and Kitlyn, then blushed ever so slightly. "Forgive me for asking, highness, but how can we know who truly speaks for Lucen? Some teachings appear to have been... incorrect."

A mixture of shocked gasps, pained silence, and one or two affirmative hums came from the crowd.

Despite the woman's evident discomfort at the idea of two women—or likely two men—together, her sincerity and openness put Oona at ease. She held out one hand and summoned her little light orb.

Annora stared at the glowing sphere. "Does it have... eyes?"

Kitlyn grinned.

True, two small white spots quite reminiscent of eyes on the tomato-sized ball of blue light often gave off a sense of emotion by changing shape. Oona thought of her as a little friend, so perhaps the magic reflected such.

"All who carry the true gift of Lucen can beckon a light like this." Oona pivoted so the crowd in the street could see. "Not every true servant of Lucen will summon one with personality, but they will be able to call Lucen's Light. The glow feels like you have a friend watching over you. False light offers no sense of companionship."

"Forgive me," whispered Annora. "For believing falsehoods."

"Worry no more on the past. Lucernia has much work ahead to recover." Oona directed the light ball to float up over her shoulder.

Annora bowed. "Thank you, highness."

"Shall we check the woods?" Kitlyn took a step toward the door.

"In a moment. Let me invoke a blessing on the house… to be sure only the one demon infested it." Oona approached the joining door. She braced herself, expecting the memory of blood-stained walls, but the home appeared quite peaceful. *Thank Lucen.* "The blessing will not take long."

6

THE FACE OF DESIRE

KITLYN

*W*hile Oona went from room to room in the house to ensure no other demons skulked about, Kitlyn waited outside with the soldiers.

The crowd filled the streets for quite a distance in all three directions. Little activity went on elsewhere she could see, making her wonder if the entire town came to watch the spectacle. A stocky man in nice—for Shimmerbrook—clothing at the front edge of the crowd caught her eye both for being short, only as tall as her, and having an air of authority about him.

To his right stood a thirtyish woman in the robes of an Orien prioress, yellow with red trim on the sleeves and around the collar plus an orange sash. She looked quite young for her rank—right below high priest—perhaps the youngest Kitlyn had ever seen. Considering the remoteness of this town, she'd probably been promoted because no other abbot or abbess wanted to live this far away from civilization. Generally, every temple had a prior or prioress stationed there to manage it.

On the short man's other side stood a middle-aged man in the robes of a Lucen abbot—curiously not a prior, pure white trimmed in silver. The prioress had to be the head of her temple here, but it would be most unusual if an abbot ran the Lucen temple. Kitlyn didn't remember hearing anything unusual about this town's temple situation, which meant it had to be recent.

The short man puffed up his chest while approaching her. "Highness?"

"Yes?" She nodded in greeting.

"I am Ernald, mayor of Shimmerbrook. It is an honor to have you visit."

"Thank you."

Ernald pursed his lips.

She winced mentally, certain she'd forgotten some pointless step of etiquette. Her father would likely never have spoken directly to someone as 'low' as the mayor of a small, remote town, barring an extreme circumstance. However, a demon more powerful than the one Oona destroyed could likely be in the woods nearby, so she didn't care to waste time on needless pomp. Introducing herself also appeared pointless as the man obviously recognized her.

"I'm glad we were able to help."

The mayor blinked, paused a moment as if uncertain what to say, then gestured at the priests. "Please, allow me to introduce Savaric, Abbot of Lucen and Charrah, Prioress of Orien."

Kitlyn exchanged bows with them.

"I understand a demon found its way into the home here?" asked Savaric. "How is that possible?"

"Earlier teachings claiming Lucen made it impossible for demons to enter Lucernia are either distortions of the truth... or such protection faltered as a result of the former king's treachery."

Murmurs of alarm arose in the crowd.

Kitlyn waited for the people to quiet before continuing. "There is no need for fear, only vigilance. Lucen clearly protects us by empowering his priests and priestesses to destroy such fiends."

"Oy, can ya make the light like the queen?" shouted an anonymous member of the crowd.

Kitlyn raised both eyebrows. During Aodh's reign, no one would have dared openly challenge a priest of Lucen to a test of veracity.

Her surprise shifted to a smile. She gestured at him, bidding him humor the man.

Savaric extended a hand, closed his eyes, and whispered to himself. Seconds later, a pure white orb appeared floating above his palm. As Oona mentioned, the radiance it gave off bathed her in a feeling of protection.

Most of the people close enough to see murmured thanks to Lucen.

He does not seem insulted by the request. "Thank you, Savaric."

The priest stepped closer. "I am curious why you burdened yourselves with coming here in person. I certainly could have dispatched a demon."

His eyes ask the question he dare not speak. Why did Lucen send Oona and not him?

Kitlyn lowered her voice. "Lucen did not personally send us here. The omen came from Tenebrea. She seems to have a certain rapport with my wife."

"Tenebrea? Why would the Mistress of Twilight favor Queen Oona?" Some color drained from Savaric's cheeks.

"I understand she has Orien's favor as well." Charrah made a reverent hand motion.

Kitlyn glanced back at the house. *Is she almost finished in there? She likely found an adorable doll in the girl's room and is amusing the child.* "The favor Tenebrea shows her does not take the form of a magical gift."

Savaric tilted his head. "I am unsure what you mean…"

"A more direct favor. Visions, warnings, and so forth." Kitlyn bowed her head in gratitude. "She even warned us of an assassin."

"Most unusual." Savaric shifted his jaw side to side while thinking.

"Consider how most citizens react to Tenebrea or her faithful." Kitlyn folded her arms. "Then consider how citizens react to people like my wife and I? Oona never feared or avoided Tenebrea for being who and what she is."

"Ahh." Savaric bowed his head. "I understand."

"I am not a priestess of any of our gods, so I do not speak for them." Kitlyn glanced back as the house door opened.

Oona stepped outside, went wide-eyed at the crowd, then seemed distracted, gazing around while making a face as if smelling something foul. She gave up in a few seconds and hurried over to stand beside her. Mayor Ernald and the two priests repeated their introductions, after which, Kitlyn caught her up on the conversation.

"Lucen detests demons and seeks to protect our people as much as he can," said Oona. "I don't claim to know why he does anything. If I had to guess, I would say he expected you to sense this demon, but you didn't due to the stronger dark energy coming from the woods."

"It has always been so." Savaric grasped the holy symbol around his neck. "Though, now that you mention it… the energy does seem somewhat more potent."

Kitlyn indicated the man's robes. "Is there a prior or prioress here as well? Are you the only agent of Lucen in Shimmerbrook?"

"I've recently been promoted." Savaric grimaced. "Quite recently in fact. Prior Garniel vanished a mere two weeks ago. I've not been in Shimmerbrook a full two days yet."

"Vanished?" whispered Kitlyn. "Does anyone know what may have happened?"

Savaric leaned close, lowering his voice. "Some have mentioned he was unhappy the 'demonic savages' in the east would not face destruction. He also made some rather alarming comments about Lucernia having two queens."

Kitlyn tensed, hurt and angry a prior of Lucen would abandon his post over his hatred of her. She could guess at the 'alarming comments,' likely along the lines of a woman laying with a woman would make Lucen turn his back on the kingdom and give it to the demons. *If he longed for the murder of Evermoor's citizens, he may have lost Lucen's favor. It does not surprise me he failed to sense the demon here.*

The crowd whispered questions amongst themselves about what it could mean for the Dusk Goddess to be so close to the queens. Not one person spoke the goddess' name.

"Tenebrea guides us to her realm when our time comes." Oona gazed out over the crowd, projecting her voice. "She is not an agent of death, but a protector and companion to those who must take the journey between worlds. It was not yet time for the people who live in the house behind me to go to her. She asked me to help them."

"The Goddess of Death *saved* life?" blurted a woman somewhere in the crowd, setting off another whisper storm.

"Did you not hear the queen?" rasped a younger-sounding woman. "Tenebrea does not make people die. She helps them after they do."

"You said her name," wheezed a man.

"Why should we not?" the same woman yelled back. "She is a goddess, not a demon. They all help and protect us."

Oona, Charrah, and Savaric joined the discussion, which grew somewhat heated when a young man said he thought Orien and Tenebrea were rival siblings—life and death—and not friendly to each other.

It seems my dear wife has started something. We shall be here most of the night. Kitlyn smiled to herself as the citizens struggled to debate the nature of a goddess whose name itself terrified most of them. The average person believed speaking her name could attract her attention and potentially hasten one's death.

"Begging your pardon, my queens, would you do me the honor of joining me for dinner?" Mayor Ernald smiled a little too earnestly, tapping all his fingertips together in front of his belly.

Kitlyn sensed no malice in the man, more a desire to feel important. Surely, if the queens visited his home and ate at his table, he would derive a sense of status from the affair. It appeared harmless enough. Her father would have ignored the question entirely, which encouraged her to accept.

"My dear mayor, we would of course join you for tonight's meal." Kitlyn nodded graciously. "There are, however, a few small matters in the way."

Ernald's jowls drooped. "Matters?"

"We must attend to a small issue in the woods first. Also, I trust you intend to provide food for our escort as well. I'll not have them standing around while we eat."

"B-b-but of course." Ernald kneaded his hands, eyeing the soldiers.

Oona returned from the crowd, her expression part frustration, part satisfaction. "Let us go now and discover the source of this evil."

If we can find it... Kitlyn nodded to her, then spent the next few minutes extricating herself from a conversation with the mayor, who appeared to believe the longer he stood near the queens, the more important he became as though he could absorb prestige in the manner of a literal sponge. He even started following them past the western edge of town into the woods until realizing they searched for a demon. At that point, he 'remembered' he needed to go make arrangements for a large dinner and hurried away.

Savaric and Charrah accompanied them, both greatly concerned at the potential presence of a demon so close to the town. Once they'd gone far enough into the woods where they could no longer see Shimmerbrook behind them, Kitlyn crouched to press a hand into the earth. She reached out to the Stone, asking to see its memory of Bertelis Kol's passage. Soon, pressure walked up her back, much heavier than the delicate patter she felt when seeing the memory of her childhood journey through the hidden passages in the castle.

She looked up from where her fingers sank into the dark brown dirt, trying to visualize the man's route into the woods the magic allowed her to feel. "How dangerous do you think this entity is?"

Oona furrowed her brows. "Dangerous, but not worse than the fiend the lich summoned as a guardian."

We should not take chances. She stepped out of her boots. As soon as her feet touched soil, her entire body tingled in response to the magic flowing into her from the Alderswood. The soldiers grew nervous. To them, Kitlyn removing her shoes meant the situation had become serious. Elemental or spirit magic, the kind common to Evermoor, remained largely mysterious and, to a point, frightened the people of Lucernia. However, the castle guard and most of the soldiers now understood she drew power up from the earth. During the war, they'd thought the Evermoor rootcallers savages for wearing little clothing beyond loincloths or skirts, but in truth, they did so to strengthen their magic. Rootcallers absorbed power from the plant life around them. Clothing over their bodies weakened the connection like dirt on a window weakened sunlight. Stonecallers drew power up from the earth in much the same way.

Kitlyn followed the ephemeral sense of footsteps into the woods while explaining to the bewildered priests how being in direct contact with the ground strengthened her magic and gave her much greater awareness of their surroundings. She compared wearing boots to attempting to have a conversation with a towel wrapped around her head.

The woods ahead appeared darker than they ought to be. Even without a connection to the gods, Kitlyn sensed a malign presence somewhere ahead. *The demon we hunt charmed a man. I should have the soldiers and Savaric remain behind.* She shifted her jaw side to side. *It may be female.* She glanced at Oona. *Will its charms work on us? Or... no. Tenebrea would not have sent her here if it could steal her mind.*

"What do you think of the mayor?" asked Oona.

"He seems reasonably nice, but insecure. You?"

"Honestly, the man reminds me of a gloamwraith, only he attempts to leech respectability rather than life."

"Gloamwraith?" Kitlyn looked over at her. "What sort of books have you been reading? Is that a real fiend or a flight of fancy?"

"The book sounded sincere. They're a form of weak undead, a sinister sort of ghost known for draining the life force of a living person, making itself stronger as its victim withers."

Kitlyn couldn't help but chuckle. "Yes, that does sound like him. You read an awful lot."

"Perhaps."

"Too much even."

Oona scoffed. "No such thing."

Fleeting humor gave way to worry. Kitlyn peered back at the soldiers following them. "We hunt a demon capable of poisoning men's minds. Should we ask them to stay here?"

"Lucen will protect us," said Savaric. "I can call upon his power to shield us while Queen Oona destroys the fiend, or we could do the reverse."

"What if you fall victim to its charms?" asked Kitlyn.

Savaric's eyebrow twitched. "Lucen will not allow it."

Kitlyn cringed inside. "Pardon. I spoke before thinking. I did not mean to question your dedication."

He nodded once. Though he didn't speak, his expression said he understood her to be young, inexperienced, and presently frightened —or at least nervous enough not to think clearly. Lucen's faithful were supposedly immune to any mind-altering charms from demonic sources. If the more powerful demon lurking out in the woods had the ability to seduce men via supernatural power, it shouldn't work on him.

I'm not as scared as he thinks me to be. Concerned, yes. She didn't mind his lack of deference or even object to his regarding her as something of a naïve child. She often felt like one, constantly questioning her fitness to sit upon the throne. She wondered if Aodh ever doubted himself. He'd been crowned much younger than her, too young to have the ability to truly consider how his actions affected others. Perhaps taking the crown at such a tender age explained his arrogance. Having everyone bow and praise him from childhood molded his sense of how the world should be. Kitlyn's life had been the exact opposite—mostly derision and contempt.

I am too doubting of myself. She looked out at the dark woods at a sudden snap not far off. To avoid scaring the demon away, neither Oona nor Savaric had made light orbs. Half the soldiers carried ordinary lanterns, which did not give off much light by comparison. The earth sense revealed the footsteps of deer too far off in the dark to see, so she disregarded worry.

For years, she'd been screamed at and belittled for the slightest errors. Even now, as queen, she caught herself thinking the same ways, going over an action or choice ten times out of fear she'd make a mistake. The last year had been the worst, but in a paradoxical way, Fauhurst's extreme contempt helped. He often shouted at her even if she performed a task perfectly, purely because he adored putting her down. The man taught her some people would scream for any reason, and her committing an error or not had nothing to do with it.

The best I can do is follow what I believe to be right. She sighed mentally. *I cannot be a worse ruler than Aodh.*

A little over twenty minutes after leaving Shimmerbrook, the Stone's memory of the leatherworker's passage led them to a small clearing, heavy with a smell akin to moldy fur and dead birds.

"It is near," whispered Oona.

Most of the soldiers coughed on the rancid air. Charrah merely scrunched her nose. Savaric, like Oona, showed no reaction whatsoever.

Kitlyn drew her sword, surveying the trees, a small stream, and the weed-strewn ground in the midst of the clearing. Her gaze settled on a brown lump, a small animal perhaps dropped by Bertelis a day or two ago.

She advanced toward the carcass, shifting her concentration from visual to sensing. The weight of the soldiers, priests, and Oona manifested in her mind, revealing their location around her. As she neared the center of the clearing, three distinct sources of motion emerged at the edge of her sensing radius. Heavy, small points like fat broom handles being pushed into her skin conjured the image of wolves in her mind. They weighed too much for their size and stalked like cats, three trails curving inward toward their group.

"Beasts approach. Be ready!" called Kitlyn.

At her shout, the creatures burst from the underbrush and charged. Three jet-black beasts set upon them with such speed even her warning didn't offer enough time to avoid them—though likely made the difference between injury and death.

Two of the beasts pounced on Savaric, dragging him to the ground. The third knocked Oona flat on her front and remained standing on top of her. Kitlyn screamed the bastard offspring of a war cry and a shriek of desperation, swinging her sword at the head of the monster attacking Oona. The blade bounced away from a hardened shell with a dull *clank*. She failed to injure the monster, but did succeed in distracting it from biting Oona's neck. It lifted his head to stare at her, a singular glowing red eye in the middle of its face brightened.

The creature had the general proportions of a dog covered in a chitinous shell rather than fur. Clear slime dribbled from its translucent needle-like teeth as it snarled, its creepy elongated mouth taken straight from a nightmare of the deep ocean.

Oona growled, shoving at the ground in a futile effort to get up. The fiend standing on her back weighed too much for her to lift. Clanks and pings came from the soldiers attacking the two beasts attempting to drag Savaric off. Their swords bounced off the hard shells, no more effective than a pack of children walloping an armored knight with sticks.

Kitlyn called a rock spike from the ground beside Oona, ramming it diagonally into the monster's side hard enough to launch the fiend into the air. It crashed to the ground a short distance away on its side. Steaming yellow ooze leaked from a serious crack in the chest plate where the rock spire stabbed it.

"How… interesting," said a fairly deep woman's voice.

While helping Oona up, Kitlyn glared toward the sensation of an approaching person waking on the earth.

A nude woman sashayed into view, only she appeared quite far from human. The skin on her face, shoulders, and the outsides of her arms and legs had a dark reddish-orange color marked by black leopard spots. Her chest and stomach lightened to a pale yellowish color. Two shiny black horns extended upward from her temples, and a long, fleshy tail swished around her legs.

In complete disregard of her bizarre appearance, Kitlyn stared in shock at the most beautiful creature she'd ever seen. Her body tingled in all the wrong places. Mouth slightly open, she gawked, sorely tempted to forget entirely about everyone nearby and rip her clothes off so she could make love to this gorgeous being.

The men among the soldiers appeared to have similar thoughts. They all ceased fighting the dog creatures and gawked at the demoness. Neither of the two women appeared to even notice the newcomer's presence, continuing to attack the hard-shelled beasts.

"Hit it in the eye," yelled a female soldier.

One of the beasts tearing into Savaric's arm let go of him and pounced at her, suggesting it had the intelligence to understand her —proving her idea worthy.

Oona scrambled to her feet. She looked at the demonic woman

for a few seconds with raised eyebrows before shaking her head as if clearing a fog. "Foul beast! Lucen shall—"

Two soldiers ran at her.

Kitlyn, too, sensed the stunning goddess' dread fear of Oona and desire to destroy her. She looked away from the being of perfect beauty toward a slender blonde girl crossing swords with three men in chain mail armor. For some reason, she thought the little woman a dire threat she needed to get rid of, but also didn't want to hurt her. The girl parried one man, hacking his sword at her in an overhead chop while sidestepping another—but the third man sliced her on the thigh. Leather armor reduced a potentially crippling injury to a superficial slash.

The cry of pain walloped Kitlyn over the head like Guard Morrow's wooden training sword. Dazed, she blinked rapidly to clear her mind. *Navissa's nethers! The fiend charmed me!* She dashed over in time to deflect a soldier's sword swinging for Oona's wide-open back. She peeled him away from attacking her, but the other three men stopped admiring the demon and joined the fight.

Damn! Kitlyn put her back to Oona's, adopting a fully defensive posture. Two against six would not have been great odds in any situation, especially when the two remained relative novice sword fighters compared to seasoned castle guards. However, the men used little of their actual skill, fumbling about like half-awake puppets.

"I looked at her," yelled Kitlyn. "She charmed me."

"I know." Oona summoned a brilliant flash of light in the faces of two men, sending them stumbling off, blind. "Lucen is shielding me."

Savaric wailed in pain, then bellowed, "Lucen banish you, fiend!"

Another burst of blue-white light went off a short distance to Kitlyn's side. She couldn't spare even an instant to look, lest a soldier's sword slip past her defenses. Something heavy thudded to the ground.

"Orien grant you peace!" shouted Charrah.

Auras of yellow-golden light surrounded the soldiers. Their strikes tapered off to limp, uninspired swipes, then nothing. The men stood motionless, eyes half closed.

The she-demon shouted, "Destroy her" in a mostly human voice with a sinister echo.

Rapid, heavy thumping like falling rocks accompanied the two remaining dogs running at Charrah, who raised a quarterstaff in defense. Her worried expression said she had little faith a flimsy wooden stick would stop stone-shelled monsters. Kitlyn pushed past two of the dazed soldiers, channeling magic into the ground.

Dark emerald glow formed around her arms.

Two stone spires burst up from the earth in the paths of the charging dogs. One fiend crashed headfirst into the pillar, cracking it in half. The other swerved around it, dodging, but a beam of blue-white light from Savaric forced it to leap away from Charrah before it could bite her.

"By Lucen's light, you shall plague this land no longer!" roared Oona before hurling a blue beam in a direction Kitlyn refused to look.

The demoness screamed at the pitch of a terrified maidservant seeing a rat, but her voice rapidly fell in pitch to a monstrous howl of rage too deep and loud for any human throat to produce.

Kitlyn gathered earth up into a small boulder, directing it to fly at the disoriented beast still standing by the broken pillar it crashed into. The glow-shrouded stone crushed the demonic dog to the ground, sickly yellow goo spraying out from the smashed shell.

"Kill!" rasped a partially feminine voice.

The soldiers started to move.

Charrah held her arms out to them. "Orien's grace, be upon you. Know peace."

Gold light shrouded her hands and the men's heads. Growing anger in the soldier's expressions faded once again to placidity. She continued concentrating on the magic, shielding the men or at least pacifying them. Savaric threw another energy beam at the remaining dog. It leapt aside, suffering a minor searing burn across its flank. Enraged, it hurled itself at him, emitting a shrieking wail.

Anticipating its abnormal speed, Kitlyn shoved her arm forward, commanding a stone spear to form and stab upward from the ground in front of the priest. Her timing proved perfect; the stone spear smashed into the monster's face, impaling it in midair before its forelegs touched the ground. Yellow slime sprayed out from the broken shell around its former eye. The spire shattered from the force of impact, crumbling into pieces as the beast collapsed in a heap on its back.

Savaric projected a light bolt from his outstretched hand, disintegrating the creature into ash.

A clink of chain preceded Oona shrieking in pain.

Kitlyn spun before thinking about the consequences of looking in the direction of the demoness. Oona stumbled forward to her knees, dragged down by a barbed hook sunk into her shoulder, connected to a black iron chain coming out of the ground. The formerly beautiful she-demon no longer had a left arm. Black ichor sprayed from the stump. A four-inch tunnel bored completely through her stomach, the edges smoking and charred. Blistering char covered half her face. Small burn marks scattered around the trees suggested Oona had experienced some difficulty hitting the demon, which likely moved quite fast.

Snarling, Oona gripped the chain in one hand and raised her right arm.

Kitlyn projected a surge of magic into the ground, liquefying the earth beneath the demon into a mud slick. When the fiend attempted to leap out of the way of Oona's light beam, she fell flat on her face. Alas, Oona still missed, having aimed too high. Kitlyn summoned a tangle of roots to grab the demon, holding her down while Oona and Savaric both invoked magic again.

Two searing white energy beams struck the she-demon simultaneously. The fiend burst into a fiery cloud of ashes, emitting a scream so loud and anguished Kitlyn almost felt sorry for her.

Almost.

She rushed to her wife's side. The hooked chain disappeared to a wisp of dark black vapor. To her astonishment, she found no blood or hole in leather armor. Still, Oona clutched the spot as if hurt.

"Oo?"

"Yes?" Oona looked up at her, smiling a weary smile.

Kitlyn pulled her hand down to examine where an injury should have been. "The hook… how are you not hurt?"

"Ice magic, solid only to flesh, not a physical attack. I believe I have a cold burn." Oona shifted to sit on the ground. "Is anyone else hurt?"

"Savaric's bleeding quite badly." Kitlyn surveyed the soldiers. A few had injuries, though the worst appeared to be a broken shin. "Yes."

Charrah called upon Orien's light to heal Savaric, so Oona started tending to the soldiers. The two women had the most serious wounds from the dogs as the men had been largely under the influence of charm during the entire confrontation. The men appeared ashamed of themselves, apologizing repeatedly for being weak.

"You have nothing to be sorry for," said Kitlyn. "The fiend affected my mind as well."

They stared at her.

"I realize some of you may try not to think about it, but as you all know, I am in love with Oona. She happens to be a woman. The sight of a supernaturally beautiful monster pretending to be a woman affects me the same as it does you."

Heat rushed to Kitlyn's cheeks. Openly admitting to her love for a woman *still* came with a heavy portion of worry and awkwardness. She no longer feared actual punishment from the king and the temple of Lucen, but couldn't so quickly brush aside years of dread at mentioning a subject so forbidden for so long.

Her blunt admission appeared to relieve the soldiers of their guilt.

Charrah and Oona checked on everyone, calling upon Orien's healing gift. By the time they finished doing as much as they could with magic, one female soldier limped on a tender leg, the other had some bruises, and Savaric would likely spend a few days in bed recovering before having much desire to move. He'd been mostly stuck fending the bestial demons off himself using his light orb, which they recoiled from. The soldiers' attacks barely rose to the level of distraction against the armored fiends. This surprised neither

Oona nor Savaric, as true demons possessed exceptional resistance to ordinary attacks.

"Are there more than one of… whatever she was?" asked Kitlyn.

"I do not think so. The woods here still carry a taint of evil, but not as strong as her." Oona winced, and rubbed her shoulder where the hook had been. "Perhaps a stain from her presence which will fade in time."

"You should rest." Kitlyn squeezed her hand. "Poor Mayor Ernald will be so disappointed."

"Hah." Oona chuckled. "I am well enough to humor him. This does not hurt as much as his conversation will."

Kitlyn snickered.

"I believe we encountered a succubus," said Oona. "A demon who sustains herself by feasting on the souls of men after charming them to do her bidding."

"She got me, too… for a moment."

Oona rubbed Kitlyn's arm. "Their charms are based on attraction, not whether someone is a man or woman. She wouldn't have charmed Donal."

Kitlyn strained to remember. "The name is familiar but I can't place who it is."

"The young soldier we mistook for a spy while camping?" Oona smiled at her. "I wonder if he's told Tavin how he feels yet."

"Oh, yes. I remember him now. I hope they're happy." She glanced back at the clearing. "Why do you think this succubus was here? Did a person summon it or do they show up on their own?"

"Either is possible," called Savaric, his voice strained. "I am concerned I did not sense its presence."

"You have only been here a few days, and demons are tricky." Oona took Kitlyn's hand. "I am sure you would have sensed the fiend had you gone into the woods."

"And become food for those damned dogs," muttered Savaric.

"Perhaps Lucen knew this, so did not send you to your death," said Kitlyn. "Shall we return to Shimmerbrook and rest?"

"Perhaps," rasped Savaric.

Oona mouthed, "Yes, I think so, too."

"Highness," called a soldier. "You should see this."

Kitlyn and Oona exchanged a glance, then followed the man in the direction the demon had come from. Not far from where they'd fought the beast, the flayed remains of a man hung in an X, upside down between two trees on black chains and large barbed hooks. His skin and most of his guts were gone. A tangle of unrecognizable scraps and several glowing stones sat at the bottom of the cavity inside his torso. What little remained of his face had frozen in a grimace of horrific agony. A vertical column of demonic sigils marked each tree from which he hung, burned into the bark.

"Ugh." Kitlyn averted her eyes. "Ghastly."

Oona emitted the noise she usually made before throwing up, but didn't look away. "I believe we have found Prior Garniel."

"What?" rasped Kitlyn. "How can you tell... there isn't enough left? I barely realized he's a man."

"His robes are over there in the bushes." Oona exhaled. "He abandoned Lucen."

Savaric made a sacred hand sign, muttering, "Lucen protect us."

"What should we do?" Kitlyn shifted so she could look at Savaric without seeing the dead man.

"The demon finished whatever it intended to do to him. His soul is likely consumed already. Devoured."

Oona bowed her head. "I feel Tenebrea's sorrow. This body has become a gateway for demons. It is no longer human remains."

She and Savaric invoked Lucen's blessing, guiding their light orbs close. The former Prior's remains began to thrash and shake on the hooks holding him up, spraying dark blood from every opening. Seconds later, he disintegrated, the chains falling limp against the trees before they, too, melted away as vapor.

The grim mood of the forest in the area lifted.

Is this the fate Aodh feared would be his? Kitlyn sheathed her longsword.

Oona took her hand. "We have done all that is possible to do here. Let us return to Shimmerbrook."

"Yes." Kitlyn leaned close, kissed her on the cheek, and

whispered, "I am going to need to hold you close tonight to ward off nightmares."

"I feel the same. We shall guard each other's dreams then."

Kitlyn offered a weak smile, still numb from the horror of the dead prior. Hand in hand, they walked in the direction of town.

7

ILL TIDINGS

OONA

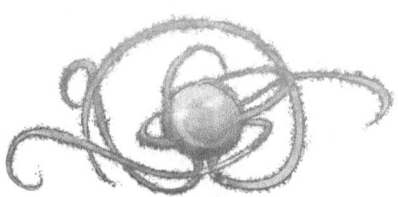

Orien's magic greatly lessened the pain in Oona's shoulder, but didn't eliminate it.

They'd taken a room at the Dancing Owl, an inn where they stopped to change before dinner with the mayor. It baffled her how something cold could burn like fire. Though the wicked hook hadn't broken skin or damaged her clothing, it left a nasty bruise. She hoped Kitlyn wouldn't notice how she mostly tried not to move her left arm while shedding her armor, but couldn't hide the pain in her face. Kitlyn helped her change without flying into a panic. Oona didn't entirely enjoy feeling like a wounded bird picked up off the ground and tended to, but at seeing her wife so concerned for her, she became misty eyed.

As they rushed out to Shimmerbrook with nothing to wear other than their armor and the basic clothing under it, they purchased some simple dresses from a local tailor. Oona couldn't help herself and selected one similar to the dress she'd worn in her dream. They looked like a pair of ordinary townsfolk rather than nobility—much less queens—but neither cared.

Predictably, Kitlyn worried over the bruise, more so because Oona tried not to move the arm.

Initially, Mayor Ernald reacted with shock to their common attire. Kitlyn rather bluntly told him they'd come here in a rush to *kill* a demon, not have a state dinner with it, so hadn't brought fancy garments. Conversation during the meal ended up being less painful than either expected. The mayor's dining room had plenty of room for all eight soldiers in addition to the man's wife, daughter, and son.

Other than a quick explanation of getting rid of the demon, their dialogue mostly felt like Ernald feeling out their intentions for policy and none-too-subtly hinting at his interest in moving up the political ladder, especially if it let him relocate to Cimril. He sounded eager to get out of Shimmerbrook, implying it small and uneventful.

Oona nearly laughed when Kitlyn asked him if he considered a succubus outside town 'uneventful.' While he struggled to come up with a response, she reframed the small town at the edge of the Shimmering Wood as important, standing between Lucernia and any potential danger coming out of the vast forest or even from the Dawnspire Mountains beyond.

After the relatively pleasant dinner ended, Kitlyn, Oona, and the soldiers returned to the Dancing Owl where they encountered a small crowd waiting for them. Sitting still and talking didn't annoy the pain in her shoulder, so Oona had no objection to spending an hour or two meeting citizens in the inn's main room. They sat in two adjacent cushioned chairs by the fireplace, a tiny table between them, and welcomed people over to talk.

She braced herself, expecting at least one person would show up to make a nasty comment about them, something along the lines of the demon being there because of their 'unnatural' love... but surprisingly, no one did. Most of the citizens merely wanted to meet them. Many commented in surprise at their young age. She doubted anyone spoke of Aodh the same way at first, though he didn't have any real power as a child. By the time he came of age for Beredwyn to step back, the people had gotten used to him.

Odd they think we are of age to marry and bear children, yet young for the throne.

Other citizens thanked them for ending the war or asked questions to straighten out the stories they'd heard about it. Kitlyn didn't pull punches, admitting Aodh's role in the conflict—though she didn't go out of her way to make him sound worse. His actions had been quite awful enough.

A few asked about the demon, questioning how such a fiend could exist in Lucernia. Oona repeated her theory about past priests misinterpreting the teachings, admitting to once having believed it as well. She refused to say Lucen didn't have enough power to permanently ban demons from being in the kingdom, since she didn't know it for a fact and it seemed wrong. Even if it ended up being true, saying he lacked power would be seen as insulting.

Whatever thread of trust she had for the old teaching snapped after seeing a succubus and a lesser demon here in Shimmerbrook. The archon they encountered while pursuing the lich had been in Ondar, not Lucernia... so it hadn't threatened the idea of Lucernia's imperviousness to demons.

Most of the teachings may have come from Lucen, but people *wrote them down. People can make errors. It is possible they misunderstood or even exaggerated things in their efforts to praise him. Not all lies are borne of malicious intent. Believing no demon could possibly tread on Lucernian soil is dangerous. It will cause complacency. I must ask Balais to warn the entire temple to be on guard.*

When the crowd started to thin, having satisfied their curiosity, Oona wondered if the citizens might really accept them much faster than she'd previously believed possible. No one commented or asked about two young women married to each other. As far as she could tell, not a single person had even glared as if to blame them wordlessly for the demon being there.

Perhaps the ones who hate us simply stayed away.

She frowned at the fireplace, so no one would see the sour look on her face. Kitlyn often told her not to let them bother her, but she couldn't get past feeling hurt by people she didn't know hating her for who she loved. Even at her spoiled worst, she'd never been mean to anyone—merely whined about life being unfair. The cruelest thing she'd ever done was force people to listen to her complaining.

"What are the Gates of Isilien?" asked Kitlyn during a lull in the crowd.

"I'd say they're the front door of wherever Isilien is." Oona flashed an impish smile.

Kitlyn chuckled. "I think we ought to find it... and go there."

"Yes, most definitely." Oona clenched her jaw expecting pain. She reached her left hand across the little table to take Kitlyn's, resulting in a stab of pain in her shoulder. "Your mother wants to protect you."

"Stop moving your arm if it hurts so much." Kitlyn stroked her fingers over the back of Oona's hand.

"It does not hurt so much I cannot bear it."

"Most would claim it doesn't hurt."

Oona smirked at her. "I will not offend Lucen by speaking false."

"It is an expression. No one would seriously understand you saying it doesn't hurt to mean there is no pain. It means you are dealing with it."

"Perhaps, but I'd rather not."

"Would you speak false to save a life?"

"Why do you ask such questions?"

Kitlyn shrugged one shoulder. "Curiosity? Exploration of the gods' desires?"

Oona sighed. "Lucen is the god of purity. I suppose one could argue that saving the life of an innocent is a pure act, even if it requires deception to accomplish. Purity may not refer to literal truth at all costs but the intention behind any action." She stared into the fireplace for a long moment, thinking. "I do not believe he would be upset at any action taken with pure intention."

"Has he told you where Isilien is?"

"Not yet." Oona smiled. "We cannot ask the gods to do everything for us. The castle has a library. I've never heard of Isilien before."

"Nor I."

"Then I shall read." Oona twirled her hair around a finger, smiling.

A man approached, clad in a green cloak and leather armor. Despite his appearing old enough to have fathered them, he gave off a sense of deference. He stood in silence until Kitlyn gave a nod.

"Pardon, my queens," said the man in a quiet tone. "My name is Kovar. I thought you may wish to know that I have seen strange creatures in the woods."

Kitlyn briefly described the dog-like monsters and the succubus. "Those?"

"No, highness. The beast I saw looked like a man, but green, its skin like moss, and too tall to fit inside this room without making a hole in the ceiling for its head. Yellow eyes. I observed it shambling along, dragging a dead deer."

"Where and when did you see this monster?" asked Kitlyn.

"Nine days ago. I was on my way to a fishing spot in the woods. Takes half a day to get there, so I usually camp a few nights, fishing and salting my catch before returning to town."

Oona nodded. "Have you seen it since? Or any closer to town?"

"No, highness."

"Perhaps he's spotted Grengwylf," said Kitlyn, trying not to smile.

A faint shiver crawled up Oona's back. She hadn't had a nightmare about the storybook monster since age thirteen, but still remembered it. "Honestly, it sounds like a forest troll."

"Those aren't real…" Kitlyn raised one eyebrow.

"They used to be, according to what I've read." Oona pictured the large book in her mind. She'd found it inside one of the concealed passages leading out of the library. It had gathered such a thick coating of grey dust, she didn't even recognize it as a book right away. "Forest trolls are generally quite stupid. They don't pose much of a threat to towns because they prefer the solitude of the deep woods. I am unsure how they would react to a single person, but my guess is they would be violent."

Kitlyn blinked. "You are taking the book seriously? It's probably a compendium of creatures from storybooks."

"It didn't seem like it." Oona shrugged her right shoulder. "Someone concealed the book in a hidden passage, certainly to protect it from whoever destroyed knowledge they wanted to hide. In the days before Lucen cleansed the demons from this land, all sorts of fiends and monsters roamed everywhere."

"Oo…" Kitlyn leaned forward in her chair. "There are no records of this land ever being overrun with demons. We know Aodh told great lies in Lucen's name. How much else of what we once held to be true is not? Besides, trolls aren't demons. They're—if they exist—trolls. Lucen protect us, but he didn't destroy every single demon or make it so they could not exist here."

"Yes, I know." Oona looked down.

"If creatures like trolls ever did exist for real, *something* is responsible for them being gone."

"True. But we know the Anthari once lived in Evermoor. No one has seen an elf in… a really long time, but they left behind statues, temples, buildings, and all manner of ruins. We know they *did* exist before." Oona swiped her hair off her face, tucking it behind one ear. "How can we say monsters like trolls never existed at all simply because no one has seen them in a long time?"

Kitlyn leaned back and sighed. "Scary to think about." She looked up at the man. "You are certain you saw this creature?"

"Yes, highness." Kovar scratched at his beard. "I didn't risk getting too close. It seemed to smell me and turned to look, so I ran before it spotted me."

"We should advise Mayor Ernald of this troll in case it becomes brave enough to approach the town," said Oona.

"He already thinks we're children." Kitlyn frowned. "If we start speaking of trolls as real, he'll believe we've been reading Grengwylf too much."

Oona exhaled. "I'd rather be thought a fool than say nothing and have someone end up dead."

"Trolls shouldn't exist," whispered Kitlyn.

"Are there tracks?" asked Oona.

Kovar nodded. "I can find the place easily, but it will take six or seven hours to reach."

Before Oona could agree to go hunting for tracks, Kitlyn squeezed her hand. "We will send word to Ernald to have some of the local garrison accompany you into the woods to observe these tracks. The good mayor can send us a report." She lowered her voice. "It'll let him feel as if he's doing something important."

Oona smiled.

"Thank you, highness." Kovar bowed. "I shall speak with him in the morning."

Kitlyn waited for the man to walk away, returning to his table, then looked over at Oona. "I know you wanted to go. It sounded fun, but we can't do every little thing ourselves. And you're hurt."

"Yes. Being queen is certainly annoying at times." Oona faked a sigh. "Responsibility is so overrated."

A few people nearby glanced over.

"My dear wife is so eager to defend Lucernia against all threats herself, she is frustrated at responsibility requiring her to be elsewhere."

"That part is true." Oona smiled for a moment before worry overpowered it. "Trolls… the small creature the soldiers spotted on our way here, could it perhaps have been an actual goblin?"

"I suppose if you are considering trolls might really exist, why not goblins, too?" Kitlyn leaned back in the chair, gazing at the ceiling. "Neither trolls nor goblins have been seen in Lucernia for centuries—if ever at all."

"So we have been told. How do we really know what's happened longer ago than the oldest living person's memory? Simply because a thing has been written down does not make it true."

Kitlyn stifled a yawn. "If these beasts truly exist, then something has changed."

"I agree," whispered Oona. "But what?"

"Do you think someone is up to nefarious deeds? Or have these creatures reappeared of their own doing?"

"It would be more worrisome to me if no person is responsible for this." Oona rubbed her hurt shoulder, grimacing. "There may be no easy way to stop them. A person doing evil can be dealt with. Life springing into existence is an act of the gods."

"Not necessarily. It could be the life or animal spirits of Evermoor. Storms, floods, earthquakes, and fires happen… not all of them are the gods' doing."

"I suppose." Oona yawned. "I am too tired to think such things."

"Then let us away to bed for the night." Kitlyn stood, then reached to help her up.

"It is my arm in pain, not my legs." Smiling, Oona still took her hand, then followed her upstairs to the rooming area.

8

TOO HEAVY TO FLY
KITLYN

*W*ater sloshed around the bathtub, echoing in the stone alcove off the royal bedchamber.

Oona sat in the tub with Evie, washing the child's hair. The little one considered the enormous, round tub more of a tiny swimming pool than a place to clean. Kitlyn toweled herself dry a few steps away, biting her lip in concern at the purplish discoloration still on Oona's left shoulder. They'd been back at the castle for three days. Oona no longer moved as if in pain, but the angry bruise worried her. It unnerved Evie, too, but the child didn't question her older sister's assurance it would heal.

Orien's magic could turn mortal injuries survivable, mend broken limbs, or even restore severed fingers, ears, and so forth. However, only the smallest of injuries vanished entirely. In most cases, it still took a while for the wound to finish healing naturally. A few priestesses at the temple of Navissa seemed satisfied Oona's injury would heal. The ones who worship the Matron of Night wielded cold magic. During the war, they often used it against the 'invaders'. Granted, they didn't usually treat the injuries of the enemy, but had still seen enough of its effect to consider her injury minor.

Oona got out of the tub, allowing Evie to play in the water for a little while more. She summoned an aura of warm blue light to dry herself off much faster than a towel could, then proceeded to dress herself. Kitlyn dropped her towel on a nearby chair and also donned her undergarments. Soon, they stood side by side in their smallclothes, arms folded, staring into the closet while Evie sloshed around in the tub playing.

"What shall we wear today?" asked Oona.

"Something comfortable."

"You always say that."

Kitlyn grinned. "Because I enjoy being comfortable. The last king always wore his robes. Why are *we* expected to confine ourselves in those ghastly, complicated, pinchy gowns?"

"Perhaps because they would look ridiculous on a man." Oona winked.

"They look ridiculous on us, too." Kitlyn sighed.

Piper picked up a towel from a shelf and approached the bathtub. "C'mon, miss. Time to get dressed."

"Okay," whispered the child.

Kitlyn plucked a fairly plain green crushed velvet dress out of the closet. It had puffy shoulders, but otherwise lacked extensive fluffery. "This shall do."

"That dress does not require a team of handmaidens, a stepladder, and invocations of forbidden magic to get into," said Oona. "The nobles will faint at the sight of it."

Kitlyn laughed.

A giggling Evie streaked around the room, running away from Piper who tried to catch her in a towel.

"I am not trying to impress nobles." Kitlyn opened the back of the dress.

"They are uneasy already at your idea to simply permit anyone to approach and talk to us."

Kitlyn smiled. "For every noble, there are a few thousand ordinary citizens. If the wealthy do not monopolize our ears, how can they ensure our decisions always benefit them?"

"But we must serve only the interests of the wealthy, otherwise the kingdom will surely crumble," said Oona in an obviously sarcastic tone.

"Quite." Kitlyn stepped into the dress. "I am wearing this."

Evie tried to scramble over the bed, but Piper tackled her, trapping the child inside the towel. Both of them lay there laughing like fools.

"Aww," whispered Kitlyn, leaning against Oona. "She is so cute. So happy. So full of life. Just like you."

Oona's face reddened. "I'm working on the happy part."

"The worst is past us." Kitlyn turned her back. "Lace me?"

Meredith, Kitlyn's official handmaiden, stepped closer, but hesitated as Oona began tying the green silk up the back of the dress. "You two are lovely together. Sometimes, I feel superfluous."

"You are not." Kitlyn smiled at her. "To the horror of the court, I consider you a friend."

Meredith fake gasped.

"Mare, you can help me contain this little dervish," called Piper.

Evie giggled, playfully trying to escape the towel.

"All right." Laughing, Meredith approached the bed, pretending to carefully approach a dangerous animal in need of containment.

"Do you think my idea is a poor one?" asked Kitlyn.

Oona shook her head. "I like it. We should be willing to hear the concerns of all citizens, even if the advisors are concerned about threats."

"While I am not so naïve as to think no one would wish us ill, we are presently more liked than not." Kitlyn gestured at Oona. "I trust in your ability to sense those who wish us ill, and our ability to defend ourselves."

"I want to wear this," said Evie.

"You've nothing on." Piper flailed her arms. "You're not wearing anything."

"I know."

Meredith and Piper sighed together.

"Come, child. You cannot go out and about without clothing."

"Oona?" called Evie. "Why don't faeries have clothes? They don't get in trouble."

Oona and Kitlyn laughed.

Kitlyn smiled, remembering the day she and Oona made love in the forest pond near Kethaba's village. For a brief moment, she envied the faeries' utter disregard for clothing—and eternal youth. Though, much like Evie, she believed faeries to be innocent. They didn't know enough to be ashamed. Then again, people in Evermoor certainly didn't appear to be ashamed of minimal clothing. While she certainly didn't want to go out in public 'dressed' like a faerie, she did think Lucernian society had some rather silly rules about fashion.

"Because," said Kitlyn. "They don't make clothes small enough for faeries."

Evie laughed. "What about doll clothes?"

"Too heavy for them." Oona walked over and encouraged Evie to begin getting dressed. "They couldn't fly in doll clothes."

"Ohhh…" Evie nodded.

"Exactly why I am wearing this." Kitlyn smoothed her hands down the front of her dress. "Those other gowns are far too heavy to fly in."

Evie laughed, holding her arms up so Piper could drape a dress over her.

"All right." Oona took a dark blue dress from the cabinet of similar simplicity to Kitlyn's. "The nobles will be aghast at us for defying fashion."

"My dear wife…" Kitlyn held her chin up. "We do not defy fashion. We define it."

"I suppose." Oona opened the back lacing and stepped into the dress.

Kitlyn helped pull it up. "Where is it written that a ruler, especially a woman, must be uncomfortable when managing their land?"

"They will be jealous." Oona laughed. "All of them standing around in seventy pounds of Amadarian silk while we can breathe."

Kitlyn pretended to gasp in alarm. "Oh, perhaps we shouldn't. If we change everyone's mind about burdensome gowns, we'd be responsible for destroying the oceanic silk trade. How will those wealthy merchants in Amadar ever survive?"

"You are so bad." Oona coughed to stop her laughter. "Come, now. We should make ourselves presentable. Or as presentable as possible in these peasant rags."

Kitlyn snickered.

"Those are not peasant rags," said Meredith. "Each one cost at least five silver crescents, enough to feed a commoner for a year."

"My dear Meredith." Oona twirled to face her. "I spoke in jest."

"Oh, yes. Of course." Meredith fanned herself. "It is unusual for me to hear the rulers of Lucernia speak in jest."

Her smile gave away her teasing, so Kitlyn didn't go off on a complaint-laced tirade about the prior king. Evie zoomed over and showed off her dress, a frilly white garment full of pink ribbons and bows that made her look like an expensive doll.

"*Now* I feel underdressed." Kitlyn threw her arms up in defeat.

"Are you joking again, dear?" asked Oona, "or should we change?"

"I am speaking in jest." She leaned over to whisper behind her hand. "I think it is allowed for us to have a sense of humor."

Oona laughed. "Stop. We're going to be all puffy-eyed and red in the face for court."

"Blame the cook." Kitlyn winked. "Dinner last night was… spicy."

They sat together on a padded bench while Piper and Meredith arranged their hair. Evie sprawled on the floor nearby playing with dolls.

Nearly an hour later, the handmaidens finished.

"Well, then. Are you ready?" asked Oona.

"Quite." Kitlyn stood.

They made it halfway to the stairs before Oona noticed her wife hadn't put on any shoes.

"Kit?"

"Yes, my love?"

"Your slippers?"

"I am aware." She smiled. "It did, after all, require me making a decision to forget them."

"If you decided to leave them behind, you didn't forget them."

Evie looked back and forth between them as they spoke, grinning.

Piper and Meredith, walking a short distance behind them, tittered nervously.

"You realize the nobility will likely faint." Oona bit her lip. "What if they accuse you of being an Evermoor savage?"

"It is already well known where my magic came from. If *that* has not already convinced them of my savagery, my naked toes will not make it worse."

Oona lowered her voice. "Are you concerned about the open court?"

"To a degree. I believe it would cause more of a stir if I spent the entire time sitting on the floor so I could touch it. Having the ability to feel an assassin sneaking up on us is part of it."

"But...?" Oona tilted her head.

"The curse," whispered Kitlyn. "My mind will not truly be at ease until the matter of it is settled."

Oona seemed about to cry but didn't. "We will break it."

"Have you had any luck determining what the Gates of Isilien are?"

"Not yet. I am still working my way around the library," said Oona. "And yes, I have prayed on it."

"What did the gods say?"

Oona hiked her dress up so she could see her feet while stepping onto the top of the grand staircase. "They answered in a feeling, not words or visions. For a brief moment, I stopped worrying about you. It must mean they are reassuring me."

Her words helped a little, but didn't fully ease the worry rattling around Kitlyn's stomach. Kovar's story of a troll sighting got her wondering what form her premature death might take. Perhaps goblins and trolls returning to existence represented the start of problems which would eventually lead to her doom. She'd also wondered as to the nature of the curse. Did the dark forces of a curse care one way or the other *how* a Talomir behaved while on the throne? It obviously spared Lady Avalina, but she'd never ruled. Despite Aodh's clear failure as king, he'd lived to thirty-seven years of age, after ascending to the throne at eleven. Branok, the brother of Aodh's father, died at seventeen, thrown from a horse after merely a week wearing the crown. How horrible a king could he have been in such a short time?

No, it didn't make sense to believe the curse cared one way or the other as to the way in which a king or queen behaved. By all accounts she could find, Eoim—Aodh's father—had been a reasonably just ruler, if not overly strict in misinterpreting the meaning of Lucen's 'purity.' Historic records of King Iastor, the first Talomir to wear the crown, all spoke of him in such praising tones they had to be magnificent lies.

Kitlyn had little faith the curse would spare her if she worked hard to be a kind and just ruler. She did not, however, feel her imminent, guaranteed death justified abusing her power. She reasoned a monarch who treated their subjects with kindness and compassion only out of fear they'd be punished—by the gods, or curses, or assassins—was not really a kind soul, merely evil on a leash.

"Do you think it's an actual place?" Kitlyn stepped off the stairs to the marble-tiled atrium on the ground floor. "Or could 'Gates of Isilien' refer to an object or even a magical portal?"

"It is possible. I haven't found any mention of it at all yet."

"Sorry. I am nervous."

Oona leaned against her, squishing Evie between them.

"Mmf!" yelled Evie before laughing.

Up ahead, the din of a large crowd echoed in the grand hall.

They followed the corridor away from it to the right, heading around to a rear entrance of the throne room. Wearing ridiculous gowns amounted to one easily disposable tradition. Shoving their way past everyone like a pair of drunks at a tavern would perhaps push it too far. Besides, any capable assassin would have too easy a time striking and disappearing in such close proximity. Granted, neither of them had Aodh's fear of vast misdeeds to stoke paranoia of assassins.

Kitlyn couldn't think of a good reason anyone would go to the trouble of assassinating them at present. Merchants made money from the re-establishment of trade with Evermoor plus new trade routes to Underholm. In turn, the nobles made money. Most of the populous loved them for ending the war. The only people who didn't like her disapproved of her love for a girl. While their hate came from an irrational place, it seemed unlikely they would kill her or Oona over it. At least, not while most of the kingdom would react with outrage. If ever opinions turned against them to the point their murderer would not be hunted to the ends of the world, it could become a risk.

For now, she feared accidents most of all. The curse had probably caused young King Branok to go flying from his horse. Perhaps Omun might accidentally step on her the next time she coaxed him out of the earth. The giant had become a statue again, deep in the Mistral Wood. His consciousness remained, but only partially in his body. If ever she needed him again, her magic could wake him from his half-sleep.

She paused at the dark wooden door leading to the throne room. Guards on either side snapped to attention, then gave her odd looks, likely for the plain dress. This spot is where she would usually work herself up into 'queen mode,' preparing to do everything possible not to make even the slightest error of decorum. The hairs on the back of her neck stood on end out of fear someone would start screaming at her over any small mistake, but today, she resolved not to obsess over pointless, overstuffed pageantry or even anyone's reaction to them wearing the 'wrong' clothes.

No one screams at the queen. As long as I don't make a mistake on the important things, we'll be fine.

9

A MATTER OF PROGRESSION

OONA

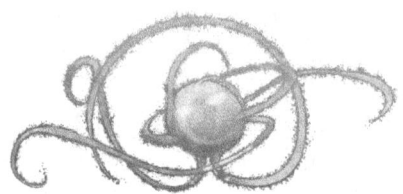

Oona walked hand-in-hand with Kitlyn up onto the dais.

By some miracle, Evie obeyed protocol and waited at the door. The throne room contained wall-to-wall people as it often did during court, most of whom had dressed in their finest. In general, people attempted to keep the strip of burgundy carpet connecting the main door to the throne dais clear. Along with the spiced potpourri fragrance the castle staff used to lessen the overwhelming odor of so many bodies packed into a single, large room, the air held the thick scent of mixed perfumes, colognes, candle wax, and wine.

Having spent much of the past five years wearing a crown as 'princess,' Oona had gotten used to it. Kitlyn, however, still sometimes didn't notice when it tilted slightly—or more than slightly if she had to wear high-heeled shoes. The poor girl still had all the grace of a newborn foal in heels, another reason she preferred slippers, or going barefoot.

"Queens Kitlyn and Oona Talomir," called Advisor Beredwyn.

The room as well as the elevated galleries on either side fell quiet.

Merchants and upper-class people stared at them in bewildered shock. Ordinary citizens continued murmuring, oblivious or unconcerned over their simpler dresses. When they sat, roughly two-thirds of the assembled gasped as Kitlyn's gown pulled up to reveal her bare feet. They likely wouldn't have cared for Oona's basic blue slippers either, but at least she wore white hose. However, no one appeared to notice her plain shoes. Some nobles gawked in shock, as if Advisor Beredwyn had exposed his backside to the room. The idea of him doing so did not seem so farfetched as to be entirely impossible, especially if he'd become frustrated at certain barristers.

Evie strolled out to the carpet at the front of the dais, carrying a small bundle of flowers. At the base, she turned ninety degrees to face the thrones and marched one step at a time up to take her place between Kitlyn and Oona. A collective 'aww' came from the crowd.

Balais Aldin, High Priest of Lucen and also an advisor to the crown, stepped forward. "On behalf of Queen Kitlyn and Queen Oona, I welcome you to the castle on this fine day." He glanced at them, seeming equally confused at their choice of attire. "In accordance with the queen's wishes, we will be inviting any citizen with questions or concerns forward to address the queens directly."

Minimal surprise came from the assembled, as they already knew this. Word had been sent around the city for days.

Kitlyn stood as Balais rejoined the line of other advisors. "I will make this, and only this comment regarding the reason many of you are staring at us. My choice of gown is not intended as a remark, commentary, or opinion on anyone or any group of people. We are all here on what could be one of the last warm days of the season. I see no point in being uncomfortable for the sake of dressing up like a peacock. Time is much better spent discussing ways to help Lucernia recover from the war than discussing fashion. This is not a grand ball, a party, a wedding, or a prestigious social event. We are here to make decisions in the interest of Lucernia."

Oona took a deep breath, expecting complaints from at least a few nobles who had nothing more meaningful to care about than where they ranked on the social ladder.

Kitlyn took her seat again.

Balais read from a scroll, going over figures and news related to the Temple of Lucen—nothing terribly out of the ordinary. When he finished, Lady Alonna, a priestess of Navissa who came from a noble family, stepped forward. During Aodh's reign, only the Lucen temple had any influence over the king. At Oona's suggestion, they appointed her as a liaison to represent the other three temples as an advisor.

Lady Alonna read for much longer, most of her time spent detailing what the Temple of Orien had been doing in regard to assisting war orphans and villages nearest the border where the most damage occurred. She mentioned a few requests from Tenebrea temples for funds to expand grave sites, which Kitlyn and Oona readily approved.

Advisor Naldun, formerly an ordinary farmer, spoke of the general mood of the middle and lower classes. For now, they seemed quite content—no surprise given the recent end of the war—though Oona wondered how long it would take before things changed. When he began bringing up multiple instances of people seeing unfamiliar creatures, she clutched the armrests of her throne. None of his stories had specifics beyond calling the various sightings 'strange.' Some of the other advisors and those closest to the front of the gallery chuckled at these reports, likely considering them flights of drunken fancy or imagination.

Oona pictured the troll illustration from the book she'd found. Never suspecting someone must have deliberately hidden it, she'd moved it out into the open. Fortunately, those responsible for purging 'unapproved' books from the library had either not noticed it or died long ago. Considering the amount of dust on it, she assumed it had been sitting in the hidden passage for centuries.

Without the need to announce new proclamations or laws, they went directly to hearing concerns from the gallery.

And so started the normal tedium of merchants and barristers quibbling tax percentages.

Oona tried her best not to fall into her old 'princess' habit of trying to fake paying attention while daydreaming or outright sleeping. Though finance and taxes bored her to tears, she endeavored to participate in the conversation if only by listening and following along. It all sounded normal and boring... until one merchant complained about the excessive import tax on ivenberries.

"Hold a moment." Oona raised a hand at the merchant, Patri, a balding almost thirty-year-old with an evident love of pastry. "There is no import tax on ivenberries."

Patri jabbed a finger at a taller, older man standing a short distance from him. "Then why does Cymuel sell them for a steel lumen apiece and claim he is barely earning a profit?"

"Either the trader in Evermoor he deals with charges him far more than the one you buy from, or he is lying to you," said Oona. "We are not levying a special tax on any imports from Evermoor."

Advisor Beredwyn nodded once, his tall, silly hat wobbling. "Indeed. We are hoping to encourage the reestablishment of trade."

Patri scowled at Cymuel.

"Why would it matter to you what he sells them for?" asked Kitlyn. "Set your price based on your cost."

"He warned me I would be hauled off for not paying the import tax." Patri's face reddened. He jabbed a finger into the air a few times, seemingly about to bark a demand the other merchant be charged with a crime… but couldn't come up with anything, finally admitting by way of silence he'd been fooled.

Now I've such a craving for an ivenberry.

Oona tried not to salivate too obviously, and asked Piper to go fetch some water. She thought of the somewhat younger girl more as a friend than a servant, but asking her to do the occasional small task kept up appearances, so no one complained about the handmaidens being 'too familiar' around the queens. Not that she would have cared about the complaining, but better to avoid hearing the whining. It would most likely come from Elsbeth, but she'd been convinced Kitlyn would cast her out or even imprison her for being so mean. Being allowed to keep her position as first maid, without even a verbal dressing down, left the woman in a perpetual state of nervousness. She believed Kitlyn wanted to let her feel safe, *then* humiliate her, even though they had no such plans. Upon realizing she'd spent four years tormenting the actual daughter of the king, Elsbeth punished herself much better than anyone else could.

The usual quibbling over trade and so forth continued for a while. Some people near the front of the gallery began chuckling. It took Oona a moment to realize the reason: Evie had fallen asleep, her head leaned to one side, mouth wide open.

This is the best part of being queen… the dreadful mundanity. No one is in peril. Oona teased a finger at Evie's cheek until the girl closed her mouth. Some of the nobility quietly grumbled amongst themselves about the queens' complete disregard for 'common decency,' meaning they'd dared to be seen in public in anything other than the most expensive, elaborate fabric monstrosities possible to buy.

Oona forced herself not to frown at the idea no one ever complained about Aodh's choice of attire. The robes of a Lucen High Priest had the same silver trim as a prior's robes, plus fancy gold-trimmed shoulder mantles. For robes, they were elaborate. Compared to the gowns worn by noble ladies, they may as well have been a nightdress. The more she thought about the annoying disparity, the more she agreed with Kitlyn. She wouldn't go so far as to avoid shoes, though. Kitlyn's magic kept her feet warm. Oona had no such gift.

No one expected wealthy women to involve themselves in warfare, exploration, or anything more demanding than sitting around sipping tea. Beyond the simple want of comfort, she and Kitlyn had valid reasons for avoiding the burdensome gowns: they might be attacked and *could* actually fight.

Any one of the ensembles requiring a team of handmaidens to get into effectively made surviving a swordfight impossible. *Some of them have enough bones in the corset to stop a broadsword.* Merely thinking about them made it difficult to breathe.

A piercing woman's scream came from the upper gallery.

All eyes went to Lady Parrington, Duchess of Tandren, standing there in her underpinnings. She'd been wearing a humungous, blooming pearlescent white gown dotted in red flowers that made her look like an enormous ivenberry-and-cream pastry. However, her gown appeared to have vanished. The woman still wore twice as much fabric as Kitlyn or Oona's dresses combined, but shrieked as if finding herself devoid of clothing entirely.

"It is here," called a man some distance away, also on the upper left gallery. He held up the missing garment.

"What?" whispered Kitlyn. "How did the duchess' dress leap off her and go so far away in an instant?"

Lord Parrington, a man who'd remained highly suspicious of Kitlyn—and not at all fond of her marrying a girl—attempted to go after the dress, but promptly fell on his face out of sight. Laughter murmured from the gallery.

Oona clamped a hand over her face to hide her smile and poorly suppressed chuckling. She thought Parrington a humorless older man, but didn't hate him. His objection to their union was entirely political. Two women couldn't produce an heir. He wouldn't have cared if not for them being on the throne.

"Faeries," whispered Evie, half awake. "They don't like mean people."

Once Oona swallowed her urge to laugh, she whispered, "I do believe Duchess Parrington will be keeping herself out of the public eye for at least several months."

"At least a year." Kitlyn smiled. "The horror. Her shoes and forearms were exposed."

"How scandalous..." Oona rolled her eyes. "Everyone saw her petticoat."

Duke Parrington rose back into view, red-faced in fury. He shouted demands to the nearest guards to locate the knave who knotted his boot laces together.

"Faeries," said Evie. "I'm sorry. They heard me talking to Pim about how mean the Parringtons are."

Oona and Kitlyn exchanged a glance, shrugged at the same time, then looked toward the gallery. It sounded so silly, but she had seen the tiny footprints out in the garden. Also, even a child Evie's size would not have been able to tie the man's boot laces together unnoticed. No explanation short of magic could explain how Duchess Parrington's outer dress vanished right off her. Even slashing the back lacing with a knife wouldn't make it possible to remove in an instant.

Once the uproar in the upper gallery died down, a series of

people from the merchant and commoner class came forward to express concerns about the war recovery, ask questions about plans for the future or seek reassurance the people of Evermoor weren't out to get them.

While she mostly paid attention to them, Oona also spent perhaps too much thought on attempting to figure out what happened to the dress and shoelaces. She could come up with only two explanations, the first being, obviously, faeries. The second possibility simultaneously made more sense while being less likely true. In the same forgotten book where she'd read about trolls, Oona found mention of many other creatures written like an encyclopedia or the illustrated journals of someone traveling the land and documenting what they found. She'd been twelve when she found the book, barely able to lift it. No creatures of the types illustrated within existed for real, but the serious tone of the writing confused her. She eventually decided it had been written deliberately to sound 'real' while being a work of fiction, something to entertain those with an imagination, or perhaps scare them.

A few of the creatures the book described used magic unlike anything she'd ever thought of. Some could disappear and reappear at will or turn invisible. Others had the ability to make locks open on their own or could levitate. Those creatures didn't have magic from the gods, or even the elemental powers someone from Evermoor might inherit. She suspected they had something in common with people called 'mages' or 'wizards' by the Lucen temple, long considered dangerous and evil.

The temples and king's army had, for as long as she could remember, treated anyone with magic not belonging to one of the four temples as a threat. In light of Aodh's deception, and no clear explanation of *why* the priests persecuted mages, she and Kitlyn decided to stop the practice along with no longer forcibly dragging everyone who possessed magic off to a temple whether they wanted to join or not.

Someone long ago clearly wanted to change history, but she couldn't begin to guess at why. Little information remained about what these mages could do. Most of what she found in the other library inside the Lucen temple made them sound like demon summoners and murderers. Oona knew enough to understand a difference existed between maleficars—essentially priests worshiping demons—and mages. The Na'vir queen Xorana had been cursed by one such individual specifically seeking knowledge of demonic magic she refused to let him have. This implied it did not come from worship but rather study. It also made a case for demonic magic being different—and a choice—separate from other forms of 'magery.'

Oona suspected a mage could use their gift to play small pranks, but she didn't believe a person smart enough to learn it would be foolish enough to wave it around in public. This, of course, got her thinking back to the more ridiculous idea of faeries.

Anyone could have planted fake faerie footprints in the garden for the amusement of Pim and Evie. She knew the kids didn't make it up since neither of them lied. Both truly believed they observed faerie footprints. Finding the tracks didn't prove faeries had been there. The footprints plus an inexplicable magical prank made a stronger case... but, she had bigger problems to think about at the moment. Specifically, determining what the Gates of Isilien were and where to find them.

The seventeenth person requesting to speak to the queens approached at his turn. He appeared to be a farmer or villager, middle-twenties with straw-blond hair and sun-weathered skin. The man removed a simple hat, clutching it to his chest while bowing. "Good day your highnesses. I am Dalin from Duskdawn Lake. The town, not the lake itself. I don't live in the water."

Chuckling came from the gallery.

Oona smiled. "Well met, Dalin."

"Speak freely." Kitlyn also smiled at him.

"Two weeks past, I was out in my boat, fishing when I seen this *creature* in the water, weren't no fish. Had arms and legs like a man, but scales. We seen 'em walkin' 'round the shore at night, too. They don't seem ta like light. Haven't come near anyone with a torch er nothin'. Think they're demons?"

"Have you taken your concerns to the temples there?" asked Kitlyn.

"Aye, highness. They think we had a bit too much ta drink. Say the lake is blessed o' the Lady of Dusk and no demons could touch its waters."

"That is true," said Oona. "Tenebrea would not allow demons near her temple."

Most of the people in the gallery flinched slightly at hearing the name aloud. The reaction annoyed her, but she didn't want to make a scene. If anyone spoke ill of Tenebrea, she would absolutely put them in their place. However, lecturing everyone because they cringed would serve only to deepen their fear.

A few people in the gallery chuckled.

"How many of you have seen these creatures?" asked Kitlyn.

"About half of us who go out to fish. Handful at night."

Oona sensed no deception in the man's heart. "Dalin has seen something he truly believes to be a creature of mysterious type. I see no falsehood in his words."

"Very well." Kitlyn looked over at the row of advisors. "Send a message to the magistrate of Duskdawn Lake—the town, not the water." Chuckling again emanated from the gallery. "Ask them to be more vigilant along the shore at night in case these creatures pose a threat."

Beredwyn nodded.

"I have seen something as well," called a woman near the back of the room by the main doors.

"Come forward." Kitlyn beckoned her with a wave.

A woman in her later forties hurried down the carpeted aisle. The middling quality of her dark yellow dress placed her squarely in the commoner class. "Thank you for hearing me out, highness." She curtseyed.

"What is your name, good citizen?" asked Oona.

"I am Jarah. I live in the village of Teryn, stone's toss from the wall."

Oona picture the small village in the meadow roughly a half mile from Cimril. Numerous tiny hamlets surrounded the capital city, mostly populated by farmers and the merchants who sold goods to them. It occurred to her she'd never been to one, and decided to suggest they make a habit of visiting the nearby outlying villages.

"Northeast of the city…" Kitlyn narrowed her eyes in thought.

"Yes, highness," said Jarah. "A few days ago, I was on my way to visit my sister, not a far walk. She lives closer to the meadow than us. I saw a critter out in the grasses unlike any beast ought to exist. At first, I figured it might be a boy riding on a big ol' wolf, but was only one beast. Had four legs, two arms, a chest like a small man. Didn't get a good look at its face, too much hair."

She is telling the truth. Oona swallowed.

High Priest Balais stared at the woman, his mouth slightly open in surprise. He, too, likely asked Lucen to reveal truth on her.

The gallery fell silent.

Dalin glanced at Jarah in disbelief.

Balais made eye contact with Oona. She nodded once. He began murmuring to the other advisors, likely telling them the woman legitimately believed she saw such a creature. Of course, the one slight problem with Lucen's magic revealing truth is it depended on the speaker's intention rather than reality. If someone tricked Jarah with a bit of runaway taxidermy, Oona couldn't tell.

"Thank you for telling us," said Oona. "We will send trackers and scouts to help determine what, exactly, you saw."

Jarah curtseyed again.

"What if these things are dangerous?" asked Dalin.

Fearful muttering spread over the gallery.

"We will, of course, take all necessary precautions." Kitlyn stood. "There is no reason to allow fear to run away with our imagination. It sounds as though unknown beings may be appearing near the city. However, this man's sighting occurred weeks ago and no one has been hurt yet or even made direct contact with the… fish person. We should be on guard, but remember not *everything* is going to be dangerous or even hostile."

Oona stood. "Yes. There are stories of fur-covered beings in the far north reaches of Ondar. Merchant traders from Amadar tell of dervishes, intelligent snakes as big as men, and great lizards. Some are highly dangerous, but not all. I would urge everyone to be wary, but our first reaction should not be to resort to violence without provocation."

"Is it true you discovered a demon in the west?" asked a younger woman in the front row.

"It is." Oona nodded at her. "Tenebrea granted me a warning vision. Kitlyn and I rushed to Shimmerbrook and destroyed the fiend before it could harm a family."

Lady Alonna smiled. She adored Oona's lack of fear toward Tenebrea.

A brief discussion of how a demon could exist in Lucernia followed. Oona and Balais re-explained their theory of a misinterpretation of former writings. Lucen didn't make it such that demons could absolutely not tread on Lucernian soil, rather gave his faithful highly effective tools to destroy them. Admittedly, Oona's blue light beam didn't work well on living people. When she tried to stop the assassin from fleeing the throne room, her spell bothered him less than a stiff punch.

Eventually, fear settled and the room became relatively quiet again.

"Is there anyone else who has a question or concern?" asked Kitlyn. "I'm sure you are all becoming as hungry as I am. It's about time for lunch."

A fair number of people chuckled.

Oona resisted the temptation to make a joke about everyone surviving a session of court while the queens wore plain dresses without anything catching fire, but held her tongue. Better not to call attention to it again. If she and Kitlyn disregarded fashion 'rules' often enough, they would create new ones.

A middle-aged man with grey fringing the edges of his otherwise black hair walked up to the dais. "Pardon the asking, highness. How do you intend to continue the Talomir line? Or do you?"

The gallery emitted a collective gasp.

Oona opened her mouth, then closed it. She couldn't speak openly about Queen Solana having loved a woman. Not only was it a personal matter, saying such a thing would absolutely invite people to accuse her of making it up as a ploy to 'persuade people not to object to immoral pairings' or some nonsense. The woman was dead, no need to disturb her memory. However, she had been like Kitlyn, like Oona… yet bedded Aodh to produce a child.

Neither she nor Kitlyn faced such a situation as they'd married each other. Neither would end up in a political union to someone they didn't love. She doubted Evie would be eligible to ascend to the throne, barring a significant change to tradition. Had she been Kitlyn's sister rather than Oona's, it would not be an issue.

"The kingdom's had enough Talomirs," muttered a deep voice from the back of the gallery.

Kitlyn's gaze hardened, but she didn't say anything in response.

"This one's better than the last," replied an anonymous woman.

"Aye, true," said the deep-voiced man.

"I am less…" Kitlyn stood. "I am less concerned with keeping the throne in my bloodline than making sure the people of Lucernia are safe and prosperous. I will do what must be done to ensure the prosperity and security of all citizens."

A few people clapped.

"She's a bit young yet ta worry about that, ey?" whispered a man over an awkwardly timed moment of silence.

"Odd how they have such bad luck," said a blonde woman three rows in from the front.

Oona clenched her jaw, worried about Kitlyn.

In her dreams, Oona had sometimes pictured them having children—either by magical means or the whim of the gods. She dared not pray to ask for such a thing, fearing it sounded too much like a story she'd read about where a baby conceived via magical means grew up to become a great evil tyrant. It had been nothing more than a fictional story, but she couldn't escape the worry.

She would adore having a son or daughter to take care of—or both. However, aside from the obvious political complexities of selecting a father, she didn't much care to go through with the physical requirements of having a child. Kitlyn shared her disinterest in becoming intimate with a man. She didn't even like talking about the uncomfortable questions, like which one of them should be the mother, or both... same father?

The kingdom will need to accept a child we adopt—Lucen knows the war made far too many orphans—or the crown simply passes out of the Talomir line when we are dead. The people are not ready to hear Kitlyn's idea for rule by council, or even selecting a new monarch by voting. May Lucen protect us long enough that the people do not suffer under the nobles warring for the throne.

Kitlyn leaned close to whisper, "I am about ready to declare this court at an end. Are you ready for lunch? I am famished."

"Yay!" cheered Evie, thrusting her arms up.

"I am somewhat too worried to eat but I shall do so anyway." Oona took her hand. "But there looks to be at least two more people with questions."

Kitlyn glanced at a pair of men waiting in the aisle. "So be it."

10

TOPICS MOST ARCANE

KITLYN

The main doors swung open with an echoing *clonk*, abruptly quieting the din of people preparing to leave the gallery. A man in a black hooded cloak entered, surrounded by a strange air. Merely looking at him made the hairs on Kitlyn's arms stand on end. He didn't give off a sense of dread or evil, more an unearthly power reminiscent of Mother's ghost.

This man did not appear to be a spirit, his body quite solid.

Guards near the door stepped in behind him, following at the ready but not yet attempting to stop him. Kitlyn sensed them waiting for her to give a command one way or the other. The newcomer didn't carry any obvious weapons, though a traditional assassin could conceal dozens of killing tools under a cloak. Assassins did not, as a matter of routine, walk straight up to their target in the open. Also, given the present political climate, she doubted anyone would move against her—yet.

Two or three nobles she could think of might possess such a strong desire to claim the throne they could conceivably try to remove such a young, inexperienced queen... but none would be so foolish as to strike so soon after they earned the adoration of two entire kingdoms. Once it got out—and it *would* eventually get out—

who did it, they'd face intense backlash. Blackmail, after all, could go on only so long. Hiring assassins always left a trail of money and those who knew who did what. Such information could be worth a fortune, virtually guaranteeing it would not stay secret.

The hooded figure made little noise as he moved down the aisle, curiously taking a place third in line behind the two men rather than ignore them and approach the queens as his intense presence implied he would. One, in a nice blue tunic, appeared to be of the merchant class while the second man in line wore commoner's garb.

"Yes." Kitlyn waved for the merchant to approach.

"Highness…" The man bowed. "I am curious what, if any, rules or controls you plan to enact on trade with Evermoor now the war is ended."

Argh. Kitlyn resisted the urge to scream. Discussing mercantile concerns proved tedious enough without being hungry. "For the time being, trade is open. If it becomes apparent an imbalance is proving disadvantageous to Lucernia, we will re-evaluate the situation at the time."

"You are not, then planning any import or export tax?"

"Did we not already discuss this?" whispered Oona.

"As of now, no. We are not considering levying any specific additional taxes on goods going to or coming in from Evermoor."

The merchant bowed. "Thank you."

At least he gave up quick.

"Highness…" The second man approached. "I've come to appeal for a pardon of my brother, Geson. He was imprisoned four years ago for the crime of smuggling ivenberries. Seeing as how it's now not illegal to trade them…"

Oona gasped.

She'd give him a medal for heroism. "Ahh. Yes. Quite understandable you would seek to have him freed. Did your brother do anything worse than smuggle goods in from Evermoor?"

"Run away from the guard, tried not ta be arrested." The man chuckled, as did most of the gallery.

Kitlyn looked toward Beredwyn. "Please have the magisterial

clerk check the records on this man, Geson. If he's done nothing more than import fruit, see that he is released."

"Of course." Beredwyn smiled.

"Thank you, highness." The man bowed deeply. "You are kind and just."

"Why'd he go to prison for selling berries?" whispered Evie. "That's silly."

"I'll explain later." Oona neatened the girl's hair.

Again the gallery fell quiet as the odd man in the black cloak approached to take his turn speaking. The guards behind him tensed, as did the advisors. High Priest Balais appeared particularly nervous. Oona, however, didn't react much to the man beyond staring at him. Perhaps she did seem poised to leap protectively in front of Evie.

"Queen Kitlyn. Queen Oona." The man reached up to pull his hood back. "I am Ulfaan Khera, and I have a simple question."

He appeared close in age to the former king, if a year or three older. His short, neatly arranged black hair and thin jawline beard gave him an air of importance or wealth despite his common black tunic and loose pants. Several pouches hung from his dark maroon belt, along with a single ornate dagger.

This man is not from Cimril. Perhaps not even from Lucernia. Something feels odd about him. "Where are you from, Ulfaan?"

"I have lived in many places over the years. Most recently, in Ondar. However, it would be my preference to return to the land of my birth."

An exile? What for... "What question is it you wish to ask?"

Ulfaan clasped his hands in front of himself. "Do you intend to preserve the prior king's laws in regard to magic? Must all those with the gift be forced to join temples or be put down?"

Put down? Kitlyn managed to stop herself from gasping in horror, though couldn't hide the shock in her eyes. She, of course, knew the various temples didn't give people the choice of joining once they displayed a gift from the gods. Had Aodh not required a decoy, Oona would surely have been taken to the Lucen temple once she grew old enough. In her case, she'd have been happier there than remaining with Ruby.

"No." Kitlyn shook her head. "We have come to understand that not everyone who possesses some degree of magic or another receives it from the gods. The former king retained enough to fool everyone into believing him a dedicated servant of Lucen, but had long ago lost the portion of his magic Lucen gave him. I can think of no clearer proof magic originates from places other than the gods. Those who *do* receive their gift from Lucen, Navissa, Orien, or Tenebrea would already be of a mind to seek out a temple. It serves no one's interest to compel anyone."

"What of those whose magic is not of the gods?"

He does realize who he is addressing? "A person should be judged by how they use any abilities given them, not simply for having those abilities."

"I am pleased to hear you say this, Queen Kitlyn." Ulfaan offered a shallow nod of appreciation.

"You mentioned put down. I do not recall hearing of any such thing." Kitlyn glanced at Beredwyn, who grimaced. "Oh, no."

"I am afraid so." Beredwyn stepped forward. "If a person demonstrated magic clearly not from the gods, the former king decreed them spies from Evermoor or minions of demons depending on the form their magic took."

"Please elaborate." Kitlyn stared at him, heartbroken at the thought the man she thought of more as a father than her actual father might have been complicit in the murder of innocent people.

"If someone manipulated stone, fire, or plant life, Aodh considered them an Evermoor spy. To my knowledge, no one native to Lucernia ever displayed such talents except for you. As you well know, the elemental or spirit magic had been severely weakened by the absence of the Heart from the Alderswood tree. All the children who showed magical talents did so in accordance with one of the gods. In a few rare cases, citizens were observed using magic not originating from the gods nor Evermoor."

"Mages?" whispered Oona.

Kitlyn narrowed her eyes. "What was done to them?"

At the anger in Kitlyn's voice, Oona grasped her hand.

"A few did go to Tenebrea." Beredwyn looked down. "The reports claimed these individuals attacked when confronted. In light of what we now know, I suspect Aodh's growing paranoia led to this. He feared them as demons, though I disagreed."

"It was beyond the doing of the former king." Balais stepped forward. "Temple doctrine has long stated all magic not of the gods is of the demons."

"The Na'vir told us of others who must somehow learn their magic from writings. We also know the elementalists and spiritualists in Evermoor are not in league with demons." Oona thrust an arm out at Kitlyn. "You do not consider her a demon. The power of the Alderswood is part of her very soul. The former king obviously did not truly believe it demonic or he would never have asked Queen Solana to drink the sap of the Eldritch Heart while carrying her in pregnancy."

Balais walked up to whispering distance, speaking so quietly only Kitlyn and Oona could hear him. "I fear you are correct. We are in the process of beseeching Lucen to provide guidance on many of the old texts. Aodh did not represent Lucen, yet he added to our writings. It appears he may not be the first to do so. I ask you do not speak of this yet as the kingdom is in a delicate time. Creating distrust in all the temples would help no one."

I doubt they are all as prone to distortions. Aodh and those before him used the faithful of Lucen as tools. No one would question the words from the lips of those who serve the God of Truth. Becoming furious made her feel too much like her father. He had a wicked temper. In fact, Piper first realized Kitlyn's true identity in a moment of rage. Kitlyn's emerald eyes and the shape of her nose so resembled the former king, it left no doubt in the girl's mind. The man had been perpetually angry for years. Kitlyn spent so long keeping her head down, afraid to look people in the eye, no one else noticed.

Kitlyn stood, raising her voice to be heard throughout the gallery. "Magic is a tool. Those who have it will not be punished simply for possessing a gift. Like any weapon, only those who use it for dark purposes will be considered in violation of the laws of Lucernia.

Manipulating the powers of demons is still an affront to all the gods and will be dealt with appropriately. Any who receive their magic from the gods would be wise to seek out the temples. However, no one will be forced."

"Ulfaan?" asked Oona. "What do you know of this magic not of the gods nor of elemental spirits?"

"Yes, highness. Theirs is a gift most ancient, though uncommon. It requires tenacity, determination, and study. Many reach the end of their lives without ever realizing they have the gift as it cannot manifest by accident, such as by unintentionally igniting a chicken."

Oona covered her mouth.

Kitlyn blinked. *How does he know... oh, wait. Oona's told the story multiple times. Everyone in the kingdom has likely heard it by now.*

"I didn't really light the poor thing on fire," said Oona. "Knocked a few feathers off."

Ulfaan chuckled.

Oona looked at Kitlyn. "Queen Xorana mentioned the man who cursed the Na'vir searched for demonic magic."

"Is there a link between this other magic and demons?" asked Kitlyn.

"Arcane magic exists in many forms, similar to different languages. One can choose to speak infernal or not speak infernal." Ulfaan slightly shook his head. "Those who do are fools. Demons only pretend to give power in the way a fisherman offers food to the fish."

Balais relaxed visibly.

The strange man appeared to be waiting for something.

Kitlyn considered for a moment, ignoring a growl in her stomach. "Those who have a magical gift other than what is traditionally seen in Lucernia or Evermoor will not be persecuted. They will, however, be expected to abide by the laws of the kingdom in the use of their gift. Any trafficking with actual demons or infernal powers will continue to be dealt with as it always has been."

Ulfaan bowed graciously—then vanished in a swirl of blue sparkling light.

The second collective gasp of the day arose from the gallery. A few people fainted.

Kitlyn suspected no one much cared she didn't have shoes on anymore.

Evie nudged her. "I think that man has magic."

11

INNOCENCE

OONA

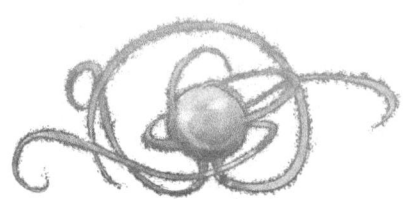

*A*ll through lunch, Oona thought about Ulfaan.

Mostly about him vanishing into thin air.

She continued trying to sort out how she felt about witnessing—she assumed—someone use a form of magic she had previously considered to exist only in stories told to scare people. Or, if not entirely made up, lost… or simply not present in Lucernia. What he'd said troubled her more than a strange man capable of disappearing. The idea of people being killed for merely having magic horrified her. Common practice had been for temples to take children with magical talents from their homes around age twelve. As far as she knew, the priests didn't prevent the children from visiting their families, merely brought them to live at the temple where they could be trained.

Given all the other lies come to light as of late, she dreaded worse things happened than forcible recruitment.

After lunch, she and Kitlyn attended a meeting with the advisors and a handful of magistrates to discuss matters of law, regulation, and taxes within Cimril. She tried her best to pay attention; however, her mind filled with nightmares of sinister figures dragging screaming young people off in chains for having 'forbidden magic', potentially even murdering the ones they considered dangerous. Such horrors could be one reason the castle library contained so little of substance about the past.

It couldn't be possible Lucen would allow his priesthood to commit such crimes.

History has a tendency to change over time... especially when writings disappear. Could the 'demons' we believe Lucen purged from the land have been 'mages'? She furrowed her brow in consternation. The random idea both mages, as well as actual demons, had been driven from the land came out of nowhere. Alas, no inexplicable feelings soothed the sick feeling in the pit of her stomach over what innocents might have been hurt by overzealous priests and soldiers.

In all honesty, everyone who died in the war Aodh started had been innocent. More recent crimes had to far outweigh anyone mistreated over magic, considering its rarity in Lucernia. Her wayward light bolt at age three had been so shocking, word reached the king himself in mere days. She couldn't even remember why it happened. Her earliest memories were of happy times playing with Kitlyn around age five or six. Kitlyn also had no real memories of her life prior to age five.

While Kitlyn dealt with the magistrates, Oona pulled High Priest Balais aside.

"You seem troubled, highness," said Balais in a tone too low for anyone to overhear.

"I cannot get Ulfaan's story out of my mind, nor do I trust anything Aodh claimed. What has the temple done in regard to those with magic?"

"Ahh. I will have to examine our records to be entirely sure. However, I feel comfortable estimating the four temples have collected fewer than sixty people over the past four decades."

"What is done with any who refuse, or who have this 'arcane' magic?"

Balais paused for the span of a breath, eyes closed. He might have been thinking, frustrated, or guilty. "Individuals chosen by the gods are almost always discovered quite young. Few refuse as they know it is their calling to serve the gods. Some are too immature and resist separation from their families. It is a simple matter to relocate the entire family nearer the temple."

"But there have been some cases where—"

"Yes, highness. A small number of individuals were imprisoned."

Oona gasped. "Imprisoned?"

"It is not as harsh as you assume. They remained at the temple in a bedchamber, not a cell, in hopes they would see the wisdom of the gods." Balais offered an apologetic smile, though he likely had not been responsible personally. "All have since been released."

"How many died?"

"None gifted with the magic of Lucen, Navissa, Orien, or Tenebrea. Anyone else would have been assumed in league with demons and the local magistrates would have dealt with them. If the temples had been involved, it would've been handled by the local prior or prioress, not sent to the high priest."

Oona sighed. *I hate not being able to make things right. Chasing this down will take years and prove to be folly. I trust in Lucen to see justice done where needed.* "Thank you."

"Of course."

She returned to her seat.

Two exceptionally boring hours later, she and Kitlyn escaped the castle to the garden for desperately needed quiet—and an ivenberry. They sat in the grass beside the large, gnarled tree at the garden's center, the same one she'd gotten stuck on as a child due to her fear of heights. Careful not to dribble juice on her dress, Oona spent a few minutes plucking the fingerprint-sized seeds off the giant berry. The fruit tapered from wide to a rounded point at one end, requiring the use of a dagger—or long fingernails—to dislodge the smaller seeds nearer the tip.

"This one's larger than Evie's head." Kitlyn whistled. "Where did you find such a big one?"

"It is fully matured." Oona cut it in half, handing one wedge to Kitlyn. "The smugglers would pick them too early so they wouldn't rot before arriving here. With trade open, we can get them as they should be. They're much sweeter."

"Oh, yes. I suppose that makes sense." Kitlyn took a bite, her eyes widening.

"A bit stronger than you expected?"

Kitlyn nodded while chewing, leaning to one side so the juice dripping from her chin landed in the grass.

Ivenberries tended to vary a little between sweet and tart, the darker red ones being on the sweet side. Oona eyed the tip of the mostly triangular fruit wedge in her hands, glistening red-pink in the late afternoon sun. "I've always adored these."

"I know," mumbled Kitlyn past a full mouth.

"Seems I've a taste for sweet magical treasures from Evermoor."

Kitlyn shifted her gaze to Oona, narrowing her eyes while chewing.

Oona leaned over and kissed her atop the head, then took a bite of her ivenberry. The cool, juicy flesh practically melted in her mouth. Sweetness with a hint of tart burst into her senses. "Mmm."

"You should not make such noises. People will think we are doing something less innocent than having a snack."

Oona blushed.

They feasted on ivenberry while discussing everything from the still-fruitless search for the Gates of Isilien to Ulfaan to the dreadfully boring meeting. Kitlyn asked about her aside with Balais, and ended up agreeing with her determination it would be next to impossible to track down anyone responsible for killing an innocent person suspected of being a demon. Considering the rarity of magic, it amounted to disassembling the entire castle to find one lost article of jewelry. Kitlyn also expected the magistrates in outlying villages hadn't kept detailed records. A simple 'destroyed a demon today' note, if even as much.

It didn't take too long for conversation to give way to playful stares and soon, kissing. They'd barely managed to mess each other's hair before high-pitched giggling approached. Oona and Kitlyn hastily disentangled themselves, exchanging a longing look of amused frustration.

"It's like they know," whispered Kitlyn.

So much for romance in the garden. Oona let a soft sigh leak from her nose. She didn't mind the interruption, however. Merely seeing her little sister's smile filled her with such joy she could forget almost any worry.

Evie and Pim darted into view, running along the garden trail out from the huge bushes. The children hurried over, both smiling a little too widely, as though they intended to ask for something.

Oona looked up at Evie, one eyebrow raised. "Finished your lessons for the day?"

"Yes." Evie nodded, grinning wider when Oona gave her the last third or so of her ivenberry.

Kitlyn offered Pim a hunk roughly the same size.

The boy grinned, thanked her, and devoured it.

"You ate almost a whole one by yourself before," chirped Evie. "How can you keep eating?"

Pim shrugged. "Pa's makin' pie outta 'em."

Oona fake swooned into Kitlyn. "Pie? We haven't had ivenberry pie in the castle in years. I am overcome with joy."

Kitlyn laughed.

"Can we go swimming?" asked Evie.

Aha. That's what she wanted. Oona waved a hand around, testing the temperature. The early autumn day seemed unseasonably warm, and there likely would not be too many more opportunities until the spring came. "All right. It'll be too chilly for swimming in another week or two. May as well enjoy it while you can."

The kids cheered.

Oona rolled to her feet. She and Kitlyn followed the children deeper into the garden. A large pond occupied the corner farthest from the castle. Dark ivy covered the walls behind it, so thick not one stone could be seen. Trails of leafy vines draped in the water. Stray leaves and fallen flower petals drifted across the surface, the small rowboat half on the shore remained upside down, untouched for months. Though the manmade pond was fairly large, it didn't have enough space to truly enjoy paddling around in a boat.

Evie and Pim sprinted to one of the small stone benches close to the edge and shed their clothing. Evie waded in, squealing in surprised glee at the chilly water. Pim let out an adorable war cry and dove in headfirst.

Oona and Kitlyn sat relatively close to the shore in the shade of the dense trees.

Once Pim's head popped up, Oona called, "Don't go past where your feet can't reach the bottom."

"Okay!" yelled Pim.

Evie, evidently too cold to move her jaw, nodded.

"She looks exactly like you the time I stuffed snow down the back of your dress," said Kitlyn.

Oona shivered. "I'd forgotten entirely about that."

The tiny blonde girl made the cutest face of determination ever, closed her eyes, and dropped underwater.

"I think the water's a bit colder than she expected," whispered Oona.

"Pim doesn't seem to mind."

"He's like you." Oona tickled Kitlyn's side. "You never thought the water cold."

Kitlyn brushed her hand at the grass, coaxing a tiny bright green vine up to coil around her fingers. "I've good reason."

"I don't understand how they do it."

"They're children. Swimming comes naturally." Kitlyn chuckled.

Oona laughed. "No, I meant people with arcane magic. You've been using yours since we were tiny. It's no different from walking or speaking. I cannot imagine having to spend hours studying specific words… and what if you say them wrong?"

"Then you summon a creature like Fauhurst," deadpanned Kitlyn.

"Do not even jest about him. He has already marked this place in my memories. Every time we are here, I cringe inside, expecting him to show up and ruin it at any moment."

Kitlyn took her hand. "We will make many more wonderful memories here. Soon, it will be as though he never existed."

"I long for the day."

The kids dove under, popped up, laughed, and played in the water.

"Remember when we could fling off our clothes to jump in the pond and no one would be shocked?" Kitlyn leaned against Oona.

"We still can."

"We still could go swimming together." Kitlyn examined her fingernails. "If we were alone, it perhaps would not be quite so innocent, though. People would be shocked."

"They couldn't be shocked if they don't see us." Oona winked.

Kitlyn bit her lip. "Middle of the night?"

"Oh, I don't know." Oona fussed at her hair. "It might be possible some beautiful nature spirit might tempt me into doing something exciting and naughty I'd not normally be inclined to do"

"Mmm." Kitlyn lay sideways, her head in Oona's lap. "The next several hours are going to take too long."

Oona stroked Kitlyn's hair. "The water will be quite cold after dark."

Evie squealed.

"Seems it is rather cold already." Kitlyn chuckled, then flashed an impish smile. "I can keep you warm."

"I like the sound of that," whispered Oona.

PERHAPS AN HOUR LATER, OONA CALLED THE CHILDREN OUT OF the water, lest they catch a chill.

It would be time for dinner soon, and after spending a while in chilly water, she wanted to bring the children inside to warm up. She and Kitlyn had spent the time watching them play. In the absence of getting romantic, they discussed Oona's search of the library. Thus far, she hadn't been able to find even one mention of Isilien at all, and only the one old book contained any information about strange beasts without being obviously intended as fiction.

Given multiple recent sightings of 'monsters,' Oona decided to consider the book seriously rather than as a fanciful compendium. Someone took the time to conceal it in a hidden passageway many years ago, most likely to protect it from the purge. It didn't make sense anyone would try to preserve—or eliminate—a book full of storybook monsters.

"It's simply frustrating." Oona sat up and rested her chin in both hands. "There's so little information in the library about anything older than the first Talomir king. It's like someone tried to erase everything else. Destroying books is as bad as lying."

Kitlyn stretched out in the grass. "I agree, though I doubt my great, great grandfather would have much reason to get rid of ancient history. Those who came before him likely all disposed of whatever parts they didn't want anyone to know."

"Keeping people ignorant is not a way to protect them." Oona fumed. "It's the reverse. We don't know how to cope with these new monsters."

After some dawdling, Evie and Pim emerged from the pond. They whispered back and forth for a moment before running off toward the trail into the garden.

Oona cupped her hands around her mouth, shouting, "Evie, Pim! Come back here and get dressed."

Kitlyn laughed.

The kids vanished behind a giant green bush.

"Faeries don't have to get dressed!" yelled Evie.

Oona bit her lip to keep from laughing as well. She collected herself then called, "You two are not faeries."

Kitlyn muffled her continued laughter in the crook of her arm.

Evie and Pim walked back into view.

"But we are wet," said Evie, flailing her arms.

Oona summoned warm blue light around them, drying the children in a few seconds. "Now, you are not."

The kids obediently crossed to the stone bench and dressed themselves before running off again into the garden.

"The girl is obsessed with faeries," said Oona.

"So were you." Kitlyn sat up.

Oona fake pouted. "The real ones never visited me."

"You think they're real?"

"You don't?" Oona blinked.

"Maybe they are." Kitlyn sat up. "But no one else in Lucernia believes they exist. Do you think people will say we're still acting like children if we tell them faeries exist?"

Oona shrugged. "Not if they *do* exist. I suppose it's possible those footprints could be false. But Lady Parrington's dress? Lord Parrington's boot laces?"

"Why would faeries who won't show themselves to Evie and Pim leave the garden, go into a crowded throne room, and play a prank on two people?"

"I…" Oona sighed. "Cannot answer you. Unless it is true they overheard Evie complaining about the Parringtons."

Kitlyn took her hand. "We have a little time before Meredith or Piper come to tell us dinner is ready."

"Not enough." Oona managed a weak smile, too worried about the curse to let her guard down. "Do you think it is wrong to miss being innocent and having no worries?"

"You wish to be a child again?"

"I didn't mean innocent in that sense." Oona snuggled close and kissed her on the side of the neck. "I adore not having *this* innocence any longer. I meant not having people expect anything of us or worries about war, death… everything."

Kitlyn kissed her on the lips. "I think it is normal to long for happier times when we were free of responsibilities. Merely because we have them now does not mean we cannot find happiness."

"Yes." Oona hugged her close, clinging as if to let go would mean she'd lose her forever. "I fear I cannot be truly happy until the curse no longer threatens you."

"Did not the gods reassure you?"

"Yes." Oona chuckled. "Perhaps some of me yet remains a child for I am impatient. I desire you safe right away."

Kitlyn brushed a hand over Oona's hair. "I would prefer to be safe as well."

"How can you stay so calm?"

"I'm terrified. Merely hiding it well." Kitlyn fussed at the grass between them. "I had years of practice concealing my fears."

"A lesser woman would have taken revenge." Oona squeezed her.

"Every day, I thank the gods for having met such a kind and loving person."

"Laziness," deadpanned Kitlyn.

"What?" Oona blinked.

"Going after them all would have taken too much effort to be worth it."

Oona stuck out her tongue. "You'd have felt horrible after. Don't deny it."

Kitlyn smiled. "You know me too well."

"It's like we're in a storybook," whispered Oona. "Childhood sweethearts, even if we didn't really understand why we liked each other so much back then... now married. I am coming apart inside with worry we're going to drop the book in the pond before finishing it."

"What book?"

"I'm being metaphorical." Oona exhaled hard. "I mean, I'm terrified the curse is going to hurt you before I even discover what Isilien is."

Kitlyn held her for a few minutes in loving silence. "We will find it, whatever it is. I shall ask the spymaster to send his people to the edges of the kingdom, beyond if necessary."

"And I will pester High Priest Balais." Oona nodded once. "He may know something."

"What of the odd one... Ulfaan?" Kitlyn glanced at her.

Oona's eyes widened. "Dare we confide in such a man something so important?"

"If anyone can determine the nature of his intentions, it is you, my love."

"I am still but a novice compared to some."

"But Lucen's gift is strong. One does not have to spend thirty years sitting in a temple to listen when he speaks."

"You are right." Oona gazed up at the sky. *Lucen guide me.*

THE SILENT GARDEN

KITLYN

A loud, high-pitched squeal came from the garden.

Kitlyn twisted to look. She couldn't tell if the cry came from Evie or Pim, or if it had been excitement, fear, or one of them stepped barefoot on a thorn.

"Evie? Pim?" called Oona.

"Did that sound like a squeal of delight or a scream of fear to you?" asked Kitlyn.

"Evie? Pim?" yelled Oona, taking a step onto the trail. "I… could be either."

Kitlyn called their names louder.

When they didn't respond, Oona bolted up to a run. Kitlyn scrambled to her feet and chased.

They ran along the arbor path the kids followed away from the pond, weaving among trees, bushes, and old ivy-shrouded statues. Every few seconds, they repeated calling for them while hurrying back and forth, searching. In a few minutes, their shouting attracted three castle guards.

"Highness?" asked a soldier by the name of Peranor. He wore the somewhat heavier armor of a soldier assigned to guard the outside areas. "Is something amiss?"

"Evie and Pim are missing." Kitlyn stopped by the guards while Oona kept jogging into the garden. "I don't know if they're misbehaving or if something happened. One of them screamed, then they stopped answering when we called for them. Help us search the garden and alert the outer guards. Make sure no one leaves the castle."

"Yes, highness." Peranor motioned for the other two to go with Kitlyn, then ran for the garden walk and the door into the castle.

Kitlyn raced around the garden, continuing to shout for the children while searching under every bush. She only half paid attention to high branches, as she didn't believe the kids would knowingly climb a tree and keep quiet when she and Oona sounded so worried.

More guards arrived to help locate the children. Shouts spread over the entire castle grounds.

Within forty minutes, she'd personally searched the entire garden except for the southwest corner opposite the pond containing the dense tangle of old, petrified growth. Kitlyn couldn't even see the ancient tree beyond the brambles despite it being less than fifty feet away from the start of the dense, dead growth. Evie and Pim had been drawn to this area before. Again, she flattened herself out on the ground and tried to look in. Even at their small size, the kids would have had great difficulty dragging themselves in under the brambles on their stomachs. Evie's fancy dress would certainly have left a ribbon or two stuck on thorns, yet she saw none—and no sign of the children in the small open patch between the gnarled roots of the ancient tree.

Still, she called their names a few times, receiving no response.

Oona's continued tearful pleas for the children to come to her echoed over the garden, twisting a knife in Kitlyn's guts. Hearing her wife's anguish aloud changed her worry into fury. She doubted the kids would've run into the castle on their own. Annabelle, Evie's governess and teacher, might have collected them, but not this late in the day, especially when they'd been with Kitlyn and Oona. Annabelle watched her when they couldn't, unlike how Aodh left

Oona in the care of Miss Harper and rarely spent time with her aside from occasional 'visits.'

Made sense now, considering he hadn't really been her father.

The more Kitlyn stood there thinking, the angrier she became. Everything pointed to the children being abducted. Apprehension changed her memory of the shriek from ambiguous to a scream of fear.

Kitlyn stormed toward the castle. Obviously, the children were not in the garden. She could do nothing productive outside. Had the nobles finally decided to make a move? How could they be so brazen as to abduct Evie and Pim right off the castle grounds while she and Oona sat not far away?

Twenty paces from the garden walk, Kitlyn caught herself letting anger cloud her thoughts. She stopped, crouched, and pressed her hand through the grass to the dirt below. Soon after focusing on her magic, her mind filled with numerous individual prodding sensations, the weight of everyone walking around. Each time someone stepped, she felt their weight as though she'd become the earth. Nothing moving seemed small or light enough to be a child. Stationary people and animals proved much more difficult to detect, but given enough concentration, she could sometimes notice them from the motion of breathing.

Especially children who couldn't stand perfectly still.

She poured energy into the ground, straining to feel out every tiny detail. For an instant, she gasped in surprise at detecting a faerie running along the ground—until she realized it had four legs.

Merely a squirrel.

Confident the children absolutely did not remain in the garden, she opened her eyes, swallowed the urge to cry, and stood. Oona's ragged calls for Evie and Pim sent a ripple of rage down her back. She would not be cruel, but would absolutely make an example of whoever took the children.

I swear on my life if the children are found alive, I will not order anyone be executed.

The kitchen door swung open, revealing Elsbeth, the first maid, who promptly stopped short and stared at her in fear.

Kitlyn walked the rest of the way across the grass to the garden walk, slipping through the gap in the arches onto the paved path under the overhanging roof of the castle's second story.

Like a mouse frozen in terror while a cat stalked toward it, Elsbeth cringed, seeming ready to run away.

"Elsbeth," said Kitlyn.

"Yes, highness?"

"You do not need to be afraid of me. I have more important things to take up my time than wasting an ounce of thought on anything you said or did to me in the past."

Elsbeth swallowed. "Highness, you look ready to… I mean… King Aodh, whenever he…"

"I am not him." Kitlyn closed her eyes, searching for calm. "Have you seen Evie or Pim?"

"Not since they went out into the garden almost two hours ago… why?"

Kitlyn opened her eyes. The cluelessness on Elsbeth's face started to make her angry, so she looked away. "They are missing. Did you see them leave the garden?"

"No… but I did see a strange man."

A shocking realization smacked the anger out of Kitlyn's brain. It made no sense how the children could disappear from the garden — unless a man wielding magic capable of disappearing had taken them. *Does Ulfaan seek revenge for what past kings did to mages?* "W-what did this man look like?"

Elsbeth flinched.

Kitlyn grabbed her by the shoulders.

Elsbeth squeaked.

"I am not Aodh. No one innocent of wrongdoing will ever bear the brunt of my wrath for something else gone poorly."

After a few breaths, Elsbeth peeled her gaze up from the floor and made eye contact. "Black hair. Curly. Somewhat long, past the shoulders. He wore a castle guard's mail armor, but he seemed a bit too thin to be a real soldier."

"How old?"

"Older than us. Not much. Perhaps twenty." Elsbeth gestured

out at the garden. "I saw him over there by the ivy. He neither appeared to be guarding nor going anywhere in particular."

Kitlyn pictured Ulfaan, as best she could remember. He, too, had longish hair, but straight. Definitely much older than twenty. His black tunic hung too loose on him to reveal the figure beneath it. *Doesn't sound like him, but a man who can disappear can probably change his appearance.*

Oona dashed over in tears. She clung to Kitlyn, shaking from silent sobs.

"We'll find them." Kitlyn squeezed her.

"I thought he might be a spy or dissenter," whispered Elsbeth. "I ran to fetch a guard, but the man had disappeared by the time we returned."

"How long ago did you see him?" asked Kitlyn, rubbing a hand up and down Oona's back.

Elsbeth bowed her head. "Beg your forgiveness, highness, it's hard to say. I've been so busy today time is rushing by. Maybe twenty minutes before all the shouting started."

"All right." Kitlyn nodded at her. "Organize the maids and have them check the castle, anywhere they think the children might have gone to hide."

"Yes, highness." Elsbeth rushed off, entering via the kitchen door.

"They're gone," whimpered Oona.

"They are not in the garden. Don't say 'gone' yet. We will find them." Kitlyn grasped Oona's face in both hands, staring into her eyes. "If someone took them, they will make demands."

Oona sniffled, struggling to compose herself. "You're right. We should have been watching them more closely."

"Do not blame yourself. We were in the castle garden. Walls on all sides. Guards. Staff. There is no safer place in all of Lucernia."

Oona's eyes said she didn't think the garden particularly safe anymore, though she merely rested her cheek on Kitlyn's shoulder and fought back tears.

TOO MANY MAYBES

OONA

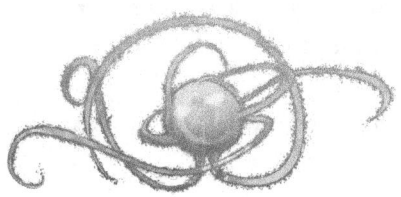

Somehow, Oona went from the garden walk to the throne room.

She didn't remember walking there clinging to Kitlyn, but must have. They stood at the base of the throne dais with the advisors: Beredwyn, Lanon, Balais, Naldun, and Alonna, plus Guard Captain Lorne.

The daze of dread, guilt, and worry released Oona's mind about the same moment Kitlyn finished explaining to the advisors what Elsbeth told her about a strange man in the garden—and how she thought it might be Ulfaan disguised.

"What makes you suspect him?" Beredwyn's fuzzy grey caterpillar eyebrows crept upward.

"A weak assumption." Kitlyn folded her arms. "Evie and Pim disappeared out of the garden, which is enclosed by a wall two stories high. The only way in or out is to go through the castle. Even if they somehow scaled the wall, guards outside would have seen them. Ulfaan disappeared in a flash, right in front of us. I only thought of him because the children also disappeared."

Beredwyn rubbed his long beard. Lanon winced in the way he did whenever he disagreed with Aodh but feared saying so. Alonna's expression gave no indication of her opinion on Ulfaan being responsible. Balais narrowed his eyes, evidently agreeing with her rather circumstantial assumptions.

"Are you certain the children are not hiding as a game?" asked Naldun. "It doesn't seem likely an unknown person could have reached them. Even if this Ulfaan took them, would he not have needed to walk into the garden? Or is he capable of appearing wherever he wants to be?"

Kitlyn and the advisors took a few seconds to agree they had no idea what the man could do.

"We heard a shriek," said Oona. "I'm sure it came from Evie, but it… I don't know. I'm questioning myself. She sounded more startled than frightened. As if Pim snuck up on her and put a frog down her dress."

Beredwyn almost smiled.

"We do not know what this man might have conjured for her to see." Balais stuck his hands into opposite sleeves, folding his arms. "We also do not know for certain he is involved."

"You don't trust him," said Oona.

"For many, many years, the sacred writings held that all magic not of the gods came from darkness." Balais let out a slow exhale. "There must have been some basis for this. Even if the teachings had become distorted over time, I find it impossible to believe some ancient servant of Lucen decided on a whim to regard arcane magic as evil. It may have been one person using magic to kill a priest, king, queen, or someone of importance. Or perhaps a large number of them preyed like bandits on travelers… even tried to take over the kingdom."

"There have never been a 'large number' of anything in Lucernia with magic." Advisor Lanon shook his head. "The reason the war dragged on for so many years is we had one priest to every forty of their rootcallers and firecallers. And only Navissa's faithful are terribly effective at making war."

Beredwyn chuckled. "To be fair, rootcallers made bridges more than war."

Oona thrust her arms out to either side. "We don't know! The library contains *no* information on any history older than the reign of King Iastor. It's possible 300 years ago everyone in Lucernia was a wizard who rode goblins instead of horses or flew on faerie-pulled chariots."

The advisors and Captain Lorne stared at her.

"No, I am not being sincere. My point is, we do not know. Mages might have been more common. Why are there no history books?" Oona shot a pointed look at Balais, then an asking one to Beredwyn. "Someone destroyed or removed these books. Does anyone know of a hidden library?"

All assembled shook their heads to the negative.

"Are you certain Elsbeth is being truthful?" asked Beredwyn, his voice full of grandfatherly gentleness.

"I do not possess Oona's gift, but I believe so." Kitlyn set her hands on her hips, scowling at nothing in particular. "She made life rather difficult for me before, but she thought me a peasant breaking the rules of status."

"The rules of status can go to the Pit." Oona waved dismissively. "There is nothing inherently wrong with having status or even being proud of it. It is wrong to be cruel to those with less."

Piper rushed in from the servant's entrance, acting like a frightened sister. She hurried over and grasped Oona's hand in both of hers. "The cook's son, Pim, is missing."

"Yes." Oona squeezed her hand. "We are already looking for him."

"Where is Evie?" whispered Piper, tearing up.

"They were together," said Kitlyn in half a voice.

The main door at the far end of the throne room opened. Elsbeth, face red as an ivenberry, entered, a young man in chain mail behind her. The two made their way down the carpeting to the dais. Elsbeth kept her head down, while the man appeared mildly nervous. Oona blinked at them, confused as to why a relatively new soldier would be barging in on the throne room in the midst of a meeting with the advisors. Upon noticing Kitlyn giving the man a smoldering glare, she nudged her.

"Did this man do something?" she whispered.

Kitlyn slightly shook her head. "I am not angry with him. Nor Elsbeth. My vexation is at the present circumstances."

"Have you found them?" asked Advisor Lanon once the duo stopped beside the group.

Guard Captain Lorne looked at the man. "Dunisen, I trust you bring important word and are not merely interrupting the queens to familiarize yourself with the throne room?"

"Forgive me, highness," said Elsbeth.

Kitlyn eyed the man in chain mail. "I believe there has been a misunderstanding. This is the man you saw?"

"Yes, highness," said Elsbeth. "Dunisen has recently been promoted to the castle guard. He was charged to spend the day walking around the castle to familiarize himself with it."

"I feel I've missed something here," said Captain Lorne.

"It is my fault, captain." Elsbeth finally looked up from the floor. "I did not recognize him and thought perhaps a spy disguised themselves as a guard. The queen was searching for the children and I told her I'd seen a man..."

Kitlyn raised a hand to stop Elsbeth. "You meant no harm. I would rather you stay vigilant than pay no attention to someone you do not recognize simply because he is dressed like a guard. I appreciate you coming to us as soon as you discovered the truth."

Anxiety forced the breath from Oona's chest. A sighting of a suspicious person had been the only clue to explain Evie and Pim disappearing. It turning out to be an honest mistake left them nothing. While Ulfaan still might be involved, the chances of it now seemed less likely. Kitlyn only thought of him due to the sighting of an unknown man.

"Elsbeth." Oona nodded to her. "Thank you for your honesty and efforts to keep the castle safe. Please go and see if the staff have found anything."

"Thank you, highness." Elsbeth made a pained, confused face at her before hurrying away.

I almost pity her. She thought me of royal blood and I am truly a commoner. Kitlyn, the reverse. The woman doesn't know what to think of either of us now.

"You've been patrolling the castle all day," said Captain Lorne. "Did you see anything out of the ordinary?"

Dunisen hesitated. "Erm, well, no, sir. Nothing pertaining to the disappearance of the children."

"Anything out of the ordinary could be important, no matter how trivial." High Priest Balais held his chin a little higher. "We may be dealing with a sorcerer."

"Of course, your grace." Dunisen bowed to him. "I observed one of the groundskeepers climbing out of the moat earlier this morning. The man had no clothing on, and by his demeanor, I suspect he did not intentionally jump into the moat."

Shock spread over the advisors to varying degrees. Captain Lorne appeared to be fighting the urge to laugh.

"Was the man inebriated?" asked Oona.

"As far as I could tell, he did not appear to be so. He claimed to have tripped, but could not explain the absence of his clothes, stating they simply vanished. Also, I observed an ivenberry pie exiting the kitchen late this afternoon."

Everyone exchanged a momentary confused glance.

"Someone made off with a pie?" asked Alonna. "How is that worthy of mention?"

"Perhaps as the cook's son Pim is one of the children missing?" Beredwyn's fuzzy eyebrows crept together.

"The unusual part was no one did the stealing," said Dunisen. "The pie drifted off the windowsill by itself. By the time I'd gone out the door and 'round the side, it had vanished."

Faeries! We saw footprints, the magical pranks... oh, no! Some stories claim faeries steal children! "Faeries took them!"

The advisors mostly stared at Oona in stunned disbelief. Kitlyn appeared lost to deep thought. Beredwyn blinked, seeming skeptical but not entirely ready to dismiss the idea.

Piper gasped in shock, whispering, "Oh, no! How do we get them back?"

"Faeries?" asked Guard Captain Lorne. "Perhaps, my queen, Beck's wooden blade has made contact with your head a few too many times?"

Advisor Lanon gawked at him. Surely, anyone suggesting the former king had been pummeled into delirium would have regretted it. Balais kept a stony face. Alonna almost laughed but her expression went pitying, as if to say she thought despair had pushed rationality from her mind.

"I do not believe childish fancy will serve any interest," said Captain Lorne.

"Hold judgement a moment." Kitlyn held up a hand. "We did see tiny footprints the other day. You'll remember Lady Parrington's dress removed itself from her in a crowded room. Pies flying from windowsills? A groundskeeper in the moat claiming his clothing disappeared?"

"Likely drunk last night," muttered Advisor Lanon. "Staggered out of his dwelling in a fog and didn't wake until crashing into the moat. Thought his clothing vanished because he'd never put any on when he got out of bed."

"There must be less fantastical explanations for this." Balais paced. "Small footprints could be made by anyone with an artist's touch. I admit the Lady Parrington's garment disappearing is more difficult to explain, but we all witnessed Ulfaan remove himself from our presence."

"No one has reported seeing an unfamiliar person enter the castle." Kitlyn folded her arms. "If Ulfaan could remove himself, he could perhaps do the reverse. However, I do not see him going to the trouble of planting false footprints, stealing a pie and mortifying the Duchess of Tandren only to abduct Evie and Pim. However unlikely the idea of faeries may be, we should not disregard it entirely."

Balais gestured at the floor where Ulfaan had been standing. "Only Lucen knows what goes on in the minds of those with magic."

"Your grace," said Oona. "Be wary of trusting tradition purely because of it being tradition. Truth is truth, but a misunderstanding or deliberate lie does not become truth simply because many people have erroneously believed it for a long time."

"I..." Balais closed his mouth, pondered momentarily, then sighed. "You may be correct. I caution against being too trusting, but we should also resist the temptation to assume the worst."

Kitlyn faced Oona. "What would faeries intend to do with them?"

Piper cringed.

"There are many stories," said Oona a touch louder than a whisper. "I do not know which ones to believe if faeries actually exist. It changes depending on the storybooks one reads. Some merely wish to have tea parties. Others? Much worse."

"I'm sure those books are wrong." Piper sniffled.

"The stories may differ based on where they came from." Beredwyn rested a hand on Oona's shoulder. "Perhaps faeries in different places behave in different ways? People certainly do."

Captain Lorne pinched the bridge of his nose as if unable to believe people around him sincerely discussed the possibility of faeries.

"For now," said Kitlyn. "Continue the search. Have any wagons or parcels large enough to conceal children checked before leaving the city. I also still wish to have our spies locate Ulfaan. Even if he is uninvolved, I'd prefer to know where he is."

The advisors and Captain Lorne nodded.

Oona bowed her head, offering a moment of reverence to Tenebrea. The goddess had forewarned her of harm befalling a family halfway across the kingdom, yet sent no visions, messages, or even odd feelings in regard to Evie and Pim.

I have to believe the children are safe.

EVIE'S SEAT AT THE DINNER TABLE TORMENTED OONA WITH ITS emptiness.

The child did not have a particular penchant for being loud, but her absence covered the dining hall in thick silence. Oona stared at the violet cushioned rectangle on the chair's back. Flickering candlelight glinted in the high-polish of the wood around it. She gazed away from the chair at the ironwood shelves covering the walls. The dark décor made it gloomy on the best of days, but tonight, it steeped the room in dread.

Their handmaidens joined them for the meal as they usually did. A quiet sadness clung to Meredith. Red ringed Piper's eyes from crying, though she'd mostly calmed.

No reports had come back from the soldiers or staff with any news, good or bad. If anyone had slipped into and out of the castle to take the children, they would have needed to be invisible. Not a single person saw anyone out of the ordinary. The exterior guard reported no one leaving the keep. Other than one unfortunate groundskeeper, no one disturbed the moat. Even if the children somehow managed to climb the garden wall, they would not have been able to leave the castle grounds without swimming the moat.

Oona didn't believe Evie would willingly jump into water so foul. Even Pim would refuse.

It also made no sense whatsoever to imagine the children trying to run away. No, someone or something took them. The more she thought about it, the more it made sense to her faeries had to be involved. Though her worries did their best to twist the sound in Oona's memory, the squeal Evie let out could have been a delighted reaction to seeing a faerie.

She'd managed only a few bites of food before clinging to Kitlyn's left arm. Her wife continued eating, though seemed not to enjoy the meal as much as perform a mechanical task. Oona focused on her hope the lack of warning from Tenebrea proved the children would be found safe. She tried not to wonder for too long if the only reason the goddess might have intervened came down to a demon being in Shimmerbrook.

At a nudge from Kitlyn, Oona allowed her trust in the gods to help her eat a little more. Becoming weak and exhausted would not help her think. She somewhat reluctantly ate a bit of ham and potato, chewing in no great hurry.

"Who would want to take them?" whispered Oona. "Fauhurst doesn't have many—if any—sympathizers left."

"No, he crossed a line with them when he tried to murder us. It's one thing to demand we 'give up evil' and marry a man like 'proper women' ought to... attempting to assassinate us while filthy and drunk showed everyone what sort of man he was."

Oona nibbled on a potato hunk.

"How convinced are you faeries have them?" asked Kitlyn.

"I'm not convinced. It makes the most sense, except it makes no sense."

Kitlyn gave a sad chuckle. "I've been thinking the nobility might be involved. There are one or two who don't trust me because of Aodh. Some view us as weak and think we could be easily displaced to seize power or even manipulated due to our inexperience."

"You aren't as inexperienced as they believe." Oona defiantly stabbed her fork into a bit of ham. "It wouldn't be logical for them to take the children. Pim's the cook's son and Evie is not a true heir according to tradition, merely the daughter of a peasant."

"Her title wouldn't matter. They believe we would do anything to keep her safe."

Tears rolled down Oona's face while she chewed. She couldn't justify choosing Evie's life over the lives of many. Most likely, however, if the restless nobles took her for leverage, they'd demand Kitlyn and Oona abdicate the throne or perhaps even kill themselves. To save Evie, she might agree.

If they hurt her, Kitlyn will send Omun to trample their estates.

"I don't believe this is political." Kitlyn grasped her water cup. "If a person working for those nobles could get into the garden—and out—without being seen, they could have killed us."

Oona stared sideways at her. "You are trying to ensure I am never able to sleep again, aren't you?"

"No. Merely attempting to be practical. The unrest among the nobles isn't yet to the point where I believe they are ready to take drastic action. They are on edge, believing my ideas are too favorable to the commoners and a threat to them."

Oona managed a weak smile. "Why must they infer being fair to commoners means we will be unfair to the wealthy?"

"Because they are used to a ruler who favors the wealthy at the expense of commoners. In their minds, the only possible change is the reverse. It is beyond them to consider we can be fair to everyone."

"Taxes again?" Oona sighed.

"It is deeper than simple taxes. The nobles prefer laws not apply to them in the same way they do to untitled people." Kitlyn drank the last of her water.

A woman in a plain grey dress standing by the wall picked a pitcher up from a small table beside her and approached.

"Thank you." Kitlyn held the cup for her to pour.

"Most welcome, highness." The woman smiled.

Oona much preferred to see the staff smiling rather than scurrying about fearfully in the presence of the royals. She'd never acted cruelly to them, though had a little too often been bratty and demanding prior to her ill-fated attempt to run away. Sitting for days in a prison cell deep within a nation of people who all wanted her dead made everything else she'd ever cried about feel beyond shallow.

Even if doing so would make the nobles drop dead from shock, she'd apologized to all the staff for her earlier petulance. Granted, she had done so prior to the wedding. Even though the entirety of the kingdom thought of her as the princess, she'd technically been a 'mere peasant girl' at the time she apologized to the staff. The minor nuance proved sufficient to prevent scandal among the nobility.

Of course, not all the nobles treated commoners and peasants poorly, but the nicer ones didn't present a threat to the kingdom's stability.

"I cannot think of anyone else who'd want to take them," said Oona. "The nobles cannot reconcile you being Aodh's daughter while having grown up as a peasant. Even to save their lives, most of them wouldn't dare force their children to suffer the 'cruelty of wearing common clothing in public, much less toil at actual work for years.'"

"The horror," deadpanned Kitlyn.

Oona took Kitlyn's hand, smiling past a few tears. "It is what makes you such a good leader. You can truly consider both sides. That you do not loathe the man says much of who you are."

"Do I not? What kind of daughter stands idle while her father dies?" Kitlyn glanced off to the side.

"The man was only your father in the most elemental of ways."

Oona pulled Kitlyn's arm into her chest, holding it like a doll. "No different from a soldier who spends one night in a village and leaves behind a daughter he's never seen. Beredwyn is more your father than the former king."

Kitlyn chuckled into a sigh. "Speaking of Beredwyn. He assures me there are no present reports of dissent reaching the level of direct action. It seems ending a two-decade-long war has won us some goodwill."

"We have much work ahead of us still."

"Yes. I don't mean to say otherwise." Kitlyn reached up and caressed Oona's cheek. "Your earnest sweetness shall win over even the most heartless."

Warmth rushed to Oona's face. "Faeries. I'm sure of it."

Piper smiled as if to call them adorable. "I've been all over the passages and didn't see Evie or Pim."

"Do you think there are faeries, Piper?" asked Kitlyn.

"My ma and grandma did. But tis different where I grew up in the moor. Different even from the forest. Bog faeries are nasty and mean. The ones up north in the woods can be nice, but ya have'ta give them treats an' such. I don't know anything about what sort of faeries would be in Lucernia, other than they'd likely be obsessed with social status."

Oona gave a halfhearted laugh.

"Maybe we should try ta pay a faerie's ransom of muffins or sweet breads?" asked Piper.

Kitlyn shrugged. "They already took an ivenberry pie. Do you think it will help?"

"According to my grandma, yes," said Piper. "Giving is much different than taking. They likely took it to punish us for being mean to them."

"How do you think anyone's been mean to them?" asked Oona.

"Bakin' pies and not giving them some." Piper winced. "Grandma said they adore baked sweets."

Meredith finally looked up from her plate. "Are you saying *not* giving them pies is something they feel we should be punished for? Did they steal the children over pies?"

Kitlyn looked over at Piper. "I think she meant they took the pie because no one gave them pie."

"Yes. Faerie laws don't really make any sense." Piper got up to fetch herself some water. "Grandma said there are two important rules to remember. Don't be rude to them, and if you have baked sweets, share."

"Sounds simple enough." Oona ate a little more of her dinner.

"It does, doesn't it?" Piper sat, wagging her eyebrows. "But bog faeries are nasty no matter how polite you try to be around them. Meadow faeries always play tricks on people. Only difference is, the tricks are whimsical if you're nice to them, not dangerous."

Oona hurried to finish her mouthful. "Is it possible they took Evie and Pim because someone was rude?"

Piper's smile evaporated. "I don't know the faeries here would be the same as the ones in the moor… but according to the stories I've heard, they only take children if someone killed a faerie. They'd be of a mind to keep them forever. Life for a life."

Oona shivered in dread. Evie should have been safe in the castle. Not even six months had gone by, and she'd already failed as her guardian.

"No one has admitted to believing in faeries." Kitlyn leaned her head against Oona's. "If someone found and killed one, they'd be showing the remains off and telling everyone about it."

"Yes…" Oona exhaled in relief. "True. I am not sure what will be harder. Finding them or convincing everyone we haven't lost our senses."

NEVER A SINGLE CRISIS

KITLYN

*T*wo rapid knocks came from the dining room door before it opened.

A young man in the pale blue tunic and green tights of a castle page entered. "Pardon, highness. There is a girl here who says Aowyn's Crossing was attacked. She is injured and appears to have been riding for hours."

Damnable timing. Kitlyn nodded once to the page, then looked at Oona. "I will deal with this. Rest and collect yourself."

"I'd rather come along. I cannot allow myself to fall to pieces. We have to put the kingdom above ourselves. And the girl is injured."

Kitlyn bowed her head, doubting herself all over again. If the day ever came where she needed to choose between the kingdom or Oona's life, she couldn't say with total certainty she would act in the interest of the kingdom. If she didn't have to look into the eyes of those her decision would kill, she might not be able to follow the nobler path if it meant her wife's death.

Oona's composure is hanging by a single strand of hair. She loves Evie like her own child. How could anyone not? The girl is almost too sweet and innocent to be real... just like her older sister.

She knew Oona would, without any hesitation, sacrifice her life to protect others. Kitlyn would do the same. If forced to choose between her own life or some number of her citizens, she would definitely save the people—not so easy if she had to sacrifice Oona rather than herself.

Beredwyn mentioned some confusing notion about weighing the greater good. Apparently, some number of casualties existed wherein he considered it better for the kingdom that she preserve herself. How could she put incremental value on lives? What number of innocent people needed to be in peril before she should sacrifice herself versus letting them die? Twenty? A hundred? Thousands?

I do not have time to debate such morbid questions. She sighed out her nose, wondering if it would be cowardly to choose they both die rather than make the decision to sacrifice Oona.

Kitlyn nodded, took her hand, and walked after the page.

Meredith and Piper followed them, as they often tended to do. As proper handmaidens, their only official responsibilities entailed being near the queens to help them. For most of the day, they effectively acted as friends and companions. Oona had, perhaps, a degree more familiarity with Piper than traditionalists would consider proper, the two of them acting similar to stepsisters rather than queen and handmaiden. Oona, and to a degree Kitlyn as well, felt responsible for the death of the girl's parents—who'd been killed fighting in the war—even though it happened nearly three years ago. Despite being only one year younger than Oona and Kitlyn, Piper's short height and scrawny size made her look closer to twelve than fifteen.

The page hurried down the hall to the throne room, rushing to open the door for the queens.

Kitlyn entered to find three soldiers and two of the castle servants standing around a young, teen girl clad in a commoner's knee-length dress. Broken leaves and branch bits littered her long, brown hair. Several superficial cuts on her arms leaked blood, and a small arrow stuck out of her left thigh. She appeared road weary but full of urgency.

The staff gave the girl water and a bowl of stew while the soldiers hovered close as if to catch her if she started to faint.

"By Lucen," whispered Oona. She hiked up her dress and ran to the girl. "Someone fetch a seat for her."

A soldier jogged to grab one of the numerous padded chairs along the walls, dragging it back toward them.

"Highness." The girl attempted to curtsey, but her left leg buckled out from under her.

The remaining two soldiers plus Kitlyn caught her.

"Argh," grunted the girl. "I'm sorry."

"It's all right." Kitlyn kept holding her up until the soldier slid the chair under the young woman. "What is your name?"

"Kemma. Aowyn's Crossing is under attack. I was near the road when it started, got on the first horse I saw, and rode to find help."

Oona cupped her hands around the arrow as soon as the teen sat. "By the grace and kindness of Orien, may your wounds be cleansed." Golden light welled up beneath her fingers.

The girl squeaked, squeezing Kitlyn's hand tight. A faint squishing sound emanated from the wound as the arrow shaft wobbled. The glow shifted entirely to Oona's right hand. She grasped the arrow in her left, gently tugging at it. A moment later, a crude, stone arrowhead emerged. By the time the puncture hole in the girl's leg sealed to a scab, the other tiny cuts on her arms had vanished.

"Praise Orien," rasped Kemma.

"Under attack?" Kitlyn's mind raced, trying to guess who might be threatening a village in the middle of the kingdom so close to the capital. Aowyn's Crossing sat about thirty miles away in the fork where the road north out of Cimril split northeast to Imric and northwest to Gwynaben. Reaching Aowyn's Crossing took a day at an unhurried pace, but this girl likely rode as fast as the horse would tolerate.

"Yes, highness." Kemma looked up at her, face smeared in dirt, blood, and bits of leaf. "They attacked us from the north meadow. The sheep and goats stampeded into town, giving us some warning. I did not see much of what happened after. Lerash saw me standing near a horse and shouted for me to ride to Cimril and bring aid."

"I have never seen an arrow like this before." The soldier who fetched the chair held the arrow up to examine. "It is neither ours nor from Evermoor."

Kitlyn looked at the arrow. Roughly two-thirds the size of a normal one, it had an unusually thick shaft and a triangular stone head. Brown fletching resembled the feathers of common forest birds.

"They weren't even human," said Kemma. "I looked back after mounting the horse, and saw them."

It cannot be the Nimse again. They no longer exist… and didn't have the intelligence to use bows. Kitlyn clenched her jaw. *What new monsters plague us?*

"And?" asked Oona.

"I'm afraid to say." Kemma stared up at Oona like a child caught stealing cookies. "I don't want to offend Lucen."

"Would you be lying?" Kitlyn tilted her head.

"No, highness. The sight was so strange. If I speak of it, anyone hearing me would think me out of my mind."

"Oona will know if you speak truth." Kitlyn smiled. "I do not think you are out of your mind."

Kemma braced a hand on her leg where the arrow had been. "I was galloping fast away from town so maybe didn't see quite well, but they looked like small green-skinned men riding huge wolves."

"How many?" Kitlyn glanced at the three stunned soldiers, then Oona, who also had a surprised expression.

"Ten, maybe fifteen. It is difficult to say. Everyone was running around screaming, fighting. Arrows…" Kemma gestured at her leg. "They saw me leaving and tried to stop me. Two chased, almost caught me, but their wolves became tired much faster than my horse."

"This is unsettling." One of the soldiers, the eldest, shifted his jaw side to side. "This girl speaks of strange beasts smart enough to recognize the need to stop a rider going to summon aid."

Kitlyn nodded.

"Kemma speaks truth as she understands it to be." Oona waved for Yana, one of the castle staff, to give the girl more water. "Please see that she is given a bath, a clean dress, and a place to sleep for the night."

"Right away, highness." Yana bowed. "Come with me, girl."

"You are most gracious and kind. May you be our queens for a long time." Kemma grunted in discomfort as she stood, then limped after Yana.

"Perhaps goblins riding wolves?" asked Oona once the throne room door closed again.

The soldier holding the arrow chuckled. "There are no such things as goblins."

"If for some unexplained reason, goblins do exist…" Kitlyn raised an eyebrow at Oona. "How dangerous are they?"

Oona shrugged. "It depends on which book you read."

"The big one you think might be real."

"In an open fight, they are not too dangerous, especially to a trained soldier. Goblins are cowardly and don't like being caught in the open. They prefer to hide and ambush and are not supposed to go anywhere near towns or villages. A raid like this on a village does not seem like anything a goblin would do—assuming the book is accurate." Oona grimaced. "They do like to eat humans and will often attack the injured, the elderly, or the young."

All three soldiers looked about ready to burst out laughing, but kept quiet.

"It would not make sense then for goblins to raise an army and attack a town." Kitlyn tapped her foot while thinking. *Aowyn's Crossing has no garrison of soldiers but thirty some town watch. No need to station any there since the town should not be in danger being so central.* "The girl might have mistaken fur cloaks or some attempt at a disguise for a monster… except the arrow."

"Aye." The soldier holding it held it out to her. "I cannot say why any man with sense would use such a poor weapon. It would have to be fired from a smaller bow. The heavy, stone head shortens the range and this fletching is crude at best."

Kitlyn beckoned the same page who summoned them to the throne room. When he jogged closer, she took the arrow and handed it to him.

"Seek Captain Lorne. Give him this and tell him to send forty soldiers north to Aowyn's Crossing. Scout the area before rushing in. We know someone or something attacked, but not exactly what or how many."

"Right away, highness." The page bowed before running along the carpeted path to the door.

Kitlyn thanked the three soldiers for escorting Kemma inside. They bowed, then hurried out, returning to their posts by the front gate.

Worried, Piper stared at them. "What's happening in Lucernia?"

"Do you think this is Lucen's punishment for what Aodh did?" asked Meredith.

"No. It is not Lucen's doing." Oona wrapped her arms around Kitlyn. "I half expected you to lead the charge."

"We can't do everything ourselves." Kitlyn hugged her back. "If the kids weren't missing, I probably would have wanted to go see these 'monsters' for myself."

Oona chuckled into a sniffle. "I know you too well. Shall we seek Lucen's counsel in the temple?"

"There is little else I can think of to do in order to find them until we retire to our chambers and stay up all night in worry."

"You know me too well." Oona rested her head on Kitlyn's shoulder.

VANISHED

OONA

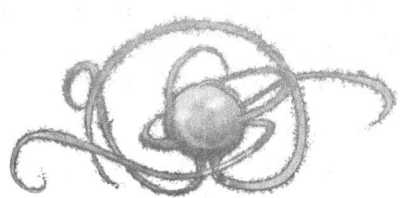

Oona closed her eyes and let her head loll back against stone.

She sat on the waist-high wall separating the garden walk from the grass, leaning against one of the archway columns. For most of her life, whenever she had too many emotions storming around her head, she'd perch here and search for peace. Except during bad, windy storms, the spot allowed her to enjoy the outdoors while staying out of the rain.

Other than being somewhat windy, the day promised to be pleasant—but only in terms of weather. She hadn't slept much at all. The two hours she spent in the temple of Lucen the previous night succeeded only in conveying to the gods how desperately she wanted to find Evie and Pim alive. She chided herself for expecting an answer. No matter how unusually often the gods sent her messages or visions, it would be wrong to assume they'd answer every time she wanted or needed help.

She caught herself starting to feel disappointed at the complete lack of response—and pleaded with them to forgive her. The gods choosing to contact her was a rare privilege, not something they owed her or *needed* to do.

Soon after she prayed apologies, a presence manifested beside her. Though it made no sound nor appeared in any way the eye could see, she knew the presence conveyed understanding. For no specific reason, she believed Tenebrea wanted her to know she didn't have anything to apologize for. The moment left her feeling like some of the castle staff who'd been thoroughly shocked when she, as queen, told them they could freely talk to her and didn't need to avoid eye contact.

Following that, Kitlyn practically carried her to bed. She'd spent most of last night drifting in and out of sleep trying to come to terms with the confirmation she *did* have a connection with the gods—or at least Tenebrea—different from anyone else.

It had, at least, given her something other than Evie and Pim's disappearance to think about.

She'd come to take the gods' non-reaction to the children's situation as a sign she needn't worry.

Birdsong from the garden didn't offer its usual serenity, only deepening her questions. Oona sat on the wall, gazing at the trees, trying to understand what happened. Voices drifted back and forth across her memory of the morning meal an hour earlier. Beredwyn joined them, mostly to discuss the spymaster's frantic efforts to explain how his people hadn't been able to find any trace of the children—or a potential abductor—in Cimril.

At the metal *click* of the kitchen door opening not far behind her, Oona lifted her head from the column and opened her eyes. Mereld, the head cook, stepped out onto the garden walk. The pale red stains of ivenberry juice on his white apron and green tunic almost made him resemble a butcher recently done slaughtering a pig. He, too, appeared to have not slept well, his eyes half-lidded.

For the most part, the kitchen staff considered themselves a different class from the rest of the castle workers. Despite being on the same social level as the maids who dusted and cleaned floors, they acted superior as if being entrusted with feeding everyone conveyed higher status on them. They'd been less than polite to Kitlyn over the years—except for the head cook. To the horror of all, he spoke to 'servant Kitlyn' in the same respectful tone he used when talking to 'princess Oona.' Too polite for one, too informal for the other—or so said the clucking hens.

He'd never been frightened of her the way the rest of the staff used to be. No one had ever feared what Oona would do, rather Aodh's wrath if she whined about them being 'mean' to her. Despite not intending to be such a little tyrant as a younger girl, she had been. Her and Kitlyn's treatment of the castle staff since becoming queens mostly assuaged the guilt. Oona had even insisted people cease using the term 'servant,' preferring to call them 'staff' or workers.

The pettiest among them still acted aloof, but Mereld, she'd always been fond of.

Oona shifted to face the walkway rather than stretch her legs out on the wall, more polite than continuing to sit with her back to him. "I am sorry."

"You've nothing to apologize for, highness." Mereld approached and stood beside her, gazing out at the garden. The fragrance of baking bread and a hint of fruit clung to him.

"I should have stayed closer to them. Not let them run out of my sight."

"In the garden?" Mereld shook his head. "'Tis nothin' you did or didn't do ta regret. There's nary a safer place in the entire kingdom to be."

Unless you are a princess an entire nation wishes dead. "It is much safer here now than it used to be."

"Aye. They'll find them, highness."

"I should share your confidence." Oona looked down at her dark blue slippers, toes hovering a few inches above the stone. "Perhaps I would be able to if not for feeling as though I should be doing something more than simply waiting."

"Agreed. I find the wait rather vexing."

"I am unsure if I am merely worried or if the gods are trying to tell me to act. Do you feel as though you are remiss as a father not to be out there searching?"

"In a way." Mereld nodded. "Though, what more could I possibly do that all the soldiers and spies can't? If I thought it would make a difference, Lucen knows I'd be out there… somewhere, tryin' to find them."

Oona absentmindedly tapped her dangling feet together. "I feel like a child standing outside a burning house watching everyone carry water in the wrong direction, away from the house. Except, I don't know where the burning house even is."

"Perhaps the gods are speakin' to ya." Mereld resumed staring out at the garden, quiet for several minutes before abruptly speaking again. "The kitchen is so quiet without Pim. Used to appreciate the peace when he'd run off ta play with little Evie. Gracious of you to allow it."

"It never came into question. What does it matter if the head cook's son and the queen's young sister are friends? If social status doesn't matter to children, why should it matter to anyone? If they wish to remain friends, I refuse to allow something as superfluous as the opinions of the nobility to pull them away from each other."

Mereld looked away from the garden, a whimsical smile on his lips. "What if they someday fall in love?"

"Then your son may well be king someday, I suppose. But commoners simply don't marry royals." Oona twirled a lock of her hair around a finger. "Oh, wait. I believe we've ignored that rule."

He chuckled.

"You think too far in the future, Mereld. They're eight and six. We should not be rushing them to grow up or arranging their lives for them. They are far too small to worry about romance yet."

"Aye, highness. Merely trying to have happy thoughts to get me through the not knowing."

Oona rested her hand on his arm, making him jump. For an instant, he appeared worried of committing a social error by touching the queen. "I understand. Thinking of Kitlyn helped me endure being imprisoned in Evermoor."

"Suppose they do grow up and become fond of each other. You would not object?"

"Consider where I came from and ask me that again." She smirked.

"No one thinks of you as a young woman from a farm in Llanoen.

You are still the princess in their eyes, now the queen."

Oona slid off the wall to stand beside him. "More proof it is all nonsense. For years, they mocked or ignored Kitlyn. Now, they pretend none of it happened. She *is* royal. I merely pretended, even if I didn't know the truth. They did not cast me aside when the truth came to light, nor subject me to the scorn she had to endure. Simple nonsense. A title is nothing more than someone's opinion."

"Opinions have power. It does not bother me to occupy a fairly low rung on the ladder. I find it peaceful. Some people are able to find happiness with wherever they are. Others are driven to climb. Some even prefer to jump down."

"Yes." Oona watched the leaves flutter, some already beginning to fall for the season. It wouldn't be much longer before the cold made the garden dreary and frightening. Leafless trees and bushes devoid of flowers unnerved her... at least until snow turned it magical. The garden had always offered a sense of solace and remembrance of many happy moments.

"You are a good person, highness. It is not right for you to know this pain," said Mereld.

Oona peered up into the cook's eyes. "You are a good person as well, and do not deserve to wonder what has become of your son." *Is it not cruel enough the war took his wife?* She sighed, turning her gaze back to the garden. "How is it possible for a pair of small children to leave the castle grounds unnoticed?"

"I have been asking myself the same question. It is impossible. As if they simply vanished."

She thought of Ulfaan disappearing in a swirl of magical light. Kitlyn already considered and mostly dismissed the idea the man had been involved, but they'd been thinking he snuck into the castle to take them. No one knew anything about what this 'arcane' magic could do. Perhaps he took them from far away.

"Maybe they did exactly that!"

"Highness?" asked Mereld.

"The children! They simply disappeared. I must speak to Kitlyn at once." She hiked up her dress and ran down the garden walk to the door.

READING FLEAS

KITLYN

A dozen or more papers littered the table in front of Kitlyn, all containing accounts from various citizens, soldiers, and even commanders.

Alas, not one had anything to do with Evie or Pim. It appeared Lucernia had a rapidly growing problem with 'monsters.' The advisors sat around the table in the former war room, now repurposed to something of a council chamber as no war presently went on. Even if she read each letter fully understanding the tendency of citizens to consider everything even slightly unusual as demonic, no one could argue at least some letters detailed encounters with legitimately dangerous beasts.

All but two described sightings from a distance, offering dubious accounts of supposedly non-human beings. Most accounts sounded as if the unknown creatures had been as keen on avoiding people as the author of the letter had been at avoiding the 'demon.' One note from the commander of the military garrison at Torlach said he lost three soldiers to 'an unidentified four-legged beast twice the size of a horse and covered in dark blue scales.' The other account containing more than a fleeting glimpse came from the commander of the troops stationed at the Lucernian side of the Arch of the Ancients. Her letter described a group of 'great hawk-like birds of a size capable of carrying off young children flying overhead, snow falling from their wings.'

The advisors believed someone had accidentally put certain mushrooms in the fort's stew the previous night. However, with so many reports of unusual beings, Kitlyn couldn't summarily dismiss them all as folly, imagination, or people making up stories for attention. She had witnessed Ulfaan remove himself from the throne room in an instant—obviously by use of magic. Could he have something to do with the sudden proliferation of magical beasts?

I should not decide his guilt or innocence before understanding the entirety of the situation. He may be connected to this, but perhaps not responsible. For all we know, he may simply be another magical being appearing for the same reason.

Advisor Lanon repeatedly asked what they planned to do about the situation. High Priest Balais suggested the creatures—if real—could not possibly be demons or Lucen would have made him, Oona, or other priests aware of the need to prepare. Alonna announced her plans to confer with the high priests of the other three temples. Advisor Naldun brought up multiple cases of people telling him about unexplained creature sightings. A few sounded much like the behavior of goblins as detailed in the huge book, though such creatures should not be brave enough to approach a city the size of Cimril.

Kitlyn knew only one thing for certain: they would not reach any sort of agreement soon.

While the advisors debated, she stared at the pile of papers, balancing her chin on her hand. Perhaps twenty minutes later, they all appeared to notice her abstaining from the argument at the same time and stopped talking.

"What are your thoughts on this, my queen?" asked Beredwyn.

She let her hand fall away from her chin, then sat up straight. "There is no reason for us to surrender to fear, assume some dire plot threatens the security of Lucernia, or spend days in here guessing. We have too many sightings to dismiss them all as imagination, lies, or the product of drink. It is clear to me something is happening.

Creatures not seen for centuries seem to be showing up once more. The question I have is: why? Are these beings genuine or costumed rogues?"

"We await word back from Aowyn's Crossing." Advisor Lanon stuffed his hands into opposite sleeves.

"Good. Hopefully, the attack was not as destructive as Kemma believes." Kitlyn gestured at the letters. "Most of these accounts talk of seeing 'beasts' from a good distance away, often in fields or forests. It would not be terribly difficult to fool the eye using disguises."

The advisors murmured agreement.

"However, we must ask what anyone or any group would gain by frightening citizens all over the kingdom. This would require a great deal of effort and resources." She swiped her hand at a parchment. "This came from Gwynaben." She flicked another one. "This from Pembrook. Two from Eastmarch."

"Someone may be trying to undermine trust in Lucen even more so than Aodh did." Alonna frowned.

"They cannot be demons, or surely Lucen would have acted." Balais shook his head.

"I do not disagree with you." Alonna bowed to him. "My point is, the citizenry tends to regard everything scary as demonic even when it is not. If an enemy of the crown understands this, they could sow widespread fear and later claim a surge in demonic activity is a direct result of… whatever they want."

The door burst open as Oona raced in, eyes wide, expression urgent.

Hoping for good news about the children, Kitlyn leapt to her feet.

Oona rushed around the table and grasped arms with her. "I think Ulfaan has them."

"A vision?" asked Kitlyn. "You are sure?"

"No…" Oona deflated. "The gods have thus far remained silent, which I am certain means Evie and Pim are not in peril."

"Why do you so suddenly think of him then? Is it not Lucen's doing?" Kitlyn squeezed Oona's forearms.

"I was talking to Mereld on the garden walk. He said there's really no way they could've left the castle and it's as if they simply disappeared. It had to be magic. We don't know he *needed* to sneak into the castle to take them. He might simply have pulled them away. No priest of Lucernia nor caller of Evermoor could do this."

"Oo…" Kitlyn brushed a hand over her love's cheek. "Why would he show himself to us, ask if we intended to persecute mages, then days later use magic to abduct Evie and Pim?"

Oona blinked, considered for a few seconds, then lowered her gaze to the floor. "I admit it does not sound probable when you put it like that. Doing such a thing would convince us mages could not be trusted."

"Perhaps," said Advisor Lanon, "his question and display were intended on purpose to announce himself in preparation for future demands?"

"This may be a trap." Beredwyn fidgeted. "If young master Pim and Lady Evie are being held somewhere, I fear our queens will charge off to recover them."

You are correct. Kitlyn narrowed her eyes.

Oona emitted a pained noise. "Of course we would!"

"A trap of what kind?" asked Balais. "What sense would it make for a man capable of seizing children from afar to lure the queens anywhere? Would it not have been more direct to abduct the queens directly if he could simply cause anyone he chose to vanish?"

Alonna held up a hand in pause. "Irrational people do not act in rational ways."

"The people are content," said Naldun. "Everyone is war weary and grateful for quiet. I have heard no discontent from the citizenry, only tales of strange creatures."

Kitlyn looked at a waiting page at the far end of the room. "Please inform Spymaster Hinlor I require an update on the search for Ulfaan Khera as soon as possible."

The young man nodded once before rushing off.

"Some *do* believe demons are returning," said Advisor Naldun.

"Unlikely," muttered Balais.

"I agree." Oona let go of Kitlyn's hands and faced the advisors. "Except for the one, I have not been warned of actual demons."

"The one?" Balais raised an eyebrow.

"Shimmerbrook," said Oona. "The succubus."

Every man in the room squirmed. Alonna scowled.

"Ahh, yes. One small group of actual demons does not an invasion make. My thoughts are this succubus sensed Prior Garniel abandoning his trust in Lucen to anger, jealousy, and resentment... and used his weakness as a means into his mind." Balais grasped his Lucen symbol. "I shall, however, seek guidance."

Kitlyn flung a wave at the pile of letters. "These creatures are all different and only two of them, plus the attack on Aowyn's Crossing, sound dangerous. I do not believe we are facing a singular foe or a coordinated campaign of aggression. We are squinting at fleas dancing on a page and mistaking them for words we cannot figure out."

"Highness." Advisor Naldun held up one finger. "Could one such creature have entered the castle? Perhaps the children found it and it took them somewhere?"

Kitlyn gestured at another page standing by the door. "Please advise Spymaster Hinlor I wish to know where Ulfaan came from, who and where he is, and what he wants. Also, if any evidence suggests he is somehow responsible for these monster sightings."

"Yes, highness," said the man.

"Illusions?" Oona raised both eyebrows. "In some cases. Obviously, illusions could not put an arrow in a girl's leg."

"Already done," called Beredwyn, waving for the page to stay put. "Hinlor is already working on the same request from me."

Kitlyn smiled at him, grateful to have at least one person she considered a wise father. "Thank you."

"What now?" whispered Oona.

"We wait. Perhaps search the castle again for any signs of an invisible creature." *I hope I am strong enough to do what is best for the people of Lucernia. This situation with the mysterious creatures seems mild, yet I already feel as though I am committing an error.* She looked into Oona's deep blue eyes. Her wife gave off hope, trust, and more than a little nervousness.

I am not facing this alone. Together, we will find the answers.

A VAST AMOUNT OF NOTHING

OONA

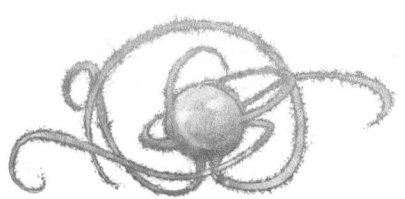

Oona screamed in frustration and slammed the cover of the large, dusty book in front of her.

The sudden noise in the otherwise tomb-silent library made the three girls at the other end of the table jump and yelp, Laura so much so she fell out of her chair. Rowan and Mary, startled several shades paler, clutched their chests, staring at Oona across a forest of book piles.

"Sorry," whispered Oona.

Laura's hands appeared, grasping the table edge, then her head rose into view between them, but only up to her nose. "Why did you yell?"

"Is there a mouse?" asked Mary.

"She wouldn't scream over a mouse." Rowan slouched, fanning herself.

"I would have at your age." Oona rested her elbows on the table, grabbing her head in both hands. "I would have a few months ago, too. Perhaps not now."

Two guards ran out of the bookshelf maze.

"Is everything all right, highness?" asked one.

"Yes. Merely frustrated at the astounding lack of information in this library." She huffed at a stray strand of hair dangling in front of her eyes. It stayed clear for only a few seconds before falling over her face again.

The clicking of hard-soled shoes preceded Margaret, the head housekeeper, emerging from the 'maze'. "It has been a while since such a sound echoed down the halls of Castle Cimril."

Laura, Mary, and Rowan tensed, heads bowed as if waiting to be scolded for a misdeed.

Oona blushed.

Wearing an uncharacteristic smile, Margaret approached and rested a hand on Oona's shoulder. "Are you all right, dear?"

Though barely past forty, the woman's black hair already had plenty of silver threads. The famously dour woman often let down her guard around Oona, suggesting a far bigger heart than she allowed the world to see. Since the end of the war—rather the absence of Aodh Talomir from the castle—she'd softened quite a bit, even smiling when people might see her doing it.

"I'm vexed." Oona sighed hard.

"Yes, I can tell. I know that frustrated scream well." Margaret patted her back.

"I do not mean to be the brat of a princess I used to be."

"You are not her anymore, dear. You've changed."

"As have you." Oona managed a weak smile. "I am quite fond of the new Margaret. I used to be quite afraid of you."

Margaret waved dismissively. "Oh, pff. No one was afraid of me. What is bothering you?"

"This library. There is no information of substance here. No history older than the first Talomir king." She held up a finger. "No, I am not merely losing my composure over books. Kitlyn's life is in danger."

The three twelve-year-olds gasped in unison.

Oona slapped her hand on the huge book. "I've at least skimmed every book in here other than the made-up stories, looking for information about the Gates of Isilien. Nothing."

"Gates of Isilien…" Margaret folded her arms. "I can't say it's familiar to me. How is this threatening Kitlyn?"

"The spirit of Queen Solana visited her, bearing a warning about the curse on the line of Talomir. She said the answer we seek would be found in the Gates of Isilien."

Rowan sucked in a faint breath. She opened her mouth, but closed it.

"What?" Oona looked at her.

"Just something silly from a storybook." Rowan's cheeks reddened almost to match her hair.

"I think we saw the ghost, too," whispered Mary.

Margaret raised both eyebrows. "Solana's spirit roams the castle?"

"She does not haunt us. Merely visited briefly before returning to Tenebrea's realm," said Oona.

Relief spread over Margaret's face. "I see."

Does she dread Kitlyn's mother for being a spirit or her dreadful arrogance? Oona fidgeted. After what Kitlyn told her about the woman, she understood where the horrid attitude came from, but still didn't excuse it. While somewhat guilty of also allowing misery at her own life to affect others, Oona never reduced castle staff to tears or made them run away in the night.

"Rowan?" asked Oona. "I don't care if it's silly. Every idea is helpful."

"Well, umm…" The girl bit her lower lip while fidgeting at the book in front of her. "Nothing specific, but it sounds like an elven word from *Blade of Sorrows*. I know it's a storybook, but it sounds like a name the elves might have given something."

"Elves aren't real," whispered Mary.

"They are!" Laura looked back and forth between her two friends. "Or were. They're gone now, but they used to be real."

"The Anthari didn't particularly like being called 'elves.'" Oona managed a feeble smile. "I confess I doubted their existence, too, until seeing Evermoor in person." She furrowed her brow. "Could Isilien be in Evermoor?"

Margaret traced her fingers over a nearby stack of books. "If so, it would explain why we have no information about it."

"It is a crime we don't." Oona frowned. "We have lost so much information because Aodh or those who came before him didn't want anyone knowing the truth about Evermoor or the past. I don't even know how much we don't know."

Laura snickered—until Margaret glanced at her. "Sorry. It sounded funny."

"She is not upset with you. She always has this expression," whispered Oona.

The girls covered their mouths.

Margaret fake frowned at Oona. "Well, I have work to do. Are you sure you are all right, dear?"

"Whatever the opposite of all right is, I am. Evie and Pim are still missing. I've not been able to find anything about the Gates of Isilien, and it feels like I've got an answer straight in front of me but can't see it."

"Is there anything I can do to help?" Margaret reached over to neaten Oona's hair.

"Thank you, but unless you know where to find either the children or Isilien, I can't think of anything." She exhaled hard.

"Perhaps a soothing cup of tea will help you think?"

Oona smiled.

Margaret drifted off into the corridor of shelves, the clicking of her shoes growing fainter with each step. Laura, Rowan, and Mary exchanged glances of surprise before slouching in relief.

"Unless you're running off before you're done what she's asked you to do, she won't scold you simply for being here and reading." Oona flopped face first over the book and sighed. The scent and flavor of dust filled her awareness. She sighed again.

How much history did we lose because it didn't fit what Aodh or past kings wanted people to know?

The three young maids resumed reading, the library quiet save for the occasional sound of a turned page. Oona remained draped across the closed book, debating if Kitlyn was right and the entire concept of royalty was inherently bad. Her council idea didn't necessarily offer a perfect remedy. While it would be more difficult for an entire group to succumb to the same manner of avarice as Aodh, spreading power over multiple people didn't make it impossible. A wise monarch was better for the people than a corrupt group of senators and wouldn't suffer the paralysis of debate, wasting precious time in a crisis arguing over what to do. On the other hand, a bad monarch led to catastrophes like twenty-year wars and the potential destruction of entire kingdoms.

The people are used to a monarchy. I pray Lucen gives us the wisdom to protect the people from another like my fa —. Oona picked at the edge of the book in front of her eyes. *Should I even think of him as my father?* She knew next to nothing about her real father, having no memories of home before the former king whisked her off to the castle at age three. Not long after Evie's birth, her real father had been conscripted into the army… only to die somewhere near the border with Evermoor. Of those who met a similar fate, he'd been fortunate. His body made it home for a proper burial. As horrid as her mother was, Oona thought it good the woman hadn't been left wondering if her husband lived or died.

Why do I not feel anger toward Aodh for killing my father? Does it make me pathetic? Is it proper to be unable to mourn a man I never knew?

Oona sat up, wiping dust from her cheek, and gazed around at all the bookshelves. Rowan's suggestion the word 'Isilien' could be of Anthari origin did sound plausible. Perhaps someone had written a fictional story where the characters spoke of real places. It would take years to read, even skimming, all the fiction books in the castle library she hadn't already finished. In all likelihood, Kitlyn would die to the curse before she completed half of them. Worse, Oona had no idea *if* any book offered the information she wanted.

Margaret returned, bringing her a cup of tea. She patted Oona on the shoulder before leaving once more to attend her duties as head housekeeper. Having no other ideas, she started skimming fiction novels where Anthari played a role in the story. Alas, the tea did little to calm her mind.

Searching storybooks for true information is truly a sign of desperation. What a useless library. We are —library! Oona blinked, struck by the sudden thought of the Na'vir, an ancient people who had been cursed into the monstrous Nimse creatures trapped in Underholm.

Their queen, Xorana, told of a human who had come seeking knowledge of demonic magic they refused to share.

The Na'vir have a library so vast I cannot even imagine a fraction of what might be there. They're also an ancient people. Perhaps they know what the Gates of Isilien are.

Hope might have sent her running down the hall to Kitlyn, but she couldn't think of leaving the castle on a journey to Underholm while Evie and Pim remained missing. True, Kitlyn's life could potentially be spared by information found there, but without knowing for a fact the information existed *and* Kitlyn faced imminent death, she couldn't justify leaving until they found the children.

Tears gathered in Oona's eyes at a crash of worry for her sister. She bowed her head. "Tenebrea, please don't take them yet. They're far too young."

After a minute or two of silent prayer, something small bumped against her right foot. She opened her eyes, astonished to find the skeletal remains of a rat prodding its skull into her slipper, effectively a tapping finger trying to get her attention. For some reason, the sight of its dry, dusty bones didn't fill her with the urge to shriek. Of course, a single skeletal rat didn't seem scary at all compared to being trapped in a tall canyon between two armies of armed human skeletons charging at her.

"Thank you," she whispered to Tenebrea.

Her heart swelled in hope, gratitude, and excitement. She jumped to her feet. The skeletal rat scampered off across the carpet surrounding the table. When it reached the stone floor, its bony paws clattered like a clumsily worked wooden puppet. The girls looked up as Oona rushed off in pursuit of the undead messenger, though none spoke.

After weaving around the mazelike bookshelves, the rat zipped across the sitting area by the library entrance and ducked under the door. Oona chased, shoving the door out of her way and running into the hall, leaving it open. She hurried after the bony rat, jogging to the top of the grand staircase. Worried the small creature couldn't navigate the steps, she stooped to pick it up—but the rat skeleton flung itself forward, bouncing down the stairs to the first floor.

A passing maid's scream carried up from the ground floor. The woman fell silent at the sight of Oona running past her.

"Highness? Shouldn't you be running *away* from the horrid little creature?" called the woman.

"No!" yelled Oona, not slowing down. "And don't call him horrid. He's a messenger from Tenebrea!"

The bony rat led her across the castle and out to the garden walk. It meandered to the gap in the wall at the middle arch, pausing at the edge of the grass. Once Oona caught up to it, the undead rodent peered up at her, jabbed its head in the direction of the garden, and promptly fell apart into a pile of loose bones.

Oona stared over the grass between the walk and the garden. "They're still here?" She blinked, then yelled, "They're still here!"

Thank you!

18

HERE THERE BE FAERIES

KITLYN

*K*itlyn leaned on the railing of the castle's grand balcony, directly above the main entrance, gazing out over the city.

So many people. How is it right for one person to have so much power over others? Most of the people in Cimril are older than me. Am I a woman or a child? Do I deserve to wear this crown? Beredwyn should be in charge as he was when Aodh remained a child. Maybe he is... I'm just repeating what he suggests. Sixteen...

Thinking of her age offered a momentary distraction from the emotional drain of Evie and Pim disappearing. It would have been bad enough without also having to watch Oona suffer. Lucernian law regarded sixteen as an adult in most cases depending on circumstances. A person of such age could seek marriage, suffered the same punishment as adults for crimes, could be conscripted into the army in times of need—but couldn't own land until turning twenty-four unless married. An unmarried person of sixteen could still be considered a 'child' in the eyes of the law if their mother or father demanded it—unless they volunteered to join the military.

For all its societal flaws, Lucernia generally treated women and girls well, not like some of the kingdoms north of Ondar she'd read of. While not a matter of law, society did draw some differentiations. For example, women of age would be gasped at for traipsing about the cities bare from the waist up while no one cared if men did the same. However, shirtless women didn't elicit much of a reaction out in the countryside. Due to that, immodest women tended to be viewed as lower in social class.

People also generally expected women to wear gowns or dresses, keep house, and take care of the children—but no one called them demons if they didn't. Mostly, it varied based on social strata. The higher up one went, the more pressure existed for girls to be 'traditionally feminine.' And of course, men like Guard Morrow existed. Though he didn't think it laughable for Kitlyn to train with a sword any longer, he still harbored no small amount of resentment. Still, his animosity might have come from her being young, small, and a 'filthy peasant' more than objecting to a girl wanting to fight. The army had plenty of women soldiers, after all.

She watched people walking back and forth on the street beyond the wall at the edge of the castle grounds. Even if she often felt in way over her head for wearing the crown while still too young to purchase land, the sight of so many citizens going about a reasonably normal life without fear of dying in war or losing loved ones made her smile.

We saved two kingdoms from my father's treachery, but cannot locate a pair of children...

"Highness?" asked an unfamiliar man behind her.

She jumped, but not enough for him to notice. "Yes?"

"Beg your pardon. Beredwyn has sent me to request you join him in the war room. Some soldiers have returned from Aowyn's Crossing with news."

"Excellent." Kitlyn pushed away from the wall, turning to look at a page. "Thank you. I will go there right away."

He bowed and ran off.

Having something to focus on, even if an unpleasant task, proved tempting enough she jogged at a rather un-queenly pace to the former war room, where Beredwyn, Guard Captain Lorne, and two men in leather armor waited, one blond, one ginger.

"Ahh, here she is." Beredwyn smiled. "Where is Oona?"

"In the library." Kitlyn hurried around the table to take her position, but didn't sit.

"Ahh. I assumed you two would be together." Beredwyn smoothed a hand down his beard.

"I can relay this to her later. I'm certain she would not want to be interrupted for anything other than finding the children or discovering the location of Isilien." Kitlyn looked at the two light-armored scouts. "What news from Aowyn's Crossing?"

"Scout Ryd, Highness," said the blond man. He hesitated briefly, his eyes betraying his shock at perhaps the queen being younger than him. Or he simply saw too much of Aodh in the set of her eyes. "Looks like some manner of large dogs attacked."

"Wolves?" asked Kitlyn. "The girl who rode here to warn us mentioned possibly goblins riding on wolves."

Ryd shook his head. "I don't believe so. The tracks were too wide for wolves, at least no wolf ordinarily in this area. Don't know about goblins, highness, but we didn't see any unfamiliar tracks other than the dogs. Plenty of blood and a spot or two where I'm certain something died. Drag marks indicated a corpse—or maybe a severely injured animal—was removed by someone or something. If 'goblins' rode these dogs, there would have been footprints around where the steed fell. Nothing."

"The attackers also used many arrows like the one you sent me," said Captain Lorne. "The soldiers found dozens of them all over the town. They're crude and don't fly straight or far. In the right circumstances, they could kill, but I'd consider a thrown rock deadlier."

"What would be the right circumstances?" asked Kitlyn.

A woman's scream came from the hall outside.

Everyone looked at the door.

Captain Lorne rushed out of the war room. The two scouts and sergeant moved to the doorway, hands on their sword hilts.

"What happened?" asked Captain Lorne, his voice somewhat distant.

A woman murmured too low to hear.

"You are certain?"

She murmured again.

Heavy footfalls echoed in the corridor, growing louder until Captain Lorne appeared at the door, hesitating for a moment, his expression bewildered. "One of the maids claims to have seen a rat skeleton scurrying around."

Beredwyn coughed. "And you are not alarmed?"

"She said Queen Oona had been following it and"—Captain Lorne paled—"the rat came from…"

"Tenebrea," said Kitlyn.

The soldiers cringed.

"Speaking her name will not shorten your lives." Kitlyn looked at Lorne. "Please, continue. In what situations would these arrows be deadly?"

He returned to his spot next to the table. "You would need to be using an unusually robust shortbow and be within twenty to thirty feet of a drunken fat man."

The scouts chuckled.

"Drunken fat man?" Kitlyn tilted her head.

"For any chance to hit a target on purpose, you'd need to be firing at something huge and stationary." Lorne smirked. "Any other successful strike would be pure luck. For stone, the head is reasonably sharp, but almost any respectable armor would laugh them off. Close enough, and lucky enough, they could strike a person and kill them, but it would be far from reliable"

Kitlyn tapped her foot, thinking. "I'd ask if you think these would be the sort of weapons made by goblins, but I neither expect you to know nor believe goblins exist."

"In terms of folklore?" Captain Lorne let out a long, beleaguered breath. "Yes, I could see goblins or creatures similar to them making these. Even the barbarian tribes of Ondar's northlands use metal arrowheads and know how to fletch properly."

"Just so I understand," said Kitlyn, "I am to believe wolves or some manner of large dogs attacked the village using crude arrows. How are canines supposed to fire bows?"

Ryd scratched his head. "I cannot answer that. The arrows have such short range it's not possible a supporting force fired from the meadow. Also, the angles at which the arrows stuck out of buildings don't indicate arcing fire. You are more than likely correct in believing something rode on those dogs, but I cannot explain what or why none of the riders left footprints."

"What happened to the villagers?" asked Kitlyn. "Why is everyone still guessing about what these beasts are? Did they kill everyone? Not one witness?"

"No… the town was entirely empty when we got there," said Ryd. "Not even a single dead person."

"Kitlyn!" Oona's shout echoed in the hallway.

For the second time, everyone in the war room twisted to look at the door.

Oona burst in seconds later. "Kitlyn! Evie and Pim are still in the garden."

"How? We've searched it over and over, except for the thicket in the corner… but I didn't feel anyone moving around in there."

"I don't know precisely, but Tenebrea sent me a message." She pointed to her right. "The children are definitely in the garden."

Kitlyn nodded to her, then looked at Ryd. "What happened to the villagers?"

"According to the tracks, everyone picked up and ran to the southwest while about a dozen town watch held off the attackers. Lieutenant Randen only started following their evacuation path when we left to bring word back to the castle. She thinks the townspeople evacuated during the fighting. Unless the raiders took *all* the dead with them, it appears none of our people were killed."

"We think the watch most likely went to tell the villagers they could return home," said the other scout.

Unbelievable. Not one person killed? Oh, Lucen let it be true. Kemma had been so frightened… "I will be in the garden. Ryd, you are a tracker, yes?"

"I am, highness. Ceryl is as well, but I'm better at it."

"Good. Please come with us." Kitlyn jogged out of the war room and down the hall to the garden.

Oona rushed after her, as did both scouts, Beredwyn, and

Captain Lorne. Kitlyn dashed down the garden walk, crossed the grass, and made her way along the trails directly to the pond in the corner.

"Ryd... they climbed out of the water about there"—Kitlyn pointed at the pond before twisting to indicate one of the three trails leading back into the garden—"then went down that trail."

The scouts crouched by the water's edge, looked around for a little while, then moved to the trail start. Both appeared somewhat frustrated.

"Trackers already tried this," whispered Oona. "I showed them the path the kids walked six times at least."

"I'm sorry, highness... the searchers have trampled any sign of the children's passage. I don't even see a single child's footprint." Ryd rose to his feet.

"Grr," muttered Kitlyn.

"Hmm?" Oona peered at her.

"I'm not thinking." Kitlyn kicked her slippers off. "I didn't feel them two days ago, but perhaps enough time has passed for the Stone to remember their trail."

Oona clasped her hands together, eyes overflowing with hope. "They are still here. I know it."

A moment after focusing on her inner magical core, Kitlyn reached out to the earth. Tingles washed up over her feet, crawling up her legs to the rest of her body. Emerald green light appeared in wisps between her fingers.

Evie... Pim... where did they go?

Like a mouse scampering over her while she slept, a sense of little footprints trailed up her back. Tapping the memory of Stone let her feel the children walking as if on her body, leading her to the walkpath. Small footprints continued poking her randomly on the back as she followed the route the children took, weaving around the garden trails past the central circle, over a stone bench, and along another branching path.

Oona followed close, the scouts, Captain Lorne, and Beredwyn a few paces behind her in single file. Evie's prints stood out from Pim's, lighter, mostly on her toes whereas the boy weighed a little more and tended to step flat. Being able to discern such detail frustrated Kitlyn due to her earlier doubt and feelings of helplessness.

I should have tried this yesterday.

She hadn't asked the Stone where the children went the day they vanished because she knew it took time before such trails could be read. Sensing people, animals, or other objects moving across the earth in the moment didn't work the same as reading history. An enigma as old as the Stone couldn't measure time well. Tracks thousands of years old felt the same as tracks from a month ago. She'd assumed it took weeks, not merely two days. Kitlyn had allowed the distraction of everything going on, plus self-doubt to cloud her mind.

The children's footfalls led Kitlyn to the northwest corner of the garden. They'd wandered along the trail leading into the old, overgrown part. She felt them exploring the area for a while before stepping off the path, hiding in the live bushes across the trail from the thick, dead brambles. Small hands and bony knees poked into the earth. The children had been hiding, but didn't seem in a panic. More as though they played a game.

"Here." Kitlyn gestured at the spot. "I feel them crawling into the bushes and hiding."

"They aren't there." Oona squeezed her arm.

Ryd stepped past her, pushing branches out of the way. "Yes. She's right. There are footprints here. "

"Where did they go?"

"Wait… they're still hiding." Kitlyn nudged a little more magic into the ground. "I am sensing the past as it occurred."

Beredwyn, Lorne, and Cerul kept quiet, watching.

Oona and I had been talking. The kids had gotten quiet, then she let out a squeal.

Evie's phantom crawled out of her hiding place first, Pim following seconds later. They both stood and walked straight across the trail into the thick, dead brambles—which shouldn't be possible. Even crawling on their bellies, small children couldn't have made it into the dead corner, much less upright. Kitlyn stopped at the wall of petrified brambles, but sensed the children's footsteps proceed forward, all the way up to the base of the enormous old tree — and vanish.

They hadn't even stopped to stand in place before disappearing. Both children had been in mid stride when their next step failed to touch the ground. Neither made any effort to dodge away from anything, nor had any other footfalls approached them.

"I don't understand," whispered Kitlyn. "They somehow walked into this corner as though none of this dead foliage blocked the way... and then... gone."

Oona shook her head, rapidly muttering, "no" over and over again about ten times. "They are still in the garden. Tenebrea made it quite clear."

"It's going to take some doing." Ryd rubbed his chin. "We can hack our way in. Swords aren't going to do the job, though."

"Kit... roots." Oona nudged her. "Can you move them?"

"These are dead. It would be easier for me to dismantle the wall." She gazed into the tangle of dead brown thorn-studded bushes. "My magic is much stronger on stone."

Beredwyn's fuzzy eyebrows leapt up. "Dismantle the wall... indeed. Perhaps *try* moving the bushes first?"

"All right." Kitlyn widened her stance, dug her toes into the earth, and raised her hands. "I've never attempted to control dead roots before."

"It's like their lifecallers," said Oona. "You're drawing the essence of life from the Alderswood, only for roots instead of people and animals. Maybe you can make them alive again for a little while?"

"Once something dies, it stays dead."

"Try pulling life into it to soften them." Oona rubbed a hand up and down Kitlyn's back to encourage her. "Evie and Pim have to be inside."

Rather than try to touch the essence of the withered plants, she called out to the Alderswood itself, the same way she did when they dispelled the curse from Queen Xorana's crown. As Kethaba taught her, Kitlyn concentrated on the magical core in her chest, picturing the green orb of energy, dark emerald globs twisting around each other within a brighter green sphere. Magic surged down her arms, shrouding them in a bright green glow. To her utter surprise, she sensed a connection to all the roots, vines, bushes, and dead wood in front of her. Apparently, she *could* exert some degree of control over them. However, moving dead wood took far greater effort than asking live plants to reshape themselves, proving even more fatiguing than reshaping stone.

Grunting as though she attempted to shove a heavy rock aside, Kitlyn leaned forward, pushing her hands at the air. Thorny brambles crackled, quivering for a few seconds before curling inward away from the opening she wished to create. The air erupted with crunching, though no vines appeared to be snapping apart. Gradually, a tunnel widened in the massive wall of dead, brown-grey foliage, creating an open path to the little clearing in front of the gnarled root base of the largest tree in the entire garden, its trunk as thick as four outhouses standing together.

A space of open dirt in front of it about the size of Kitlyn's former tiny bedroom contained a scattering of white and violet flowers. The tree had grown into the corner of the wall, deforming like a clay sculpture, swelling forward as it could not expand any further into the large stone blocks. Thick roots roughened the earth, rising in tangled gnarls from the soil. Dark green ivy covered most of the trunk, the top almost as high as the castle's spires.

This tree is ancient.

Kitlyn released her magic, taking a moment to lean against Oona and catch her breath.

"Are you all right?" whispered Oona.

"Yes. Tired. I can evidently move dead roots as well as living ones, but it is exhausting."

"Evie?" called Oona. "Pim?"

No reaction came from the small clearing.

Ryd entered the narrow passage she'd made first, looked around, and backed out to the trail. "Nothing in there. Just some flowers, grass, and a bunch of old junk. The children did leave tracks on the dirt. No idea how they got in there."

"Old junk?" Kitlyn peered up at him.

"Candlesticks, cups, little forks and spoons, a plate or two.

Dolls…" He shrugged. "All of it looks like it's been back there for centuries. It reminds me somewhat of how ravens collect shiny baubles."

Kitlyn let go of Oona and crept down the twelve-foot 'tunnel' she'd made, keeping her gaze on the ground, following the sense of where the children's footfalls had stopped. She pictured them walking next to each other into the clearing—right up to where they should have stepped into a ring of purple flowers, which gave off far too strong a scent. An overwhelming fragrance of plants saturated the innermost part of the dead corner, from no apparent source.

Both children should have put their foot down inside the ring, but left no memory of it in the Stone. Their footprints, though shallow, crossed the bare dirt between the root tunnel and the clearing in front of the tree. Exactly as she sensed, the tracks led to the ring, but didn't disturb the dirt inside it.

Oona bumped into her when she stopped short, grabbed her from behind, and peeked over her shoulder. "What? Why did you stop?"

Kitlyn pointed. "They walked into that ring of flowers, but never touched the ground inside it."

"Eep!" Oona gasped. "I think it's a faerie circle."

"It's simple flowers," deadpanned Ryd from the tunnel.

"In a *ring*." Oona jabbed her finger at it, pointing. "Who plants a ring of flowers in a tiny spot of garden no one's been in for centuries? It has to be a faerie circle."

Kitlyn shifted her jaw side to side. She hadn't read much of anything for fun since twelve, before the castle staff made her work. The phrase 'faerie circle' sounded familiar from old stories, but she couldn't remember if the book had been scary or cute.

"No…" Oona stumbled forward, falling to kneel beside the circle. She pawed at the ground a few times before bursting into sobs.

"Shh." Kitlyn knelt next to her. "Why are you upset? Tenebrea led you here, right? We can find them. They're still in the garden."

Oona closed her eyes, sorrow shifting to determination. "You're right. I… faerie circles are doorways to another world. The faeries took them. They could be old now."

"Old? In two days?"

"Maybe." Oona shivered. "The stories are all different, but most of them say time is strange in the faerie's realm. Maybe I have it backward. It might be people who leave the faerie world find everyone they knew has become old."

"Do you want to see this?" asked Ryd in a low voice.

"I don't think so. I'd lose my hat in there," replied Beredwyn.

Oona got up. She stepped one foot over the flower circle, tamping at the dirt inside. Nothing unusual happened.

"Is it that simple?" Kitlyn stood.

"Evie squeaked! She must have seen one." Oona 'knocked' on the ground inside the circle with her foot. "I know there are faeries here!"

The dense wall of dead foliage behind them vanished.

Kitlyn stared around in shock at a lush forest of widely spaced trees stretching as far as she could see in every direction. The rush of fast-flowing water came from somewhere off to the left. They still stood inside a ring of violets, only brightly colored mushrooms had appeared out of nowhere around the circle as well. The ground had gone from bare dirt to soft forest duff, layers and layers of dead leaves and mulch undisturbed by human activity.

"Uhh…" Kitlyn whistled. "What happened?"

"We're on the other side of the circle." Oona bit her lip. "I don't know how I did it, but I somehow made it work."

A giggle echoed out from the distance.

"Evie!" yelled Oona before sprinting off in the direction of the voice.

Kitlyn ran after her, following for a little over a minute before Evie and Pim raced out from behind a tree up ahead. Oona shouted a noise in no way even close to a word, as if relief and happiness combined into a release of raw, audible emotion. She zoomed over to the children, scooping them up in her arms before breaking down in happy tears.

Overjoyed, Kitlyn hurried over to join the embrace, hugging the kids into Oona.

"Why are you crying?" asked Evie. "We found faeries! They're playing with us."

At a chorus of whispers overhead, Kitlyn relaxed her grip on Oona and looked up.

Dozens of tiny people sat or stood on branches overhead, watching them. Each had a set of delicate filament wings emitting soft glowing light in white, green, or blue. They didn't look as cute as she expected faeries would be. Except for being about five inches tall, they resembled a drawing Oona once showed her of an Anthari.

They also seemed rather annoyed.

Oh, no… we might be in trouble.

19

A RANSOM OF BERRY TARTS

OONA

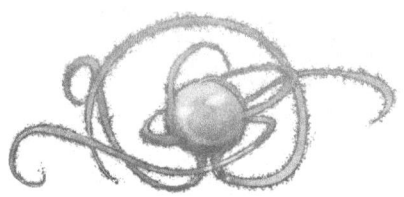

Overcome with joy, Oona clutched Evie and Pim close.

All the anxiety and dread she'd steeped in for the past two days released its grip, stealing her voice and leaving her unable to do anything more than cling to the children while mentally thanking Tenebrea. After a minute or so, she realized the children's hair remained damp.

"Why are you scared?" whispered Evie. "The faeries are nice."

"Is it time to eat yet?" asked Pim.

Kitlyn rapidly patted Oona on the shoulder. "Look up."

Sniffling, Oona relaxed her desperate grip on the children—somewhat—so she could peer up at the branches. A gathering of tiny people watched them, their expressions difficult to discern on such little faces. Some wore bits of leaves or garments made of cobweb, though the raiment appeared intended for decoration rather than any attempt at modesty. Most of them didn't even bother. Their hair ranged in color from white through various shades of brown and green to black. All had comparatively large dual filament wings in two pairs, similar to those of dragonflies, aglow in pastel colors. Whenever the wings moved, they flared brighter.

I knew it! Faeries are real. Momentarily gripped by childish awe, Oona gazed around at them.

"What's wrong?" asked Evie. "Why are you upset?"

"We couldn't find you." Kitlyn brushed a hand over the girl's hair. "Everyone has been searching for the two of you."

Evie flailed her arms. "Why? We just got lost in the garden."

"You've been missing for two days." Oona hugged her again.

"No…" Pim scrunched up his nose. "Don't be silly. We haven't been lost *that* long."

Oona kissed Evie atop the head and set her back on her feet. "We went across a faerie circle into their world. Time is not the same here. What felt like a few minutes here really was two days. I've been so worried."

The kids gawked.

"We saw a faerie an' then the scary giant bush opened." Evie grinned. "The faerie wanted us to follow her. We played chase."

"They're fast." Pim kicked his toe at the dirt. "I couldn't catch them."

Evie twirled. "We danced with them."

Did we do something wrong? I don't know which stories are true… if any of them are. Oona looked up at the group of faeries. *Are they afraid of us? They played with the children but are staying up high now.*

"Hello? I am Oona. This is Kitlyn. Evie is my sister. We are sorry for disturbing you."

The assembled faeries continued watching them, none making a noise beyond the occasional faint rustle of wings to maintain balance while standing or sitting on narrow branches.

"We should leave this place before too much time passes back home." Kitlyn took Pim's hand. "Lest things fall to disarray."

"Yes." Oona grasped Evie's hand, then looked up at the faeries. "Please accept our apologies. I am afraid we do not understand your ways. If there is anything you would ask us to do to make amends for disturbing you, please tell us."

The faeries remained quiet. A few tilted their heads.

"Perhaps they do not understand us?" whispered Kitlyn.

"Did they speak to you before?" Oona nudged Evie.

"No. Only giggled." Evie pressed herself against Oona's side. "They look like they're mad at us now."

Kitlyn started walking. "We should respect their realm and remove ourselves at once."

"Yes... I..." Oona stood still for a moment, watching the faeries. When none said anything or moved, she offered an apologetic smile, then scurried off after Kitlyn.

Buzzing arose behind her as the faeries leapt to wing, sounding so much like a swarm of giant insects Oona involuntarily cringed. Some twenty or thirty faeries followed them, zipping from branch to branch or gliding along at a slow hover. None ventured too close, as if afraid of being grabbed or swatted. In flight, their wings glowed brightly enough to be mistaken for a lantern at night.

Kitlyn reached the faerie circle and walked into it — but nothing happened. She reversed and crossed the spot again, but didn't vanish. Hoping it probably waited for them all to be together, Oona rushed over to stand with her and the children inside the ring of violets and mushrooms.

The swarm of faeries flew around the area once before gathering like songbirds in the trees nearby. Some sat on branches well out of reach, but a few braver ones clung to the trunks at head level.

Oona smiled politely at them before stepping into the circle. When nothing happened, she tapped her foot at the ground trying to prod the magic into working. *Oh, how did I make this open before?* She'd simply wanted it to do something and it had.

Green light flickered over Kitlyn's hand. "I don't feel anything other than ordinary ground here. Did you read about how to make a faerie circle work?"

"Not really. It let us through earlier. Perhaps *I* didn't do it?" Oona looked at the nearest faerie, a woman clinging to the side of a tree like a squirrel, long kelp-green hair down to her knees. "Will you please help us go home?"

The small woman kept staring at her, surprisingly not flinching away when Oona took a step closer. Up close, the faeries looked like Anthari rather than humans. They had slender bodies, prominent ribs, dark almond-shaped eyes, narrow faces, and pointy ears. None had hair anywhere except for atop their heads and eyebrows. Oona would've had difficulty telling the females and males apart had they not been largely naked.

"Again, please allow me to apologize for invading your world. My sister and Pim did not mean any harm or disrespect." Oona smiled. "If it isn't too much trouble, can you please help us return home?"

The faerie leapt off the tree, her wings brightening to a lantern-like intensity while beating at blurry speed. Her sudden buzzing almost made Oona yelp and jump back, but she managed not to flinch—much. Seeming curious, the tiny woman glided up to within a few inches of Oona's face. Much like having a large wasp too close for comfort, she held perfectly still.

"She doesn't look angry anymore," whispered Kitlyn.

Evie reached toward the faeries up in the branches, smiling and laughing. "Come down and play."

"You cannot leave," said the faerie, her voice squeaky but not as much as her size implied it should be, pitch closer to that of a six-year-old than a talking mouse.

"We must..." Oona blinked. "We do not belong here, and many people depend on us."

"They saw," said another faerie with glowing lavender wings while gliding down toward Kitlyn.

Not until Oona looked over did she realize him male; the voice offered no clue. "Who saw?"

"The small humans saw us," said the female faerie. "They would speak of us. Other humans find us and again do what they did before."

Kitlyn held her hand under the faerie by her, offering him a seat. "We are not old enough to remember. Until this moment, we did not think your kind existed."

"Yes," said the female faerie. "We have hidden on purpose."

The male faerie dropped to stand on Kitlyn's palm. "Humans swat and yell and crush and trap. We are vermin to them."

"How awful." Oona gasped. "Why would anyone want to hurt you?"

"No!" wailed Evie. "I love faeries!"

"You aren't vermin," said Pim. "People shouldn't be mean to you."

Oona pondered a moment. "You brought the children here because they saw one of you?"

"Yes. Hiding and trick us." The female faerie folded her arms, tapping her foot on air. "But did not be mean."

"Children," said the male faerie. "They have not been teached to hate us."

"The big ones not children," called another voice from above. "Not mean."

Evie grinned up at Oona. "Pim and I hid, trying to find a faerie. We saw them walking out from the scary place. I squeaked from being happy."

And the faeries tricked you into the circle. Oona sighed mentally. *Then grabbed Kit and me when I yelled about knowing they were real.*

"We will not allow anyone to harm faeries purely for you being faeries," said Kitlyn. "I give you my word we will regard any act of aggression against your kind no differently from a human attacking another human."

"Why all humans would do as you say?" asked the female faerie.

"Not *all* humans." Oona gestured at the circle of flowers and mushrooms. "Only the ones in our land. Kitlyn and I are the humans' leaders. We are queens."

"Two queens?" asked the male faerie.

Oona and Kitlyn nodded at the same time.

"We are married." Kitlyn put an arm around Oona. "Umm. Mated?"

The faeries emitted a collective noise of acknowledgement. Their casual, almost non-reaction made Oona feel all warm inside.

"Kitlyn and Oona are the queens. They get to tell everyone what to do," chirped Pim. "My pa makes the best treats, but he can't tell people what ta do… unless they work in the kitchen."

"I don't tell anyone what to do. It's not nice," whispered Evie.

More faeries glided down from the branches, collecting in a hovering mass. The male standing on Kitlyn's hand flew up to join them. They appeared to be speaking to each other, though the buzz from their wings drowned out their voices. Oona suspected they used an entirely different language—and probably much higher-pitched voices when talking to each other, since the tones they spoke in earlier should have been louder than the noise of their wings.

A smaller group of faeries, apparently uninterested in the debate, circled Evie and Pim, playing with their hair. She laughed, adoring the attention. Pim didn't appear to mind.

Finally, the green-haired female zipped up to Oona. "We know you queen the humans as you say. Others seeing you be important. You can law them to not vermin us?"

"Yes." Oona nodded.

"We can certainly do so, but it would require us to tell everyone faeries are real. You've been hiding for so long nobody believes you exist. We could not make a law to stop people from harming you without revealing you exist." Kitlyn paused, giving the faeries a moment to consider her words. "Since you brought the children—and us—here to conceal your existence, we could also keep your secret instead if you would rather."

Oona squeezed the kids' shoulders. In a way, the faerie forest represented a dream come true. A place to live with Kitlyn completely free of responsibility, violence, or anyone who might hate them. *If we stay here, would it protect Kitlyn from the curse like Lady Avalina?* A somber sigh slipped out of her. Only a spoiled child would put her wants above all the citizens. Without them, the nobles would certainly start a cycle of vicious internal wars. "It is important for us to return. We will keep your secret or protect you, as you choose, but please, we must go back to our world."

The faeries debated inaudibly for another few minutes before the green-haired woman faced Oona and Kitlyn. "How can we know you mean no harm when small humans set trap for us?"

"I love faeries," chimed Evie.

"My sister believed you were real and wanted desperately to know you're real. She meant no harm. They hid themselves only hoping to see you."

"The harm would be the telling," said a black-haired male. "More humans looking for us."

"They found us." The green-haired woman, apparently the one closest to being in charge here, shook her head to the negative. "I knowing you have reasons for going back, but it dangerous for us."

Oona's thoughts raced back to the giant book, old folklore, and childhood bedtime stories. "If you allow us to return home, we will give you a treasure of ivenberry muffins—and decree in law no human shall harm a faerie in the absence of cause."

The hovering faeries all stared at her.

"What is absence?" asked the green-haired faerie.

"Oona means we will make it against the law for people to attack faeries unless the faerie does something to provoke the attack." Kitlyn proceeded to get into a complicated back and forth about 'appropriate response,' trying to clarify that a person would still be punished for attempting to cause serious harm to a faerie over a harmless prank.

They eventually accepted it meant a human hurting or killing a faerie would only be tolerated when it could be proven the faerie initially tried to cause serious harm or death to the human first—a circumstance the faeries claimed next to impossible.

Negotiations ended with the faeries accepting a 'tribute' of ivenberry tarts, muffins—and other as yet to be determined baked goods—in addition to legal protection. Within seconds of all the faeries smiling and flitting around in celebration, the vast forest changed in an instant to the garden path by the dead corner. The tunnel Kitlyn previously opened in the brambles had closed, making the small clearing with the faerie circle inaccessible to anyone larger than a faerie.

It also appeared to be the dead of night.

"Oh, no…" Oona whistled. "We've been gone for hours, likely. I'm sure Beredwyn and the others are in a panic."

"It's bedtime," whispered Evie. "Are we in trouble?"

"You are not in trouble." Oona squeezed her hand.

"She's so happy to find you safe you could probably do almost anything for a while and not even be scolded for it." Kitlyn winked at her.

"Do not corrupt the innocent." Oona tickled Kitlyn's side.

Kitlyn laughed. "Beredwyn, Lorne, and Ryd would have seen us disappear. I am sure they are not fruitlessly searching around for us. However, we should go inside quickly."

The green-haired faerie appeared, landing on Oona's shoulder. She pointed at the wall of dead bushes, causing them to curl back into themselves like a pair of doors swinging apart.

"Thank you." Oona waved at the faerie.

Kitlyn took Pim by the hand and headed out from the 'dead corner.' Oona followed, leading Evie by the hand.

"This is going to be fun to explain," said Kitlyn over a hint of a chuckle.

"It certainly will." Oona smiled. "But not difficult."

"Do you sincerely think they will believe us?"

Oona laughed. "I did not say that. It will be simple to explain. The difficult part comes in convincing them we have not indulged on dreamstem."

20

THE BURDEN OF ROYALTY

KITLYN

Kitlyn awoke to an overabundance of warmth and a growling stomach.

Not only had she and Oona worn nightgowns to bed, the reason they did so—Evie—nestled between them. Almost being abducted by faeries hadn't bothered her at all, as the children believed they'd been lost for only a little while. She asked to sleep in their bed, mostly for Oona's sake.

I thought we'd never fall asleep…

The prior night had been interesting, to say the least. Upon their return to the castle, they found the advisors screaming at each other in the war room—mostly. High Priest Balais had been the calmest, urging the others to stop shouting. Advisor Lanon tried to simultaneously not accuse Beredwyn of lying while also refusing to accept his explanation of Oona and Kitlyn vanishing into thin air. Advisor Naldun believed the story as well as Beredwyn's assumption faeries had something to do with it.

Alonna tried to convince Beredwyn and Lanon they needed to hasten the search for Ulfaan, believing him responsible for abducting the queens in the same manner he'd disappeared from the throne room.

In the midst of the advisors debating how best to keep the kingdom from panicking while hunting down 'the rogue mage,' Kitlyn and Oona walked in. Beredwyn momentarily dropped all sense of decorum and rushed over to embrace them.

The resulting explanation of events stunned everyone. Hearing both Kitlyn and Oona speak seriously of faeries caused the expected amount of laughter, except from Balais who sensed the truth of it courtesy of Lucen's gift. Evie relayed the faeries told her they'd played tricks on the Parringtons due to overhearing her telling Pim about them making her cry by referring to Oona and her as 'filthy peasants' when the duke and duchess thought themselves alone in a hall. Evie had been behind a curtain playing hide and seek with Pim at the time.

This, of course, proved faeries had been in the castle already, but no one knew for exactly how long.

Kitlyn approached the situation as if dealing with a neighboring sovereign kingdom. Technically, it *was* neighboring, only in an adjacent reality rather than an adjacent land mass. Perhaps thinking her childish and a bit eccentric, the advisors hadn't offered any serious objection to the decree making it illegal to attack faeries. More specifically, she worded the decree to grant 'personhood' to faeries. Violence committed against them would be evaluated the same as people attacking each other—with considerations for size. Throwing a shoe at a human did not count as a deadly attack.

They took a light supper due to the late hour, sent word to the kitchen staff to prepare a tray of goodies to be set out in the garden by the dead corner, then retired to bed.

She opened her eyes to daylight appearing much later into the morning than she usually woke up, unsurprising due to the skip they'd experienced. Close to five hours had passed during the few minutes they'd spent in the faerie world. Despite it having been quite late at night when they went to bed, it felt as though she'd tried to sleep much too early.

Kitlyn lay still, not particularly motivated to move until Evie stirred and an accidental knee bumping her brought attention to how full her bladder had become. Grimacing, she made her way to the garderobe down a corridor saturated in the fragrance of sweet baking. By the time she returned, Oona and Evie were awake and showing no sign at all of having stayed up past bedtime. Seeing them both full of energy chased away the last of Kitlyn's sluggishness.

They traded their nightgowns for comfortable dresses and went downstairs to the small dining room to have breakfast. As per usual, Piper and Meredith joined them for the morning meal, eager to hear the story of what happened the previous night. A page poked his head in, announcing the advisors awaited them in the war room with news.

After breakfast, Annabelle collected Evie for her daily lessons.

Kitlyn walked with Oona to the war room, unable to resist the urge to keep looking around in case she caught sight of a visiting faerie. Having the children back—and discovering a relatively innocent explanation for their disappearance—made the other problems facing her seem completely within her ability to handle. She'd failed to heed her own advice. While asking everyone else to not assume every strange creature would be a dangerous threat, she'd gone straight to the most sinister theory possible regarding the children's disappearance. A seemingly insurmountable problem ended up being a minor misunderstanding.

"Discovering faeries as the cause changes everything," said Kitlyn.

"Hmm?" Oona glanced over at her as they walked down the hall. "Talking to a ghost or thinking?"

Kitlyn grinned. "I am so relieved Evie and Pim are safe."

"As am I, but how did the faeries change... whatever changed?"

"Well, first, they showed me what I thought would be an awful situation was, in fact, not. Ulfaan had nothing at all to do with the children disappearing from the castle. We do not need to worry about a... mage being a threat."

"Oh. Yes." Oona's eyes brightened. "True."

Kitlyn glanced briefly at the corridor to avoid walking into an armor stand. "Second, we saw faeries. *Real* faeries. I am still young enough to be thrilled."

"If I should live to be a little old grandmother, the sight of faeries will still stir within me a childish delight." Oona spun around as she walked. "Oh, these ordinary dresses don't flare very much, do they?"

"No, but it is worth it to be able to move." Kitlyn pressed a hand to her stomach. "And breathe."

Oona laughed.

"Now, we know faeries are real. If they exist, it is reasonable to consider other sorts of creatures everyone thought made up also exist. Obviously, no nefarious individual is setting *faeries* loose across Lucernia to create a panic. With the children, I jumped to thinking someone took them on purpose. Discovering faeries are real puts everything else in perspective."

"Oh, yes, well… what about the Nimse and Na'vir? We'd already met an entire civilization not of humans. And a lich. Oh, and a massive stone giant."

"Yes, wife, you are correct. My head has not been on straight."

"Wife…" Oona flashed a sly grin. "I rather like the sound of that."

Kitlyn stopped at the door to the war room. "Feels strange to use the word."

"How?" Oona's eyebrows notched up in worry.

"I expected to spend my entire life alone, scrubbing floors and fetching linens."

"I expected to die before reaching my eighteenth year," said Oona.

"Wife."

Oona smiled. "Wife."

Kitlyn took her into her arms, kissing her deeply right in front of the war room door, between a pair of castle guards who politely pretended not to notice. Oona held her close, their kiss not one of steamy passion, rather a silent acknowledgement of devoted love. After a few minutes, their embrace became a simple hug.

"You are more precious to me than life," said Oona.

"I could no more imagine existence without you at my side than everyone in Lucernia floating off into the sky."

They held each other for a moment more.

"I'd burn every demon out of existence to keep you from harm." Oona clung tighter.

"I'd tear this castle apart stone by stone to protect you," said Kitlyn.

Oona snickered.

Not the reaction I expected. "Oo? I wasn't trying to be funny."

"I'm sorry, Kit." Oona leaned back to make eye contact. "It made me giggle because you actually *could* tear the castle apart. I thought we were exchanging romantic hyperbole, not making actual promises... and I do kind of like the castle."

Kitlyn hung her head, trying not to burst out laughing.

"Not sure Lucen has given me enough power to destroy *all* the demons, but I would absolutely take as many of them with me as I could."

"Says the girl who hid under a blanket from a man in a dress." Kitlyn winked.

"Hmph!" Oona huffed. "Ordinary men are more dangerous than demons... at least to me."

Kitlyn booped her on the nose. "You're also a touch braver now. As am I, with you at my side."

"I love you, Kit."

"I love you, Oona. And... we should likely go inside before they grow old."

Oona chuckled. "Yes."

The guard on the left stealthily wiped a tear, pretending to have a fly buzzing at his face.

Kitlyn pushed the door open and walked into the war room. Beredwyn, Lanon, Balais, Alonna, Naldun, and two unfamiliar men in the light armor of scouts stood around the table, all turning to look at the creak of the moving door. Beredwyn, Lanon, and Naldun all wore the off-beige tabards over green robes of the castle advisors, complete with ridiculous tall tube-like hat. The gold decorations on the shoulder mantle of High Priest Balais glinted in the sunlight from the windows. Alonna's ceremonial version of Navissa's priestly raiment had a tight-bodice, more like a gown than robes, in dark blue. Her long auburn hair possessed almost too much color for a follower of the Night Goddess, though she also had a far sunnier personality than most in that temple.

"Ahh, good morning, highness." Beredwyn held his arms out wide in greeting.

"Are you addressing me or Oona?"

"Both of you." Beredwyn raked his fingers down his beard. "Highnesses sounds a bit clumsy, don't you think?"

It does, but he is certainly adroitly explaining his error. He is not used to greeting two *monarchs. Queen Solana had been dead for so long, and uninterested in the affairs of the kingdom... for reasons I now understand.* Kitlyn approached the table, feeling sad for the woman she once thought insufferably mean to the staff. How often had her mother sat alone somewhere in the castle pining for a love she could never act upon? *Did Aodh know? Is that why he gave us his blessing without any objection? Or had it been simple guilt for what he'd done to me?* She sighed. "Especially coming from you, dear Beredwyn." She looked at the advisors and scouts. "What news?"

Oona stepped up beside her.

"My queens," said the shorter scout, a dark-haired man not much older than them. "I am recently back from Aowyn's Crossing. We located the villagers several hours off in the outskirts of the Mistral Wood to the southwest. They described creatures difficult to believe, but all who saw them had the same story."

Kitlyn nodded once. "Perhaps not so difficult to believe as one might think. Go on."

"The villagers spoke of monstrous creatures part wolf, part something else. They had four legs and the bodies of enormous canines, but where the wolf's head should be, the upper half of a small man. People described the human part as having green skin with a leathery texture. The beasts had long, pointed ears, large noses, and yellow eyes."

As none of the advisors reacted much to hearing this, Kitlyn assumed they'd already been told. "I see. What do you have to report of casualties or damage?"

"One dead, a young man who'd been out in the fields north of the village attending goats when the attack started. Many others suffered wounds of varying severity, but none went to Tenebrea. The local guardsmen tallied some thirty or more of the fiends killed before the remainder fled."

"How much of a remainder?" asked Oona. "You say thirty were killed. Did the dead amount to half of the attacker's force? More?"

"The watch did not know the exact number but said a much greater group left than they'd killed." The scout tilted his head side to side. "If I had to guess, I'd say if they killed thirty, perhaps three times that number initially attacked. It seems as though the attackers returned after the guardsmen went to inform the townspeople they could return. We found no dead creatures and the townspeople claimed much of their livestock had gone missing. Food stores had been broken into as well."

"A simple raid then..." Kitlyn narrowed her eyes. "Whatever these creatures are, they act with intelligence and malice. This was not a misunderstanding, but a deliberate hostile act."

"Highness?" Advisor Lanon held up a finger. "Am I to understand you do not question the existence of a creature such as this? The townspeople were obviously in distress and not thinking or seeing clearly."

"All due respect, sir," said the scout, "We spoke to twelve members of the Aowyn's Crossing town watch who engaged these beasts in sword-to-sword combat. They all saw them quite close."

"And defeated them without losing a single person?" asked Oona. "That is impressive for village guardsmen."

Beredwyn chuckled. "Twelve fending off sixty to ninety of anything is more than impressive... it's implausible."

"Oona held back thousands of Nimse." Kitlyn put an arm around her. "However, she did have Lucen's light to aid her. The creatures could not bear the pain of coming close."

The scout nodded to Beredwyn. "It does defy tactical reason. The watch may have exaggerated the numbers of attackers. We do know the raiders entered the village mostly from a single direction. The defenders claimed the beasts did not possess much skill in combat, and attacked using crude hatchets or clubs made of wood and stone, easily destroyed by steel blades."

"If I may, highness?" asked the other scout, an older man in his middle thirties, several scars on his left cheek.

Kitlyn nodded to him.

"In my opinion, these creatures are much more effective at a modest distance where they can run as fast as a wolf while lobbing arrows. In close quarters against one of our soldiers, the beasts wouldn't stand much of a chance barring an overwhelming difference in number. A dog is nimble because it's low to the ground. The goblin-like upper body would be quite easy to strike with a blade, especially when one can slice through the stick they're using to defend."

"Like centaurs?" asked Advisor Alonna.

"Aren't those part human, part horse?" asked Balais.

Advisor Lanon rubbed the bridge of his nose. "Are we taking these claims to be serious? And speaking of centaurs as if they exist, too?"

"I am not implying centaurs exist." Alonna glanced at him, a hint of irritation in her green eyes. "Fictional or not, everyone in this room understands what a centaur looks like."

Kitlyn gestured at the scouts. "We have a dozen or so soldiers who all claim to have fought these beasts, many more villagers all describing the same manner of creature. Ryd, another scout, found large dog tracks but not one footprint from any riders. Kemma said she believed she saw goblins riding wolves. She'd been terrified and rushing away from the village, so it is plausible to believe she mistook such an odd creature for two different beings."

"A woman mentioned seeing a similar beast in court the other day." Balais stroked his beard. "Though, she neglected to mention the upper part had been green. Too far away, perhaps?"

"I think it's obvious what's going on," said Oona.

Kitlyn looked at her. "Obvious?"

"Well, yes. To a point." Oona waved a hand about as if trying to pluck words out of the air. "Magic of one form or another has always been part of the world. We know demons are real. We know undead exist. You've all seen Omun—an immense stone giant. We saw the Nimse all change back into the Na'vir as the curse wore off. Our people have been seeing unknown creatures for several months. Reports continue arriving from every corner of the kingdom. Ulfaan used magic to disappear himself after inquiring about how the law will regard 'mages.' Now, we've seen faeries with our own eyes and these... half-goblin, half-wolf creatures. It's obvious to me, magical energies are rising within Lucernia."

"You are quite ready to believe all of the stories are true?" asked Balais.

"Not every single one, no." Oona shook her head. "But generally, yes. We should accept the idea creatures not seen for many hundreds of years are, for some reason, returning."

Kitlyn folded her arms. "We cannot even say for certain how long they have been absent. Our library is bereft of information older than the reign of King Iastor. We should also consider the possibility such beings *did* exist before or during his time but all mention of them has been purged. No one alive today would even know anyone who lived when Iastor ruled."

The advisors murmured amongst themselves, discussing the likelihood of 'magical creatures' reappearing in the kingdom and to what degree they would become a threat.

"Aowyn's Crossing." Kitlyn looked at the two scouts. "Did the creatures attack first, without provocation?"

"According to everyone we spoke to, that is correct." The younger man nodded.

"And it appears their intention was to raid the village for meat and other supplies. Whether or not they intended to kill humans, we cannot determine."

The scout cringed. "Pardon, highness, but they did slay one young man who had the misfortune to be out in the field with goats as well as unarmed. They showed clear willingness to kill humans. It is my opinion they simply failed to be able to do so when confronted with steel armor and trained—somewhat—warriors."

"Very well," said Kitlyn. "These creatures should be considered hostile and dangerous for now."

"I concur." Oona faced Beredwyn. "Please have word sent to all towns and villages to be wary of these creatures. If it is true they have recently reawakened somehow, I am sure after sufficient losses, they will realize the folly of attacking our towns and establish a territory safely away from any people."

"They will all think us crazed," muttered Lanon.

"Should we not be concerned about *why* this is happening?" Advisor Alonna clasped her Navissa amulet, a two-inch disc of shiny jet-black inlaid with a white crescent moon hanging at her chest.

Beredwyn pursed his lips in thought.

Advisor Naldun's expression made him look like a farmer trying to figure out the best way to remove a cow from a ditch. The stocky, square-faced man had spent most of his fifty-three years on a farm and still largely carried himself as an ordinary person despite being elevated to the rank of royal advisor. His salt and pepper hair had a bit more salt than before, but his demeanor remained unchanged. Despite the misgivings of Advisor Lanon, some of the snootier members of the castle staff, and the nobility, Kitlyn liked the grounded perspective he lent to their discussions. Also, having 'one of their own' in the queens' ear—and them being willing to listen to him—endeared them to the people.

"They will understand," said Naldun. "Perhaps not at first, but the citizens are already speaking about strange creatures. I think it would be a mistake to pretend they are not returning. The people do not believe it the work of darkness, but a natural change."

Advisor Lanon fidgeted. "These creatures are *unnatural*."

"Like us," muttered Kitlyn.

He cringed. "Apologies, highness. It is not my intent to imply there is anything whatsoever wrong between you and Queen Oona. The gods have quite clearly blessed your marriage."

Kitlyn blinked. *He didn't refer to it as an arrangement?* The man admitted to being uncomfortable at the idea of two women—or two men—in love with each other, but didn't think his feelings should guide anyone's life but his. Over the past several months, he had become somewhat less awkward around them. "What are you trying to say, Lanon?"

Having nothing further to add, the scouts bowed and hurried out of the room to return to their commander.

"If there are any left in the kingdom who seek to stir dissent, they could try saying the appearance of unnatural creatures is a result of an—in their words—unnatural union. My only point is we should prepare a response if this happens."

High Priest Balais smiled at him. He, more than anyone else in the kingdom had shocked Kitlyn. Having been steeped in the 'teachings' of Lucen prior to his arrival in the city, he'd been aghast at the notion of two women in love, to the point he nearly called them an offense to the gods. However, upon learning of Tenebrea's message, he reserved judgement until the wedding ceremony, which he performed. The instant the flame ignited showing Lucen's approval, he'd become one of their most ardent defenders.

"We need no defense for a union blessed by Lucen himself." Balais held his arms out to either side. "Any who questions it, questions Lucen. The temple held hundreds of witnesses."

Oona snapped her head up, wide-eyed. "The Eldritch Heart!"

"What about it?" asked Kitlyn.

"Restoring it to the Alderswood sent a great amount of life energy into Evermoor." Oona patted the drawing of the giant tree on the big map covering the table. "Old magic doesn't care about kingdoms. What if the life energy kept spreading outward and is bringing about a resurgence of magical beasts? The Heart being absent from the tree drew magic out of the world and weakened these creatures so much they stopped existing."

Kitlyn stared at the little wooden soldier figures on the map, presently representing nothing more than the laziness of not putting them away. "These creatures have been gone for far longer than the twenty years or so since Aodh ripped the Heart from the Alderswood."

"Oh... yes, true." Oona tapped a finger to her chin in thought for a few seconds. "But perhaps the great tree becoming whole still released such a powerful surge of life energy, it awakened old magic?"

"I suppose it is a possibility." Beredwyn pulled a hand repetitively down his beard.

"Sometimes, things simply happen." Advisor Naldun seemed

about to spit to the side, but caught himself.

Kitlyn looked away so she didn't chuckle at him. *He is so rustic.*

"What should we do if returning the Heart to the Alderswood is truly what's caused all these creatures to appear?" Advisor Lanon pointed at the map. "It may soon reach Ondar."

Oona pointed at him. "We are *not* even going to consider removing it."

"Absolutely out of the question." Kitlyn folded her arms. "Separating the Heart from the Alderswood dooms an entire civilization to a long, horrible death and would certainly rekindle the war. A few creatures popping up here and there is hardly a 'catastrophe' worthy of such mass death."

"Agreed," said Balais.

Alonna nodded. "Definitely. It would undo all the goodwill our queens have made and cause untold suffering."

Advisor Lanon offered a sheepish smile. "I did not mean to suggest we kill the tree. One does not cut their child's head off because they have an insect bite on their face. Does anyone believe dissenters might try to make the appearance of these creatures sound like an affair worse than the war and blame the queens for it?"

"There are always idiots," said Naldun. "No matter what a ruler does, *someone* will complain about it… even if it helps them."

Everyone murmured agreement.

"Yes. Removing the Heart is as stupid and self-destructive as burning every farm in Lucernia to the ground because a few people got stung by bees. I feel we cannot change this and must adapt to a new reality." Kitlyn looked among the advisors. "Send word out to mayors, magistrates, our generals, and the titled. Inform them we believe there is a reemergence of creatures once considered to exist only in stories. Please emphasize there is a differentiation between actual demons and other creatures. We do not want panic, but caution."

"Also…" Oona swept her arm to the side, suppressing a smile. "Please inform Spymaster Hinlor he can now speak of these creatures without fear of being ridiculed. I'm sure he's known about them for months already."

The advisors laughed.

Oona waited a moment for the laughter to die down. "We will need to begin surveys, scouting Lucernia all over again to determine what sort of creatures have appeared and where they are. It is important we learn what we can of them in order for us to best protect our people."

"I will draft letters to King Lanas of Evermoor and King Harl of Ondar, advising them of what we are seeing." Kitlyn drummed her fingers on the seatback of the chair in front of her.

"Ondar is already somewhat accustomed to certain unusual creatures," said Beredwyn. "Most of them are in the northeast portion of their kingdom where few people dwell."

The war map focused primarily on Lucernia and Evermoor—for obvious reasons—but she remembered studying Ondar while they 'graciously allowed the peasant girl' to accompany Oona during her tutoring lessons. All the major cities clustered fairly close in the southwestern portion of the kingdom with only a handful of medium-sized towns progressing northwest toward the sea. Something like ninety percent of people in Ondar occupied eight percent of the land, at least in terms of official citizens. Vast areas of 'uncivilized' areas in the east, northeast, and far north contained barbarian tribes.

Did magical creatures disappear from Lucernia because humans tamed it? Did the gods play a hand in it? Or... perhaps mages? But where, then did the mages go? Could their absence be the cause? A room without candles attracts no moths.

While the advisors fell into discussing the particulars of how to word the letters sent out to the various officials, commanders, and nobles, Kitlyn mulled over the potential ramifications of magical beasts returning. Barring an extremely large number of creatures or deliberate action by a hostile entity, it should be no more problematic than ordinary bears or wolves. Nature had no shortage of ways to kill humans. In fact, two or three of the large bears common to the forest near Imric would have done more damage to Aowyn's Crossing than the goblin-wolf-centaur creatures did. Bizarre or magical did not inherently make a beast more dangerous than any creature considered 'natural.'

"Kit," whispered Oona, leaning close against her. "I want to go to Underholm. With Evie and Pim safe, I cannot wait any more."

"Underholm?" Kitlyn didn't care they had an audience and snuck a quick kiss. "For what reason?"

Oona's cheeks pinked. "Their civilization is ancient and they have an immense repository of information. A library so vast I cannot even guess at its size. They may know what the Gates of Isilien are."

Ack! Kitlyn squeezed her hands into fists. She'd been so thrilled at finding the children alive and relieved at realizing Ulfaan likely had nothing to do with the 'abduction' or the appearance of magical creatures, she'd gone a full day without once thinking about the curse. *How did Aodh put the worry of it aside—or did he? Is hoping the Heart could help him escape the curse what drove him to betray his friend and start a horrible war? Perhaps he didn't even realize the curse existed.*

"What's wrong?" Oona brushed her thumb over Kitlyn's cheek, below her eye. "You look suddenly sad."

"To what ends would we go to escape this curse? I wondered if it drove Aodh to his madness."

Oona rested her head against Kitlyn's shoulder. "It may be. But you are not him. You are neither mad nor cruel. Visiting the Na'vir to ask for information is hardly an act of a deranged mind."

"What shall we do if they refuse?" asked Kitlyn.

"I don't see why they would, but if they do... perhaps Kethaba would know."

"She is not as old as her grandson claims." Kitlyn snickered to herself, picturing little Alin saying his grandmother was there to watch the Alderswood be planted as a seed.

Oona evidently had the same memory and stifled a laugh. "If she doesn't know, we could visit King Lanas. The spiritcallers might be able to pull the knowledge out from the realms beyond."

"You have not mentioned praying for this knowledge."

"Because I have already done so... often." Oona bowed her head in reverence. "The response is a feeling of reassurance. Surely, the gods mean to tell me this answer is within our grasp. I dare not bother them by demanding we be led like children."

"Wise," muttered Kitlyn. "Frustrating, but wise."

"If you lay wounded, I would absolutely beg them for help." Oona clung tight to her side.

"Consulting the Na'vir is a wonderful idea. We should be proper and send a messenger first to request an audience rather than show up unannounced."

Oona sighed past a smile. "Yes. You are correct. We are, after all, queens. Oh, the cumbersomeness of royalty."

"Only as cumbersome as we allow it to be." Kitlyn again stole a quick kiss. "I abhor pointless ceremony for no sake other than boasting. We can dispense with all nonsense we deem unnecessary."

"Fluffery."

"Yes, fluffery." Kitlyn fake-preened. "Some fluffery is fun, but we do not need thirty wagons, five massive tents, and 250 soldiers escorting us."

Oona covered her mouth to hold in a conspiratorial laugh. Sometimes, when alone with only Kitlyn or perhaps their handmaidens, she'd forget herself and giggle like a child. In public, she tried to project a more mature air, and largely succeeded. However, Kitlyn still adored the moments where her purity and innocence showed.

"An official request to visit is, however, a matter of respect. I do not mind doing so." Kitlyn headed over to the shelves she'd dusted innumerable times and selected a piece of suitable parchment for the letter. "As I know you are beyond eager to take this journey, I shall begin writing this very moment."

Oona pulled out a chair for her.

Kitlyn parodied Lady Aubrin on the walk to the chair, exaggerating an overly dainty, girlish manner. Or tried to… she lost patience at the slow gait halfway there and surrendered to her normal stride. Fighting not to laugh so loud she disturbed the advisors' discussion, Oona plopped down to sit beside her on the same chair, the two of them mostly fitting on the oversized cushion together.

"Esteemed Queen Xorana," said Kitlyn, while starting to write.

THE LIBRARY OF UNDERHOLM

OONA

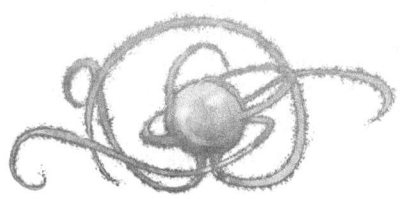

Six days later, Oona and Kitlyn departed the castle for Underholm.

A messenger made the back and forth trip relatively fast, bringing a welcome response of acceptance from Queen Xorana. Out of worry asking directly about the Gates of Isilien in a letter might upset her or be refused outright, their missive expressed the desire to discuss a matter of importance to the kingdom and the Na'vir.

Kitlyn rationalized if the curse killed her, Lucernia would fall into disarray as the nobility split the land up into multiple small nations and warred for the crown. Even if by some act of the gods such a fracture did not occur and the nobility managed to agree on the next monarch, much of the wealthy class retained attitudes similar to those of Aodh. Essentially, everything not human had to be a demon. Whatever ruler followed them could likely be a threat to the Na'vir. After all, a human already destroyed their civilization once. As children, Kitlyn and Oona had been taught some great agent of Lucen 'cleansed the Underholm of demons.'

Obvious nonsense.

Oona couldn't blame Aodh for it, however. The story was older than recorded history—meaning about 200 years. Sadly, the library in the temple of Lucen didn't have any more information about the past. Worse than simply disappointing, it reinforced her fear misguided priests had been responsible for the original purge. Someone had been so insistent on rewriting the past, they didn't even keep a copy of the truth hidden.

Or perhaps they had, and no present living priest knew where to find it. Lucen would surely have guided her to it if he deemed it necessary.

Much to Beredwyn's displeasure, they'd taken only a group of six soldiers along as an escort. They'd wanted to travel alone, relying on their unadorned leather armor and cloaks to disguise their identity. People in Lucernia still hadn't become accustomed to their new queens' habit of avoiding ostentatious displays of wealth or power, so would likely not expect them to be riding around dressed like a pair of scouts without any guards. Also, the people viewed them favorably, so fear of attempts on their lives was low.

However, Beredwyn convinced Kitlyn to consider the convenience of being able to travel faster and freer didn't outweigh her responsibility to the people. Having at least a small retinue of guards along drastically reduced the chances of misfortune, and virtually eliminated accidental death to something stupid, such as being thrown from their horses and starving to death helpless on the side of the trail, both legs broken and no one to fetch help before ants devoured them.

The old man exaggerates… but he cares for us like a grandfather.

Beowyn, the huge former deserter they'd found living in exile in Ondar, had to count for at least five men. In light of their exposing Aodh's lies, the commanders and other soldiers no longer regarded him—and the other deserters—as traitors. It hadn't made everyone happy to welcome them back, however. Oona didn't understand the mindset of soldiers. Beowyn and the others couldn't fight in a war they knew to be unjust. The entire kingdom now understood the war to be unjust, yet many among the military considered them cowards for leaving.

What should they have done? Turned on their commanders? Joined

Evermoor? Attempted to assassinate the king? Every other option is worse and really would have made them traitors.

Rakden, a lieutenant, officially commanded the small escort. The eldest at forty, he'd survived the front lines of the war, spending the last two years as a subcommander of the garrison at the Arch of the Ancients. Once the war ended, he'd been recalled to Cimril where he ended up at a desk pushing paper around. Upon hearing the queens wanted volunteers for a small escort, he leapt at the chance to 'get some air.'

The remainder of their group consisted of Lliard, Danos, Yerbin, and Imoa, all seasoned soldiers in their late twenties. Oona felt awkward hearing Rakden refer to people she thought of as 'somewhat old' as a bunch of kids. He probably regarded her and Kitlyn as literal babies. Thankfully, he said nothing of the sort. Kitlyn already doubted herself due to being young, though following the recovery of Evie and Pim, her confidence had grown.

While self-doubt plagued Kitlyn, Oona's worry went in an entirely different direction. Whenever she had a moment not spent agonizing over the curse killing her dearest love, she worried about the question of an heir. Had they not been queens, taking in one or more orphans would have happily satisfied her desire to become a mother. She still considered herself a bit young for the responsibility, so had no desire to rush into anything yet. Guilt over Evie and Pim disappearing made her even more inclined to wait a few years. However, as queen, any child they didn't bear would not have a solid claim to the throne to follow the rights of succession.

If the curse—or sheer bad luck—killed them both before they could reshape the government of Lucernia from monarchy to some other system, she had no doubt the gentry would do everything possible, including assassination, to keep Evie off the throne. Her fear of this reached such a peak she and Kitlyn already considered enacting a decree officially declaring the girl ineligible to assume the throne, hoping it would spare her life. Besides, Evie would be too easy for unscrupulous advisors to manipulate—too loving, trusting, and innocent.

If they adopted a war orphan, the child would face a similar threat should Kitlyn and Oona die early.

Of course, if they somehow gave birth to a blood descendant, the nobility might still attempt to usurp power, though it would be far more difficult. There would be no legal path to take, guaranteeing war or assassination attempts. If enough time passed for such a child to reach adulthood, or at least their later teens, it might not be as much of a problem.

Granted, their having a baby to begin with presented a far greater issue. Doing so would require a magical intervention of the gods. Alternatively, one or both of them could do things with a man they only wanted to do with each other. Not only did it feel like the greatest betrayal to her love, the idea made her squirm the way Advisor Lanon used to squirm whenever he saw them kiss.

She spent a while smiling at how the man no longer did so.

If magic is returning to Lucernia, perhaps there will be a way Kit and I can bear each other's child. While fantastical, unbelievable, and tempting… she pushed the thought to the side of her mind. *Not yet. We're too young.*

They'd married at an age many considered the bare minimum. Most commoners tended to marry between the ages of eighteen and twenty, and often had children soon after. Nobility occasionally married even younger than Oona and Kitlyn. While Lucen temple weddings required the participants to genuinely love—and be right for—each other, any priest of any temple could legally officiate a wedding. A common joke involved noble weddings happening at Tenebrea's temples because the young girl eagerly awaited her older husband's death. Noble marriages almost always involved shifting prestige, power, or money around. 'Rare as a noble groom in a temple of Lucen' had become an idiom poking fun at how infrequently the upper class married for love.

Oona spent the three-day ride to Underholm alternatively worrying about the curse and the future. Sticking to roads made the trip longer, but would be safer than cutting straight across the meadow. Also, it allowed them the nicety of sleeping on an actual bed. Night one, they took rooms at the army garrison by the Arch of the Ancients, at which they'd arrived two hours past sunset. The second day, they rode north to Wick Hollow and spent the night at an Inn where they enjoyed a fine meal and the voice of a somewhat inebriated minstrel. They hadn't gone out of their way to hide, but no one recognized them.

The third day, their group rode up past the town of Crow's Corner, following the faint ghost of an ancient highway across the meadow east toward the Churning Deep, a massive canyon separating Lucernia from Evermoor, impossible to cross without a bridge—or the power of flight. Underholm spanned the divide, far beneath the great, violent river. Thousands of years ago, the Na'vir excavated miles and miles of tunnel, creating a passage between the two kingdoms. At the middle of the underground roadway, a vast city stretched north and south.

They reached the Lucernian entrance to Underholm shortly before noon and decided to stop for a lunch of bread and cheese before continuing down the half-mile long ramp. The passage descended below the surface between walls of plain grey stone. Statues of four-armed people Oona now understood to be representations of Na'vir gods stood in facing pairs at regular intervals. The deeper they went, the smaller Oona felt. By the time they reached the enormous stone doors at the bottom, she imagined herself a mouse in a narrow box.

Looking at the statues made Oona think about gods and the Evermoor spirits. Unlike what she'd been taught growing up, the four gods of Lucernia were not the only powerful beings. The Pit existed, but so too did Banefallow, an equally awful place the people of Evermoor believed evil souls went after death. Honorable souls ended up in the Glimmering Grove, much like Tenebrea guided people to her realm. The Na'vir had gods of their own, as did the people of Ondar. Certainly, the barbarians did as well—not to mention the land of Amadar and other kingdoms north from Ondar. Whatever lay beyond death had to be a confusing tangle of various planes. No wonder Tenebrea needed to guide souls to her realm. A ghost could seriously end up lost without help.

Kitlyn didn't need to use her magic to enter as the titanic doors had been left open. Since their last journey to Underholm, they'd learned the doors had only been closed a few times in thousands of years. Centuries ago, Queen Xorana ordered them shut in hopes of protecting the outside world from the curse ravaging her people mere hours before she fell victim to it. The Na'vir normally had a lifespan of about eight-hundred years, but the Nimse curse effectively froze them in time.

The great subterranean highway connecting Lucernia to Evermoor once carried traders, explorers, and travelers in large numbers. Oona much preferred this route, several times wider than the Arch of the Ancients, to the bridge due to her discomfort with heights. Crossing the arch on Omun's shoulder had been the second most frightening experience of her life, the first being the time assassins nearly forced her to ingest poison. Visiting Evermoor by carriage still made her nervous, but at least she couldn't see over the side of the bridge from inside the coach, with her eyes closed... and possibly a blanket over her head.

Oona summoned her orb after entering the vast tunnel, flooding an area around them in intense light. Long shadows stretched away from every rock or pebble on the ground, swinging around as the group advanced. The little orb's 'eye spots' widened in awe as if the magical energy ball gazed around. Considering the size of the Na'vir —the average adult stood to a height of about three feet—she couldn't imagine what possessed them to make an underground road four stories tall. According to Kitlyn, the stone giant Omun had no trouble walking in this passage, though his head nearly brushed the ceiling.

Did they make the tunnel tall enough for stone giants or the stone giants only as tall as the tunnel? Oona gazed around at the dark, almost black stone walls and thick, square columns. Since the last time she'd seen the place, the Na'vir had been quite busy. They'd cleaned up all traces of destroyed wagons or skeletons of long-ago traders. The stonework still appeared ancient and abandoned. However, she remembered there being more damage—especially to the columns— before. Traversing Underholm didn't set off her fear of heights but did come with mild concern of cave-ins. If the Na'vir intended to fix anything, the columns holding up the roof seemed the best place to start.

The mood in the tunnel had definitely changed since their last visit here. Cloud, Oona's highly skittish horse, barely hesitated at the entrance. He still didn't like going underground, but no longer acted terrified of doing so.

"So it's true? The Nimse were real?" asked Imoa, the only woman among the soldiers.

"Yes..." Kitlyn recounted the story of their last journey here as well as the curse placed upon the Na'vir by an ancient maleficar.

For them to be reduced to mindless, savage beasts yet remain aware they had once been civilized... Oona cringed at the cruelty of such a curse. The Na'vir possessed keen intelligence and an incredibly high regard for knowledge. To them, information had as much or more value than money. Of course, being traders as well, they also accepted coins, gems, and so forth as they could then give those 'worthless' things to others in exchange for necessary commodities such as food and textiles.

A mile or so into the tunnel, the downhill grade leveled off. Kitlyn's voice echoed around them, her descriptions of Nimse giving the soldiers, including Beowyn, the jitters.

"There is no need to worry about the Nimse," said Oona. "No more of them exist. When the curse ended, they all changed back to Na'vir."

"Nice ta think," said Yerbin. "But the shadows down here keep moving around like critters."

"Don't say that." Imoa gripped her sword. "Now you're going to have me jumping at everything."

Oona coaxed stronger light out of the glowing orb floating above her head. "The Nimse were not true creatures. Only a product of a curse. However, if for some unexplained reason some still exist, they cannot stand bright light."

"Praise Lucen," whispered Rakden.

They continued riding into the depths, no faster than a walk. The occasional alcove on the wall held clusters of glowing amethyst stones. With the Nimse all gone, it might be safe to disturb the piles, but no one bothered. Torches and Oona's magic provided enough light. Kitlyn believed the Nimse attacked her because she'd taken some of those rocks to use as a light source. No idea if the Na'vir also considered them sacred, but she didn't want to risk offending them if so.

The deeper they went, the nicer the walls and columns looked, suggesting the Na'vir actively worked to repair their city. Except for Omun ripping his way to the outside world, most of the damage had been due to collapse or simple neglect.

A bit more than two hours after entering the tunnel, they reached the city.

Except for having a ceiling and nearly everything being made of stone, the Na'vir capital city of Underholm looked more or less like any other city Oona had ever seen. They'd carved or used magic to create the façades of buildings on most surfaces, no free-standing structures other than fountains to be seen. Half-sized Na'vir shops, homes, and taverns covered the walls in eight tiers, connected by various walkways, ladders, or stairs. Every so often, a shop spanned two (Na'vir) stories, amounting to an almost human-sized room. Undoubtedly, those had formerly been places involved in trade with outsiders. Oona didn't think it likely humans or even Anthari would have been inclined to literally crawl into shops with five-foot ceilings.

I wonder if merchants would bring their children along to help. Oona grinned to herself. Evie was a little on the short side for six, but would seem tall here. Queen Xorana, large for a Na'vir, stood about as tall as a nine or ten-year-old human child. The traces of Anthari in the Na'vir—pointed ears, almond-shaped-eyes and delicate bodies—diluted with human traits such as less narrow faces and rounder eyes *did* somewhat make them seem cute and childish, but only in terms of appearance. An unscrupulous Na'vir thief, for example, could disguise themselves as a child among humans. Easier for the women as they didn't need to shave, merely required some moderately loose-fitting clothing to hide their curves.

Oona gazed around in wonder at the hundreds of tiny windows and doors, all teeming with activity. Only the two-story-tall shops intended to trade with outsiders had light inside them since the

Na'vir could magically see in total darkness. This likely explained why their eyes glowed various pastel colors to match the shade of their irises, making the distant reaches of the city beyond the range of her orb a starscape of multicolored 'fireflies' in the dark.

Hundreds of small people raced around busily at work restoring their city to its former glory. They all now had clothing thanks to Kitlyn and Oona urging the mercantile guild to send large quantities of fabric here in trade. The Na'vir had vast stockpiles of gemstones, which they did not place as much value on as humans. To them, handing over glittery rocks for fabric had amounted to a welcome gift from the surface dwellers. Nimse, being mindless beasts, had no regard for clothing. When the curse wore off, it left them quite exposed. Due to the length of the curse and total absence of contact with the outside world, the Na'vir initially lacked any usable cloth, for it had all rotted.

However, Underholm changed in the relatively short time since they'd last visited. Other than everything being roughly half the size, she may as well have been in the merchant district of Cimril.

The Na'vir tended to stop in their tracks upon noticing Oona's bright blue light sphere, though didn't seem at all pained by it. Oona surmised the Nimse had been repelled by Lucen's purity more than the sensitivity of their eyes. After all, the one who cursed them had been a maleficar, a summoner of demons.

A few small tools or devices carried by various small people exploded as they went by, making their owners scream in surprise and swat out any resulting fires. Queen Xorana admitted the Na'vir sometimes made use of extremely weak demonic entities to power magical devices. Likely, being too close to Lucen's light destroyed the demonic energy. Since she considered it her duty to purge demonic things from the world, she did not feel guilty, nor did she stop to explain what happened. If anyone asked, she would freely admit it, but in the interest of diplomacy and Kitlyn's life, she walked a thin line of truth in keeping her mouth shut.

The soldiers whispered to each other, awestruck at such a civilization existing underground. Except for Lliard sincerely asking what happened to all the adults, their comments remained respectful. Seeing clear evidence of a non-human civilization shocked them.

How are people going to respond to seeing faeries? It will eventually happen. Spymaster Hinlor will certainly attempt to recruit a few. By Lucen, faerie spies would be... ridiculous. Highly effective, but I would hate to put them in danger.

Kitlyn led the way by memory, turning left at the grand plaza in the heart of the city. The palace sat all the way at the end, it's grand and laughably oversized façade taking up the entire wall at the end of a subterranean street. The palace glittered as they neared, thousands of gemstones embedded in the walls, window frames, and decorative columns catching the light of her orb and the soldiers' torches.

Six Na'vir guards, perhaps some of the same ones who, as Nimse, had put themselves between them and their queen, stood by the huge onyx doors. Their armor appeared worn and ancient, though the clothing under it quite new. All carried polearms twice their height. Two small men in purple tunics rushed out and down the stairs, hurrying over to Oona and Kitlyn.

"Welcome, Queens Kitlyn and Oona," said one, bowing. "Queen Xorana is waiting for you inside. We will take care of your horses."

"Thank you." Kitlyn smiled at him, then dismounted.

"You are most kind." Oona jumped down from the saddle, patted Cloud on the neck, then greeted another man approaching to take the reins, who had white hair and glowing red eyes.

Kitlyn fished her crown from her saddlebag and set it upon her head. In line with the general aesthetic of austerity in Lucernia, the normal crown consisted of a plain platinum circlet set with green gems. The 'queen's crown' as it was officially known, matched it except for being gold. Kitlyn wore the 'king's crown' for no reason other than Aodh being her blood relative. If anyone assumed she did so for being 'less delicate', they assumed incorrectly. Up until they forced her to scrub floors and clean the castle, she would have been as equally likely as Oona to scream at mice.

Not so much anymore for either of them.

Both had brought their 'travel crowns,' lighter and less expensive replicas they didn't mind losing.

They walked together up the steps, Oona's heart racing from excitement and hope they might soon learn what they needed to stop the curse. Despite their leather armor and soldiers' clothing, they took a moment to collect themselves into royal demeanor before walking in.

Several richly dressed Na'vir in the grand hall turned to look at them, conversations trailing off to curious silence. A feminine whisper came from the innermost end of the room, speaking in a language Oona didn't recognize. In response, patches of decorative stone on the walls and columns began to emit light, brightening the palace interior enough for humans not to need torches.

Oona called her light orb down to sit in her hand. "Thank you, my friend." She patted it.

The two tiny white spots tilted into a shape resembling 'smiling eyes.'

She always felt guilty about dispelling her little friend due to it seeming alive. So, she dimmed the light as much as possible and let it continue gliding along over her shoulder until the duration of the spell ran out naturally. *They are half as tall as us, yet their throne room is twice the size.* Oona nodded in greeting to everyone she noticed looking at her.

A thankful, welcoming—yet ever so slightly suspicious—mood pervaded the room.

Queen Xorana waited for them in her enormous onyx throne. Fortunately, the cushions hadn't been made of rock, too. She remained beautiful, simultaneously a woman in her later twenties and a child not yet twelve depending on how the light fell on her face. Her little body vanished in a lush, velvety turquoise gown trimmed in gold and silver thread. The generous neckline offered a peek of decidedly un-childlike cleavage, the most obvious indication of her not being human second to her glowing amethyst-hued eyes. Curly blue-grey hair draped over her like a waterfall, still so long it would touch the floor if she stood.

Oona and Kitlyn approached the dais, expecting the tedium of a formal introduction process.

Xorana stood and descended the six steps to the floor. Her hair did not in fact touch the stone tiles, though it came within an inch of doing so. "Kitlyn, Oona, welcome to Underholm."

"Thank you, Queen Xorana," said Kitlyn, along with a polite half bow.

"We are grateful to you seeing us." Oona also bowed in greeting. "I understand you are still not quite ready to open Underholm to the outside."

"You are correct. Please, call me Xorana. We are contemporaries, are we not? My people still have much work ahead of us." She waved for them to follow, then walked off to her right. "Let us move to more comfortable surroundings."

Oona and Kitlyn followed her across the room.

Near the archway leading to a hall, Xorana paused to gesture at a man in a fancy blue-and-cyan robe. "Show our guests' escort to their rooms and see they are provided for."

"Yes, my queen." The man snapped his boots together, bowed, and hurried over to Rakden and the other soldiers.

Xorana led Kitlyn and Oona down a wide corridor, its ceiling low enough their hair touched it. The dingy blue rug underfoot appeared in dire need of being replaced. Holes and tears exposed white stone tiles beneath it. Any noble from Lucernia would have been horrified at the sight.

This is grand and large for them... Beowyn couldn't fit in here. Oona ignored the condition of the rug. Xorana obviously didn't want outsiders seeing the city until they'd fixed it up, but made an exception for them. *If someone saved me from an 800-year curse, I'd help them as much as I possibly could.*

Xorana abruptly turned right, entering a square room containing an octagonal table, eight chairs, a fireplace, bookshelves, and various bits of artwork—mostly statuettes. Surprisingly, the red velvet cushions on the chairs did not appear the least bit dirty or old. The tall chair backs came up to Oona's face despite the seats being sized for Na'vir.

Oona brushed her hand over the soft pad on the seatback. *They couldn't have expected official guests so soon... has magic been used to clean this room? This furniture looks new.*

"Please, sit." Xorana extended one arm toward the table as she walked around to take the chair facing the door.

To her, the chairs appeared decoratively large, wide and unnecessarily tall. Oona had to stretch her legs out forward as the table got in the way of her knees otherwise. A chair a Na'vir could sit on and not have their feet dangle proved slightly awkward for a human. Being young and flexible, plus not terribly large, Oona and Kitlyn managed it gracefully. She imagined poor Beredwyn attempting to sit in these chairs and doing awful things to his back.

The overly wide table had plenty of room underneath for human legs, resulting in an ultimately comfortable, if odd position. She couldn't remember ever sitting with her legs stretched out straight in front of her except for reading in bed.

A man and two women in nice but not rich clothing swooped in, giving them each a goblet of water and leaving a tray of assorted finger snacks. Some appeared to be baked goods, others possibly meat. None of it smelled bad, but she had questions about where any 'meat' would've come from this far underground.

"It is most gracious of you to welcome us here so soon." Kitlyn picked up her goblet. "Thank you for the food and water."

"Something to nibble on." Xorana smiled. "We shall have a proper meal in due time."

They spent a little while on small talk about the state of their respective lands. The Na'vir worked feverishly to restore their city to its former glory. Their first priority had been to restore the vast moss gardens to keep the air breathable. Queen Xorana expected it would take years to fully recover to the city's former grandeur, but planned to open Underholm to trade once they'd restored the parts of the city visitors would see. Conversation about the goings-on in Lucernia eventually led to the appearance of faeries and other unidentified beings.

"Wyrg," said Xorana upon hearing the description of the creatures spotted at Aowyn's Crossing.

"We know nothing of them." Oona sighed. "The library at our castle is woefully lacking in books on history, magic, creatures... anything more than how 'wonderful' our past kings were."

Xorana gasped.

"Oona is quite upset, too," said Kitlyn. "Though we understand a human cannot possibly feel pain over the loss of knowledge to the degree you can."

"I'm close." Oona flashed a weak smile. "I did actually cry the other day over it. Though, I admit the emotion came more from not being able to answer the question I needed to answer than anything else. Do we really need seventeen treatises on King Iastor's prowess as a hunter?"

"Depends on if they are substantively different." Xorana sipped from her goblet.

Oona risked trying one of the snacks, a white brick roughly the size of her thumb. Biting into it revealed a consistency—and taste—similar to fish. "Mm... this is actually quite good."

"Perhaps I shouldn't tell you what it is then." Xorana winked. "Most humans who try it find it delicious, but cannot eat it once they know."

Oona froze, staring at the half-nugget pinched between her thumb and index finger, doing her best to talk around the small mouthful without sounding as if she had anything on her tongue. "Is it going to make me sick?"

"Not at all."

"It's a bug, isn't it?" asked Kitlyn.

Oona again, glanced down at the innocuous white fishy lump. She chewed once. Still rather enjoyed the flavor, so she swallowed.

"Cave spider." Xorana watched her intently. "Humans compare it to crab, though I have never partaken in crab flesh."

Kitlyn cringed, expecting a loud scream.

Spider. Oona narrowed her eyes at the small meat nugget. *I have had crab before and she is right. Hmm. As far as I am concerned, this is crab.* She ate the other half.

Xorana pretend clapped. "I am impressed."

"So am I." Kitlyn blinked.

Once she finished chewing, she gestured at the tray. "It *does* taste exactly like crab. Try one."

"What is a wyrg?" asked Kitlyn. "How dangerous are they?"

"Not very. They are cousins to goblins, even less intelligent. Greedy, primitive... easily scared. Your people should have little trouble from them once they grow accustomed to the sight." Xorana shifted her gaze to Oona. "I suspect you did not urgently come here to ask about wyrg."

"No, you are correct." Oona gave Kitlyn an 'eat the spider, I dare you' side stare for a second. "The reason these creatures are all of a sudden appearing is the second most worrisome thing on our minds."

"We think it may be due to restoring the Heart to the Alderswood," said Kitlyn, conspicuously not looking at the tray.

"Spider," muttered Oona.

Kitlyn pretended not to hear.

"The great tree did send forth a tremendous surge of life energy." Xorana gazed off into space. "Most Na'vir felt it pass through us as it radiated outward. I did not understand its origin at the time, but have determined it did originate from the Alderswood."

Oona grasped the tray and slid it closer to Kitlyn. "It is good to have at least one mystery solved."

A barely audible sigh escaped Kitlyn's nostrils. She picked up the other spider nugget. Grinning, Oona pushed the tray back to its original position and selected a small orangey-brown loaf. They bit their respective treats in half at the same time. Oona's eyebrows rose at the unusual experience of sugary cake seasoned with herbs more appropriate for a baked ham. Not too unpleasant to finish, but she likely wouldn't willingly eat another one.

"It is not the reason you are here?" asked Xorana.

"There is a curse following Kitlyn's family line." Oona hastily ate the second half of the oddly flavored mini-cake. "The spirit of her mother returned with a warning, confirming our suspicions of a curse as real. She told us to find the Gates of Isilien. Yet, we do not know what Isilien even is. Our library is useless."

Xorana made a pensive face, idly tapping her fingers on the table edge. "It sounds somewhat familiar. I feel as if I've heard of it, but cannot recall. For what reason do you wish to know about the Gates of Isilien?"

"My mother's spirit told me my life lays beyond the Gates of Isilien." Kitlyn eyed the second half of the spider-meat nugget. Her expression said 'hmm, not bad.' "Is it an artifact or a place called Isilien with actual gates? We haven't the slightest idea what to find there, only it has something to do with breaking the curse on my family."

Oona leaned forward, clutching the table. "I need to know what or where this is to protect Kitlyn's life. We understand your hesitation in sharing information with humans after what happened here. We're not seeking magical knowledge... at least, I do not believe we are. I know nothing of Isilien. Please, you are our best hope of protecting Kitlyn's life from this curse."

"My dear Oona, please do not become upset." Xorana raised a placating hand. "I do not fear sharing information with humans in general. Much can be learned from *how* a question is asked, who does the asking, and what the question is. The one you refer to demanded forbidden knowledge knowing it forbidden. I dare say he did not even 'ask.'"

Kitlyn and Oona nodded in unison.

"I honestly do not recall the meaning of Isilien, only the word sounding familiar to me." Xorana interlaced her fingers, hands resting on the table edge, and smiled. "I shall have the archivists look for this. While we wait, please join me for dinner. I'll have someone show you to a room so you can rest from your journey for a short while before the meal, and unburden yourselves of your armor if you would like to be more comfortable."

"That would be lovely," said Kitlyn.

"Thank you." Oona bowed as graciously as possible while seated in a short chair.

I surprise myself by thinking this, but if we are to have spider as a meal, it would not particularly vex me.

22

A CURSE MOST ANCIENT

KITLYN

One small nugget of spider meat swam around Kitlyn's stomach for the entire duration of dinner.

Oona had been right. It *did* taste like crab, which she had on occasion — certainly not as often as 'the princess' enjoyed it. Beyond the flavor, she couldn't fully get past the notion of consuming a bug. Seeing beetles, worms, spiders, or other insects with far too many legs for any one creature to possess didn't bother her. *Eating* them, however, crossed a line. Worse, she had a feeling the cave spider she ate was quite a bit bigger than any spider she'd ever seen before. Out of politeness and to prevent Oona's increasingly obvious teasing from escalating to rudeness, she'd acquiesced.

Between the two of us, it is completely opposite for her *to be the one ignoring etiquette in an official social setting.*

She suspected the Na'vir's small size and partially elven features caused Oona to relax her sense of decorum, as if she'd been left to entertain the monarch's young daughter rather than the monarch herself. However, Xorana also adopted a far more casual attitude than she expected from a head of state.

We are all queens, so perhaps she regards us as equals and sees no need for unnecessary ceremony out of the public eye?

An attendant showed them to the bedchamber they'd be using for the night so they could change prior to the meal. Their saddlebags had already been brought in and set on the table. After swapping their leather armor and plain tunics for matching blue dresses—expensive but nothing elaborate enough to require handmaidens to help get into—they relaxed for a little over an hour and a half before the attendant returned to lead them to the dining hall.

The main dinner consisted of various root vegetables prepared in different ways, breads made of the same root vegetables, spider-meat cakes—similar to crab cakes, though Kitlyn avoided them—and fish from an underground river. Oona rather fancied the spider-cakes, though didn't overindulge.

Conversation during the meal mostly involved the restoration of Underholm as well as various, random meanderings. Xorana encouraged them to share more of the story regarding what happened with the Heart and the war between Lucernia and Evermoor. Oona brought up the distorted versions of Na'vir history. One claimed a sorcerer wiped them out while the second most prominent tale told of a Lucen priest 'purging demons' from Underholm. Xorana believed both stories had roots in truth, namely the 'sorcerer' referred to the maleficar who cursed them. The purge story matched her memory of a surface dweller attempting to wipe out the Nimse, not understanding their origins. However, the supposed Lucen priest didn't survive, nor did he kill many Nimse.

Having been trapped in a twisted version of her body but largely in possession of her mind—so she could watch her former subjects suffering as savage beasts—Xorana remembered the attack. A handful of other humans from the same expedition successfully escaped.

Oona guessed the survivors, or someone official at the temple, made up lies about the 'great cleansing' to cover up the absolute failure or perhaps prevent anyone else from going down there and being killed. She spent the rest of dinner doing her best not to act as angry as she'd obviously become. Learning Aodh had not been the first servant of Lucen to so grossly throw aside all regard for truth infuriated her, especially if done over simple pride of refusing to admit failure.

After the meal, Xorana entertained them by bringing in dancers and musicians to perform a play. While neither Kitlyn nor Oona knew the first thing about ancient Na'vir romantic tragedies, the performance enthralled them, largely due to the use of props infused with magic to create illusions of blood, ghosts, and even changing the main character from a young man to older-middle-aged when the story skipped ahead 400 years.

Eventually, Oona and Kitlyn found themselves escorted back to their well-appointed guest bedroom. Before she left, the attendant who led the way informed them the soldiers had enjoyed a banquet meal in a sitting room to which all their guest rooms adjoined and spent the night relaxing.

The relatively large room appeared much like any other guest bedroom in a wealthy person's estate, other than it not having any windows or lamps, and mere inches separating the top of Kitlyn's head from the ceiling. Oona's light orb intensified, gliding in a lazy circle around the room. The deep shadows it painted on the walls wavered and stretched in time with its slow orbit.

Oona paced, muttering to herself in annoyance at not being able to go into the library here.

Kitlyn stepped out of her slippers. Her bare toes went numb within seconds of touching the stone floor. Soft green light swirled momentarily around her arms as she tapped her magic for warmth. "Undress quickly. It is quite chilly in here, my love."

"I will," replied Oona in a grumpy voice.

"Did you expect they'd set us loose in their library?"

"I'd hoped to see it at least. The Na'vir library is supposedly massive. Shelves taller than our castle in corridors stretching for miles. So many books, scrolls, tablets, parchments, and so forth even a Na'vir would grow old and die before they could read it all." She clutched her hands to her heart and fell over backward onto the bed. "It makes me dizzy to think about all those books in one place."

Kitlyn turned away so she could scowl and not upset her. She'd once enjoyed reading books, too… back when they'd been children and the castle didn't have a Fauhurst lurking around every corner to scream at her. He, Elsbeth, and some of the other servants would always tease her if they caught her reading. His favorite taunt had been 'why are you wasting time reading? No book is going to help you scrub floors any better.'

I must make time to read. It will give us something fun to talk about. She's always referring to stories I don't know.

Oona emitted a frustrated mix of sigh and growl, which she typically only made when attempting to escape an elaborate gown on her own.

Expecting to see her squirming around on the bed like a fish, Kitlyn peered back over her shoulder. Oona sat on the edge, bent forward with her head in both hands, hair draped down in front of her face, nearly to the floor.

"Oo? Are you all right?"

She sat up, flipping her hair around behind her back. "Yes. Merely frustrated. I understand they're highly protective of their library. It should not disappoint me so."

"Need I point out you didn't ask to see it?" Kitlyn pulled her dress off and draped it over one of the chairs at the table holding their saddlebags and piled-up armor.

"Yes, yes…" Oona rolled her eyes while kicking her slippers off. She had the benefit of a small carpet close to the bed to protect her feet from icy stone. "It is gracious of her to have the archivists do the searching for us. They will be much faster."

Kitlyn shed her undergarments and slipped into bed. Surprisingly, the bedclothes didn't smell musty or damp. It seemed odd for there to be a soft bed here already in a guest room, but… Xorana did have over a week's notice to prepare for their visit.

Squeaking at the cold in the air, Oona hastily undressed and crawled into bed as well. Fortunately, they had two sheets and three blankets. Kitlyn rested her hand on Oona's stomach, sharing the warmth her magic provided. Oona stopped shivering in a few seconds, emitting a soft moan of contentment.

Their heads almost touched the board, their feet an inch past the foot end.

"It's nice of her to let us use the largest bed in the palace." Kitlyn grinned.

"Quite. Though this bed is not exactly... erm... *queen* sized." Oona winked. "An inch or two shy of it."

Kitlyn groaned. "Depends on the size of the queen in question. It is charming in a way."

"I don't mind the coziness." Oona traced her hand over Kitlyn's side, down onto her hip.

"Nor do I."

Oona snuggled closer. "I have come to a realization."

"Oh?" Kitlyn raised an eyebrow. "What?"

"My mind is no longer too troubled with worry to think *other* thoughts." Oona flashed an impish smile.

Kitlyn caressed her wife's cheek, brushing her fingertips down over her neck. "What manner of 'other' thoughts?"

"I think you know the sort of thoughts I'm having." Oona half closed her eyes.

"Ahh, yes." Kitlyn leaned in to kiss her. "I believe I do."

KNOCKING AT THE DOOR WOKE KITLYN FROM A PLEASANT, dreamless sleep.

She opened her eyes to Oona's gaping mouth and tangled blonde hair splayed about as if she'd been struck by lightning. Oona's light ball sat upon a little table beside the bed, dim enough not to bother them while sleeping. Kitlyn assumed she also resembled a faerie who'd flown at high speed into a window.

Due in part to the small bed, they'd ended up entwined together in a tangle of limbs. Her face prickled from the cold air. Autumn in Lucernia had nothing on being miles underground in a stone chamber for chill.

"Yes?" called Kitlyn. "What is it?"

"It is morning," said a female voice higher in pitch than a woman but not exactly childish. "Queen Xorana would like to know if you would join her for breakfast in an hour."

A sudden unwanted mental image of a spider-egg omelet nearly launched whatever remained of last night's dinner across the room. She managed to dispel the horrifying thought in time by concentrating on her memory of the reasonably safe vegetables.

"Thank you, that will be lovely," called Kitlyn.

"Why are you awake?" rasped Oona.

"We've been invited to breakfast."

Oona made no effort to move or even open her eyes. "It's morning already?"

"I assume. The attendant said so."

"Ugh... how can they tell?"

"An innate sense? Maybe they have devices to tell the time." Kitlyn played with Oona's hair. "It may be small, but this bed is so wonderfully cozy and soft it's making me not want to move."

"I concur," said Oona in a sleepy voice.

"I've already conveyed our acceptance of the invitation, though I suppose she would understand if we preferred to sleep all day."

Oona opened her eyes. "This bed is *too* cozy to spend all day in. We can't straighten our legs out and be comfortable. If you desire to spend an entire day under blankets, we should return home first."

"Now I am having fantasies, my love."

"What manner of fantasies?" Oona tried to smile but ended up yawning.

"The two of us relaxing for an entire day wearing nothing but the bedclothes."

"Tempting." Oona disentangled herself enough to stretch, but stayed under the covers. "My face is cold."

"It is rather chilly in here. We did not start a fire."

"There is no wood."

Kitlyn concentrated on her magic for warmth, sharing it with Oona.

"Mmm. Better. Now I do not need to pull the blankets up over my head."

"We should get out of bed."

"Are you certain it's morning? It feels as though we barely slept at all."

Kitlyn sat up, examining her fingernails. "Not surprising, really. You did rather wear yourself out last night."

Oona gasped in fake shock, but started laughing when Kitlyn tickled her. To defend herself, Oona pounced and held her down, straddling her while pinning her wrists to the bed on either side of her head. Long blonde hair spilled off her shoulders, falling upon Kitlyn's chest like the gossamer breath of ghosts.

"We are going to be late for breakfast." Kitlyn peered up at her.

"Oh, darn." Oona leaned down to peck a kiss on her cheek. "I suppose we cannot have fun then."

Kitlyn patted her on the rear end. "We absolutely can, but it would be rude of us to do so right this moment, and I'd prefer not to rush things."

Oona overacted a disappointed sigh, then swung her leg over to get out of bed. Kitlyn grabbed her wrist before she got too far.

"I thought you wanted to get up?" Oona hopped on one foot, glancing back at her.

"We really ought to. But, if I stop touching you, the magic responsible for you not shrieking at the cold will stop."

"Eep."

Kitlyn crawled out of bed after her, keeping hold of her hand. "Should we put the dresses back on or the armor?"

"The armor will be a little warmer, but might imply we are in a hurry to leave and come off rude." Oona fidgeted. "Dresses. If we are to leave soon, we can always change."

"All right." Kitlyn patiently kept one hand in contact with Oona while she dressed enough not to freeze, then hurried into her garments.

They doubted Xorana would care about them wearing the same dresses, not like Lucernian high society who'd be less shocked at a murder than someone wearing the same outfit two days in a row.

Kitlyn couldn't help herself and habitually started making the bed. Oona attempted to assist as best she could while making fun of herself for being poor at it.

"Oh, it's all right. You don't need to distract the peasant girl from remembering she spent four years peasanting." Kitlyn chuckled. "I don't feel ashamed of making my own bed."

"It's silly of me to be more intimidated by bedclothes than a man trying to cut my head off."

Kitlyn nudged her. "Oh, how did your little friend stay here all night? Doesn't the spell run out eventually?"

"The brighter she is, the more I need to concentrate on giving her energy. This dim, she might be able to exist for a whole day before needing to re-cast the spell."

As if aware of being talked about, the small orb levitated up from the table, brightened, and glided over to her.

Something is clearly unusual about her little pet. It's almost alive. Other priests simply make light orbs... no eyes. Or personality.

They took a short while to neaten each other's hair as much as possible, then exited the bedchamber. A palace attendant waited for them in the hall, showing them to the same dining room where dinner took place last night. Queen Xorana already sat at the head end of the long table. To her left sat a Na'vir man who appeared to be in his early forties. He wore elaborate robes the same shade of slate grey as his hair, composed of layered gold-trimmed triangular sections descending from an abnormally wide, pointy shoulder mantle. A small gem at the middle of a thin gold circlet across his forehead glowed the same shade of amethyst as his eyes.

Kitlyn approached, sitting where another attendant pulled out a chair for her. She sat, arranging her legs under the awkward low table as gracefully as possible.

Oona took the seat at Kitlyn's right.

"You are early. Grand." Xorana smiled, then waved at a nearby attendant in a 'proceed' gesture. "I am hungry this morning. You slept well, I trust?"

Numerous attendants hurried off into small archways.

"Yes, thank you." Kitlyn nodded.

"Quite well," said Oona.

Xorana indicated the man to her left. "This is Archivist Merix. He has the information you have asked for. I am pleased to share it with you. It is far less than any reward you deserve for your efforts in ending the curse on my people."

"You are most gracious, Queen Xorana." Oona bowed.

Attendants scurried about, bringing everyone water, hot tea, and bowls of steaming... something. The porridge appeared part way between being extremely runny scrambled eggs and oatmeal, it's aroma closer to that of eggs. Dark bits resembled mushrooms. Small green flecks reminiscent of parsley had to be some manner of seasoning. A hint of potato came from it as well, likely her imagination filling in for another form of root vegetable.

Perhaps I will enjoy this more not knowing what it is. Eggs, mushrooms, potatoes mixed together.

She tasted a spoonful. Clearly, she did *not* eat eggs with potatoes. It somewhat had the flavor of mashed turnip. The dark hunks did appear to be mushrooms at least. Even though her magic kept her warm, she welcomed the hot breakfast, not caring exactly what it came from. The Na'vir had great amounts of knowledge about so many things, it would be highly unlikely for them to feed her a meal a human couldn't endure.

"You are looking for Isilien?" asked Merix.

"Yes." Oona nodded. "Ooh, this is quite good. What is it?"

Darn. She had to ask. Kitlyn braced herself for tragedy.

"A combination of pureed root vegetables, mushrooms, and a form of lichen with properties quite similar to the whipped contents of bird eggs. Humans do eat bird eggs, correct?" Xorana tilted her head.

Plants. All plants. I can do this. Kitlyn ate another spoonful. It honestly had a fairly mild flavor. Easy enough to pretend she consumed mashed turnips with an egg thrown in.

"It's wonderfully warm," said Oona. "Sorry. Yes, it is very important we find the Gates of Isilien. Is it an object or a place?"

"A place." Merix sipped his tea. "Isilien is deep in the southeastern part of Evermoor, quite well into the swampy region. Its exact location is not recorded here. The closest specific point to it is a town called Kolbrin's Quay... which due to the age of the information we have, may or may not still exist."

Since Oona had a spoon stuffed in her mouth at the moment, Kitlyn asked, "Is Isilien a city or village?"

Merix shook his head. "It was a school, which became a ruin more than 2,500 years ago."

Kitlyn coughed.

"What manner of school was it?" Oona stirred her spoon around in the breakfast mush.

"One where they taught arcane magic." Merix glanced at Xorana, who nodded in a 'go ahead' manner. "I understand neither of you are learned in such magic?"

"No," said Oona.

"We are not." Kitlyn held her arm out, focusing a little power into the floor. A small patch of stone liquefied, extruding upward at her command. The gloopy liquid rock coalesced into a small sphere, which she then directed to fly around between her hands, a tiny comet shrouded in green light. "I carry the magic of the Alderswood."

Oona nodded toward her light orb. "Lucen and Orien have graciously bestowed their gifts upon me."

"Ahh, yes. I see. Interesting." Merix ate a few spoonfuls of his breakfast. "Neither one of you seem to have any reason for pursuing the secrets which might dwell within a ruin like Isilien."

"We aren't looking for magic… I'm honestly not sure *what* we're trying to find." Oona bowed her head. "There is a curse on the Talomir family line. It seems any who remain on the throne of Lucernia find themselves suffering an early death. The spirit of Kitlyn's mother briefly returned from Tenebrea's realm to tell us the way to protect her life is beyond the gates of Isilien. Suppose she meant actual gates."

"Arcane mages are capable of doing a great many things with their magic. Elementalists"—Merix gestured at Kitlyn—"are potent, but fairly limited in scope. Those who channel the powers of gods also have the capability to wield significant power, but again, they are somewhat limited in what the power can do."

Kitlyn allowed the tiny stone meteor to return to the floor. "How can power be significant but limited?"

"In the sense you had the power to reopen the tunnel to Underholm, but everything your magic does involves stone or earth." Merix gestured at Oona. "Likewise, her magic follows the sphere of influence associated with the particular god or goddess from which it comes. Your magic is at an instinctual level, requiring little intellectual exertion on your part to make it work. The same way a bird is born with the ability to fly, you two wield magic."

"A bird cannot offend the god of flight and end up a chicken stuck on the ground," said Kitlyn.

"Yes, yes... a minor issue not relevant to what I am trying to explain." Merix chuckled. "An arcane mage does not simply create magic whenever they wish something to happen. It is not a reflex for them. They must study ancient formulas to tap powers not of this world, drawing them through and manifesting in wondrous ways. Where everything you do magically involves stone or earth, an arcane mage could do almost anything if they found the proper formulas. Summon rocks, fire, lightning, water... feathers. Make objects move, bring statues to life." He waved his hand around dismissively. "The variations are too numerous to list."

"Disappearing," said Oona.

"Ahh, teleportation, or did you mean invisibility?" Merix tilted his head. "Both are possibilities."

"The man she's thinking of did not merely go invisible. He stopped existing."

"Teleportation then." Merix raised both eyebrows. "No small feat. This person you saw is likely quite skilled. He is not the one sending you to Isilien, is he?"

Oona shook her head.

"No." Kitlyn finally picked up her tea, not quite hot anymore. "He has no idea we are even searching for it."

"Are you certain this man did not send the spirit?" asked Xorana.

Kitlyn blinked. "I have no reason to suspect he did. The spirit told me things he could not have known. I'm sure I spoke to my actual mother."

"If this teleportation requires great skill, wouldn't this man have been able to locate Isilien on his own?" Oona exhaled. "It would not make any sense for him to have us try to find it. We didn't have the first idea of where to begin looking until we came here."

"Does Isilien contain something dangerous? Arcane magic we should not disturb?" asked Kitlyn.

Merix grimaced. "It pains me to say this, but we do not know. It is potentially a source of great knowledge."

"If we are able to find it, we will happily share its location with you." Oona smiled.

"How could such a place as Isilien be connected to a curse on my family?" Kitlyn glanced at Oona. "If it became a ruin 2,500 years ago... the Talomir line has not occupied the throne of Lucernia for anywhere near so long. They all die early, except for the first... Iastor lived to sixty-four. Branok died in a week. Eoim ruled from age nine to thirty-seven, also dying suddenly. Aodh, my father, ascended to the throne at eleven and died months ago at thirty-seven."

Oona gasped. "Eoim and Aodh both died at the same age. I wonder if the curse is so specific?"

"Then I still have plenty of time, I'm only halfway there..." Kitlyn smirked.

"What of your ancestors before Iastor?" Merix gestured for an attendant to refill his hot tea.

"We do not know." Kitlyn titled her bowl to scoop out the last of the food. "We have no records of any history earlier than King Iastor's reign. If they still exist, they've been hidden. No one knows if the monarch prior to Iastor was a Talomir or otherwise."

Merix covered his mouth in shock. "They destroyed knowledge?"

"It seems that way." Oona sighed at her lap. "Most humans do not value it in the way the Na'vir do. Some of our rulers believe they can hide or effectively change the past to better make people do what they want—or to conceal their misdeeds."

Queen Xorana set her spoon down beside the empty bowl in front of her. "It must be quite a powerful curse indeed to follow your family line for 2,500 years. Such a thing does not seem possible. It is far more likely the curse originated with Iastor's predecessor, whose deeds must have been so vile they have been erased."

The idea of a distant relative committing such an atrocity the priests and kings after them erased all mention of it horrified Kitlyn —for a moment. Considering what Aodh did, it certainly sounded possible for an older descendant to have accomplished worse. *Posterity is the great arbiter of justice. I will decree all deeds of politically significant individuals from the royalty to priests to nobles be recorded, made known, and preserved.* She narrowed her eyes at the table. *Until the king or queen after us decides to change it. We must encourage the people to value the truth and demand to know what their monarch does. There must be some way to protect it from future evil... but how?*

"I've been wondering what made them do such a thing." Oona frowned.

"If I may..." Merix raised a finger. "If we assume an ancestor prior to Iastor is the reason the curse is on your family line, it surely would have occurred within the last two centuries. Maybe three. Quite less than the time Isilien has lay in ruins."

"Indeed." Xorana nodded. "If such a curse has been on your family for so long, the chances of the line surviving thousands of years are not good."

"Our library is woefully incomplete." Oona picked up her tea, cradling it in both hands. "There is too much we have lost."

Kitlyn looked at Merix, considering asking the Na'vir to send an emissary to Cimril as a scribe. Preserving history in the Library of Underholm might protect it, but could also threaten them. History could only protect the citizens from misdeeds at the hands of their rulers if everyone knew it would be preserved. *I must think.*

A woman who appeared only somewhat older than Kitlyn and Oona—which likely made her close to 160 years of age—rushed in, also wearing elaborate multi-layered robes in the same style as Archivist Merix, only pale green. Her bright cobalt blue hair hung in disarray around her face, as askew as Oona's had been before she awoke. Her eyes gave off light the same shade of blue. She rushed over to Merix without hesitation, disregarding the presence of everyone else, handed him a scroll, and ran back out.

"It seems the junior archivists have located a related record." Merix unfurled the scroll between his hands, holding it up to read.

The fragrance of damp ink wafted in the air. "Hmm. We have records of another inquiring about Isilien."

"Remarkable you are able to find it," whispered Oona.

Merix peered around the scroll to smile at her. "We utilize minor incantations and spells to create 'finders.' Small points of floating light, somewhat like your companion. They guide us to the necessary information. We have been searching all night for references to Isilien."

"Thank you for helping me protect Kitlyn." Oona took a deep, wavering breath, struggling to rein in her emotions.

"This mention of Isilien…. Hmm." Merix read over the scroll. "Quite a long while ago, before the curse befell us, a human came here seeking information about it. According to our records, one of our seers attempted to divine its location. Her writings indicate the gates of Isilien were sealed by ancient and powerful magic of a kind lost to human comprehension. She speaks of a key thusly:" He cleared his throat, then read directly from the parchment. "Those who seek Isilien will know the key when wrathful amber dwells beside innocent emerald. It is at once large and small. Fragile, yet deadly with proper training."

Oona's expression fell from hope to dread.

Kitlyn pondered the words. "Could this key be not a literal key but… perhaps a sword? Maybe a dagger—small for a weapon but large for a key."

"Oh, perhaps." Oona perked up. "The soldiers don't think of daggers as dangerous, but in the hands of a master, they are deadly."

"I am sorry to say we have no information about what became of this person who searched for Isilien so long ago. Whether or not they located the key or found the ruins, I cannot say." Merix smoothed the parchment out on the table, conjured a quill from thin air in his hand, and began writing. "As I am sure you are curious, this note will go permanently into the library. I am documenting the two of you asking these questions and our responses."

Will someone a thousand years from now hear of us? Kitlyn could scarcely grasp the concept of so many years in the future. Being queen already ensured people would talk about her and Oona for years to come. She found it awkward, not being terribly fond of fame or believing herself deserving of such effort to remember.

Maybe the past kings were not cruel but incredibly humble… Kitlyn sighed. *Unlikely.*

"Can you perhaps offer any idea of where we might begin looking for this key, whatever it is?" asked Oona.

Merix glanced up from the parchment. "My apologies. If we possessed such information, I would have already given it to you. Queen Xorana has instructed us to share knowledge of Isilien freely with you."

"We thank you for your most gracious assistance," said Kitlyn, bowing her head. "Truly, if your great library does not contain the key's location, we have a daunting task ahead of us."

Xorana blushed slightly. "You are too kind. Our knowledge is extensive but imperfect. We can only try to improve it. You are, of course, welcome to stay as long as you desire. I suspect, however, you are eager to dispel this curse before it catches up to you."

"Yes," said Kitlyn on a long sigh. "My dear wife is already beside herself with worry for me."

Oona squeezed her hand.

23

A QUESTION OF RECKLESS CONCERN

OONA

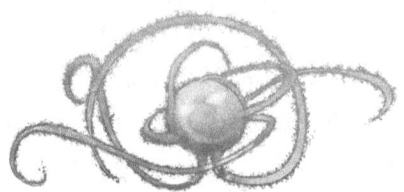

*A*fter the 'business' of their visit concluded, an hour or so of polite socializing with Queen Xorana passed in a foggy blur. Oona's mind hadn't been in the room with them, too lost to worries over Isilien and shock at the potential truth a past Talomir monarch might have committed an atrocity so horrible it had to be erased from history.

They'd debated the meaning of Solana's message for a while, wondering if 'beyond the gates of Isilien' might be far simpler than the need to physically go there—namely, the curse could be broken by a mage using the type of magic once taught there. Xorana and Merix considered it an unlikely interpretation. They didn't believe the spirit would be so cryptic in referring to such an obscure ancient ruin as a roundabout way of referring to arcane magic. Something about Isilien itself had to be crucial. Oona inexplicably felt the urge to agree with them. Considering her hunch to be a nudge from Tenebrea, she accepted they would have to go there.

Not only did the exact location of Isilien remain unknown, they wouldn't be able to find whatever Kitlyn's mother sent them in search of without some manner of complex key. Worse, how could they search for a key when they didn't even know what form it took? It *could* be a literal key, or a dagger, or perhaps even a bottle of magical water. Emerald and amber obviously suggested a physical item of some form set with jewels. A literal key could be fancy, but so could daggers or swords. It might also refer to a green bottle holding amber liquid.

Oona spent most of the time they'd socialized trying to think of an object simultaneously bejeweled and deadly. The riddle complicated things to the point of frustration. It had to be something deadly not by mere existence but training. Even a dagger could be deadly in the hands of someone who'd never been in a fight before. One did not need to be a master duelist to murder a sleeping person, or a chicken.

The 'small yet large' most likely implied the item was bigger than a key ought to be, yet not of a size to be burdensome. Perhaps a small version of something also existing in a larger form. Kitlyn's idea of a dagger fit the logic: small as blades go, but large for a key.

I cannot fixate my thoughts on it being a dagger or my mind will close to a different truth.

"Are you planning to ride home like that, my love?" asked Kitlyn.

Reality intruded upon Oona's mental debates. She found herself in their guest bedroom, standing in her smallclothes beside the bed. Evidently, she'd removed her dress and become lost in thought.

"No. Of course not."

Sighing, Oona collected her tunic and breeches, then donned her armor. Each time she put on the scout's leather, she mentally stuck out her tongue, making childish faces at the nobility, who'd certainly gasp at her. It bothered her greatly how they admired a king or nobleman for showing valor on the battlefield, but a noble lady *must* at all times wear the height of fashion. She couldn't truly say it came entirely from them considering women too delicate for warfare. The nobility had no reaction to women of the lower classes being soldiers and scouts.

It will be far easier to locate this key than explain the inner workings of a noble's mind.

She continued agonizing over the key problem the whole time they collected their saddlebags and made their way out of the palace to the courtyard where Rakden, Lliard, Imoa, Danos, Yerbin, and Beowyn readied their horses in preparation of departing Underholm. The soldiers spoke of their morning meal in grateful terms, apparently having enjoyed temporary lodgings much fancier than ordinarily provided to soldiers.

Kitlyn hung her saddlebags on Apples after an attendant led him over. "What say you, wife?"

"Hmm?" Oona grunted as she hurled her saddlebag up into place on Cloud. "About?"

"Shall we proceed straight on to Evermoor now, or resist the urge to be impulsive?"

Oona faced her. "Where would we go? Kolbrin's Quay? If such a town still exists, will anyone there even know *of* Isilien much less be able to find it? I also don't think it is wise to spend weeks exploring the swamp in search of a ruin we couldn't even enter if we found. The key must come first."

"Yes... and I suppose it is folly to set out on an expedition likely to take weeks or months without proper planning. And it would be cruel to Evie for us to go off and not at least tell her."

Oona's heart sank at the thought of being away from her sister for a long journey, especially while she remained so small. "Well, we *are* queens, are we not? We have a network of spies. Since we now know Isilien is a place, we can send someone in search of it. It's not lazy of us, is it?"

"It is not laziness because we have responsibilities elsewhere. It would be foolish of us to spend months exploring the moor when we are needed at the castle. All right. Let us return home for now." Kitlyn hugged her. "Even if they find it, we can do nothing until the key is located. I also wish to evaluate the idea Ulfaan may be involved."

Oona pulled herself up into her saddle. "Involved? As in he tricked you with a false ghost?"

"No, I..." Kitlyn fidgeted at the reins. "When she told me how she loved someone other than Aodh, a woman, it felt genuine. It also makes sense for my mother to have had the same kind of love we do. I am her daughter."

"I suppose I got it from my father then if such things are passed from parent to child." Oona rolled her eyes. "Certainly not Ruby."

"Indeed." Kitlyn mounted her horse.

Apples flicked his ears. He didn't fidget anywhere near as much as Cloud, but she had no doubt both horses looked forward to seeing the sky again.

"Do you think it is such? Passed from parent on? Or do our souls simply find love with another soul regardless of the body they wear?"

"I know not, nor does it matter to me." Kitlyn maneuvered Apples closer and took her hand. "I care only that my soul, for whatever reason, has become one with yours. And no force, be it curse, goblin, faerie, or closed-minded fool will change anything."

Oona stared into Kitlyn's dark emerald eyes. "I have never been at ease without you by my side. Our souls have always known."

"You were so miserable when he dragged you off to Ondar."

The memories she had of the official visit four years ago fell far short of being pleasant. In light of discovering Kitlyn's true identity, she understood now why Aodh refused to bring her. The trip would have been pleasant, perhaps even fun had they been together. Alone, she'd spent the whole time sullen and crying, refusing to talk to anyone or even move, forcing someone to carry her about. Aodh had ultimately cut the trip short due to her excessive gloom.

I wonder if he didn't feel as sorry for me as he claimed. Difficult to convince a foreign king to arrange a marriage between his son and a ball of sadness.

"Yes. I only wanted to be with you, though I didn't yet understand love." Oona looked over at her. "Did it pain you as well?"

Kitlyn gazed down. "Yes, but I did not have the time to dwell on it. I feared they would throw me out into the street if I didn't work as hard as they demanded."

"They wouldn't have."

"Obviously," grumbled Kitlyn. "I realize that *now*."

"We are ready, highness," called Rakden. "We are to return to Cimril, yes?"

"Yes. To Cimril... we must think on what to do next."

Oona waved at the Na'vir around them in the palace courtyard, then steered Cloud into line with the rest of her group. They rode through the heart of Underholm, alive with thousands of Na'vir working to restore the once grand city, most little more than points of colored light in the dark beyond the reach of her glowing orb. It pained her to think how followers of Lucen wanted to wipe the Nimse out, not realizing the only reason they existed at all had been their attempting to refuse power to a maleficar. Oona couldn't truly fault the Na'vir for not destroying the man. As far as she knew, anyone other than a follower of Lucen had little chance of defeating demons.

Forgive me, but I am glad the priest failed.

ONE DAY AFTER ARRIVING HOME, OONA AND KITLYN MET WITH the advisors in the throne room.

The previous day went mostly to rest and catching up on a handful of minor decisions. Peace made for quite the leisurely existence, at least compared to managing a kingdom at war. They had ample periods of quiet time to themselves. Of course, the constant possibility of abruptly needing to make a life-or-death choice affecting their citizens tempered the idleness. Advisor Lanon told Oona she cared too deeply about people to ever know true happiness so long as she had power over others' lives. He did not mean it as an insult or to say she would be better off hardening her heart, more to reassure her the feelings were normal. She resigned herself to enjoying whatever moments of happiness she could find strong enough to momentarily obscure her worries. Alas, such moments would be few until they dispelled the curse stalking Kitlyn.

She endured a three-hour session of court which had mostly been rote matters of policy, law, or deciding on minor disputes between citizens. Barristers from the mercantile guild had become extremely frustrated dealing with Oona as they could no longer glibly lie to the monarch. Aodh had lost his ability to sense truth, allowing the smooth-talking guild representatives to manipulate him by stroking his ego. Lucen allowed Oona to see their deception, forcing them to make arguments for whatever they desired based on actual laws and/or logic. This, naturally, led to many entertaining episodes where someone attempted to argue a blatantly ludicrous point.

As court came to an end, Kitlyn bid the advisors to delay lunch for a private discussion. Once the throne room emptied of citizens and nobility, she explained to the advisors what they learned of Isilien as well as its connection to the curse.

Evie and Pim had evidently gotten into the sweets, as they ran around and around the upper galleries, their energy as boundless as the angled rays of late afternoon sunlight crisscrossing down the middle of the chamber. Childish laughter echoed off the walls, lifting Oona's spirits. She'd spent most of the past few hours drifting between quiet prayer, general anxiety, and mental gymnastics in an effort to discern what the key riddle could possibly mean. Once Kitlyn finished the summary and moved on to talking to the advisors about her intent to find and go to Isilien, Oona cast aside her daydreams and paid attention.

Both Balais and Alonna agreed the curse likely real if Tenebrea sent Queen Solana's spirit back with a warning. Lanon, as usual, took a more pragmatic view, not ready to blame anything more than coincidences and bad luck for the odd deaths among the Talomir line.

"What became of the monarch prior to Iastor?" Naldun lightly elbowed Beredwyn. "You were a boy then, yes?"

Beredwyn laughed.

"We have no idea... nor do we know if they came from the Talomir line." Oona slapped her hand on the throne's armrest. "Unless there are records hidden somewhere, our history does not exist."

The advisors exchanged glances of resigned helplessness. All understood full well the dearth of information pertaining to the past.

Would one of Tenebrea's priests be able to speak to the spirit of a long-dead king or queen? Or can they only find spirits of relatives?

"Isilien," muttered Beredwyn while stroking his beard. "I've honestly never heard of it before."

"Nor I." Advisor Lanon furrowed his brow. "And we have spent a great deal of time studying the layout of Evermoor."

"Oh, I am surprised." Oona rolled her eyes. "There is no information in our library. For a man who claimed to adore truth, Aodh certainly destroyed any he didn't like."

Beredwyn offered a conciliatory head bow. "Much of this happened before Aodh's time, else there would be some alive today who remember stories of what happened prior to King Iastor's reign."

"Please request of Spymaster Hinlor he send people in search of Isilien. They need not venture inside—likely, they could not. Credible information as to the whereabouts are their objective."

Oona sat up. "Also, I will write to King Lanas. Perhaps they have records."

The main door opened, drawing everyone's attention to a woman in an ordinary loam green dress, black bodice, and boots. Disheveled black hair gave her the look of someone who'd recently been riding at speed. While the queens had a policy of being open to speaking to any citizen, they generally did so during court or by request. Citizens, even the nobility, did not make a habit of barging in whenever they cared to.

Both guards by the door moved to intercept the woman, but after a brief exchange of quiet words, they let her pass.

Oona raised an eyebrow, whispering, "Who is she?"

"I do not know other than someone who has permission to be here, if the guards let her pass." Kitlyn watched the stranger approach, her expression part curiosity, part vigilance.

Lucen help me discern truth. Oona focused on the woman.

"My queens..." The woman bowed upon reaching the bottom of the dais. "I have returned from Gwynaben with news regarding Ulfaan Khera."

"You are one of Hinlor's agents?" asked Kitlyn.

"Yes, highness. I am Abria." The woman bowed again.

"Are you certain?" whispered Lanon to Beredwyn. "She looks like a common citizen."

Beredwyn raised an eyebrow. "That is rather the point, is it not? To be inconspicuous? Shall we have our spies all wear black uniforms, hooded cloaks?"

The other advisors, and Abria, chuckled.

"What news do you bring from Gwynaben?" Oona leaned forward in her seat.

A long, happy squee echoed from the upper gallery.

Oona glanced up at a delighted Evie chasing after a small flying creature. The child's reaction plus the buzzing of giant dragonfly wings hinted something more wondrous than a bird flew around inside the castle.

Everyone, even Abria the spy, watched the child run for a few seconds, smiling.

She is so happy she could melt any icy heart. Oona clenched her jaw. *Except Ruby's.*

"Highness... Ulfaan has gathered several individuals who are openly using magic. They have secured the use of a modest home in the city. I've observed him and at least three others meeting there."

"What manner of magic? Anything dangerous or suspicious?" Kitlyn shifted to lean back in her seat, bare toes peeking out from under the hem of her dress.

"What I saw appeared to be mostly small tricks. Making quills levitate or igniting candles. Nothing any rational person would consider an immediate danger. My impression is that he is teaching them."

"It seems he is starting a school of sorts." Balais tapped a finger to his chin. "We should watch this carefully. I am not suggesting we distrust magic, but we would be foolish to expect all who learn will be responsible."

"Did you determine the intent of their activity?" asked Kitlyn.

Abria pursed her lips. "At this point, it appears they are merely practicing and sharing knowledge. Only Ulfaan has demonstrated any ability beyond simple tricks. I was unable to locate documentation or materials suggesting any motives more sinister than practicing their arcane ways."

Oona looked at the advisors. "Please send a friendly message to Ulfaan with the intention of establishing contact and inquiring as to his intentions."

"Abria," said Kitlyn, "you have our thanks. Please pass along our gratitude to Hinlor."

The spy bowed again before taking her leave.

This mage is either as peaceful as he claims or quite talented at hiding his true goals. Oona closed her eyes. *Lucen watch over us.*

NINE DAYS LATER, OONA SAT AT THE DINING TABLE, STUDYING A piece of parchment bearing a largely indecipherable mess.

A lopsided circle with some dashes in it connected via a long, curved line to a sideways vee at the opposite end. Four other lines traced upward from the curve, closer to the circle. Evie stood next to her wearing an enormous smile of pride.

It took Oona a moment to figure out her sister had attempted to draw a faerie in flight. Thankfully, she didn't need to ask the girl what she drew. "It's a beautiful faerie."

Kitlyn, seated next to her, leaned over to look. "Yes, that is absolutely a faerie."

Evie bounced on her toes, clapping.

As the staff brought their mid-day meal in, Evie scrambled into her seat.

Oona thanked the kitchen maid before picking at the various slices of fruit, bread, and cheese on her plate. Pim joined them for lunch today. Oona and Kitlyn encouraged it, not wanting them to grow up believing they did anything wrong or improper by spending time together. The boy would, in all probability, end up working with his father in the kitchen as a cook. For now, though, she wanted both of them to enjoy childhood.

Frustration had again built up to the point it kept her awake at night. A letter arrived a day ago from King Lanas, stating they did not know the location of Isilien beyond it being somewhere in the southeastern moor. His writing spoke of 'many old Anthari ruins' littered around Evermoor, but almost no one knew the names they'd once been called.

Word from Spymaster Hinlor was equally unhelpful. He'd sent a few of his people off in search of Isilien. Admittedly, it had not yet been two full weeks, but they'd found nothing more than a weak rumor of 'someone in the vicinity of Kolbrin's Quay *might* know about it'. They'd thus far been unable to locate this individual. However, they did confirm the town Merix mentioned still existed.

Oona took out her frustrations on an apple slice.

Piper, seated across the table from her, looked up with a bit of a grin at the faint snarl she'd made.

She's from Lamneth... the city's at the southern coast of Evermoor, right next to the swamp. "Piper?"

"Hmm?"

"Have you ever heard of a place named Isilien? It's supposed to be in the moor."

Meredith glanced over at the younger girl, a note of surprise in her expression. Few in the castle knew Piper's true origin, and those who did easily forgot she hadn't been born in Lucernia. As far as it truly mattered, she may as well have been.

"I remember stories of Anthari ruins all over the moor... but no one really goes out there." Piper cringed, shaking her head. "Not only is it an inhospitable swamp, the deep moor is full of monsters and elder magic. It is always gloomy. Even in Lamneth, it's often raining or about to. We don't get much sun. They say if you go far enough into the swamp, it's permanently night."

"Sounds a little overstated." Kitlyn nibbled on a slice of cheese. "I'm sure it's dark and foreboding, but permanent night would require magic, would it not? The canopy couldn't be so thick as to entirely block the sun."

"Yes, I think you're right." Piper fidgeted her fork around her plate. "But some of the stories tell of the ruins having powerful enchantments to protect them from thieves. No one really knows, but I have heard people tell of the Anthari using magic like Kitlyn's. Elementalists wouldn't be able to make it dark all the time."

"Kethaba is a spiritcaller." Kitlyn gazed off into space, thinking. "If the Anthari had spiritcallers, which they certainly would have, it is possible they summoned ghostly ancestors as guardians. The presence of such beings could create darkness or feelings of fear strong enough to cause people to believe they see darkness."

Piper shivered. "Can we pretend it's only enormous snakes and insects the size of cats. They are less scary."

"Bugs as big as cats?" blurted Pim, gawking.

"If you go deep enough into the swamp, yes." Piper cringed.

"You don't remember anyone ever going out there in search of old ruins?" asked Oona.

"No. I'm sure it's happened, probably not during the war. Lamneth isn't in the moor, but it is fairly close. People in the city think the moor dwellers are either brave or crazy." Piper twirled a finger in a circle beside her head. "I know there are villages and little towns all over, but the people who live there can be as dangerous as the giant bugs. They wouldn't live way out in the swamp if they liked having people around."

Over the rest of the meal, Piper shared stories about the moor. Most sounded like the sorts of tales people told children of brave explorers hunting for valuables in long-abandoned places, fighting a monster or two, and either being chased back to civilization or discovering valuable relics.

Oona thought it far better to find the ruins for their potential value in knowledge of the past rather than hope for any physical valuables. Though the idea of exploring the lost remnants of ancient civilizations struck her as romantic and fun to daydream—or read— about, she had little interest in doing it for real. She would, however, absolutely venture into the swamp to stop a curse from harming Kitlyn.

FLAT ON HER BACK, OONA STARED UP AT THE CEILING OF HER bedchamber, mostly out of breath.

She lay with her arms out to either side, legs slightly apart, as if she'd fallen from a wagon and lacked the strength to move. Kitlyn's breath washed warm over her chest. Her wife curled up beside her, both of them glowing in the aftereffect of a spirited bit of romance doing the sorts of 'vile things' Ruby likely had nightmares about.

Another week passed and still, no one brought any useful information. Ulfaan replied to their letter to say he would be pleased to answer any questions, repeating his gratitude for them reversing the prior king's laws regarding magic. His 'stated intention' claimed he wanted to help those who had hidden their gifts either by teaching them or reuniting families separated by fear. It all sounded noble, though Oona's gift to detect lies did not work on written words.

His reply to their second letter asking if he'd ever heard of Isilien surprised them. Ulfaan wrote that he'd read of it in many books containing arcane knowledge. It had, according to him, been a prominent source of learning in the magical arts but its exact location had been lost to time. He didn't know where it was other than 'somewhere in Evermoor,' and cautioned them not to approach it recklessly if they somehow managed to locate it.

Kitlyn and Oona didn't quite agree on how to feel about him. Oona wanted to believe his intentions pure, while Kitlyn clung to some suspicion. Too little to act on, but she thought it best not to cast aside all doubts of his intentions yet. Oona admitted to being perhaps overly optimistic and naïve, so trusted her wife's decision to limit the information sent to the unknown mage. For all they truly understood, he still might have set all of this in motion.

As the surge of exhilaration and joy from making love to Kitlyn waned, Oona again found herself worrying about the curse and becoming vexed at the situation.

Despite lying about nude, she didn't worry too much about accidental intrusions unless it happened to be someone other than Evie, Piper, or Meredith. Merely being naked wouldn't bother their handmaidens who helped them bathe—or Evie who bathed with them. As long as no one walked in on them in the midst of *other* activities, Oona wouldn't die of embarrassment. In a short while, once the sweat and warmth disappeared, they'd crawl under the covers and try to sleep.

Nothing is going to happen if we keep waiting. "I think we should go to Evermoor."

Kitlyn sighed a blast of warm air over Oona's chest. "Are we to run off in the middle of the night again?"

"No." Oona chuckled. "It isn't one of *those* feelings. Just… I can't help but think if we start walking, Lucen will guide us."

"No horses?"

Oona tickled Kitlyn's side, making her squeal. "You are silly. I don't mean literal walking. We can't expect the gods to bring us everything we need on a golden platter. They set it on the table at the other end of the room. We can at least get up and go to it."

"I see." Kitlyn traced her fingernails over Oona's stomach.

"Eep!" Oona curled up, grabbing the hand. "I'm ticklish!"

Kitlyn wagged her eyebrows. "Why else would I tickle you?"

Fingernails lightly scraped Oona's side, above her hip. Again, she squealed—then retaliated. Minutes later, they collapsed on the bed facing each other, out of breath for the second time that night.

"What salacious rumors do you think the staff will be spreading after hearing us?" whispered Oona.

"I am sure they will not think such naughty things due to the amount of laughing."

Oona cracked up, burying her face in the pillow to quiet herself, lest the entire castle staff think a pair of giddy children sat on the throne.

"I think the people enjoy how happy you are. Aodh was far too angry and dour."

"How happy *we* are." Oona scooted closer and rested her head on Kitlyn's shoulder. "I would be so much happier if I could stop worrying about you."

Kitlyn stroked Oona's hair. "You will always worry about me. We sit on the throne."

"Fair enough, but we can manage the ordinary risk of death based on our actions. This damnable curse does not care how well or poorly we govern." Oona huffed. "I feel we should go to Evermoor soon. The gods will lead us where we need to be."

"All right. We shall visit Kethaba." Kitlyn yawned. "If we are done waiting for our spies to report, we may as well journey to seek her wisdom."

"What of Omun? Or the Stone?"

"I've already asked." Kitlyn grumbled. "A name given to a place means nothing to the Stone. I'd have to picture it in my mind so vividly as can only come from having been there. Omun rests. I do not think this worthy enough to disturb him."

"Let us make preparations tomorrow and set off in a day or two."

Kitlyn sighed. "As much as I would prefer we slip off on our own, it is likely reckless for us to travel by ourselves."

"Not so reckless. In our armor, we blend in. No one expects the queens to travel without soldiers, though I do believe people are coming to understand we are not terrified of being seen in commoner's clothing. The armor may not be as effective a disguise for much longer."

"What have we to hide from?" Kitlyn sat up to grab the bedding, pulling the sheets and blankets over them before snuggling close again. "People in both kingdoms seem to like us."

"Some nobles might want to arrange an accident. And what of bears?"

"Bears?"

"Yes, bears." Oona mimicked a growl that made Kitlyn snicker. "Large, furry, claws. They'd make a snack of us. And bandits, too."

"Bringing soldiers with us might increase the chances of bad things happening, since it would be obvious someone important is traveling. Bears, and other animals tend to leave me alone. I think they sense my link to the Alderswood."

"I don't want others to get hurt for me wanting to go traipse around Evermoor after some curse." Oona kissed Kitlyn on the forehead.

"What happens to Lucernia if we disappear? Do you think the nobility will select a new king or usher in another twenty years of war over the throne?"

Oona fake pouted. "It is quite unlikely they will all agree on which one of them should be king or queen."

"Settled then, we will ask a small group of volunteers to accompany us. We shouldn't be reckless. After all, we're adults now." Kitlyn made a silly face and tickled Oona on the stomach again.

SPIRIT WHISPERS

KITLYN

Six days later, Kitlyn and Oona crossed the Arch of the Ancients into Evermoor.

The same six soldiers who'd accompanied them to Underholm volunteered to escort them again, though none expected such fine food and lodgings this time, Beowyn joking they had 'earned' a little rough camping to balance the scales of luxury.

Kitlyn missed the freedom of being able to run off on her own with Oona whenever they wanted, even though neither of them ever truly had it. *What would have happened if Fauhurst won and I'd run away?* Most likely, Aodh would have been furious. If he discovered it had been Fauhurst's incessant abuse that drove her off, he'd likely have put the man to death—conveniently forgetting his part in her being a servant. Also, Fauhurst's continued attempts to get her kicked out of the castle continually failing—which she now knew had to be due to her being the true princess—frustrated him to the point of madness and worsened his treatment of her.

Oona hadn't even been allowed to visit the merchant district of Cimril, much less travel freely out into the countryside. They'd both essentially been trapped in the castle. The 'freedom' she and Oona enjoyed for a mere few days after running away took a terrifying turn when they'd been abducted by Evermoor spies. Fortunately, they'd both survived—barely.

I nearly drowned in a river and Oona was almost murdered.

To take her mind off the bad memories, Kitlyn daydreamed about the two weeks they'd spent at the castle between their return from Underholm and departing on this journey. She already missed the quiet time of being a family with Oona and Evie, and looked forward to returning. Evie wanted to come along, mildly upset at the idea of being apart from them for potentially months. Kitlyn almost caved in and suggested they bring Evie at least as far as Kethaba's village, leaving her there to visit until they returned.

Under no circumstances did she want to bring a six-year-old into the moor. Even if Piper's stories about monsters and dangerous old magic turned out to be simple peasant folklore, a swamp held all manner of mundane threats. Also, if something truly awful happened and they never returned, Evie would be stuck in the village of Ilde Brae—which might not be a bad thing. If nothing else, being there protected her from any nobles trying to keep her off the throne.

For similar reasons—not wanting to endanger them—they'd asked Piper and Meredith to remain at the castle. With the queens elsewhere, their handmaidens had essentially become residents of the castle with no official responsibilities, though Piper would likely spend much of her time keeping Evie company.

Despite her fondness for quiet days in the castle, venturing out into Evermoor excited her. Maybe she hadn't quite become old enough to sit still like a boring old queen and sip tea all day.

May as well have some adventure while I'm young… before the curse kills me, anyway.

She looked over the group of soldiers, again debating if bringing them had been wise. A group of eight required additional effort and resources, plus attracted more attention than a pair of cloaked figures riding together. Both queens going out and about, rather than staying safe in the castle, could be considered foolish. Aodh certainly lived in perpetual fear, but then again, the man knew he'd turned on Lucen and no longer had any hope of divine protection. In fact, he likely feared the gods' wrath, never mind the same assassins coming after 'the princess' would have gladly killed him, too.

Threats are fairly low. The war is over. Even the people who hate me for being in love with a woman have fallen quiet. Relations with Ondar are stable. We're friendlier with Evermoor than we've been in decades, even before the war.

She squirmed in the saddle, uncomfortable at having an entire nation think of her as saving their lives, even if it had been true. Kitlyn didn't believe she deserved praise considering her father put everyone in danger in the first place. It wasn't as though some titanic monster rose up from the depths of antiquity to destroy the people. No one even hinted at blaming her for what he'd done. She hadn't even been born until four years *after* he stole the Heart, condemning the people of Evermoor to a slow, withering death. Given the circumstances of her life, she'd rebelled against him much sooner than any reasonable person could have expected her to.

Would I have done the same thing if I grew up as a princess? Kitlyn shook her head, throwing the idea out of her mind. Oona said a person could do nothing but drive themselves to madness dwelling on all the ways a life could be different. It didn't matter at all how Princess Kitlyn would have reacted because she didn't exist.

They spent four days riding and camping their way to Ilde Brae.

Rather than take the road around in a long detour, they diverted north along the plains west of the Faunhollow River. Kitlyn much preferred to observe the river while not being in it, even if the water remained fairly calm this far south. She'd plunged into it some distance north of Ilde Brae and plunged over the waterfall. Thankfully, she didn't remember much of it, only being blasted off the bridge, landing in the water, and later waking up in Kethaba's hut. The old woman told her she'd actually started to die, claiming to have herself gone into the spirit world to grab Kitlyn's ghost and bring her back from 'the path.'

Obviously, she hadn't *fully* died. Kethaba did not resurrect her, merely healed her body to prevent death, then gone to inform her she could return. Ever since, she regarded the old one as her grandmother.

The energy core of magic inside her chest thrummed. She

suspected her happiness at visiting Kethaba somehow let the old one know of their approach, a notion proved true when they arrived in the village and discovered the elder had prepared enough dinner for their entire group.

As they did last time they visited, Kitlyn and Oona would sleep inside the house while the soldiers made camp in the woods behind it. Little Alin, Kethaba's seven-year-old grandson, practically bounced off the walls, happy to see them. The entire time they ate, the boy kept running back and forth to show them various rocks, sticks, coins, and other baubles he'd found—and assumed magical, making up stories to explain each one.

After dinner, Kitlyn and Oona felt like a pair of ordinary young women visiting their grandmother, helping out with cleaning the dishes and then simply spending time and talking. Once Alin went to sleep in the two-bed alcove off the side of the hut, Kitlyn decided to bring up the serious questions. Kethaba appeared to sense it coming, bid her wait a moment, and put a kettle over the fire.

Soon, they gathered around the little table, staring into steam wafting up from wooden bowls of tea.

"We're trying to find a place called Isilien. Have you heard of it?" asked Kitlyn.

"The name is known to me." Kethaba stirred honey into her tea. "It is a ruin somewhere in the southeast, quite deep in the swampy moor. Not so much sun down there."

Kitlyn thought of Piper. The pale girl fit in unnoticed in Lucernia. Most who lived in the northern two-thirds of Evermoor had brown skin, a fact Aodh had used to claim them demonic. Those from the dense moors tended to be fair-skinned, which allowed Piper not to stand out as an obvious foreigner, leading to her being selected as a spy.

We are fortunate the girl has a big heart and questioned the lies she'd been told about Oona.

"Can you help us find it?" asked Oona, before explaining about the curse and the warning from Solana's ghost.

"Hmm." Kethaba leaned close, squinting at Kitlyn. "I do not sense a curse on her."

Oona glanced back and forth between them. "Is it possible a curse exists you cannot detect?"

Kethaba twirled her hand dismissively. "Anything is *possible*, dear. However, I find it unlikely."

"So there is no curse?" Kitlyn gripped the sides of her seat, lightheaded from conflicting emotions.

The old one's right eye widened, left eye shrinking to a slit. "Not necessarily. Spirits are seldom prone to warning of curses when no curse exists. This curse is simply not on *you*."

Oona started to gasp, but quieted at Kethaba raising a hand.

"Before you rejoice, let me finish."

"Sorry," whispered Oona.

Kitlyn took her hand, unsure exactly who comforted who.

Kethaba rose from her seat and ambled across the room to a shelf containing various jars, bottles, bowls, and small boxes. "Curses are as varied as anything else in the world. They can be placed on people, families, places... items."

"Like crowns?" asked Oona.

The absence of metal sitting atop her head made Kitlyn feel lighter—and safer.

Pottery clinked and clattered as the old one rummaged the shelf. "Yes, perhaps. In this case, however, I believe the curse does not rest upon any person or even family line."

"Every other Talomir to sit on the throne has died early. Only Lady Avalina survived to old age... and she refused the crown." Oona scratched her head. "I don't understand. How could the curse not be on the Talomir line?"

Kethaba turned to face them, smiling, a bundle of small jars and candles in her arms. "The curse is most likely on the castle. Or perhaps even Cimril. Did this Avalina remain in the city?"

"No, she moved far off to the countryside." Kitlyn slouched. "Do you think it matters she did not become queen? Would the curse leave me alone if I ruled from some other city?"

"Ehh..." Kethaba returned to the table, bending forward to set all the stuff she'd collected from the shelf down before sitting. "I do not know enough to say. What of past kings before the Talomirs?"

Oona and Kitlyn explained for the seeming hundredth time about the lack of history in the library while Kethaba arranged candles, small piles of grey powder, glass marbles in varying colors, several feathers, pieces of small creatures, and three bronze coins on the table in front of her.

"Hmm. Regrettable." Flames sprang up on the candle wicks as Kethaba waved her hand over them. "Your belief this curse is on Kitlyn's family is based on you not knowing anything about rulers who came before. Curses on family lines mark their victims. There is no such mark on Kitlyn or I would have brought it up the first time we met."

I've not reached seventeen years, yet twice I've come close to Tenebrea's arms, and twice magic has spared me. Is the curse responsible? "Perhaps I slipped free of the curse by nearly drowning?" Kitlyn held a hand to the left side of her neck. "Or when the assassin nearly slit my throat."

Oona squeaked.

"Hmm." Kethaba pondered. "Possible, but I believe the curse would still have left a residue on you."

Kitlyn leaned against Oona, exhaling in relief. Three people in the entire world existed who she trusted implicitly: Oona, Beredwyn, and Kethaba. If the old one said the curse didn't affect her family line, she believed her. However, Solana's ghost felt too genuine to disregard as a trick. Ulfaan's responses to their letters further muddied the situation. While he might advise them against going to Isilien even though he wanted them to, such subtlety of manipulation didn't fit a man who'd teleported right out of the throne room. He'd obviously meant to make a statement by doing so, but what?

Still, such a display of magic conveyed a pronounced *lack* of subtlety. If he'd eagerly suggested they go find Isilien, it would've made him seem involved. But if he wasn't involved, he wouldn't have any reason to care what Kitlyn thought of his motivations.

Argh!

"Can you tell if the spirit who came to visit me was really my mother?" asked Kitlyn. "Or are the Glimmering Grove and Tenebrea's realm too different?"

"I may be able to determine. Be still for a moment and allow me to concentrate." Kethaba snapped her fingers, setting fire to a bowl of powders in front of her.

Glowing fumes wafted up into her face. In seconds, her eyes glazed over, losing focus on the world in front of her. The fluttery wisps of smoke rising up from each candle straightened to thin trails. Darkness swam into the edges of the hut, making it difficult to see anything more than six feet away from the table. Ghostly energy gathered in lazy orbiting strands, encircling them. A powerful sense of otherworldly energy settled over the room.

Oona shivered.

Kitlyn sat still, afraid to move the slightest bit lest she disturb the goings-on.

Minutes passed. Kitlyn kept still, watching the luminous white ribbons circling them. Kethaba occasionally muttered or whispered too low to make out words. She leaned side to side, tilting her head back and forth.

At a white light moving to her left, Kitlyn jumped, twisting to look at the faint image of Solana. Her mother's apparition remained visible only long enough to nod once before fading away. Kitlyn stared, captivated, into the darkness where the ghost had been.

"You will need a key," said Kethaba.

Kitlyn almost leapt out of her seat at the sudden break in the silence.

Oona emitted a startled, "Eep!"

"Yes," whispered Kitlyn. "The Na'vir archivist mentioned a key but it's a riddle. We don't know whether the key is actually a key, a weapon, something else, or even where to begin looking."

Kethaba opened her eyes, both completely white and faintly glowing. "Isilien is far older than I imagined possible."

Oona squeezed Kitlyn's hand, seemingly too nervous to breathe.

"Key..." Kethaba's eyes flared brighter for an instant. "I feel you will not need to search for it."

"I don't understand," said Kitlyn. "How can we find something we don't even look for?"

A smile formed on the old one's lips. "When Isilien is ready to welcome you, it will send you the key." She shuddered, grimacing and twitching for a few seconds before going still again. "The key will appear to you only for a fleeting moment, lost forever if you do not seize it fast and guard it well."

"How will we know what the key is when we find it?" Oona leaned away from a drifting spectral trail gliding near her head. "Is it an actual key? A dagger? Something else?"

Kethaba swooned side to side. "Torjin... the key is there."

Ice blue pupils reappeared in the old one's eyes as the eerie spirit light faded. She slumped forward, elbows resting on the table. The spectral whorls vanished. Kitlyn and Oona leapt from their chairs, rushing around to check on her.

"I am fine, dears. Merely tired."

The darkness saturating the hut faded away, receding like black smoke being drawn out through the walls.

Kitlyn squeezed her shoulder. "My mother's spirit appeared. She nodded to me. I think she wanted to tell me she really visited."

"Yes," rasped Kethaba.

Oona fetched a cup of water for her.

"Thank you, dear." Kethaba drank most of it in one swig, set the cup on the table, then extinguished the candles with a stare. "A curse does threaten you so long as you rule over Lucernia."

A chilly swirl circled Kitlyn's heart. "Then we must find a way to dispel it."

"You said Torjin... who is that?" Oona slipped back into her seat.

Kethaba touched two fingers to her forehead. "I believe it is a where, not a who, though the name is unfamiliar to me. It must be relatively new, most likely a fort built during the war or small village."

"If it is in the moor, I doubt it's a fort." Kitlyn offered a wan smile. "There would be no need to establish defensive fortifications so far in from the border. The former king's army never crossed the Churning Deep."

"Yes, child." Kethaba shifted her jaw around in thought. "I feel the spirits tried to tell me it is in the moor. Isilien, is quite ancient. As old as the Alderswood. Seek the Ebon Mire."

"Sounds lovely," whispered Oona.

"It is the thickest part of the moor. You will only be able to ride as far as Kolbrin's Quay. To venture any deeper will require boats." Kethaba leaned back, stretching.

Kitlyn exchanged a glance with Oona at the name 'Kolbrin's Quay.'

Our spies found rumors of someone supposedly in that town who might be able to find Isilien. Merix said it's the closest known location to Isilien. Kethaba talking about it as well has to mean something.

Kethaba stood. "I am drained and must sleep. Tomorrow, we will have time to discuss more. I do hope you'll be able to visit awhile."

No real rush… might as well. "I think we can —"

"We have to go." Oona grabbed Kitlyn's arm, her face pale, eyes wide.

"Demon?" asked Kitlyn.

Oona bit her lip, gazing around as if listening for someone to whisper in her ear. "No. At least, I don't think so. It's extremely important we hurry."

"Okay. Should we race off without our escort?" Kitlyn pointed a thumb over her shoulder at the window.

"I…" Oona shook her head. "I think we can sleep here, but we need to leave early and ride fast."

Kethaba glanced at her, shrugged, and scratched her side. "If her god's givin' her a nudge, you might as well listen to him. Or her."

Oona's grimace said she didn't know which god sent the message.

"We will definitely return to have a longer visit as soon as we are able." Kitlyn walked to the door. "Back in a moment. Going to tell Rakden we need to leave early in the morning."

Oona went over to the second bed, normally Alin's, the same one Kitlyn awoke in after the elder fished her out of the water.

KOLBRIN'S QUAY

OONA

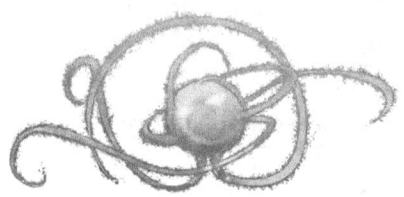

The gods woke Oona early the following morning.

She rarely sprang out of bed on her own so easily before the sun finished rising. Kethaba and Alin remained asleep. Not wanting to disturb them, she nudged Kitlyn awake, making as little noise as possible. After getting dressed, they crept outside to the soldiers' camp, surprised to find them already packed up.

They rode south from Ilde Brae following the Faunhollow River. The bridge east of Dorwick had been repaired, allowing them to cross to the eastern side a day sooner than taking the bridge on the road leading from the Arch of the Ancients to Ivendar. Driven by her inexplicable sense of urgency, they pushed the horses a little, riding in ten-hour stints rather than eight. Cloud didn't seem to mind the pace. Apples put up with it, though appeared to be grumbling.

Not entirely sure where to go, they kept following the river south since Kitlyn remembered the maps, and knew this route would take them to Lamneth. Certainly, someone in such a large city would be able to direct them to Kolbrin's Quay.

A few hours into their third day of riding, they neared the town of Thiobel, which mostly sat on the opposite (west) side of the Faunhollow. Multiple root bridges spanned the river, none of which appeared large enough for horses or wagons to cross. Not far from the town, they encountered two young men tending a large herd of goats who pointed them back to a path—more a horse trail than a road—leading east from Thiobel into the Gloamwake Forest. According to them, the trail went straight to Kolbrin's Quay.

Oona sensed no deceit on them, so suggested they take the route as it would be much faster than going all the way south to Lamneth and back up. The forest gave off an ancient, primeval energy that put Oona on edge the instant she looked into its depths. Trees unlike any she'd seen in Lucernia or anywhere else in Evermoor stood off the ground on legs of ropey, gnarled roots twisted together into warped trunks of irregular width, as if some mad old god made them by wringing cords of clay together haphazardly. Some trees had so much open air between the base of their trunks and the ground, a person could crawl in. Leaves dark to the point of appearing black formed a dense canopy overhead.

Hissing, bird calls, and a constant susurrus of various insect noises emanated from every direction. Violet lichen clung to the sides of some trees. The soil here looked like the ashy muck left over after throwing water on a campfire. A heavy odor somewhere between outhouse and flowers tainted every breath.

Maybe it really does always appear to be night in the deepest parts of the moor.

The trail forced them to ride single file due to thick vegetation on both sides. Soon after entering the woods, the horses occasionally balked when the ground they tried to step on proved to be squishy grey-black mud rather than dirt. Cloud neighed in protest each time he feared getting too dirty. Apples trudged into the muck, ears flat, thoroughly unimpressed with the moor.

Oona lurched forward when Cloud stopped short for the umpteenth time, hugging him around the neck to stop herself from flying headfirst to the ground. "Am I imagining things or does this mud smell like..."

"An outhouse," said Beowyn. "And yes, highness. It does."

"It's not though," called Imoa, behind them. "We're smelling dead moss and plants rotting."

"Ugh," said Kitlyn. "No wonder people in Evermoor aren't terribly concerned about clothing. Easier to wash this gunk off skin than get it out of fabric."

The soldiers laughed.

Oona stared into the gloomy, wet forest around them, wondering what kind of people lived there. Would they see the 'naked savages' she'd been erroneously taught to believe occupied all of Evermoor? Piper's stories of Lamneth sounded quite normal, but the city also didn't stand in the middle of the swamp.

A sense someone would die if they took too long still gnawed at her, neither having weakened nor grown more intense since it started days ago in Kethaba's hut. It came out of nowhere as soon as the old one suggested they visit for a while, proof enough to Oona the gods sent her a message.

Before, it felt like Lucen stood beside her pointing at Shimmerbrook and prodding her to hurry up and stop the demon. Her present need to reach Kolbrin's Quay as fast as possible seemed more pleading in nature than demanding. She half wanted to describe the feeling as 'please hurry or you'll be really sad.' From this, she inferred no demon would be involved. The message might have come from Orien, who by all accounts had a huge heart and was considered quite sensitive and loving. It might also be Tenebrea or even Navissa, as their followers often described them as quiet. Navissa *could* become loud and wrathful if angered, but otherwise, tended to be subtle.

The definite sense someone would die if she took too long made her doubt the message came from Tenebrea. Unless... she didn't think the goddess decided when people died, simply escorted spirits after. Could she sense when outside forces conspired to kill someone before their designated time? Did people even have designated times? *She warned us of Fauhurst's treachery.*

Official temple doctrine regarding Tenebrea's role as the Goddess of Death didn't make it terribly clear on that point. If any of the gods would know when a person was about to die, it ought to be her. Why would Tenebrea need to ask a mortal to interfere to prevent a death she objected to? It would imply she couldn't prevent or cause death directly. Or maybe she could, but direct action from the gods might set off some worse consequence.

She is *Lucen's daughter. Maybe she has to ask permission.*

Oona smirked, remembering her arguments with Aodh about going shopping.

The worst part of sensing impending death came from not knowing who would die. It could be the curse acting on Kitlyn as easily as some random stranger experiencing grave misfortune. She'd spent at least an hour each time they'd camped after leaving Kethaba's hut praying to thank the gods for their help. Trusting them, she hadn't asked for anything, believing they already gave her the necessary aid.

Beowyn, riding at the front of their group, waved an arm over his head. "Stay to the trail. The mud's getting soupy. If it thins much more, we'll need to get off and let the horses walk."

"If it thins much more, we'll need a boat," called Imoa.

The soldiers chuckled.

They continued moving in single file, weaving around the bizarre trees. Small blue-purple lizards darted up the trunks away from their approach, black tongues flicking. Eventually, patches of water appeared at varying distances off the trail, most with reeds or odd flowers sticking up out of them. An occasional small splash revealed the existence of fish or perhaps snakes eating fish.

The deeper they traveled, the marshier the outlying areas became. As Beowyn predicted, they ended up dismounting and walking at the three-hour mark. Oona's boots sank into the trail up to her ankles on the most solid areas. Missteps swallowed her leg to the knee. The horses didn't appear to enjoy the trip but only made noises of displeasure. Even Cloud had given up whimpering.

A little over four hours after entering Gloamwake Forest, the fragrance of cooking food and burning lamp oil occasionally slipped past the overpowering stench of rot rising from the mud. Oona's skin crawled at the idea of having such foul-scented muck on her boots. If not for her need to protect Kitlyn and the gods' message pulling her forward, she'd have had serious second thoughts about continuing.

Kitlyn didn't seem to mind at all. She'd obviously been through worse messes in her life as a castle servant. The poor girl had even 'slipped' into the moat once or twice. Oona had no doubt someone pushed her, but Kitlyn either didn't know who did it or preferred not to have anyone punished for her sake. Considering every garderobe in the castle emptied into the moat, she thought it too horrid to count as a mere prank.

Another hour or so later, they reached the edge of an odd town. An interwoven network of brackish waterways ran like narrow streets throughout the settlement, dividing it into dozens of separate islands. Some amounted to little more than mud piles five or six feet across, while the larger ones supported small shops or private homes. Wooden walkways and platforms built on poles similar to river docks connected occupied islands. Some had railings, most didn't. About a third of the town's buildings wrapped around the trunks of huge trees, likely for increased solidity against the squishy ground.

The trail they'd been following led to a huge mushroom-shaped island upon which stood a reasonably sized inn. Three horses sheltered under an awning partially covering an attached horse pen on the near side of the building. From the looks of the town beyond the inn, horses would have a near impossible time navigating the narrow wooden walkways.

People here appeared normal if a bit dirty—definitely not primitive tribal savages. Despite the drab coloration of their clothing, they wouldn't seem too out of place in most other cities except for not a single woman in sight wearing a dress. Every adult had some variation of breeches plus shirts or tunics. The children wore simple knee-length tunics, no shoes, and a good deal of mud.

Oona gazed around at the dense foliage, rickety wooden bridges, uncountable number of flying bugs, and general filthiness of everything. Even the 'clean' people here resembled the beggars in Cimril, though appeared much happier.

Kitlyn headed for the inn. Oona followed. They led the horses into the penned area, where Oona spent a while brushing and cleaning the mud from Cloud's legs. Kitlyn gave Apples a brushing as well, bribing him with an apple or two for putting up with the swamp. The soldiers also tended to their horses. Yerbin went inside the inn, returning a short while later carrying enough feed for all the animals.

After making sure the horses were comfortable, fed, and had water, Kitlyn and Oona headed around the building and went inside. Less than a dozen people seated at a scattering of small, round tables glanced at them briefly, then went back to their food, drinks, or conversation. Kitlyn approached the inn's proprietor, a fortyish man with a few extra pounds. His copious mustache looked like his sideburns decided to meet for a tryst under his nose. The grey skin around the man's empty left eye socket had withered, pockmarked with tiny pits. Other than the small dead area of his face, he appeared normal and relatively pleased to see new people arrive.

Somehow, Kitlyn managed to show no outward reaction to his nasty scar while talking to him and arranging board for their horses.

Oona, however, couldn't help but stare as she walked up to the counter, wondering if the gift Orien gave her might help lessen the disfigurement.

"… probably two to four days for the horses. I'm not sure how long we will need rooms," said Kitlyn.

The innkeeper shifted his eye toward Oona. "Doom needle."

"Sorry?" Kitlyn blinked.

He indicated Oona with a nod. "Your friend there's wondering what happened to my eye. Got stung by a doom needle."

"How long ago?" asked Oona.

"Least ten years by now."

"Oh. I'm sorry. I didn't mean to make you uncomfortable." Oona clasped her hands in front of herself. "Orien has bestowed a healing gift upon me, but such an old injury is…"

"Ahh, you lot are from Lucernia." The innkeeper chuckled. "Wondered how long it would take before we got some travelers in so far from the border. Don't often have outsiders here in the moor. What brings you to Kolbrin's Quay?"

Kitlyn set a silver crescent coin on the counter. "Is this enough to cover the care of our horses?"

"Aye, more than. Thank ya, lass." He picked up the coin.

"We're looking for a place called Isilien." Oona spoke loud enough to be overheard by everyone in the room.

"Huh... never heard of it. If you're planning to go any deeper into the moor than this town, you should find a local willing to guide you so you don't end up like this." He pointed at his missing eye.

"What *is* a doom needle?" asked Kitlyn.

"Ya know what a wasp is?"

They both nodded.

"Picture a wasp the size of a rabbit. Damn thing came from nowhere. Sunk its stinger straight into my eyeball. Felt like getting stabbed by a red-hot icepick. Only good thing is, I didn't feel it for long. Blacked right out. Woke up a couple days later."

The soldiers groaned, cringed, or gasped.

Oona shuddered.

"Why did it attack you?" Kitlyn squirmed at the thought.

"Don't rightly know. Best guess, something else ticked it off and got away. Left the spirits-forsaken thing in a mood and it came after me for being there. Ya shouldn't see any of them devils unless you head into the moor. They don't usually come around town."

Imoa whispered, "Helmets."

"Don't think it'd help much," said Beowyn. "Wasp that size'd have a stinger at least three inches. No problem goin' through an eye slit."

She and Beowyn got into a whispered debate as to whether or not the wasp deliberately aimed for the man's eye or simply happened to hit it.

Kitlyn leaned against Oona. "Do we have time to look around here?"

The urgency didn't flare up, so she nodded. "I think so, yes. It feels as if we still have time."

After finalizing arrangements with the innkeeper, Kitlyn bid the soldiers to pair up and make their way around Kolbrin's Quay, asking everyone they found about Isilien, planning to meet back here by nightfall. She and Oona headed off together as well. Rakden protested, but Kitlyn insisted so they had four pairs to search town and could cover all of it in the hours remaining before sunset. Oona reassured him by promising to send up a brilliant blast of light if they encountered any trouble.

Kolbrin's Quay spread out from the 'mushroom island' in the general shape of a tree, expanding wider the deeper it went into the moor. Oona and Kitlyn headed right up the middle, walking across the often bouncy wooden plankways connecting islands. Opaque dark water came up to within a foot or so of the bridges. Every time a loud buzz went by, Oona ducked, frightened it might be a giant wasp hunting for eyeballs.

They wandered from door to door, visiting numerous homes and a few shops, asking everyone they met if they knew of a place called Isilien. The people seemed—mostly—friendly enough, but none offered any useful information. Once they neared the outer edge of Kolbrin's Quay, they observed dozens of small boats moored to tiny docks or tied directly to the bridges anywhere the waterways offered an unobstructed pathway out to the moor. The largest ones looked capable of holding four people while most were one or two-person affairs.

"This place smells like moldy shoes and fish," muttered Kitlyn.

"I'm trying not to breathe." Oona chuckled. "When we get back to dry land, I intend to spend at least an hour in a bathtub."

Six unhelpful small dwellings later, they traversed a treacherous walkway not only lacking railings, but the wood had become slick from some manner of mold or moss. Both Oona and Kitlyn nearly slipped into the water multiple times while making their way across the fifty-foot bridge.

A little boy watching them from another walkway yelled, "Don' gotta be scared. It ain't too deep."

It's not drowning I'm afraid of, it's smelling like rotting corpse for the next month. Oona shivered.

Clinging to each other for balance, they carefully made their way to solid ground in front of a leatherworker's shop, or so she assumed based on pelts of unrecognized furry animals hanging from the porch awning. Three had white fur with black stripes, four plain brown, and two dark blue spotted in white.

Kitlyn pushed the door—rather a large leather curtain—aside

and stepped into the shop. Oona coughed at the overwhelming smell of new leather. The humble store didn't have much of a display, only a few sets of thigh-high boots and leather tunics—more waterproof clothing than armor.

An older man with long, grey hair sat at a worktable covered in various tools, busily stitching flaps of leather into what would likely become a large boot.

"Hello," said Kitlyn.

The man jumped and spun to look at them. "Ach! Didn't hear you come in."

"Sorry. We didn't mean to surprise you." Oona offered an apologetic smile.

"Oh, that's some fine workmanship." He set his needle down, stood, and leaned closer to examine their armor. "This is from the west, isn't it? Ya find it on the dead? Wait, no. Ya didn't. Fits too well. This was made for ya. You *from* the west?"

"Yes, we are," said Kitlyn. "We don't mean to take up too much of your time. Have you ever heard of a place called Isilien?"

"Hmm." The leatherworker sat in his chair again, rubbing his chin. "Doesn't really sound familiar, but I don't pay much attention to anything outside my shop. There's a man comes in here every few weeks, name o' Aztian. He's gotta go pretty deep into the moor to get some of those pelts he brings in for trade. If there'd be anyone around here who'd know where to find the place you're looking for, it'd be him."

A strong surge of anxiety came out of nowhere, churning butterflies in Oona's stomach. She sucked in a gasp, pressing a hand to her gut. "W-we can't wait for him that long. Do you know where we could find him?"

Kitlyn grasped her arm, giving her an 'are you okay?' glance.

"Ehh, if he's anywhere other than out hunting," said the man, "he'd be in a little village bit southeast of here. Locals call it Torjin, but no one outside o' Kolbrin's Quay'd know it by name."

"Torjin!" whispered Oona.

Kitlyn went wide-eyed. "Where is this place?"

"Gonna need a boat ta get there. It's not *too* far. Head south from the Quay, you'll eventually see a big ol' tree covered in bright green lichen. Go to its left and follow the water. This whole area's basically a bunch of tiny rivers running between little islands, least until ya hit the Ebon Mire. Then it's all marsh, only a handful of spots with anything close to solid ground. If you stop seeing rivulets between mounds of dirt, ya gone too far. Anyway, once ya go left past the green tree, think of it as being on a road made outta water. Follow its path, don't take no turns, and you'll go right to Torjin."

"How long does it take to get there from here?" asked Oona.

"Three hours maybe." He shrugged. "Depends on how fast ya paddle or pole."

The alarm in Oona's gut settled to the same nudge haunting her since they left Kethaba's. She weighed the options of leaving right away or waiting for sunrise to avoid going into the moor at night. Neither thought changed the strength of the pull.

"It should be fine if we leave in the morning. It's almost dark now." Oona rubbed her stomach, waiting a moment to see if anything changed. When nothing did, she nodded.

"You have our thanks." Kitlyn bowed to the leatherworker. "If Aztian visits you before morning, will you please ask him to find us at the inn?"

"I will." He smiled. "You two seem a little young to go running off into the moor. If I were you, I'd not go past Torjin unless you can convince Aztian to join you as a guide. Otherwise, you'll probably never come back out."

"Yes, that is our plan." Oona managed a weak smile. "Finding a guide."

They exchanged a polite farewell with the man and left the shop. Navigating the wooden walkways connecting the various islands of Kolbrin's Quay at twilight proved unnerving. To avoid going for a swim, they crept across town at a tedious pace, arriving at the inn after dark.

Yerbin and Donal teased them a little for being late.

Over a dinner of fish, bread, and some manner of green leafy vegetable, they explained what they'd learned from the leatherworker about the village of Torjin. Imoa and Danos encountered a fisherman who also knew Aztian and mentioned the same village. Yerbin and Beowyn spent a while talking to an old woman who claimed Isilien belonged to 'the old ones' and should not be disturbed.

Oona assumed she meant Anthari, so she didn't worry too much about disturbing anything. They had no intention to loot the place, merely find... whatever Queen Solana's ghost sent them to find. Exactly what they needed to do upon reaching Isilien remained a mystery. The spirit said only to go beyond the gates. Presumably, the answer to the curse would be obvious enough for them to discover or work out on their own once inside.

During the course of dinner, she caught snippets of conversation from other tables. Those having meals here seemed to either live alone or be travelers who didn't reside in Kolbrin's Quay. Many spoke of seeing strange monsters and odd creatures, often in a frightened or complaining tone.

An older woman who'd taken over managing the place at night from the large-mustached man came by to refill everyone's drinks. Oona and Kitlyn restricted themselves to water, avoiding ale and wine so they could wake early.

"Lots of stories going around." Rakden held up his cup for the woman to pour into. "Is it as bad out there as it sounds?"

"Eh, they ought'a be happy," said the woman. "This is how things used ta be before the war. Life from the Alderswood isn't only for us humans."

"You had strange creatures around as recently as twenty years ago?" Kitlyn raised both eyebrows.

"Some, yes. There's more since. An' they kept mostly to the deep woods and the moor. You lot are from Lucernia, yes?"

Kitlyn and Oona nodded.

"Must be strange to you seeing such things." She laughed.

"We're starting to." Oona held up her cup. "Not sure where they are coming from."

The woman poured water into it. "The world is about due for a time of healing, I think. My father says magic's like water. Comes in and goes out on tides. Only, takes thousands of years. No idea if he's right or having old person dreams. Closer we get to the Glimmering Grove, the stranger our dreams become. Like the spirits know we're almost with them and whisper in our ear."

"Don't listen ta ol' Neana," yelled a bald man at a nearby table. "Anyone who can cook all the flavor out of a bogfin is destined for the Banefallow."

A small group of people erupted in angry shouting at the man, defending Neana's culinary skills. The bald man held his hands up, claiming to be joking. The confrontation quieted mere seconds before it appeared ready to escalate into a brawl. Eventually, everyone laughed about it, making it woefully unclear if the man originally meant the complaint seriously.

"I thought the fish was good," said Oona.

"Thank you, dear." Neana smiled. "Kerun's a bit of a troublemaker. Don't listen to him. Ancient forces are in motion. All these critters waking up is a *good* sign."

Kitlyn swiped her hair out of her eyes. "Even if some are dangerous?"

"The world's a dangerous place, child." Neana patted her on the head. "If you're not gonna get bit in the ass by a bear, it's gonna be a manticore draggin' ya off. Don't much matter how many horns or glowing parts the critter has, does it?"

"Umm, I suppose not." Kitlyn grimaced.

"I prefer my backside unbitten," whispered Oona.

"Aww," whispered Kitlyn while fake pouting.

Danos, Yerbin, and Imoa found their plates quite interesting all of a sudden, refusing to look at them. Neana either ignored the remark or hadn't heard.

Oona's face burned. She whispered, "Must you? In public?"

"I could not miss such an easy opportunity to tease you." Kitlyn took her hand. "However, there shall be no rump biting until we are safe at home."

Mortified, Oona shrank in her seat, hiding her face behind her hair.

26

MONSTERS

KITLYN

$\mathcal{A}$ pleasant dream of walking in the garden beside Oona momentarily changed into a nightmare earthquake—until she woke up to Oona shaking her.

Kitlyn blearily looked up at the silhouette of her wife's head hovering over her, backlit in the blue glow of her little magical orb. The window behind the headboard remained as dark as a swath of black ink.

"We have to go right now," whispered Oona. "Or death. I'm about to throw up."

The urgency in her voice slapped the drowsiness out of Kitlyn's brain. "All right. I'll—"

Oona dragged her out of bed, pulling her to the door.

"Oo!" Kitlyn set her heels. "What are you doing? We don't have anything on!"

"There isn't any time. We have to go right this second."

Kitlyn grasped her by the wrists, pulling her around to stare into her eyes. "You are panicking. We are neither faeries nor can we fly. Running off into the swamp naked and unarmed is not going to help anyone. We'll be the ones dead."

Oona closed her eyes, breathing deeply for a second or two

before she nodded. "You're right. I wasn't fully awake. No time to argue."

Seeing her wife in so much of a panic-fueled rush she almost ran out the door with nothing made Kitlyn anxious to the point her hands shook. She scrambled to dress as fast as possible. Oona fumbled to secure the buckles of her leather chest plate due to her haste. Already dressed, Kitlyn finished them for her. Clearly, Oona believed someone—possibly one of them—would die soon if they didn't move fast.

Oona rushed into the hall.

Kitlyn stepped out of their room, pointing back over her shoulder. "I'll meet you outside. Going to wake Rakden and the others."

"We don't have time!" rasped Oona, whirling. "We're already late."

Never before had she been so rattled by one of the gods' messages. The shock of seeing Oona in such a panic kept Kitlyn from arguing. They ran down the hall to the inn room, empty except for the man with the enormous mustache cleaning tables.

"Please tell the people with us we've gone to Torjin," said Kitlyn while hurrying past him.

Without waiting for a reply, they rushed outside. It still appeared to be the middle of the night, not the slightest hint of approaching dawn in the sky. Beyond the reach of Oona's floating light orb, all remained black. All the water in the area made the chill in the damp air feel worse.

Oona rushed off down the rickety wooden plankway, her light ball keeping pace above her right shoulder. Kitlyn sprinted after her, one hand on her longsword to steady the scabbard from banging into her legs. The clomp of their boots on the bridges echoed over Kolbrin's Quay like an angry mob pounding on doors. Fearless of slipping, Oona paid little heed to caution, zigzagging among the islands and bridgeways toward the south edge of town.

A few windows opened, as locals awake at the awful hour peered out at the commotion of people running.

Oona skidded to a halt at the end of a walkway to nowhere,

having reached the edge of town. The elevated wooden path simply stopped over the water. Small boats lined up on both sides, so many they bumped into each other. "Lucen forgive me… only borrowing."

"What?" asked Kitlyn.

"Hurry!" Oona looked around for a second and, seemingly at random, stepped down into a two-person boat. "We're not stealing it. We're borrowing it."

Kitlyn got in behind her, untied the rope, and pushed off from the pier, snagging a spare oar from an adjacent boat as they glided away.

"You're not protesting?" Oona seized the paddle on the floor between her feet and flailed at the water.

"As you said, we aren't stealing it. We're borrowing it, and we don't have the time to figure out who owns it and ask. You are certain someone's life is in peril?"

"Yes." After a few ineffective swipes, Oona adjusted her hold of the oar and finally began helping to propel them forward. "Oh, this works much better when I turn the oar flat, doesn't it?"

Kitlyn reached out and squeezed her shoulder. "You are out of your mind from panic. If you don't try to calm yourself even a little bit so you can think, we will be in trouble."

"You're right." Oona raked the paddle at the water. "I'll be all right once we catch up. We are still behind. We shouldn't have spent the night."

"Do you know where we are going? I can't see anything past your light."

"I'm looking for the big green tree. This feels like the way we should be going."

Kitlyn paddled on the opposite side to keep them going forward rather than in circles. Her only experience in boats came from the pond in the castle garden. As children, they'd sometimes played in the small boat; however, it had been at least five years since they touched it. Of course, at the moment, they didn't intend to lazily float around a pond for fun. Oona appeared driven in a particular direction. She grunted from the effort she put into paddling, splashing the awful-smelling water everywhere in a frenzy so desperate she had to believe Kitlyn's life hung in the balance.

Her urgency proved contagious. Kitlyn also paddled hard, trying not to worry about doom needle wasps coming out of the darkness. The man didn't say much about them other than comparing their size to rabbits, but she pictured them as all-black, invisible at night. Maybe they had glowing red eyes or something suitably demonic for such a wicked monster.

They paddled feverishly into the moor, buzzed every few seconds by dinner-plate-sized white moths attracted to the light orb. If her nearly running outside without getting dressed hadn't proved the urgency of her divine pull, Oona's complete non-reaction to giant moths—even when they crashed into the side of her head—proved the veracity of her worry.

A few slapped into Kitlyn as well, soft as being struck in the face by hairy pillows. The enormous bugs came out of the blackness, offering little time to react to their dive-bombing passes. Fortunately, the moths lacked any apparent means or intention to bite, merely flinging themselves drunkenly at the light source.

One bounced off Oona's face and hit the water, flapping about for less than a second before *something* beneath the opaque surface chomped it gone in one bite, disappearing too fast to see.

There are fish in this water big enough to eat moths the size of gophers. We should try not to fall out of the boat.

A massive pale green tree drifted into the outer reaches of their light radius. Kitlyn couldn't tell how long it had been since they left Kolbrin's Quay, between the feverish paddling, desperation, moths, fear of wasps, and everything else, the journey thus far simultaneously felt short and long. It could've been two hours in the boat or merely twenty minutes. Still, the sky showed no indication of dawn.

Oona shifted to paddle on the left, pulling the boat to that side.

The giant tree stood so high above the water's surface on a cluster of fat root 'legs,' their boat could have sailed under it if they cared to risk navigating a patch of dense green grass-like plants poking up out of the water.

Snakes probably live in there, or something equally dangerous. Definitely tons of bugs. Maybe one of those enormous fish.

Kitlyn peered up at the twisty wood towering over them. A trunk at least eighteen feet wide resembled an enormous towel being wrung out, gnarled and refusing to adhere to anything close to a straight line. The pale green lichen coating it appeared wet, as if someone had spilled a giant's pot of pea soup over the tree. She decided against touching the glistening slime, using the oar to push the boat away from the nearest root.

"What is making you so worried?" asked Kitlyn in a half whisper.

Oona continued paddling as hard as she still had the strength to. "I'm not sure exactly, but I know something horrible is going to happen... maybe to you. Maybe to... I don't know, an innocent. It feels like if we don't get there fast enough, my heart is going to shatter."

"I won't let your heart shatter." Kitlyn brushed aside her fatigue and kept raking the oar at the water. "Pace. Wearing ourselves out won't help."

"I'm trying. Still feels like we're already too late."

"No, it doesn't. Or you'd want to stop so you didn't have to see the bad thing. If we really are out of time, the pull would stop, wouldn't it?"

Oona shook her head. "Not until it's absolutely too late. I mean, if we keep going at our present speed, we're not going to make it there on time. There is still a chance we can do something, but I'm sure we are moving too slowly."

Should I have asked Omun to bring us here? He could navigate the swamp easily... or maybe get stuck. Definitely cover an hour's worth of paddling in mere minutes. He'd terrify everyone who saw us though. She considered trying to call him through the Stone, but he remained dormant in the Mistral Wood back in Lucernia. Even as fast as he could cover ground, he'd never be able to catch up to them in time to prevent whatever tragedy occupied Oona's mind.

She stopped worrying about things she could have done but didn't do, and focused on making the boat move. They paddled at their limit of endurance for a while before having no choice but to slow down from fatigue. After they caught their breath, Oona tolerated an endurance pace rather than constant sprinting.

Eventually, the moths thinned and stopped altogether. Soon after the bombardment ended, the beginnings of morning lightened the darkness around them, revealing grey-brown swamp trees dotting the moor in every direction. Scraps of daylight reflected on distant water, squiggles of white paint on black. They appeared to be following a narrow river among hundreds of tiny islands, each no bigger than a cheap inn room. Though the ground appeared solid, she suspected it to have only slightly more substance than a bowl of stew. Trying to step out of the boat anywhere would surely see her sinking waist deep.

Minutes after the first traces of daylight appeared, they spotted a few stray paddle boats drifting empty up ahead. Various bits of wood, bottles, or other debris floated around them. Early morning mist clung to the water, concealing the details enough to where she couldn't tell if any corpses occupied the boats. The pervasive stench of bog water made it impossible to determine by scent if anyone died nearby. In fact, she suspected a rotting corpse would *improve* the smell.

"We are close." Oona paddled faster.

Silhouettes of partially demolished huts appeared in the distant fog.

Kitlyn summoned a second wind for another brief sprint.

The form of a giant island slipped out from behind the curtain of mist. Numerous small homes lay in varying states of ruin. Any structure not flattened completely appeared to have suffered damage from narrow trees falling on them, split in half like bread loaves struck by a sword. A row of posts revealed where a pier had been, though all the surface planks had disappeared. More debris bumped against the prow of their little boat, as though the occupants of the village up ahead decided to randomly throw half their possessions into the swamp.

"What happened here?" Oona gasped in shock.

"Nothing good." Kitlyn stopped paddling and used her oar as a tiller to steer them over to land.

Once the prow struck mud, Oona stood and jumped from the boat. Surprisingly, she didn't sink to her knees in muck. Kitlyn stowed her oar before climbing forward out of the boat. The squishy mud only swallowed her boots to the ankles. A few paces from shore, it solidified to wet but normal ground, except for being as black as charcoal.

They walked side by side into the ruins of a village, examining the remains of approximately thirty small dwellings around a much larger building that appeared to serve as inn, trading post, and perhaps town hall. Other than having its porch demolished and a few giant slashes in the wall, the inn seemed to be the most intact of anything. Roughly half the dwellings had been reduced to piles of broken wood.

Thousands of footprints and strange troughs in the mud held tiny puddles of water, which didn't offer much information about how long ago anything happened. Wherever Kitlyn or Oona stepped filled with water in mere seconds. She guessed most of the other prints came from people running due to being much deeper. The grooves and small trenches made her picture an army of snakes crawling around. However, snakes, even large ones, couldn't demolish buildings on this scale.

She approached the inn to examine one of the gouges in the wall, a slice in the building twelve feet high and four inches wide. Splinters, green residue, and a few dark leaves definitely made it look like a narrow tree had fallen into the wall—yet no tree lay there. Kitlyn peeked through the gap at the interior. A few tables nearest the hole had also been crushed flat in a pattern most unlike what a rigid tree trunk would've caused.

"What did this?" asked Kitlyn.

"Eep!" gasped Oona.

Kitlyn whirled.

Her wife stared at a man's arm sticking out from under a slab of former wall.

They ran over to the collapsed hut. Oona struggled to lift the smashed lumber off the man to little success. Kitlyn held her arms out, fingers apart, and summoned a rock spire up from the earth to push the debris off the man.

Oona crouched, ducking in under the precariously balanced wooden slab. She didn't spend more than a few seconds checking the man over before standing up and giving Kitlyn a sorrowful look.

"Are we too late?" whispered Kitlyn.

"For this man, yes." Oona turned away from him — and gasped again. "Oh, Tenebrea guide them…"

Kitlyn twisted to peer in the same direction. Bodies lay strewn across the southern end of the island where no buildings had been, the muddy ground so torn up around them the dead were partially buried. By count of hands or feet sticking into the air, she guessed anywhere from eight to twelve people died there. Water-filled gouges crisscrossed the area as though someone had been dragging huge branches around in wild patterns. Rows of straight footprints on the east edge of the island suggested twenty to thirty people walked off in a group, likely after whatever catastrophe befell this place ended.

"This is too strange." Kitlyn surveyed the muddy carnage. "It's like a giant ball of snakes rolled around here."

Oona walked out into the field, going past the bodies while turning her head as if trying to listen for a distant voice.

"Do you hear something?" Kitlyn followed.

"No, it's merely a feeling pull — "

The partially muffled scream of a child broke the silence in the foggy woods to the south.

Oona bolted up to a sprint, leading Kitlyn to the end of the big island. A log bridge spanned a narrow waterway, leading to another island. The distant child screamed again, seemingly trying to speak but unable to. Waving her arms for balance, Oona rushed across the log. Dreading whatever monster smashed the village had dragged one of its children away to eat later, Kitlyn ran after her, opting to jump across the narrow swaths of water rather than slow down for moss-covered log bridges. Dense fog limited visibility to about twenty feet, muddy islands and trees appearing the same in every direction.

Six jumps later, Kitlyn landed on a large island where a tall grey stone obelisk stood at the center of a square stone platform. The screaming came from a pale young girl tied standing to the obelisk, her arms behind her back. Long, dark brown hair mostly covered her face. She appeared to be around ten years of age, dirty and clad like a beggar in a faded red dress, so tattered it had essentially been reduced to a shirt. Her baggy blue pants bore numerous stains and patches, as did the shabby sky-blue blanket she wore as a cloak. The relative cleanliness of her bare feet suggested she'd only recently been deprived of shoes—likely by whoever tied her ankles together. Surprisingly, multiple pouches hanging on her three belts looked full, undisturbed by thieves.

Coils of rope around her middle as well as the rope around her ankles kept her securely attached to a twelve-foot-tall stone obelisk. A wooden rod as thick as a broom handle had been stuffed into her mouth sideways, tied around her head into a gag. Split logs at the base of the obelisk implied someone intended to build a large fire. The child appeared terrified for her life, thrashing at the ropes, but could barely move. Her feverish struggle occasionally swung her hair off her face, revealing bruises and a black eye. She bled from the nose and a cut on her lip.

Upon noticing Kitlyn and Oona appearing out of the mist, the girl stopped struggling, stared at them, and screamed, "Hrrll!"

"Let's hurry this up and rejoin the others," said a man on the left.

Oona emitted a low growl.

Kitlyn glanced away from the struggling child in the direction of the voice.

Two men emerged from the trees on the left, carrying armloads of wood toward the obelisk. The skinnier of the two wore a simple tunic, belt, and thigh-high boots. He appeared quite nervous, as if frightened of approaching the little girl. The other man, clad in leather armor, had a more robust figure and carried a broadsword in a scabbard on his belt. He looked a few years older than the skinny man, perhaps in his early thirties.

"Hrrll! Nmmm gmm kmmm mmuh!" yelled the girl.

Oona rushed forward, putting herself between the men and the obelisk.

Both men screamed, jumping away and dropping the firewood. The skinny man nearly slipped in the mud and fell on his backside.

Broadsword pointed at Oona. "The little demon's summoned help!"

"Hey!" shouted Kitlyn, hand on her longsword. "What in the name of the gods are you two doing?"

27

EMERALD AND AMBER

OONA

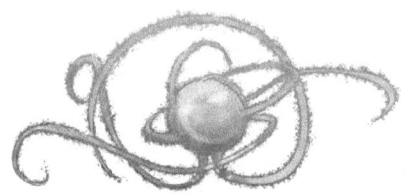

The instant Oona saw the struggling child—still alive—the overpowering urgency stopped.

Relief at not being too late left her standing there in a bit of a stupor watching the girl squirm, her mind trying to cope with the sudden lack of divine inspiration. Free from the heavy sense of duty pleading her into action, Oona's thoughts took a moment to coalesce back to reason. The ten to twenty minutes it would have taken to wait for the soldiers to get up and prepare would have killed this child.

"Let's hurry this up and rejoin the others," said a man to her left.

She forced herself to look away from the frightened girl at a pair of men, one thin, one muscular, carrying armloads of firewood. Not since the assassin tried to poison her had she felt such a strong desire to harm a living person. Despite being at least ten years older than her, the guy with chestnut brown hair didn't seem any more dangerous than a common villager. Oona resisted the urge to pull her longsword and ran forward to get between these two idiots and the child.

The men spotted her and screamed as if seeing a ghost manifest out of thin air, nearly falling over and dropping the wood they carried.

"Hey!" shouted Kitlyn. "What in the name of the gods are you two doing?"

A whimper of relief came from the girl who slouched, all her weight hanging on the ropes.

Oona stomped toward the obelisk, drawing her dagger.

Broadsword charged over. He grabbed Oona by the shoulder and belt, lifting her off her feet and carrying her away from the child. Oona struggled futilely to force the man's grip open. Realizing she'd never overpower him, she thrust one hand up toward his face, focusing on Lucen's light.

Kitlyn started to draw her longsword. "Let go of her or—"

A blinding blue-white flash exploded from Oona's palm.

Broadsword yowled in surprise more than pain, reflexively dropping her to clutch his eyes. Oona landed on her feet, taking a few steps back, hand poised over the grip of her longsword. Kitlyn hurried over to stand between her and the large man.

Oona pointed at Broadsword. "How dare you do this to an innocent child, foul brigands!"

"What's all the damn shouting?" bellowed another man, hidden behind fog in the area where the other two came from.

"It's not a child." Nervous jabbed his finger at the girl. "Wants ya to think it is, but it's a demon."

"Mmmm nmm!" The girl shook her head rapidly.

A fortyish man, wearing an angry scowl as well as a commoner's tunic and breeches walked out from the fog carrying a single-edged, slightly curved Evermoor longsword. He appeared initially surprised to see Oona and Kitlyn, but resumed glaring in mere seconds. Two more men jogged out into view behind the angry man, a young-twenties blond in chain mail armor and a second in his forties, wearing a light leather vest and a bandolier of daggers.

"Gah," wailed Broadsword, blinking rapidly. "Demons. They're demons."

"The little one's called demons to destroy us all," yelled Nervous, still pointing at the child tied to the obelisk.

"Nmmm!" the girl shook her head while struggling as if to call attention to her hands being tied behind her back.

"This child is no child at all, but a demon." Angry pointed his sword at the girl. "She tried to kill us all and we now purify her evil as Lucen commands."

"Nmmm!" tears streamed down the girl's face. "I dmmnt! Peeeem dmmm bmmm muh!"

"Lucen?" shouted Oona. "The Lord of Purity does *not* command the murder of innocent children. You speak falsehood!"

"What would you know of him, child?" snapped Daggers.

"Do not dare question her devotion to the gods." Kitlyn glared at him, looking far too much like Aodh—at least in the eyes—for comfort.

Oona drew a dagger from her belt. "I will hear this child's story from her own mouth."

All five men shouted variations of "No" or "do not" at the same time.

"If she can speak, she'll call another one," yelled Nervous.

"Nmm!" yelled the girl, shaking her head hard.

"True servants of Lucen would not fear demons. The fear you show toward this child proves your lies. Lucen does not require ceremonial burning to send demons back to the Pit." Oona approached the girl.

The men tensed, seeming ready to attack. An uneasy nasal whine came from the trembling child.

Oona stopped two paces from the girl and faced the men once more. "I am a servant of Lucen. I will know if this child speaks false."

"You are a demon lying to free your mistress," bellowed Angry.

Furious, Oona thrust her left arm up into the air, releasing a burst of light magic into a twenty-foot-tall symbol of Lucen, saturating the area in its soft blue-white glow. The child gazed up at it and ceased trembling.

The men stared in shock for a moment, then appeared to relax.

"Lucen's sacred symbol," whispered Nervous.

"A true priestess." The man in chain mail bowed his head.

Kitlyn pointed at the girl. "Look at her. She sees Lucen's light and is calmed by it. No demon would be able to bear the sight of it."

"We are servants of Lucen as well," said Broadsword. "A small group of devoted doing his work in the darkest part of the land."

Still angry, Oona pointed her dagger at the child. "Nothing Lucen commands requires murdering an innocent or performing ritual sacrifices. What is the point of all this?"

"If we merely cut her head off, the demon will return in days, disguised as another innocent," said Armored. "The fiends must be destroyed by Lucen-blessed fire."

Oona stared at him, aghast at the idiocy. "Where do demons come from?"

"The Pit," said Angry.

"And what is the Pit filled with?" asked Oona, her eyebrows going up.

The men exchanged glances for a moment before Nervous timidly offered, "Demons?"

"No, you fools. It's filled with fire!" yelled Oona. "Fire makes demons *stronger*. It is the exact *worst* way to fight them."

"Emm dmmnt mmnnn mn," mumbled the girl.

"Sorry, sweetie." Oona stepped up to her. "Let me get that horrible thing out of your mouth."

"No!" yelled Nervous. "She'll kill us all."

"Are you five men honestly frightened of a little girl who is presently tied to a stone pillar?" asked Kitlyn. "For Lucen's sake, show some courage."

"Oh, you poor thing." Oona looked over the bruises on the girl's face, cut lip, bloody nose. Finger-shaped marks darkened the side of her neck where someone had roughly grabbed her. "Hold still."

"Mmm." The girl turned her head, exposing the rope binding the stick in her mouth.

Oona rested her left hand atop the child's head to hold her steady while gently sliding the dagger blade up between the girl's cheek and the rope, then yanked down and away, slicing the cord in one quick cut.

The child spat out the rod, which fell draped over her chest.

Whimpering, she worked her jaw around. Blood dribbled over her chin. Fortunately, she didn't appear to have lost any teeth. "Ow…"

"What happened, child?" Oona glanced at the men, not trusting them.

"My name is Tamsen. I didn't call the monster. It came all by itself. I only wanted to help fight it."

Kitlyn moved a few steps to the right, standing between the men and Oona. "Lucen shows her truth. Remain still."

Relieved, Oona turned her attention back to the child who peered up at her without fear or hesitation. At the sight of her eyes, Oona momentarily forgot how to speak. This little girl staring adoringly up at her had two different colored irises, one amber and one dark green.

"They want to kill me because they saw me use magic," said Tamsen.

Lucen's gift revealed the truth of the child's words. Oona's heart melted at the sight of this girl wearing a ratty blanket for a cloak.

"They think I'm evil. Please, you truly have Lucen's blessing. Help me. Don't let them kill me." Tamsen squirmed at the ropes.

Oona spun to face the men. "This child speaks truth. Your actions disgrace Lucen's name."

"*Iazeth*," whispered the girl.

All the logs piled up around her leapt away from the obelisk as if pushed by a ghost.

"See!" yelled Angry, pointing his sword at her.

"I'm not a demon," whispered Tamsen. "They're just stupid."

28

FALSE SERVANTS

KITLYN

$\mathcal{A}$t the clatter of wood behind her, Kitlyn peered back.

The firewood lay a few feet from the obelisk, each log having slid a short distance in a straight line directly away from it.

"She makes fire from her hands," yelled Nervous.

"So?" Kitlyn scrunched her face at him. "You live in Evermoor. Have you not heard of firecallers? People commanding roots, fire, stone, water… none of those should at all surprise you."

"Untruths," said Angry. "We have been lied to. There is no such thing as the elements. Demons mislead us. Only Lucen bears truth."

"Can I please have some water?" whispered Tamsen. "I've been tied up for two days."

"Two days?" roared Oona. "You kept this child bound to a post for two days? Such cruelty offends all four gods!"

The guy in chain mail shrugged. "We had to wait for the wood to dry out."

"She hasn't been on the pillar the whole time," said Daggers.

"I was in the camp, tied to a tree." Tamsen squirmed. "Sitting down *was* more comfortable than this, but they didn't give me any food or water because they were afraid of me talking."

Oona grumbled. "Enough of this."

She reached to slice the ropes around the girl's chest. The men all shouted and raised their weapons.

"The demon tricks you!" bellowed Angry.

"Fool!" yelled Nervous.

Broadsword drew his weapon.

Oona jumped back from Tamsen, trading the dagger to her left hand and pulling her longsword from its sheath.

"As Lucenites, we cannot allow you to set a demon free." Angry pointed his sword at Oona.

"You are no more servants of Lucen than winged hogs." Oona narrowed her eyes.

Why do I feel as though these men will make any excuse for a fight? Kitlyn sized up the men, Broadsword and Angry her two biggest concerns. Armored might pose a problem, as she didn't think anyone in full chain mail would be unskilled at combat. However, she also didn't need to worry so much about his defenses. Flexible mail armor wouldn't help much against a magical rock moving at high speed. Nervous looked like a peasant man dragged along to help them 'execute the demon.' Daggers would either be a huge problem — trained assassin — or another peasant. Angry carried himself like a man accustomed to combat, as did Broadsword. Both men undoubtedly had more experience than her and Oona combined.

She surreptitiously slipped out of her boots, stepping barefoot into the cold, squidgy mud. The men, if they noticed, likely thought her crazy unless they understood how stonecaller magic worked. A fight with these five would be dangerous in the best circumstances. She couldn't afford to weaken her connection to the earth.

"Lucenites..." Kitlyn didn't like the idea of getting into a fight against five men, but she kept her expression hard. Being Aodh's daughter cursed her with a bit of a temper at times. She'd learned to stifle it to avoid harsh punishment when living as a servant, but here, she allowed herself to feel angry at these men for being cruel to a child as well as insulting Oona. Not irrationally so, only enough to mask her fear. "You men have been deceived."

"We are agents of purity and truth!" yelled Angry.

Tamsen struggled feverishly for a few seconds, then gave up and hung limp.

"No, you are not." Kitlyn scowled in frustration. Once she had officially become queen, Beredwyn and Lanon shared with her information about several clandestine efforts undertaken during the war, some of which turned her stomach to think about. One such effort—that didn't involve poisoning innocent citizens with weakening agents—came to mind. "The former king of Lucernia sent spies into Evermoor posing as spiritualists. He hoped to convert citizens to worship our pantheon of gods instead of your elemental, animal, and ancestral spirits."

"I'd nearly forgotten," muttered Oona. "Of all the deceitful... false—he believed the people of Evermoor to be savages unworthy of Lucen's true teachings, so the spies brought an entirely false version of the story. They did not sincerely want to introduce anyone to Lucen's temple, but turn you against your own people, believing all magic came from demons."

That part is fairly close to accurate. Kitlyn frowned. "They hoped to incite violence, creating a group of insurgents who would target rootcallers and firecallers to weaken the war effort. What you have been taught is not the truth."

"The creature is evil." Broadsword pointed at the girl. "She is not even human. No parents. Showed up out of the blue one day. Lucen says magic is from demons."

"No, you fools." Kitlyn squeezed the handle of her longsword, convinced these idiots would attack them any second. "Her magic comes from the Alderswood."

"I don't think my magic came from the great tree..." Tamsen wriggled. "But it is definitely not evil. When the monster attacked Torjin, I tried to help defend it even though I was afraid everyone would hate me for it. Their swords and axes didn't hurt the monster much. I had parents. They died during the war. Every other place I went chased me off, but the people in Torjin let me stay. I knew they were all in a weird magic-hating cult, so I kept it hidden—but I didn't want them to die. They're going to kill me because they think I'm evil. They think I called the monster."

"You men are fools. This child is no demon and she does not deserve to spend one minute longer tied to a post." Oona raised her sword to the ropes.

"If you free the demon, you reveal yourself as a false servant of Lucen!" shouted Angry.

Oona whipped around to scowl at him, eyes burning with fury.

Kitlyn cringed. *Damn.* "You really shouldn't have called her that..."

29

PROOF OF LIGHT

OONA

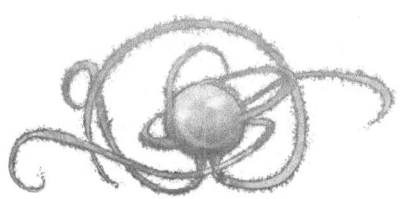

The sheer stupidity of the men glaring at her defied even the gods to explain.

Oona wanted to slice the ropes binding the girl to the stone obelisk, but feared doing so would ignite a battle. As much as it pained her to leave the girl tied, if she and Kitlyn got themselves killed, the child would die soon after. She also didn't want to kill anyone if at all possible.

"How can you still falsely claim this child is a demon after everything that has happened?" Oona looked from man to man. "I can feel the sincerity in your words. You truly believe what you say despite it being false. Do any of you desire to truly serve Lucen?"

Kitlyn shook her head. "For them, it isn't about Lucen at all. This is Aodh's fault. He taught people to use Lucen's name as a tool to justify hatred for anyone who wasn't like them."

"I do not understand why these men cling so desperately to obvious falsehoods they would take the life of a child when the truth is right in front of them." Oona put her dagger back in its sheath, freeing both hands for her longsword.

"Consider Aodh. These men fell for the lies offered them. The lies are comfortable. They believe in their own version of Lucen because it is what they want. Rather than follow the teachings of Lucen, they invent their own god to suit their will."

"Be quiet, girl." Daggers scowled at Kitlyn. "Blaspheme no more."

"What do you know of blasphemy?" Oona stepped toward them.

"Quite a lot," whispered Tamsen.

Oona peered back at her, eyebrow raised.

"I was talking about them, not me." Tamsen puffed air at a strand of hair draped over her face.

"Ahh, yes." Oona faced the men. "Do any of you bear his gift?"

The five men exchanged looks ranging from angry to nervous.

Oona held out her left hand, summoning her light orb. The little blue ball bobbed into the air, circling around her head in a playful orbit, despite its eye spots glaring at the five men.

"So pretty," whispered Tamsen.

"All who are called to serve Lucen can summon his light. It radiates his power, calming and reassuring." She directed the orb to fly past the men, weaving between them before returning to hover over her. "Show us you bear Lucen's gift. Call your light."

None of the men moved, not even attempting to do anything magical.

They admit the truth by inaction. "You have been deceived. Lucen does *not* hate magic. He despises demons, impurity, and falsehood. Those who truly serve him carry his light. Spies sent by the former king manipulated you to weaken Evermoor from the inside. I will share Lucen's truth with you if you are open to it, but I will not stand idly by and permit you to harm this child."

"Please, let me go." Tamsen grunted, futilely struggling to escape. "I only wanted to help. I did not call the monster. I know you don't trust me. I'll go away and you'll never see me again."

"There's no reason for violence here," said Kitlyn. "If this girl was a demon, she could not bear to be touched by Lucen's light. We will bring her with us away from here."

Everyone stared at each other in silence, the stillness of the moor disturbed only by the warbling of distant insects and the calls of unseen birds. Minutes passed. The men seemed poised to attack at the slightest sudden noise. Only Nervous appeared disinterested in fighting and somewhat questioning of what he'd been taught. The other four regarded her with varying degrees of anger.

They must know I speak truth and are angry it differs from what they wish to be reality. How can grown men have such blind hatred for an innocent child?

The girl sneezed, making the men jump.

"Eww," whispered Tamsen. "Will someone please wipe my nose?"

"Enough of this. Lucen led me here to stop this profanity of his name. Interfere with his will at your own peril." Oona turned to slice the ropes.

"Purge the demons!" yelled Angry before rushing at Oona.

30

WHAT BLOOD IS NECESSARY

KITLYN

Kitlyn summoned a pillar of stone to thrust up from the ground.

The rock spire rammed into Angry's crotch, lifting him a few inches off his feet and stopping his charge cold.

Wheezing, he staggered to the side, falling to one knee. Daggers yanked a throwing knife from his bandolier, hurling it at Oona in the same motion. The attack seemed intended more to keep her from freeing the child than hurting her. Oona easily dove away from the obelisk, avoiding the blade. Broadsword rushed at Kitlyn, trying to grab her.

She poured magic into the ground, liquefying the dirt out from under him. He slipped, crashing to the mud on his back, legs in the air. Dark green light surrounded Kitlyn's hands as she called a mass of inch-thick vines out of the earth, wrapping the man and pinning him down.

"Aaaaah!" screamed Broadsword, thrashing at the vines pinning his arms to his sides. "They are all demons!"

"Fool!" yelled Kitlyn. "Do you not recognize the magic of the Alderswood? If you saw an actual demon, you'd soil your smallclothes."

She sighed in her mind, knowing it pointless to attempt reasoning. The spies trained these people to regard all magic as evil. Their entire purpose had been to kill rootcallers in hopes of making it impossible for Evermoor soldiers to cross the Churning Deep anywhere they wanted. If she could keep them busy long enough, Oona could cut the ropes and get the child out of here.

Nervous ran at Oona as if to grab or tackle her.

"*Iazeth!*" yelled Tamsen.

The skinny man's charge diverted to one side as if someone shoved him. He tripped over his own feet and ate dirt next to Oona who scurried away, raising her arm. A beam of blue light shot from her hand, nailing Daggers in the forehead. He staggered backward from the force of a punch, dazed but not injured.

Kitlyn summoned a vine to wrap around Angry's legs. "I'll tangle these idiots up. Get her loose and run."

"Yes please," said Tamsen. "I really don't like being tied to a post near people waving swords around."

Angry howled in rage, stumbling, but keeping his balance. With two deft strokes of his single-edged blade, he freed himself. Kitlyn summoned another vine, tripping him onto his chest. He growled.

"Do you like being tied to a post when there's no one waving swords around?" asked Kitlyn.

"No, but it isn't as scary." Tamsen grunted from the effort she put into trying to squirm loose, but still couldn't move.

Armored bellowed a war cry and charged Kitlyn. She swung her longsword up in time to parry; the force of the blow sent her stumbling, bare feet sliding in mud. Somehow, she kept her balance.

Nervous picked himself up. Daggers, dazed from the hit to the face, threw another small knife at Oona when she tried to slice the ropes around Tamsen's chest.

These fools are trying so desperately to keep us away from that child, as if setting her free would doom the world.

Angry cut himself loose a second time. He started to charge at Oona, stopping short as Kitlyn ducked away from Armor, swiping at the air in front of him, getting in his way. He slashed at her face. She deflected his attack an instant before Armored lunged at her, forcing her to scramble to the right and drawing her defenses down and left. Rather than exploit the opening on Kitlyn, Armored swerved around her to run at Oona, grabbing her from behind while Nervous had her attention waving a dagger in her face. She screamed as he hauled her off her feet in a bear hug.

Broadsword continued growling, struggling at the roots holding him to the ground.

"We must purge all the demons with fire!" yelled Angry. "Lucen commands it!"

Realizing the men intended to kill them all, Kitlyn lost any desire to hold back, deciding to take the fight lethal. These men would murder them with no hesitation. Snarling, she called forth a fist-sized stone shrouded in glowing green magic up from the ground, levitating it to shoulder level before launching it at Angry. The rock zoomed faster than a crossbow bolt, glancing across the side of the man's head. His left ear vanished in a spritz of blood and torn skin. Howling, he lost his grip on Oona, staggering to the side clutching the wound.

Kitlyn glared. "Stand down or —"

Armored came out of nowhere on her left, lunging into a thrust. She swatted his blade down and away, but not well enough to avoid being hit. A few inches of longsword punched into her left thigh — better than her heart, at least.

Between her fury at the man for trying to kill Oona and her adrenaline, Kitlyn didn't feel much more than a pinching sensation. Angry spun to face them again, blood streaming down over his left shoulder. Manic rage made his eyes seem to vibrate in their sockets. He raised his sword in a two-handed grip, glaring at Oona as if he intended to chop her in half from head to crotch.

Oona thrust her left hand into his face, releasing an intense flash of light inches from his eyes.

The man wailed in furious agony, blindly slashing back and forth while Oona scurried out of the way. Armored swung high, his sword striking Kitlyn's defense with a bell-like clang. His advantages in height, weight, and strength sent her stumbling backward. The mud proved the victor this time, taking her feet out from under her. Kitlyn landed on her butt, her blade flung up behind her head in both hands.

Armored stepped in to attack again.

Kitlyn poured magic into the earth. A head-sized rock spat up from the mud by her feet, flying into the man's chest hard enough to carry him airborne, crumpled around it. Blood sprayed from his mouth, trailing after him. He landed flat on his back some fifteen feet away, wheezing. Traces of green magical 'fire' danced across the chain mail for a few seconds where the rock hit.

He's not going to get back up.

Oona traded strikes with Nervous, stalemated. Her sword clattered against his dagger again and again. Angry continued slashing around blind while screaming curses about demons. Amid a loud series of snaps, Broadsword tore loose from the roots. He and Kitlyn scrambled back to their feet at roughly the same time.

Armored lay flat on the ground struggling to breathe.

Growling, Broadsword engaged Kitlyn, slashing wildly. She dodged as much as parried, trying to use her smaller size as an advantage rather than a shortfall. His fifth rapid swing crashed into her sword, locking blades. She grunted, straining to hold him back while he pushed forward, inching his heavier blade's edge toward her face.

"*Iazeth!*" called Tamsen in a forceful tone.

Armored lurched backward as if shoved by a man Beowyn's size, his blade peeling away from Kitlyn's with a musical *shing*.

At the sound of the child's voice, the still-blinded Angry swiveled toward her and swung more feverishly, still blindly trying to hit anyone he could. The child looked like she wanted to scream in terror, but kept quiet, struggling to scrunch down below the height of the swinging blade getting closer and closer. The ropes, alas, had other plans, pinning her tight to the stone.

Oona growled, swatted the dagger out of Nervous's hand, then raised her longsword as if to take his head off. He screamed in terror and ran to the side out of her way. Oona rushed forward, grasping her weapon in a two-handed grip, and hacked the blade into the side of Angry's neck where it met his shoulder. Still unable to see, he offered no attempt at defense. Oona dragged the sword out of the wound. Gurgling, he collapsed over sideways, convulsing and grasping at the wound.

"Orien forgive me," whispered Oona. "Close your eyes, child."

Kitlyn's earth sense revealed the weight of someone creeping up behind her. She pretended not to notice him, waiting to attack once he'd come close enough to surprise with a sudden spin.

"I saw the monster squish people. I can handle this… and I can't help if I'm not looking." A half-second later, the child yelled, "*Iazeth!*" while staring at Kitlyn.

An "oof" came from behind her, stalling the man a little too far away for a perfect strike.

Kitlyn twisted to look at Daggers flailing his arms for balance while stumbling from the magical shove. Green glow surrounded her left hand as she called out to the roots. A vine as thick as her wrist sprang out of the ground and wrapped around Daggers. At her command, it hauled him into the air, swinging him back and forth for a second or two before whipping him against the nearest tree. He bounced off, landed on his chest, and lay moaning in pain.

Angry stopped moving.

Oona raised her longsword to slice the ropes on Tamsen, but jumped back to defend herself as Nervous charged in screaming like a lunatic. He slashed and stabbed at her in such a frenzy he couldn't possibly be trying to hit her, only drive her away from the child.

Footsteps in the earth warned Kitlyn of Daggers trying to sneak up on her again. She spun into a low slash, startling a yelp out of him and scoring a superficial wound across his lower abdomen that left a rip in his grey tunic and drew a fair amount of blood. He winced, giving her hope the wound might slow him down a little. Seeing him bleed reminded her of the wound in her leg, making it flare up in pain.

Groaning and gasping for air, Armored pushed himself up to all fours. Oona thrust at Nervous, finally done toying with him and wanting to end it. Alas, she missed, giving the man an opportunity to dart around her and run at Tamsen.

"*Iazeth!*" yelled the child.

The man's feet shot out from under him so fast his face went straight into the mud.

Blood gushing from his mouth and nose, Armored forced himself up to his feet, then staggered over to Kitlyn, swinging a half-hearted chop she easily parried. Oona moved to finish Nervous off with a stab to the back.

"Look out!" yelled Tamsen.

Daggers threw a knife at Oona, who pivoted away from Nervous. By sheer luck—or Lucen's favor—she successfully swatted the spinning blade out of the air. A faint *clink* rang out as the tiny weapon glanced off her sword. Kitlyn tried to maneuver around Armored to stop Daggers from throwing another knife at Oona, but the chain-mail-clad warrior shoulder-rammed her, knocking her back. Daggers ducked past them, sprinting at Oona.

Broadsword slashed at Kitlyn from the right, Armored pressing his attack on her left. Having two men swinging at her simultaneously forced her into a circular backpedal. The muddy ground made it near impossible to distance herself without losing her balance and ending up in a much worse position—flat on the ground. The only magic she could use fast enough to work in between parries at such a frenetic pace created slippery patches, as she'd done to Guard Morrow during their sparring session. Here, the ground was already slippery. Making it slightly looser wouldn't help.

She tried calling small stone pegs up from the earth to trip the men, which did slow them enough not to draw blood from her, even with her left leg beginning to go into full-fledged mutiny from the stab wound. Oona seemed equally up to her eyeballs dealing with Nervous and Daggers. Both men went after her with small, fast weapons. She exploited the reach of her longsword, defending as much with intentionally missed slashes to keep them away as parrying or dodging. Oona also appeared to be pressed so hard to defend herself, she had no time to use her magic.

Tamsen stopped struggling to free herself, becoming a literal captive audience to the fight. The child stared intently at them, silent until the pain in Kitlyn's leg finally got the better of her and she stumbled.

"*Iazeth!*" yelled the girl.

A magical shove fouled Broadsword's swing—an attack that likely would have cut her leg off at the thigh—redirecting his downward chop into the muck. He growled.

"Look out!" yelled Tamsen. "They have reinforcements."

Kitlyn raised her sword to block a slash from Armored, screaming from the pain in her leg as well as her sheer determination not to let these men kill Oona. Reinforcements meant she had to do something fast. Two men swinging at her afforded her no time to concentrate on summoning a fatally large rock to throw. She'd have to let one of them hit her in trade for using her magic; though she'd surely slay her target, she might die doing so.

A bellowing war cry in a wonderfully familiar, deep voice came from the fog.

Beowyn.

The big man charged into view, rounding his enormous sword overhead in a cleaving chop at Broadsword, who pulled away from Kitlyn to defend himself. The smaller man got his weapon in the way —and paid for it. Beowyn threw so much force into his swing, blocking it hurled Broadsword into a stagger. Yerbin, half a step behind Beowyn, engaged Armored, landing two quick slashes that stalled with dull clanks, failing to penetrate the chain mail. He hit the same spot the rock did earlier, causing the man to scream in pain and nearly black out.

Kitlyn poured her desperation and anger into the earth, raising a pumpkin-sized stone out of the mud. The floating mini-boulder aglow in green light hung in space for a second before rocketing forward into the armored man's chest, tearing the chain-mail apart into a spray of tiny rings. The boulder carried him into the air, striking a tree thirty feet away somewhere out amid the fog. Dense mist concealed the gruesome details, but the crunching squish left no doubt in Kitlyn's mind the man died instantly.

Color drained from Broadsword's face. He glanced back and forth between Kitlyn and Beowyn, at the other four soldiers rushing toward them, then dropped his sword, raising both hands.

The instant Beowyn appeared to accept his surrender,

Broadsword pulled a little knife from behind his neck, pivoting into a throw—at Tamsen. Beowyn lunged into a body-block, crashing into the man an instant before the knife left his hand. Broadsword tripped over Kitlyn, falling on his side.

Unable to move, Tamsen could only scream as the blade flew toward her—and struck the obelisk a hand's width to the right of her head. Without word or hesitation, Beowyn plucked Kitlyn to her feet like a kitten with his left hand while simultaneously hacking Broadsword's head off.

Lliard, Rakden, Imoa, and Danos rushed over to help Oona, who continued fighting beside the obelisk, a surprising distance away from where Kitlyn had drifted.

"We die for Lucen!" shouted Daggers to Nervous. "Destroy the demon at any cost!" Screaming like a fool, he charged Oona in an effort to grab her, leaving himself wide open.

She obligingly stabbed her longsword into his gut. Undeterred, he grabbed her in both arms, two thirds of her sword sticking out of his back, and held her out of the way. Nervous raised his dagger and pivoted toward Tamsen—who screamed.

Pthoonk!

A crossbow quarrel lodged in the back of Nervous's head from Lliard's bow, painting a spritz of blood on the grey stone above the child. The dead man stood stock still for a second before falling limply to one side. Enraged, Daggers shoved Oona back, pressing her against Tamsen and the obelisk.

Oona let go of her sword, leaving it speared through the man, to grab his wrist in both hands, fighting to hold his dagger away from the child's throat.

Imoa arrived first, seizing the man from behind and pulling him off Oona. She dragged him back and threw him to the ground. Danos and Rakden both stabbed him in the chest before he stopped sliding. Daggers writhed, rasped, "I go to Lucen," and went limp.

"Doubtful," muttered Oona.

Kitlyn limped over to her. "Are you okay?"

Lliard re-cocked his crossbow, loaded a bolt, and hung the weapon over his shoulder again.

"No." Oona placed her hand on the hole in Kitlyn's leather leg guard. "I'm upset because you are hurt."

The pain lessened as golden light appeared under Oona's fingers.

"*This*? This is what happens when you two run off alone." Beowyn folded his arms, throwing off serious paternal energy.

Tamsen stood patiently still, waiting for someone to remember she existed.

"Sorry." Kitlyn looked at Beowyn. "Oona had a vision. We didn't have time to wake everyone."

"A vision?" Beowyn raised an eyebrow.

"Yes." She gestured at Tamsen. "I understand now. If we'd taken even a few minutes more to get here, this child would have been dead."

Tamsen shrugged. "A few minutes? Maybe not dead. Definitely on fire, though."

"Did they tie her to a stone post as punishment for sarcasm?" asked Imoa.

"No," said the child. "They thought I'm a demon."

"Are you?" Danos leaned back.

"No, but would a demon really admit it?" Tamsen smiled innocently.

The soldiers, except for Beowyn, appeared somewhat afraid of her.

"This girl is far too calm for being bound to a post." Rakden looked at Oona, who still concentrated on focusing golden healing magic into Kitlyn's leg.

Tamsen sighed. "I've been trying to get loose for hours and haven't made any progress. The people who want me dead are dead. I'm merely being polite and patient. It's the least I can do for you saving me."

"I realize those men were not what one would call scholars, but why did they go to all this trouble to kill her?" Kitlyn exhaled. "Obviously, I'm overjoyed they didn't merely stab her."

"Those idiots believed they needed to use fire to destroy a demon or she'd simply come back." Oona looked up as the golden light faded.

The soldiers stared in bewildered silence for a moment.

"They wanted to *burn* a demon?" Beowyn whistled. "Such stupidity boggles the mind."

Oona pulled her dagger out, approached the obelisk, and sawed the ropes away from the child. Tamsen hopped forward. After slicing the bindings off her wrists and ankles, Oona put the dagger back in its sheath and examined the girl. She had one black eye, numerous facial bruises, a split lip, bloody nose, bruises on her neck, and the ropes had rubbed her wrists and ankles raw to bleeding.

"You're hurt."

"They hit me. The big ouch on my back wasn't from them, though. The monster did it."

"Hold still." Oona rested her hand on the child's forehead, whispering prayers to Orien.

A thin aura of golden light surrounded Tamsen. Over the course of a few minutes, all the cuts, scrapes, and bruises faded away. Her expression relaxed visibly in time with her pain lessening.

Once the last of the minor injuries disappeared, the child cried tears of rage. "Why were they so mean? All I tried to do was help."

Oona put an arm around her. "You're safe now."

Her precocious aplomb faltered. The girl clung to Oona, shivering and staring into nowhere with an 'I almost died!' expression.

"Someone please give her water and some food." Kitlyn rubbed her sore thigh. "We left ours at the inn."

"Your packs are in our boats." Imoa plucked a canteen from her side and offered it to Tamsen.

"Thank you!" The girl chugged eagerly, choking a few times before calming enough to drink without most of the water splashing down her front.

Oona shook her head at the five dead men. "So needless to spill this blood."

"War is often needless." Kitlyn embraced her. "Better their blood wets the earth than yours. We gave them every chance to see reason."

31

THE COURT WIZARD

OONA

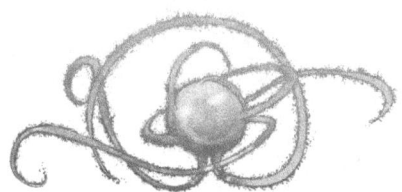

$\mathcal{A}$ village of 'Lucenites' being destroyed made Oona wonder about the nature of the attack.

Obviously, Lucen would know how they'd react to Tamsen using magic. If he had, in fact, sent whatever monster here to destroy heretics, wouldn't he have waited a tiny bit longer to avoid cutting it so close on an innocent child's life? Perhaps he had merely not protected them and the monster simply happened by.

They'd found tracks indicating quite a few survivors marched away from the village, all of them likely believers of lies.

"I think we should find the rest of the people from Torjin." Oona walked over to the corpse of Nervous and pulled her longsword out of him. "They deserve to hear the truth of Lucen."

"These men possessed heads harder than any rock I can summon. They also tried to kill us. It's also quite likely they all agreed on the plan to kill Tamsen." Kitlyn held her arms out to either side. "Do you really want to chase down the survivors who fled this village only to be forced to kill most of them? Assuming, of course, we don't lose and end up dead."

Oona shivered. "I don't want to kill anyone. I didn't want to kill *these* people, despite their heresy." She crouched to wipe the blood from her sword on the dead man's breeches. "It seems wrong not to do anything about such lies."

"I think it's already been handled." Kitlyn pointed at the ruins of the village, faintly visible past the fog, which appeared to be thinning due to the sun. "Some sort of creature scattered the villagers."

After sheathing her blade, Oona walked over to Tamsen. "What manner of beast attacked this place?"

Tamsen hurriedly finished chewing a hunk of ration. "I don't know what it's called, but it looked like a giant ball of vines or roots as big as a whole house. I'm not sure where it came from or why it attacked. I was at the inn cleaning tables and everyone outside started screaming."

"The villagers are probably on their way to seek safety in Kolbrin's Quay or even Lamneth," said Kitlyn. "Larger cities where the people didn't fall for the spies' manipulation."

"I don't think so." Tamsen scrunched up her face. "They talked often about how people chased them off for being traitors."

"Makes sense." Yerbin nodded. "Talking about Lucen or the other gods in Evermoor during the war makes someone sound like a spy or traitor."

"Yes." Kitlyn set her hands on her hips. "Explains why they settled a tiny village out here away from everyone. Unless you're feeling Lucen's call to go get involved, I think we can trust the people of Evermoor to deal with them. They aren't at all tough, picking on a little girl who can magically shove people."

Tamsen looked down. "Sorry. I'd have done more to help, but it's the only spell I can cast when my hands are tied behind my back. It's so simple it's not even really first circle. More like zero-th."

"Those fools will likely stay deep in the moor so they aren't executed for being traitors." Beowyn smirked. "Critters and such will sort them out."

"No need to say sorry." Kitlyn patted the girl on the shoulder. "You really did make a big difference. Saved my life at least once. Quite an impressive thing to do while you couldn't move."

Tamsen grinned up at her.

Whoa. She's got two different colored eyes. Kitlyn stared. *Amber and emerald. She almost died. There for a fleeting moment and lost forever if we don't grab it fast enough... by Lucen! She's the key!*

"Wwwwwhat?" asked Tamsen, raising an eyebrow. "You're giving me a strange look."

"Oona, she's the key!"

"Huh?" Oona blinked. "She's a child, not a key."

Tamsen pointed at Oona. "I agree with her."

"Hear me out." Kitlyn indicated the girl's eyes. "Emerald and amber. She is both small and large at the same time. A small person —child—yet large for a key. Fragile—again, child—but deadly with training? We're thinking of training using the key, but what if it means the *key* needs training? It has to refer to her magic."

"I'm a little worried where this is going, but I've spent a year washing dishes, scrubbing floors, and waiting tables in exchange for a place to sleep and food... so if you two want to stick me into a door I can maybe go along with it if it isn't going to hurt. Honestly, you saved my life. I owe you. No one's ever risked their lives to protect me before."

Oona looked the girl over. "Did those men take anything that belonged to you?"

"Yes. My boots. They're kinda big on me. Got in the way of the rope." Tamsen walked off in the direction the men had come from.

The island turned out not to be an elongated oval but rather an odd lopsided T shape. The men had established a primitive camp at the end of the smaller sideways spur. Shelters made of vines and leaves covered bedding taken from the wrecked village. Five small trunks sat positioned around a fire pit as seats. Tamsen retrieved a pair of tattered, floppy soft leather boots from beside a tree. They looked a bit big on her and had quite likely been scavenged from someone's trash. She sat on one of the trunks, held her legs up and squinted at her feet.

Mud and dirt fell off her for no apparent reason, leaving her clean from the shins down. Tamsen put her boots on, stood, and pointed at a tree. "That's where I spent the past two days. The men weren't lying when they told you they waited for the wood to dry out."

Oona ran over and hugged her, horrified at the implication. "You sat there for two days knowing they were going to burn you?"

"Yeah."

"You poor thing." Oona squish-hugged her.

"It was scary, but I'm okay now. I knew they couldn't really follow Lucen because they had no idea about demons, so I tried praying for help. Not easy with a wooden stick in my mouth, let me say."

Tamsen gurgled in response to Oona squeezing her harder.

"I have a feeling Evie's going to have a new friend," said Kitlyn.

If she wants to stay with us... Oona smiled at Tamsen. "Do you have any family?"

"No." Tamsen shook her head, eyes downcast. "I'm an orphan. I had nowhere to live for a while until I found the inn here. Burran let me work instead of kicking me out, so this *was* home."

"A place isn't home if you're forced to work," said Oona.

"Ouch," deadpanned Kitlyn.

Oona twisted to look at her. "You were mistreated."

"He didn't *force* me to work." Tamsen shrugged. "But if I didn't, he'd have kicked me out. It wasn't too bad."

"Would you like to stay with us?" asked Oona. "If Kit is open to the idea."

Except for Beowyn and Imoa, the soldiers grimaced or made faces at her referring to the queen as 'Kit.'

"I like her attitude and courage." Kitlyn smiled. "And your blanket cloak is adorable. Are those little bears around the edges?"

"Yes. It's my blanket from when I was little. Only thing I have left from home. I know it's kinda dingy, but I keep it because my parents gave it to me when they left me at grandpa's... the last time I saw them."

Aww! Oona's heart practically melted into a puddle. "You are no longer an orphan."

Tamsen peered up at them, a hint of hope in her multicolored eyes. "Umm, okay. Do you have to ask your parents or husbands for permission or are you older than you look?"

Beowyn leaned back into a hearty laugh.

Oona burst into laughter as well. Kitlyn snickered.

"Oh, we have our own little house." Oona smiled.

Kitlyn covered her mouth.

Oona wagged her eyebrows. "And we're married—to each other."

"Ooh, really?" Tamsen grinned. "Wonderful! You must really love each other to go wandering around this horrible place together."

"We do." Kitlyn took Oona's hand. "As a matter of fact, we are in this place because Oona loves me so much, she's demanding we run around trying to get rid of an ancient curse that's trying to kill me."

"Maybe both of us. Kethaba said it's not on your family specifically." Oona fidgeted, dreading what her death might do to Kitlyn.

"Are you rich?" Tamsen looked at Oona. "You kind of sound like it, but your wife talks ordinary."

Oona patted the girl on the head. "Kitlyn is far from ordinary."

"I mean…" Tamsen laughed. "Like 'not rich' ordinary. You're really nice for a rich person. The ones in Lamneth are *so* arrogant."

"We have enough money. You won't have to worry about anything."

Kitlyn elbowed Oona. "Stop teasing the poor child."

"Am I to be a servant?" asked Tamsen. "I don't mind."

"No. Oona's got a little sister you'll likely want to play with, and I'm sure you'll be too busy studying to have time for floor cleaning." Kitlyn winked.

Well, the queens are barely adults. Oona smiled to herself. *Why shouldn't our court wizard be a little girl?*

32

THE PATH TO ISILIEN

KITLYN

Tamsen being the key made more sense the longer Kitlyn spent thinking about it.

Kitlyn paced around while Oona fussed over the girl's shabby clothes. As cute as the blanket cloak was, it would have to go as soon as they arrived anywhere with a functional tailor's shop. Fine for her to keep due to sentimental value, but she shouldn't be wearing it. Too much about this girl aligned with the riddle the Na'vir seer relayed. The ramblings of seers didn't particularly impress Kitlyn considering the disaster of The Foretelling responsible for how their lives had gone from age three to sixteen.

However, this particular seer's words didn't involve anything as significant as the end of the world or even the end of a war. She hated the ambiguity associated with foretellings in general. Why couldn't people able to see the future be more direct? Couldn't they say 'you will need to find a child with magic' and not 'a key?'

Kitlyn still found it difficult to argue. What were the odds they'd stumble across a person who had two different colored eyes, the exact colors described in the seer's writing from a thousand years ago? A ten-year-old was small compared to an adult while being much larger than a traditional key. The part about them having only a short time to acquire the key or it would be lost forever certainly fit. If those idiots had killed her, Tamsen would've been lost forever. Neither she nor Oona knew much about arcane magic, but what they'd been told so far certainly made it sound like they gained in knowledge and power with training.

"There's one thing I'm not understanding," said Kitlyn.

"Just one?" asked Oona.

"Funny. I mean about the Isilien situation. If Tamsen *is* the key, what makes us so significant that she'd be born in time to be here to help us break the curse? Is it something about *her* specifically or could anyone who possessed arcane magic effectively act as the key? Did some greater force set all of this in motion, or did the old seer simply happen to see this moment not realizing how far in the future it would be?"

Oona rubbed her forehead. "I hate foretellings."

"Me too."

"Yeah, they're annoying." Tamsen folded her arms. "Who wrote what about me?"

Oona fished a scrap of paper out of her pouch and read from it. "You will know the key to Isilien when wrathful amber dwells beside innocent emerald. It is at once large and small. Fragile, yet deadly with proper training."

"Innocent could mean child. Wrathful? She's probably pretty upset at those men for wanting to kill her after she tried to help them." Kitlyn grimaced at a twinge of pain in her thigh. *It's going to hurt for a few days. Thank Orien, it could be far worse.*

"Okay," said Tamsen. "I can understand how you think those words describe me. Foretellings are horrible for never saying exactly what they mean. My eyes aren't wrathful or innocent. I use them both when I'm angry or making a 'please don't hit me' face. The seer who wrote it had to be using fancy language on purpose. Innocent and wrathful probably means I'm a kid, but I'm not helpless. I *could* really hurt someone if I had to."

"You?" Beowyn grinned. "You're pretty little."

"Fire." Tamsen huffed. "I didn't use it on those men because I hoped to convince them I'm not a demon. By the time the true depths of their stupidity became clear, they'd already tied me up."

"So what do we do here?" Oona exhaled. "It does sound like Tamsen might be this key, but do we really drag a child with us into a dangerous swamp?"

Beowyn's expression hinted he felt the same way about Oona and Kitlyn.

"You saved my life. I will help you." Tamsen folded her arms.

"We still don't know where to even go." Kitlyn peered back at the smashed village. "We might have to follow the survivors anyway to find Aztian."

Oona raked her hands up through her hair in frustration. "I hope he's not one of those Lucenite fools."

Tamsen cringed. "He's dead."

"What?" asked Oona.

"The monster squished him." Tamsen clapped as if swatting a bug on her left hand. "He tried to fight it."

Oh, no... Kitlyn stared at Oona. "How are we supposed to find Isilien without a guide?"

"Isilien..." Tamsen squinted. "Think I know the place you're looking for. My books talk about it. If it isn't too much trouble, can we get my books once we're done?"

"I don't see why not." Kitlyn looked around. "Where are they?"

"Hidden under the floor in my room at the Drowned Rat. Didn't want anyone finding them or they might have tied me to the 'sacred obelisk' and lit me on fire."

Oona grumbled.

"Why did you even stay there knowing everyone would try to kill you if they discovered you had magic?" asked Kitlyn.

"I liked having a roof over my head." Tamsen shrugged. "They wouldn't know I could do anything unless they caught me using magic. Books, I could pretend not to know what they were. Wouldn't really have to, now that I think about it. Not like anyone else in Torjin could read."

The soldiers chuckled.

"We're right here." Oona gestured at the smashed village. "Might as well collect them now."

"Are you sure? I have a lot of books. They're heavy and too much to carry in a dangerous place where I could lose them."

Kitlyn had to agree it made little sense to lug heavy books deep into the swamp only to lug them all the way back for no real reason. "All right. We will stop here for them on the way home."

Out of spite, Kitlyn liquefied the obelisk, commanding it and the platform to sink deep into the mud before solidifying them into an assortment of rounded rocks. After everyone took a short break to deal with the call of nature, they made their way back across the log bridges to the main island. The soldiers had brought three more two-person boats. Beowyn explained they didn't technically belong to anyone specifically, as the town of Kolbrin's Quay paid for them out of tax money. Anyone could use them to go fishing as long as they returned them.

Kitlyn and Oona got in their boat, Tamsen perched between them. Beowyn shared a boat with Imoa due to her weighing the least of the soldiers. Rakden spent a few minutes politely grumbling about Oona and Kitlyn rushing off in the middle of the night, though conceded Oona couldn't really ignore it when the gods wanted her to do something.

Tamsen pointed. "Keep going straight down this way until we get to the ruined tower."

"Ruined tower?" asked Kitlyn.

"Yes. It's really old. The Anthari made it." Tamsen peered back at Kitlyn. "We shouldn't go inside. It could fall over and crush us."

"Have you been there?" Oona padded in no particular hurry.

"Burran took me with him once to hunt for cooking herbs," said Tamsen. "We went close enough to see it in the distance. Some of my books have drawings. The Anthari called this one Noru Sendral. They built thirteen of them as defenses."

"You making this up, kid?" called Yerbin from two boats back.

"No, sir. I remember almost everything I read like I can see the pages in front of me."

Kitlyn chuckled. "Handy talent for a mage."

"It is," said Tamsen. "Makes it much easier to remember spells."

"Are there many wizards in Evermoor?" Kitlyn paddled a little faster to keep up.

"I haven't met any except for Pelar, but he disappeared." Tamsen slouched. "He lived at the end of the street from my grandfather's. His house looked empty and broken, but he said he used an illusion spell to keep thieves out. Pelar gave me all my books, told me I had magic, and taught me how to use it."

"He wouldn't take you in when your parents died?" asked Oona, her voice sad.

Tamsen sighed. "Pelar disappeared. I went there first, but his house really was broken inside, like no one ever lived there. I think he ran away from bad people who wanted to hurt mages."

So strange... how does a house turn into a ruin so fast? This child is... maybe more than she seems?

Kitlyn leaned forward, fussing at the girl's long, straight dark brown hair to get a look at her ears. Round, not pointed.

"Hm?" Tamsen twisted to look at her.

"Something in your hair. It's gone." Kitlyn blushed faintly.

Tamsen smiled. "Thank you."

She's not an elf. They have pointed ears... or so the books claimed. Part faerie? The only thing we know for sure is she is no demon. When Oona made the huge Lucen symbol, the child looked up at it exactly the way a child would look at people saving her from murderers. How much does she know about Isilien?

"What do your books say about Isil—?"

Something massive burst up out of the water to the right of their boat, creating a wave powerful enough to nearly capsize them. A flailing mass of huge whip-like roots rose into the air, protruding from an irregular tangle gathering itself off the river bottom into a spherical mass. Soldiers screamed in alarm and warning. An uncountable number of leafy tendrils whomped at the water, seemingly at random.

One came straight down at their boat.

Kitlyn grabbed Tamsen, hauling her backward a second before a vine as thick around as her leg smashed the little boat in two. The front and back halves pivoted like seesaws stomped on by a giant, throwing Kitlyn, Oona, and Tamsen into the air past each other. Kitlyn caught enough air to flip over once before falling into the water and going under.

More shouting came from the soldiers, muted by the water in her ears. Tamsen wriggled out of her grip, pushing upward. Kitlyn reoriented herself vertical, discovering the disgustingly slimy bottom much closer than expected. Even though her feet sank a bit into the muck, she stood chest high in surprisingly shallow water.

To her right, the next nearest boat to them containing Lliard and Rakden had also been smashed in half. Both other boats survived the frantic root pounding, though Beowyn and Imoa's had overturned. Danos and Yerbin jumped out of their boat, shoving it toward the closest marshy island.

Tamsen stood neck deep a short distance to Kitlyn's left. "This is not good. We should run."

Kitlyn stared straight ahead in bewildered horror at the colossal tangle of living vines. The central mass, about fifteen feet across, formed a lopsided sphere, fatter on the bottom than top, no doubt due to its weight. Numerous long, branchy tentacles sprouted all over, several reaching thirty feet in length. A few had thorns, some had leaves, many sported recent nicks and gouges from blades. Something that size couldn't possibly have lurked in water this shallow unless it had flattened itself out deliberately to hide. The sight of the roots and such whipping around explained the unusual damage to the buildings in Torjin.

"We can't run in this muck," yelled Oona. "How did you beat this thing before?"

"Umm, we didn't. We ran away." Tamsen pulled her hair off her face. "Everyone decided to hide and watch it smash buildings. It eventually got bored and went back into the swamp."

Huge roots slapped at the ground, six or seven at a time, attacking multiple people at once but mostly smacking empty space.

Kitlyn dove aside to avoid a downward-swinging root, swimming for a short distance underwater in hopes of hiding from it. *Is it after Tamsen? Were those Lucenite fools right?*

She surfaced to the sound of Oona screaming and Beowyn roaring a war cry.

Fortunately, Oona only screamed while diving out of the way of a smashing root. Beowyn trudged up to the creature's central mass, hacking his greatsword at the tangle. He may as well have been trying to kill a house, though the giant blade did manage to leave noticeable gashes.

Imoa and Rakden dueled thinner roots trying to slap them around. Yerbin slogged across the water, closing in on the creature's main body beside Beowyn, who kept hacking at it. It seemed he had a decent idea as the long whip tendrils couldn't effectively pound on anything too close to the middle.

A dull thud preceded Danos screaming. The red-haired soldier flew sideways, spinning, launched by a crossing slap from a ten-inch-thick root. He skipped twice off the water like a stone before going under.

Kitlyn reached for her longsword, but hesitated. *I'd have an easier time chopping down a tree with a table knife.* Since her bare feet made firm contact—up to the shins—with the earth, she couldn't possibly achieve a stronger connection to the Alderswood magically except for touching the tree itself. She held her hands out to either side, arms shrouded in green light, and summoned a two-foot boulder up from the depths. Despite the size of the rock, it still zoomed forward at the speed of a crossbow bolt, striking the creature's spherical center.

The boulder tore into the roots, snapping and crashing its way deep into the monster's core. Alas, the entity didn't appear to have any sort of heart or internal organs, merely a tangle of flexible branches. Still, the power of the impact made the creature roll slightly backward. Multiple root whips flailed around, giving the impression the creature became confused at anything having the power to forcibly move it.

Danos resurfaced, gasping for air. "Don't let it smack you."

"Appreciate the advice, never would have thought of that," yelled Imoa while hacking at a nearby root.

"Oh, I'm going to regret this," muttered Tamsen. She lifted her hands out of the water, weaving them together in an intricate gesture. *"Na'ava sura kaz maranhi eht."*

A blazing bolt of fire shot forth from the child's hands, giving off a roar and a blast of heat like a furnace four feet from Kitlyn's face. The glimmering orange-yellow streak washed over the upper left portion of the root sphere, lasting three or four seconds before dissipating. A few patches of burn remained on the roots.

The entire root ball undulated, bouncing in place in a manner reminiscent of a pudgy, spoiled noble brat not getting his way, though it made no sound other than the whip-crack of vines flying around.

"Yeah, I'm going to regret lighting it on fire." Tamsen dove to her left, already swimming away from the revenge she expected.

By Lucen! Kitlyn gawked at such a destructive thing coming from the hands of a girl so young. *Wrathful indeed.*

"Kit! Look out!" yelled Oona.

She looked up at a root about to smash straight down on top of her. Alderswood energy responded to her desire not to be crushed, summoning a rock spire up to block. The root whip smacked into the column, bending over and whipping the water behind her, crushing the top foot or so of the stone pillar into fragments.

Tamsen chanted the same phrase again, projecting another stream of fire into the creature.

Multiple vines swung at the child.

She shrieked and dove under, the barrage of tendril whips churning the water where she'd been.

Oona threw a bolt of blue light into the spherical mass, knocking a hunk of bark askew. Alas, Lucen's magic proved extremely effective on demons but largely weak on anything else. Kitlyn summoned another giant boulder, hoping if she punched enough tunnels into the root sphere, she would eventually accomplish something.

Before she could launch the rock, Tamsen flew up out of the water, a relatively narrow vine coiled around one leg. She appeared only for a second as the creature slapped her back down into the water.

"Tamsen!" screamed Oona, struggling to swim/run toward her.

Trusting her wife to protect the girl, Kitlyn resumed focus on her magic, firing the boulder into the root mass. The larger stone tore a path into the creature, rolling the giant tumbleweed backward. Muddy water dripped from limb vines pulled up from beneath the surface. This monster didn't appear to have any true top or bottom, flailing tendrils stuck out in all directions like the thorns of a thistle. It lacked any means to convey emotion whatsoever, having no eyes, mouth, or anything beyond being a knotted mass of roots. It also made no effort to roll forward again, evidently not caring which part of it faced in which direction.

The soldiers kept trying to kill it with blades. Only Beowyn's greatsword had any effect more than leaving tiny nicks, but even he could only sever the smaller tendrils. Yerbin went flying backward when a slender root grasped him around the middle and flung him. He landed over thirty feet away with a wet *splat*, face down on a mud island. Two large root whips sprouting from the top of the sphere swung high, rearing back to crush him.

Kitlyn called out to the earth. Two columns of mud surrounded in green light shot up from the ground on either side of the dazed soldier, bending together to join in an arch over him. She solidified it to dense stone an instant before the heavy roots crashed through it. The stone arch disintegrated, but took most of the force out of the strike, sparing Yerbin serious injury.

Imoa's scream receded into the distance, ending with a dull *thud*.

A hard, wooden root sprouted up from the brackish water, grabbed Kitlyn around the chest, and dragged her under. She clawed at the surface, lost to a momentary feral panic. Bubbles trailed up from her lips, air forced out of her as the root squeezed. Her legs drifted upward, higher than her head. She grabbed the vine where it wrapped over her left shoulder, struggling to pull it away. Thorns jabbed into her side, more annoying than deadly.

Her head pounded harder and harder as she held her breath.

Someone grabbed at her, trying to pull her upward but couldn't overpower the root holding her down. Oona's voice shouting desperately came from close by, words too distorted by depth, fear, and disorientation to understand.

Kitlyn fought the cloudiness invading her thoughts, refusing to surrender to unconsciousness. Kethaba wasn't here to bring her back from the brink of death after drowning a second time. Oona kept trying to pull her head above the surface, forcing thorns in deeper. Kitlyn latched onto the pain, grateful for it. Hurting meant she remained awake. She fought panic, trying to stop kicking and call out to the stone. If she could summon a spire to push her upward, she could breathe.

The tendril holding her jolted from a sudden impact and stopped moving. Its crushing grip around her body lost strength. No longer fighting a live root, Oona easily pulled Kitlyn upright. She gasped for air, seeing spots, gagging. The slimy water she coughed up tasted like old shoes left in the rain.

"Kit!"

"I'm"—she coughed—"okay."

Beowyn, who'd evidently chopped off the root trying to drown her, hauled his greatsword up out of the water. He trudged off to resume his assault on the central tangle.

Roaring flames drowned out Tamsen's tiny voice intoning magical words.

Bleary-eyed, Kitlyn looked up at the huge root monster. It shuddered and flailed, slapping dozens of whipping tendrils randomly at the water in what appeared to be a tantrum or response to the pain of being on fire. It rained mud. One big glob splattered into Kitlyn's face. Plumes of whitish smoke rose from the root ball's upper half, which continued to burn after the brief stream of intense fire from the child petered out.

Rakden's shouts came from the far side of the river, searching for Imoa. She responded in a moan of pain.

Tamsen gave a brief high-pitched squeal of alarm and ducked underwater seconds before five root whips pummeled the water where she'd been.

Oona scraped mud out of her eyes, momentarily blinded. "I don't know what to do. My magic isn't able to hurt it and I dare not try using a blade."

"I'm not sure I'm helping much either." Kitlyn coughed, spat to the side, and gathered her magic to summon another boulder.

Tamsen's head appeared above the surface about twenty feet away on the right. She stuck her hands out of the water and cast another fire bolt into the center of the quivering mass of roots.

Oona abruptly plunged straight down. Her attempt to scream muffled into a trail of bubbles.

Kitlyn grabbed for her in the murky water, but her fingers found only a fast-moving current. Seconds later, Oona rose out of the river twenty feet away, dangling upside down from a root wrapped around her legs. She spat out water, coughed, and managed to gasp in another breath before the root smacked her into the marsh and dragged her under.

Tamsen started to invoke the fire spell again, but something yanked her beneath the surface before she finished.

No! Dammit! Kitlyn rapidly looked back and forth between two bubbling spots. If she went for Oona, Tamsen would drown. If she tried to save the child, her love would drown. A second passed. She started to turn toward Oona's last known location, but froze, realizing she felt both of them kicking at the ground in her earth sense.

She knew exactly where they were.

Kitlyn poured magic into the earth, forcing stone to rise in the shape of flat-topped pillars under Oona and Tamsen. The touch of their feet lifted off the river bottom—a good sign—but it momentarily made them invisible. Hoping they hadn't slipped off the pillars, she continued commanding the stone to grow upward.

Oona, flat on her back, broke the surface first. A lump of soaked blue fabric—Tamsen's blanket-covered butt—appeared a second later. The child lay draped over the pillar on her stomach, arms and legs wrapped around it. Multiple root tendrils gripped both of them. Squished between crushing roots trying to drown them and unyielding stone pushing upward, they both screamed.

Kitlyn reached for her longsword to cut them loose, but hesitated. *I am a fool. This thing is made out of roots.* She stared at the vines squeezing her beloved against the stone. Rootshaper magic had a different energy, more like asking it to do things rather than commanding as with stone. She'd never tried to use it on angry, sentient plants before. This monster certainly would not do what she asked—so she tried making demands.

Bright green glow surrounded her hands and forearms. Kitlyn reached out for a connection to the life essence within the roots trapping Oona.

Release her! Let go of them now!

The usual sense of response the roots gave didn't exist—so she treated it like stone, trying to exert her willpower over the tendrils, forcing it to move as she desired. Oona's pained screams pushed her to a level of furious rage beyond the moment she'd nearly torn Castle Cimril apart.

In a burst of splinters, the roots holding Oona exploded. Seconds later, the roots crushing Tamsen shattered. Snarling, Kitlyn faced the creature, concentrating on one tendril at a time until each whipping root in sight exploded.

Tamsen scrambled upright, standing atop her column as she waved her arms around in a mesmerizing series of intricate hand motions. *"Na'ava sura kaz maranhi eht."* A loud, fluttering stream of fire projected outward from her hands, burning a deep hole into the side of the root mass.

Moisture boiling out of the twitching vines squealed like a scream of agony.

Roots flailed and shuddered, the monster pounding randomly around at the marsh.

"Yeah, I'm definitely regretting lighting this thing on fire." Tamsen spat to the side.

The creature lurched forward, rolling itself toward the child.

"Uh oh." Tamsen leaned back. "I think it's angry."

Oona's continued shouts of pain infuriated Kitlyn more. Snarling, she focused on the immense mass of roots and grasped at the air, yanking her hands apart as if tearing a bundle of straw in half. The green glow around her arms intensified. Similar light welled up throughout the root ball's core. It shuddered to a halt, no longer rolling toward Tamsen, every whipping tendril flopping aimlessly.

Weakened by fire, the burning top portion split apart first, the rip progressing downward in response to Kitlyn pulling her hands farther apart. Despite having a physical grasp of nothing, it felt as if she pulled against tough fabric, tearing it apart strand by strand. Beowyn hacked at the point where the two halves separated, chopping again and again in an effort to help.

Finally, the tension gave way; Kitlyn's hands flew apart to either side.

The giant root sphere ripped completely down the middle, each half flying off as if Omun had thrown them. Exhaustion crashed over her. She slouched forward, trying to catch her breath while gradually absorbing energy from the ground.

"Wow," whispered Tamsen. "You threw it like a hundred feet. It had to weigh as much as a house!"

Oona sloshed over and grabbed her. "Kit…"

"I'm fine. Just tired. Are you hurt?"

"Bruised. Almost drowned, but nothing serious. Got a couple thorn stabs, and a fish tried to eat me, but it spat me out once it realized I was too big."

"Ugh," said Tamsen. "This water tastes like butt."

"Imoa?" called Rakden.

"I'm here," came a weak shout from the trees. "Think my leg is broken."

Oona directed everyone to gather on a relatively solid island by where the monster initially destroyed their boat. She tended to a few minor thorn punctures and a fish bite on Tamsen, Kitlyn's bruises, and cracked ribs Danos and Yerbin suffered. Rakden and Lliard carried Imoa out of the woods from two rivers over. Oona arranged the woman's leg as straight as she could before calling upon Orien's healing gift.

Tamsen sat nearby, occasionally coughing and spitting up water.

Ten minutes later, the golden light around Oona's hands faded.

"Her leg will heal as it was before, but it will be fragile for several days." Oona looked up at Rakden. "She won't be able to hike or fight for at least a week."

"Damn," muttered Imoa. "I can sit in a boat and use a crossbow."

"Lliard, go with her back to Kolbrin's Quay." Rakden pointed at one of the two remaining boats. "Wait for us at the inn."

"Sir." Lliard didn't look happy to be the one chosen to sit out, but offered no protest.

Kitlyn handed him a few coins to pay for their lodging and food.

Oona plucked the canteen from Imoa's belt, holding it up in both hands. "May Lucen's purity transfer to this water. May it guard us from foulness and decay." Faint white light surrounded the canteen, then faded. She took a sip, then handed it to Kitlyn. "Everyone drink a little. We all swallowed bog water. I dare not think what horrors lurk within."

The canteen made the rounds, the soldiers and Tamsen all too happy to avoid coming down with a nasty disease.

Imoa scowled off to the side. "Never expected to lose a fight to a damned bush."

Most of the soldiers chuckled, Rakden patting her on the shoulder.

"Indeed." Beowyn whistled. "When we cut vines out of our way... they don't usually fight back."

Kitlyn tried to make sense of what they'd seen—and what she'd done. Tearing such an enormous monster in half seemed beyond ridiculous, but it *had* been entirely made of plant matter. The Alderswood infused her with the powers of stone and root. No creature could possibly exist *more* vulnerable to her magic than a root ball except for a solid stone being. She couldn't magically rip a living creature apart, even a mouse, so perhaps destroying a massive plant hadn't been as impressive as it looked.

Everyone stared at each other in silence as they rested, seemingly trying to process what happened.

Eventually, Tamsen broke the uncomfortable silence. "My boots are gone."

"What?" asked Oona.

Kitlyn looked at the girl. Sure enough, she sat there barefoot.

Her formerly baggy pants clung to her legs, making her appear thin and underfed. Somehow, the blanket cloak stayed on despite the vine dragging her around underwater.

"The mud ate them when I fell out of the boat. First time I stepped on the bottom, the muck pulled them right off me." Tamsen checked over the various small pouches on her belt. "I lost my satchel, too."

Drat. Mine are probably gone as well. They were in the boat and it's smashed. Kitlyn stood. "We'll get you some new ones, and some proper clothes as soon as we're back in civilization."

"Thank you."

Kitlyn wandered over to the wreckage of the boat she'd been in, her feet squishing into the mud up to the ankles. The wreckage sunk in the shallows by the river's edge, a little deeper than halfway submerged. Since she'd already gotten soaked, she waded in and fumbled around the opaque water between the two hull sections until she located her pack.

"My satchel! There it is!" Tamsen scrambled into the water, jumping forward to swim in pursuit of a brown lump floating between the stone pillars.

Oona crept over to the water's edge behind Kitlyn, watching the child go out and return to shore towing her little bag. "She shouldn't run around barefoot out here. She doesn't have your magic."

"Every child and half the adults in Kolbrin's Quay aren't wearing shoes. Besides, do you fancy swimming back and forth grabbing at muck for hours?" asked Kitlyn. "She put her feet down in the mud. Those boots are gone and buried. They'd probably fall apart if we tried pulling them out."

"Her boots were the most intact bit of clothing she had." Oona folded her arms, frowning.

"Pity your light ball only looks as if she has eyes. Sure does seem expressive sometimes."

Oona held her hands out as if cradling a kitten. Her light orb appeared a second later, the two bright spots in the otherwise blue sphere tilted in a way suggestive of a big smile despite it not having any sort of mouth. Seconds later, it zipped into the water. Glow moved back and forth in the murk for a few minutes. The orb abruptly popped up, bouncing on the surface a few yards away from shore.

"She found them!" Oona beamed—then rushed into the brownish-grey water.

By Lucen. The gods really do fancy her.

Oona waded out into chest-high water, then ducked under at the indicated spot, resurfacing in a moment holding the missing boots.

"Yay!" called Tamsen.

Oona triumphantly returned to shore and poured slime out of the boots.

"So… the princess threw herself into muddy swamp water." Kitlyn winked.

"She did," whispered Oona. "But she's not a princess anymore."

Kitlyn kissed her, mud and all. They looked at each other serious-faced for a second before the taste of the swamp got the better of them and they both made 'blech' faces, trying not to laugh too hard. While Oona handed the boots back to the girl, Kitlyn crouched in the foul water and struggled to push the smashed boat aside to free her pack. Her legs sank into the mucky bottom up to her knees, but she dislodged the front portion of her former boat. Oona grabbed the pack, helping pull it—and her—from the moor. Gooey mud squished out from under them. Oona spilled over backward, dragging Kitlyn down on top of her, nose to nose.

"Oof," muttered Oona.

Kitlyn smiled at droplets of dark brown dripping from her chin onto on her love's face, though she'd already been quite filthy. "Well, I'm covered in mud. Do you still think I'm beautiful?"

"I do." Oona attempted to wipe mud from Kitlyn's cheek, but only smeared it around. "Oh, the grand life of royalty. Mud in our hair and betwixt our toes."

"Did you lose your boots, too?" asked Kitlyn.

"No, but they're flooded."

"I really don't mind the mud." Kitlyn grinned. "At least we're in our armor and not one of those bothersome gowns."

"Wait…" Tamsen raised both eyebrows. "Did you say royalty?"

"Yes," deadpanned Kitlyn. "We're the queens of Lucernia."

The child cracked up giggling… but her laughter gradually lost strength at their continued serious expressions, until she wound up staring at them, blank-faced. "Are you teasing me?"

"No." Oona smiled at her. "But we don't take ourselves too seriously."

"We take our responsibility seriously, but don't believe we are better than anyone. I don't mind getting dirty—as you can plainly see."

Tamsen emitted a strange squeak, her right eye wider than her left.

Oona glanced down. "You are in tune with the earth… though"—she bounced, making squishing sounds come from her boots—"This *is* somewhat fun."

"It is."

"Except for the nearly being crushed by a giant monster part." Oona shuddered.

"You are really the queens of Lucernia?" whispered Tamsen. "And you're really offering to let me go home with you? Like, you want to adopt me?"

"Yes," said Oona and Kitlyn simultaneously.

The child stared into space.

After a minute, Kitlyn asked, "Are you all right?"

"I'm trying to decide if I should scream, cry, or faint," whispered Tamsen. "The choice is difficult." She looked at the soldiers. "Are they teasing me?"

Everyone shook their heads.

Tamsen's eyes crossed. She muttered something incomprehensible and fell over backward into the mud, out cold.

"I understand exactly how she feels." Kitlyn sat up.

33

MERELY IN HIDING
OONA

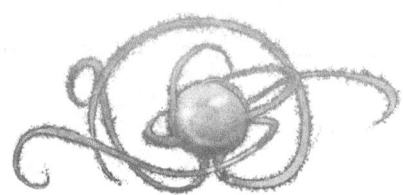

O ona gently shook Tamsen awake and encouraged her to eat a little more of a ration.

The child asked another fifteen or twenty times if they'd teased her about being the monarchs of Lucernia, bringing up various reasons for why they'd likely be pulling her leg: no crowns, too young to possibly be queens, running around Evermoor instead of being in a castle, not having a huge army with them, being 'too nice' and Kitlyn not 'talking like a rich person.'

She collected herself surprisingly fast for a ten-year-old, perhaps not fully believing them yet. Naturally, *some* degree of reaction had to be expected at learning she went from being an orphan who had to work to survive to being adopted by literal royalty. However, Tamsen resumed acting normal after only a brief display of emotion, neither becoming big-headed nor obsequious. She did, however, give off gratitude, enough for Oona to suspect her desperate need for a permanent home would've made her thrilled if even paupers took her in. That a child willingly stayed at a village where everyone would kill her if they learned her secret spoke tragic volumes.

Another odd thing, the girl's boots already appeared dry and mud-free.

I don't imagine many children her age would stand their ground in the face of a giant root monster. She's not reckless… tried to tell us to run at first, but she fought beside us.

While waiting for Kitlyn to weave two replacement boats out of summoned roots, Oona studied Tamsen's mannerisms. The child stood at the south end of the small island, gazing off into the swamp like someone trying to remember directions. She didn't really act like an orphan who'd experienced a few rough years. Most of the war orphans back in Lucernia around her age tended to be highly distrustful of everyone, clingy, or perpetually sad. Tamsen hadn't shown even the slightest bit of doubt toward Oona and Kitlyn's intentions, almost as if she could sense their inner nature. Granted, they *had* gotten into a swordfight against five men to protect her life.

I know nothing of people who use arcane magic. Perhaps it is normal for her to read people? Ulfaan appeared to expect we would tell him of our intention not to ban magic. Or am I confusing myself? She sighed into her hands, eager to get home and put this moor and the curse behind her. As long as she and Kitlyn occupied the throne, there would always be *some* fear of death. However, the small chance an assassin or enemy might crop up didn't bother her anywhere near as much as a curse promising *definite* death.

Lliard and Imoa took one boat, heading back to Kolbrin's Quay. Orien's gift allowed Oona to mend the woman's leg to a point, but it would be a while before she'd be able to fight or even handle hiking over rough terrain.

Once Kitlyn finished 'growing' the two replacement boats, the group resumed traveling into the moor. The root-boats had pointier ends, thinner and longer than the stubby paddleboats they'd taken from the town. Oona found it took less effort to reach the same speed, though the canoe-shaped craft felt more likely to roll over sideways.

They followed the stagnant waterway for a few hours, navigating around mud islands ranging in size from a few feet across to large enough for a house. Not one appeared solid enough to set foot on. Every time a loud buzz arose from the chorus of insect noises, Oona ducked, frantically searching for an attacking doom needle wasp—

though fortunately, she spotted only beetles or dragonfly-like bugs big enough to carry mice off.

Eventually, a stone tower came into view out from the trees up ahead. Decades of ivy, moss, and other growth covered it, displacing several stones and cracking many others. The narrow middle spanning between the uppermost story and the base appeared only wide enough to contain a spiral staircase. Its pointy roof and overall shape made Oona think of an enormous war mace stuck handle-first into the ground. Four large openings looked out from the chamber at the top, one facing in each direction. Dense plant growth largely filled the chamber at the top. Based on its size, she figured it had to be a watchtower or archer's roost.

Tamsen sat up tall in the middle of their boat, pointing at it. "That's Noru Sendral. You can't really see under all the dead leaves and stuff, but there is a big copper orb at the top. It amplifies magic —or did. Probably doesn't work anymore after so long. If I cast my fire spell through the orb, it would have cooked the giant root monster in seconds."

Oona gazed up at the tower's upper chamber, noticing patches of bright green in between some of the vines—likely corroded copper— encased in the tangle of plants. "By Lucen... are you sure? Sounds quite dangerous."

"I read about it. The Anthari used towers like this to defend against invading armies. Powerful, but they couldn't move." Tamsen pointed left. "Turn here."

The old tower gave off an eerie, imposing presence, worsening as they neared. *At her age, I would've been terrified of this place.* The entire area gave off a sense of being steeped in death and suffering. Nothing she'd ever read about the Anthari made them sound evil or even savage. Most likely, the land here had been the scene of a horrible battle. Death in large numbers, as often occurred during war, could permanently change the spiritual tone of an area.

They steered to the left. Oona mostly watched the water ahead of them, but at the sense of something staring at her, occasionally glanced to her right as they passed the diamond-shaped island on which the tower stood. Some of the dead brambles appeared suspiciously like human—or perhaps even Anthari—skeletons. Everywhere she looked, the shape of the moss-covered debris resembled bodies left where they'd fallen centuries ago.

I'm imagining it. She turned away, refusing to let the foul energy of the place affect her. *The dead couldn't possibly* still *be there after two thousand years.* Yerbin and Danos whispering about seeing bodies in the underbrush further rattled her. Every so often, a soft splash like someone throwing rocks into the water announced the demise of an unfortunate insect straying too close to a fish. On edge from whatever dark energy made her hallucinate skeletons, she jumped each time.

They paddled along the twisting waterway, trying to avoid clusters of beard-like leaves hanging into the water from protruding branches. She didn't really think of it as a river due to the lack of any current. The water merely sat in the channels between islands. Oona had no idea where to go, so whenever the watery 'road' split around a muddy bank, she chose left or right based on whichever way felt the most like staying on the same path. She found herself hesitating before deciding, in case Tamsen chimed in about which way to go… but the girl remained silent for now.

Why are we relying on a child to guide us? She peered back at the girl, seated in the middle of their root canoe, far too quiet and calm than seemed normal for a child. At least she gazed around at the moor with a wondrous, wide-eyed expression quite appropriate for a ten-year-old seeing a fascinating place for the first time.

Tamsen noticed her looking and smiled. "We're going the right way."

Oona returned the smile before facing forward. *The gods send messages in strange ways.*

When daylight began to weaken, Rakden called, "Highness, we should look for somewhere to make camp before darkness becomes full."

Hours spent sitting in a boat most definitely made her eager for a break.

"Agreed," said Oona. "If we can find a patch of land big enough, and more solid than an enormous pile of mud."

Kitlyn pointed her oar at a large mound of land a fair distance ahead. "There. That one appears promising. The middle looks to be at least six feet above the water's surface. Should be dry... or at least as dry as we can find in this place."

A few minutes later, the prow of their boat mushed into the squishy bank of the big island. After testing the ground for solidity with a few oar pokes, Oona got out. She groaned, stretching her legs. Kitlyn walked up beside her, covered in so much dried mud she resembled a baked treat dipped in chocolate. Rakden, Yerbin, Danos, and Beowyn trudged uphill away from the water, examining the ground in search of a spot suitable to unfurl their bedrolls.

Oona looked down at an equal amount of mud on her armor. She brushed at it.

"Tempting to rinse off." Kitlyn swatted at her leg.

"The water is dirty."

"It's clean enough to get rid of mud." Kitlyn frowned. "Might be a little improper for us to take a bath in front of the soldiers."

Oona blushed. "A *little*? I think you've been in Evermoor too long, my love. You're going native."

Kitlyn laughed.

"Do you want to go swimming for fun or just clean off?" asked Tamsen.

"I'd like to get rid of the mud." Oona kept swatting at herself.

"Easy." Tamsen made a quick hand motion at her.

The dried mud covering Oona leapt off her into a cloud of hovering dust as the still-wet muck in her boots bubbled up, running down the sides to the ground. In seconds, she'd become clean and dry—though still felt grungy. Tamsen gestured in the same manner at Kitlyn, ridding her of dirt.

Oona gawked at the display of minor magic, as impressed by it as watching the girl throw fire at the roots. "Why didn't you do that earlier?"

"I'm sorry." Tamsen offered an apologetic shrug. "You said you liked the mud. You were joking, weren't you?"

"Not exactly joking. It's complicated." Kitlyn laughed. "No need to apologize. Thank you."

The child grinned.

They headed together to higher ground where the soldiers worked to make a quick campsite. Since wood dry enough to burn proved quite scarce, they decided against building a fire. Fortunately, a meal of salted meat rations and bread didn't require cooking.

Despite looking like a little vagabond in her dingy, torn dress, baggy threadbare pants, and blue blanket cloak—bordered in cute bear faces—Tamsen didn't defensively clutch her portion of food the way many of the war orphans did.

"Thank you for letting me stay with you," said the girl upon noticing Oona's stare. "I promise you can trust me. I don't steal or do bad things."

"Not why I keep looking at you." Oona handed her another hunk of bread. "I'm trying to understand how you can be so brave."

Tamsen shrugged one shoulder. "I had to be."

"Did someone hurt you?" Kitlyn looked up from her food, worry in her eyes.

"Only the men who were going to kill me. Oh, and the man who stole my house picked me up and threw me into the street. Kinda hurt my knee."

Kitlyn narrowed her eyes. "Stole your house?"

"Yes." Tamsen bit off a mouthful of bread. "My parents left me with my grandfather when they had to go fight in the war. They died, so I stayed with grandpa until he died from being old. I lived by myself for a while until this man noticed I didn't have parents or anything, so he took my grandfather's house. He said I was too young to legally own land."

Grumbling came from the soldiers, along with various bits of commentary about the quality of the man's parentage.

Oona scowled. She almost demanded to know who, but held her tongue as she had no power over the laws of Evermoor. More than likely, this happened in a small village somewhere. She couldn't tell if the man in question seized the house due to taxes or legitimately stole it to sell for profit.

"The cruelty of some people astonishes me." Kitlyn sighed.

"I thought about taking the house back, but I was too little to beat him up and didn't want to throw fire at him, so I left. Tried to go to Pelar, but his house really was ruined inside. Waited at the ruins for a day or two. He didn't come back, so I begged for food and slept wherever I could. Got chased away from the village. Went to another one. Happened again."

Oona could no longer resist and fussed over her as if she'd found a stray kitten. "Horrible. They chased you away?"

"Yes. The war made lots of orphans. No one had much food and people didn't want *another* kid. About a year ago, Aztian saw me begging and bought me a nice dinner. I followed him until we got to Torjin. He wouldn't take me into the deep moor because it's dangerous, so I stayed at the inn whenever he went out to hunt or trap. I'd been in Torjin for eleven months before the root monster attacked and killed him."

"He was your only family?" Oona patted her back. "I'm sorry."

Tamsen shook her head. "Not family. He just bought me food a few times and let me follow him. I think he wanted to leave me there since he didn't really like having a kid to look after. I'm really happy you're letting me stay with you. Promise I won't steal or get in trouble."

"I know." Oona smiled. "I promise we won't be mean to you or make you work."

"If you're really queens, why don't you have a big army? You look like a group of bandits."

The soldiers laughed.

"Ya think we're bandits, eh?" asked Rakden, trying not to smile.

Kitlyn summoned a pair of small stones out of the ground, making them rotate around each other. "I didn't want to inconvenience twenty men for a flight of fancy."

"It's not! This is your life." Oona gestured at her, then slouched. "We took a small group because I needed to move fast. I understand now it's because of Tamsen."

"Me?" The girl blinked.

"If we took a hundred soldiers and everything needed to travel in such a large group, we wouldn't have found you." Oona bowed her head, offering a silent prayer of thanks to Lucen.

Tamsen picked up the canteen near her. "You probably would still have found me... just not alive."

Anger surged in Oona all over again.

"Did you try to escape?" asked Kitlyn.

"Yeah." Tamsen rubbed her wrist. "My magic isn't like yours. Except for little tricks like cleaning mud off or shoving something, every spell has specific words to focus the power, and hand motions. Even one finger being bent wrong can ruin it. Those men kept me tied up and put the wood in my mouth to stop me from talking. Torin's Hand only needs a word. That's the push spell."

Oona fumed. *Did those fools end up in the Banefallow because they died in Evermoor or did the gods send them to the Pit?* She had to believe men who not only twisted Lucen's teachings but used them to justify the murder of an innocent child would go somewhere bad. According to what she'd been taught growing up, all who died either went with Tenebrea to her realm or fell into the Pit. She'd come to believe in various other realms after death, again explaining why the Goddess of Death needed to guide honorable spirits to her realm. Question being, did a person's ultimate destination after death depend on the land where they died or the traditions they aligned themselves with in life?

"You are surprisingly skilled with magic for someone so young," said Kitlyn.

"So are you." Tamsen chuckled. "Pelar taught me some first circle spells like Drake's Fire and gave me the books to study more magic. But I've never torn a giant monster in two pieces."

Something buzzed in the distance.

Oona flinched. "We should sleep so we can wake up at first light."

The soldiers murmured in agreement. Rakden assigned a night watch rotation. Tamsen removed her 'cloak' and used it as a proper blanket, having to curl up to fit completely under it. Oona pictured her sleeping like that in an alley somewhere, and her heart cracked open all over again. She draped her blanket over the child, and shared Kitlyn's blanket with her.

Eager for morning to arrive, Oona tried to stop looking around every time a loud insect buzzed by and closed her eyes.

34

PAELIRRON THE WISE

KITLYN

A gentle nudging at the shoulder woke Kitlyn.

Oona, half on top of her, stirred.

Kitlyn opened her eyes to Yerbin's face hovering over her. "Pardon, highnesses. It is morning."

"Thank you." She yawned.

Tamsen had migrated in her sleep from where she'd initially curled up to laying against them. As soon as the child woke, she jumped back, somewhat red-faced. Kitlyn pretended not to notice and forced herself to get up.

Everyone rushed through the process of relieving themselves. After a quick meal of rations, they broke camp and resumed navigating the river toward the deep moor. Tamsen advised them to look for the 'tilting keep.' Over the first few hours, the waterways they followed became noticeably wider, the islands fewer and smaller. A little before noon, they spotted the ruins of a small stone building sunken into the marsh, much deeper on the left side than the right. Centuries of moss, vines, and other dead plants wrapped around the ancient structure.

"Turn right," said Tamsen.

"How do you know where we're going?" Oona peered back at the girl.

"There's a big map on the wall at the inn. The tower and this keep are painted on it." Tamsen pointed off to the right. "We're close to the Ebon Mire now. It's a big open area of water. Most of it is shallow enough to stand in, but there are some deep spots. Anywhere no trees are sticking out of the water is probably a deep spot. There isn't much land except for a few big islands. When we get to the first one, go around it to the left."

Oona looked at Kitlyn.

I can think of no reason not to at least try listening to her. Lucen leading us to her and this kid matching the riddle of the key are too coincidental to ignore. She nodded. Oona faced forward and resumed paddling.

"Also," said Tamsen, "even though the water is pretty shallow once we're in the Ebon Mire, it's really dangerous. Bad idea to get out of the boat. Lots of snakes, bugs, and other dangerous stuff in the water you won't see until it's already too late—like razor eels. They live in burrows under the muck. If you step in one of their holes, it's like getting stabbed by twenty red-hot knives... then the poison kills you."

Oona again looked at Kitlyn, whistled, and resumed paddling.

"If we end up in the water, don't put your feet down and try to get back on a boat fast," said Tamsen. "Most of the deadly stuff lives in the muck on the bottom."

A little over an hour after they passed the tilting keep, they reached the Ebon Mire. True to Tamsen's description, the myriad little of mud islands came to an abrupt end, forming almost a shoreline along the edge of a massive, foul lake. If not for all the trees, marsh grasses, and other plants sticking up from the surface of the water ahead, it could've been a sea.

Not too deep. Stay away from the bottom.

They paddled out into the bog. Kitlyn glanced nervously at vees cutting through the water here and there, possibly snakes, fish, or other deadlier creatures. She clutched the oar tight, ready to defend herself at any moment from a leaping serpent or slime-coated tentacle. An awful smell similar to rotten meat hung over the brackish water. Kitlyn tried to breathe as little as possible, taking small sips of air. Oona occasionally retched. Tamsen covered her face with her blanket cloak. Yerbin and Rakden also gagged, muttering random ideas of what they thought lay dead on the bottom of the swamp. Bubbles glooped to the surface every few minutes, no doubt releasing more of the horrid stench.

The laziness of the bubbles made the water appear thicker than it ought to have been, closer to extremely loose mud—and about as murky. A haze of brown, perhaps some kind of moss or decomposing plant material lurked an inch or so deep, under a clear water layer. Paddling hadn't become noticeably more difficult, so she hoped the muck wouldn't be too difficult to swim in if they capsized.

"Don't go into any spot with lots of bubbles," said Tamsen. "We'll sink."

"Wouldn't bubbles push us up?" asked Oona.

Tamsen shrugged. "I don't understand why. Trappers and hunters at the inn always told people not to go in the bubbles or they'd drown."

Soon after the edge of the Ebon Mire disappeared into the distance behind them, loud buzzing on the right made Oona squeal in alarm. Kitlyn almost disregarded the noise—as her wife had been flinching constantly at any similar sound—but upon noticing a fast-moving black object heading toward them, she yelled out in alarm.

Six wasps the size of housecats raced toward their group, headed for the second boat containing Rakden and Danos.

"Eep!" yelled Oona. She pointed at them, releasing a beam of blue light.

"Na'ava sura kaz maranhi eht," chanted Tamsen while weaving an intricate hand motion.

Kitlyn reached out into the earth for a stone. Sitting in a boat without touching the ground at all made the task of drawing up even a small rock tiring, but not impossible.

Oona's beam struck the second wasp broadside, smashing it in half amid an explosion of slimy yellow goop. Both pieces fell, spinning, into the water.

Fire leapt from Tamsen's outstretched palm, the roar too loud to speak over without yelling. She sprayed a three-second-long stream of fire over two wasps, roasting them to cinders in midair. The fourth one veered to its right, zooming at the child as if smart enough to recognize her as the source of the fire. Kitlyn commanded the rock she'd summoned into a projectile, aiming at the doom needle headed their way.

The grape-sized stone struck the wasp in the head with a dull crunch, leaving a neat hole as it disappeared into the insect's body. The wings stopped beating in an instant, the dead wasp falling straight down. Another wasp buzzed at Rakden, who managed to ward it off using his sword. It flew over him, circling around on the right side of the boats. Wasp Six dive bombed Yerbin, who sliced it in half, then proceeded to scream in fear as the stinger-bearing rear end landed in his lap.

Rakden's wasp flew around in a wide circle, evidently willing to sting whatever it saw in front of it—which happened to be Kitlyn. She shouted a war scream while swinging the oar in a two-handed grip. The wide part of the paddle mashed into the wasp's face, bursting the insect into a shower of yellow and green slime that rained over Tamsen and Oona. Her powerful swing imbalanced the narrow boat, throwing her into the water.

Kitlyn surfaced as fast as she could. Despite her fondness for the earth, she kept her legs tucked up, not wanting to risk sticking her bare feet into snakes or any other wildlife hidden on the mucky bottom.

Somehow, Oona managed to not only stay in the boat, she kept it from capsizing.

Tamsen, her face splattered with bug guts, stared at Kitlyn, refusing to open her mouth to speak.

Despite being afraid of unseen teeth feasting on her at any moment, Kitlyn forced herself to gingerly climb back into the boat to avoid rolling it.

"You killed it at least." Oona swiped bug slime off her chest. "Better guts all over me than stung by one of those horrors."

Tamsen waved her arm to the side in an 'away with you' gesture. All the bug guts on her and Oona leapt into the water.

"Yerbin, are you hurt?" called Kitlyn.

"Nah, he's fine." Rakden laughed. "Dead bug landed on him."

"The stinger!" yelled Yerbin. "It's the size of a damn dagger—and it's still moving!"

"Nah, merely an icepick."

"Oh, *merely* an icepick. It's longer than the width of my hand!" Yerbin shuddered. "And you all saw that man's face."

Tamsen pointed. "We should keep going before more wasps find us. There's a nest over there. Doom needles are territorial and will attack anything too close to their nest."

Kitlyn stared into the fog at an irregular dark lump about the size of a peasant hovel nestled in the branches of a swamp tree.

"Burn it," muttered Oona.

"If I light the nest on fire, a hundred wasps will come out at once. I can't burn them *all* with Drake's Fire. If I knew how to cast Dragon's Fire, then I could kill the whole nest, but it's a third circle spell and beyond my abilities."

"Hun… dred?" Oona grabbed her oar and paddled so feverishly she splashed water all over Tamsen and Kitlyn.

Chuckling, Kitlyn resumed paddling. She sometimes teased Oona for her fear of heights, but she completely agreed with her fear of enormous flesh-rotting wasps.

Tamsen flicked her fingers at Kitlyn. All the water soaked into her clothes extruded out into floating globules before falling into the moor, leaving her dry.

A FEW HOURS LATER, THE DARK SILHOUETTE OF LAND DRIFTED out of the mist ahead.

It had been mostly quiet, except for a few instances of biting fish launching themselves out of the water and one black snake jumping into Kitlyn's lap. She started to panic, expecting it venomous and wanting to bite her—but the giant fish that had been trying to eat it rammed the boat, nearly spilling them over. The snake, apparently, ran to Kitlyn for help.

Naturally, neither Tamsen nor Oona much appreciated having an extra passenger of the venomous variety. Kitlyn couldn't claim to enjoy having a snake hiding between her rear end and the boat wall, either. Between feeling pity for it and being afraid to try touching it, she let it be until it eventually felt safe enough to jump back in the water on its own.

A nervous discussion of Alderswood energy making her feel 'trustworthy' to animals followed. Oona and Tamsen both believed it the reason no fish tried to bite her during the fight against the root monster.

Upon reaching the large island, they steered left to go around it. The surface held only swamp trees, some crumbling stone ruins, and probably thousands of angry small venomous creatures.

I've never before seen a place more desperate to take the life of everyone who dares to venture into it than the Rose District. Kitlyn frowned to herself at the thought of the nobles' little paradise in Cimril. Most of the wealthy families owned at least one manor house there. The walled-in area had many ritzy shops, a park, and two theaters. Everyone who lived there tried to outdo their neighbors in one way or the other. She detested the shallowness.

"*Sa'ava auruun moh.*" Tamsen waved her hands around in a small circular motion for a few seconds until a tiny blue flash went off between her palms. She pointed ahead a little to the left. "That way."

"What did you do?" Oona squirmed. "I felt a tingle all down my back."

"Soramar's Sight," said Tamsen in a monotone voice, still evidently concentrating on something. "The spell allows me to sense magical energy. Most people use it to tell if an object is enchanted or not. I don't exactly know where Isilien is other than out here in the Ebon Mire, but, I *do* know it's full of magic. Since we're close enough, this spell should let me find it."

She is quite resourceful.

With nothing more than a child's finger pointing the way, they paddled deeper into the Ebon Mire. Heavy mist made it difficult to see the sky or tell how much time passed. Based on how hungry she'd become, Kitlyn assumed they'd gone well past the middle of the day. She didn't like the idea of trying to stop to eat on boats while water stretched as far as she could see in all directions, so they kept going.

"I see something," called Oona after another hour or so. "An island I think."

"Good, we can stop there and rest a bit. We should have brought more provisions."

"We have plenty of provisions, highness." Rakden laughed. "The problem is, they're all the same thing."

Yerbin and Danos started to get into a contest over who knew the most jokes about what the salted meat rations were 'really' made of, but Rakden reminded them they escorted the queens and to show some decorum.

Minutes later, they reached the edge of another large island. Not far from shore, the smashed remains of what had once been a fountain lay at the head of a stone walkway leading off into the fog.

"The magic is here." Tamsen scrambled out of the boat. She ran a few steps before her left boot fell off. Grumbling, she backtracked and stepped into it.

The other three boats maneuvered to the mushy bank, pulling alongside them in a neat row. Once everyone made it onto solid ground, Kitlyn approached the fountain, pausing momentarily to look over the various chunks of rock. A few bore some resemblance to human figures, likely statues so eroded by time they had lost all detail. No trace of any carving, writing, or useful information remained.

How old is this place?

Dark green moss swelled up through gaps in the tiles of the ancient walkway leading away from the water. Vines and woody roots grew everywhere, some having cracked or pushed stones out of their way. Kitlyn followed the stone path past several pairs of collapsed benches and smaller walkways leading to circles where more benches surrounded crumbling, unrecognizable statues. The place reminded her of a relaxing garden where people might have sat reading or enjoying the day. She could scarcely imagine anyone being comfortable in a rancid-smelling swamp teeming with bugs, snakes, and enormous wasps.

The crumbling footpath brought them to an old, rusted gate. Beyond it lay a paved courtyard enclosed by a twelve-foot-high wall upon which perched winged gargoyles. Most retained only broken fragments of wings, but their facial features hadn't eroded like the other statues. At the back of the courtyard, a bramble of massive, pale grey thorn vines covered a three-story tall cliff face.

Kitlyn softened the stone around the gate, allowing Beowyn to lift the entire set of bars away and set them aside, leaning against the wall.

"Someone doesn't want anyone getting inside there." Rakden entered first, gazing up at the huge vines. "Look at the size of those thorns."

"*Thorns* aren't three feet long." Yerbin whistled in awe.

Beowyn approached the back wall and examined a root thicker around than his thigh. "This feels like stone, not dead wood."

"There is nothing here… only a courtyard?" Danos turned in place, gazing around at the walls.

"No." Oona also studied their surroundings. "There has to be something here we aren't seeing."

"Look for an opening or something my size. Maybe you have to stick me in and give me a twist." Tamsen forced a laugh, eyeing the gargoyles. "Are those statues going to wake up and try to eat us?"

"I don't feel anything odd about them." Kitlyn patted the girl on the shoulder. "And I don't think you are meant to be a literal key. Maybe all you needed to do was help us find this place."

"Is this Isilien?" Oona poked at a giant stony thorn.

Kitlyn gazed up at the huge wall of impassable vines. "We'll have to go inside to find out."

"It has to be." Tamsen held her arms out to either side and let them flop against her body. "It's *so* full of magic."

Eyes closed, Kitlyn called out to the energy in the Stone, 'seeing' the formations of rock, earth, and empty space around her as forms of grey in a void. Surprisingly, the 'vines' did not appear to have ever been vines at all, but stone, suggesting a stonecaller conjured or perhaps petrified them. A flat rock wall behind the wavy tubes appeared to be the façade of an ancient structure built into the cliff face, undoubtedly covered by the false bramble to conceal it. She sensed something highly unusual at the center of the wall: a rectangular slab of pure void, blacker than the nothingness representing air-filled spaces in her stone vision. Two stories tall, a foot thick, and as wide as a castle gate, the mysterious object served as a door blocking off a long corridor leading into the cliff.

She approached the tangle of stone vines in front of the hallway, widened her stance, and raised her arms.

No need to tear all of this down. I only need to expose the... door?

Magical energy spread outward from the core in her chest, manifesting as a green glowing light around her hands a few seconds later. Kitlyn projected power into the false bramble, commanding the stone to soften. Under her control, the enormous false vines writhed and came to life one by one. The ground shook from the weight of such heavy constructs shifting around, bending and stretching to expose a glittering black-grey stone monolith the same size as the unusual void she'd sensed. Millions of tiny silver flecks in the material glinted like stars. Unlike an ordinary gate or door, the impossibly perfect block had no hinges, seams, handles, or any features to speak of.

It also didn't appear the least bit eroded or affected by time.

"You make it look so easy," said Oona.

"The Stone likes me more than the roots do." Kitlyn smiled, redirecting her focus on the strange slab... which ignored her. Her smile faded. She poured more power into her magic, the 'door' refusing to budge. It didn't even reverberate to her power in the way stone should. A crackle of lightning arced from the middle of the slab to the ground, setting off a *bang* that echoed into the moor.

"Stop!" yelled Tamsen.

Kitlyn backed off, somewhat out of breath. "It's resisting me. This looks like stone, yet it doesn't move when I try to bend it. Perhaps I should tunnel underneath?"

"Wait." Tamsen scurried over to the slab. She spent a moment feeling around the surface before pressing her ear to it, then stepping back, arms folded. "It doesn't look like it, but this is a lock."

"It's a giant block of stone... just no kind of stone I've ever seen before." Rakden gestured at it.

"Pretty though," said Yerbin. "I could stare at it for hours."

Tamsen turned around to look at everyone. "I might be able to open it if you want."

Kitlyn raised an eyebrow. "Why would you not do so after we came all the way here?"

"Magically locked doors are usually sealed for a reason. There could be something bad behind it."

"The ghost of my mother visited from Tenebrea's realm to tell me something in this place will break the curse on the throne of Lucernia." Kitlyn closed her eyes, sending her feeling into the earth. Except for the soldiers, Tamsen, and Oona, she sensed nothing moving around to the limit of her range, about a hundred yards. "There is nothing in there but a long corridor."

"Okay. It seems I am actually the key." Tamsen traced her hands around in sweeping motions while manipulating her fingers in a complicated looking pattern and chanting, "*Elaan amoath. Elaan kuur. Elaan amuun del erethin.*"

Six thin concentric circles of blue-violet light appeared at the center of the door slab. Small glowing white dots, one per circle, raced around in alternating directions like marbles on a track. Five runic sigils appeared inside the smallest circle. The rotating points stopped simultaneously, forming a straight line at the top of the rings. From the outermost to the innermost, the points winked out one by one. The circles faded next, leaving only the sigils.

A heavy *thud* emanated from the slab, which split down the middle and swung inward in the manner of a giant pair of double doors. The earth shook when the massive gates thudded into the walls on either side, fully open. Ahead lay a dusty corridor tiled in fancy marble panels, leading into darkness. Stone hands stuck out of the wall in pairs at regular intervals, each holding an opaque white glass orb. The air carried the petrichor of a recent thunderstorm, tingling with an inexplicable charge of power.

Kitlyn stepped defensively in front of Tamsen. "Whoa…"

"It's the *door's* that's impressive." Tamsen set her hands on her hips. "I can't brag. Aldren's Charm isn't a difficult spell. It's usually used by thieves to sneak into places or work magic locks because they don't *have* real keys."

"Have you ever used it to go somewhere you shouldn't be?" asked Rakden.

Tamsen bowed her head. "Yes, but only to take food when I had no other choice."

"You won't have to steal anything anymore." Oona smiled.

Kitlyn stepped past the threshold into the cavernous hallway. The glass orbs perched in the stone hands lit up one pair at a time, brighter than any common lantern, though not as intense as a Lucen priest's orb. Oona, Tamsen, and the soldiers filed in behind her. Starting a short distance in from the door, black char covered the walls, floor, and ceiling, continuing the entire length of the passage. Here and there, oddly smooth rounded stones littered the ground along with a generous coating of ash.

"You're bringing the child with us?" asked Rakden.

"Shall we leave her outside by herself?" Oona glanced at him.

Yerbin whistled up at the ceiling. "This is impressively large."

"That's what she said," muttered Tamsen.

Beowyn appeared horrified for a second before bursting into laughter. The other soldiers stared in bemused shock at the girl.

Why is he laughing at her? Kitlyn raised an eyebrow at him.

Oona blinked. "What she said?"

"Yes." Tamsen nodded. "The men at the Drowned Rat—the inn I stayed at—always said 'that's what she said' whenever anyone called something big."

The soldiers stifled laughter.

"Why is it funny?" asked Kitlyn.

Coughs and sputtering came from the soldiers.

"Because *I* said it." Tamsen rolled her eyes. "They think I'm too little to know what it means."

Beowyn gawked at her. "You, err, know what it means?"

"Yeah." The ten-year-old waved dismissively. "The men are obviously talking about their swords."

The soldiers exchanged uncomfortable glances.

"Their... swords," said Rakden, trying not to laugh.

Oona looked at Kitlyn, clueless.

No idea why swords are funny. Kitlyn shrugged.

"Look at him." Tamsen pointed at Beowyn. "He's obviously got the biggest sword here."

The large man coughed.

Discomfort radiated in waves from the men.

Tamsen tilted her head at them. "Why are you laughing? Beowyn is the only one here whose sword is so big he needs to use it in both hands."

"That's what she said," muttered Danos.

Yerbin burst out laughing.

"Ahh," said Rakden. "She's talking about our *blades.*"

"Of course I am." Tamsen sighed. "I honestly don't know why men think the size of their swords is funny. A little one can be just as effective as a big one if used right."

The soldiers, including Rakden, lapsed into uncontrollable laughter.

I sense there is something eluding me about this. Kitlyn furrowed her brow. Deciding it not worth the time to ask about, she resumed walking, leaving footprints in the ash.

"What could possibly have scorched every inch of a corridor this size?" asked Oona.

Danos paused to pick up one of the strange stones. "Bones. Bodies were burned here."

"We burned a fair amount of enemy dead during the war," said Rakden, "and I've never seen bones reduced to little rocks before."

"I have." Danos stood, tossing the bone nugget aside. "Once. Firecallers attacked us. Magic flames hotter than any ordinary fire. This child could probably do the same to a person."

"Not yet," said Tamsen in a matter-of-fact tone. "I'd have to learn a more powerful spell first."

Oona cringed. "Have you ever used the fire spell you cast at the root monster on a person?"

Tamsen shook her head. "No. I'd only ever do it if someone was about to kill me and I couldn't run away. But it's okay to use on monsters."

Whew… Kitlyn let out a silent sigh of relief.

They trudged through ash, bone nuggets, and a few mangled metal scraps apparently from melted armor. At the end of the corridor, they found a pair of ornate double doors, engraved with decorative patterns around floral shapes. Suspiciously, the green-stained wood didn't appear the least bit burned.

Kitlyn reached for the handles.

"Wait!" yelled Tamsen. "There might be a glyph."

"What is a glyph?" Oona leaned out of the way as the child ran up to the door.

"A trap. A magical one. Probably what burned the people who died here. Glyphs are incredibly difficult to make and use expensive or rare materials. No one who makes a glyph is going to embed a weak spell in it." Tamsen held her hands out to the door and made a series of intricate finger motions. *"Sa'ava auruun moh."*

The double doors took on a bright blue glow.

Kitlyn and Oona leaned back. The soldiers finally stopped snickering.

"No glyph, but these doors are enchanted. It's far too complicated for me to tell what the enchantment does, but I'm sure it won't hurt anyone." Tamsen stepped back. "Go ahead. It's safe."

"What are we looking for here?" asked Rakden.

"Mother's spirit didn't say. She only said to go beyond the gates of Isilien. I imagine what I need to find is going to be fairly obvious."

We're really trusting a kid. Kitlyn sighed and gripped the handles. *She's only six years younger than me.*

She pulled the doors open, flooding the corridor in sunlight from a vast round chamber on the other side. Her attention went straight to the skeletal remains of a huge creature facing her. Oona gasped. Tamsen tried to run past her into the room, but Kitlyn caught and held her.

A wedge-shaped skull the size of a horse-drawn coach faced the door, seemingly staring at her despite being *long* dead. It tapered evenly from a ridge of horny plates to a relatively narrow tip. Its other bones lay apart in pieces, no longer joined by any sinew or cartilage. Nothing had evidently disturbed the beast since it died, as the lay of the bones defined its forelegs, rear legs, and wings. She couldn't tell exactly how big it had been in life, but any beast with eye sockets she could use as bathtubs had to be massive.

Kitlyn gawked at the impossible skeleton for a long while before she could peel her gaze off it and take in the rest of her surroundings. The cylindrical chamber went up six stories to an opening as wide as the central atrium, covered by a domed lattice made from the same stone 'vines' they'd seen out front. Sunlight shone in the gaps between thorns. Circular hallways went around the atrium at each story, containing alcoves of bookshelves, corridors, or sitting rooms. Each story was open to the central shaft, devoid of any railings or walls.

"This is definitely not a place to explore while drunk." Yerbin whistled, gazing up at the sixth floor.

Three corridors led deeper into the earth from the ground floor at evenly spaced intervals around the circle.

Oona gestured at the skull. "You said what your mother expected us to find would be obvious. Does this count as obvious?"

"It's dead, whatever it was." Kitlyn approached and brushed her hand down the side of the skull as if greeting an enormous horse.

"Dragon," whispered Tamsen. "It was a dragon."

"Dragons aren't real." Rakden smirked.

"If they aren't real, then someone went to a great amount of trouble to create a false skeleton and seal it away in a place deep in the swamp behind a magical lock." Kitlyn lowered her arm.

"All the books." Tamsen turned in place, gawking at the gigantic library. "...and they're probably all written in a language I can't read. Nuts."

Kitlyn glanced at the corridor leading away on the left. "I suppose we should begin searching."

"Greetings, humans." A low-pitched voice emanated from overhead, its depth and volume shaking the chamber.

Tamsen gave a high-pitched squeak and darted behind Oona before peering around her. "Who said that?"

"I am Paelirron the Wise," replied the great voice.

"Eep! Kit! Kit! The eyes!"

Kitlyn glanced back at Oona who jabbed her finger in the direction of the dragon's skull. Pools of spectral light had appeared in both eye sockets. Her body went rigid in fear. *Merely a ghost. If people have ghosts, dragons must as well.*

Tamsen leaned further out from behind Oona, her jaw open, staring at the skull. She didn't appear the least bit scared—more shocked.

"Paelirron the Wise," whispered Kitlyn. "Were you a dragon?"

"I am still a dragon. My living form has merely ceased to exist."

The soldiers gazed up at dust falling from the five upper floors, shaken loose by the depth of the voice.

Mother must have intended for me to find this spirit. "I apologize for disturbing you. Is this Isilien?"

"You are correct," said the dragon-ghost.

He doesn't sound angry.

"Should we ask him?" Oona edged up beside Kitlyn. She, too, no longer appeared frightened, rather wide-eyed in awe.

"It has been far too long since any have been here to converse with. You need not be frightened."

"Pelar?" asked Tamsen.

"Hello, child." The pools of spirit fire in the eye sockets extinguished with an audible *whuff.* The ghostly form of an unusually thin man appeared standing beside the skull in long, flowing robes. An amulet of gnarled tree wood hung about his neck, studded with crystals. Pointed ears stuck two inches up from his hair, which might have been brown—though the bluish glow of his spiritual nature made it difficult to tell. "Yes. We have met before."

Tamsen appeared ready to yell 'why did you leave' but simply exhaled hard. "Oh. You're a ghost. Your house was never anything more than a ruin, was it?"

"I am afraid not, child."

"He didn't look like an Anthari when I saw him," whispered Tamsen behind her hand to Kitlyn and Oona. "And his voice wasn't so *boomy* then."

Paelirron-the-Anthari smiled, clasping his hands in front of himself. "I am neither Anthari nor human. I merely find the appearance of the Anthari more suited to these surroundings." He looked at Kitlyn. "You have come a long way to ask your question."

"Yes... there is a curse on my family, or maybe on the throne. The ghost of my mother told me I'd find the answer beyond the gates of Isilien."

"The curse is not on your family, but on any who rules Valendar." Paelirron shifted his gaze to Oona. "So long as you both occupy the throne, it shall affect you."

"I am unfamiliar with Valendar." Kitlyn tilted her head. "Is it the Anthari name for Lucernia?"

Paelirron shook his head. "Not in the way you are thinking. In the time of the Anthari, the land was known as Valendar. Many years ago, dragons came to believe humans and Anthari could be trusted with the knowledge of magic. And so, we bestowed the gift of magic on a small group and began to teach them. Isilien was one such school. For a time, humans respected this gift."

"Oh, no." Oona grimaced.

"Yes, my child." Paelirron bowed his head. "Humans eventually succumbed to greed and began using magic for horrible things. The Anthari expressed concern at the humans' carelessness with powers they had only begun to understand and didn't fully comprehend. The humans mistook this concern for the Anthari feeling superior to them and wishing to keep magic only for themselves. Fear and distrust eventually convinced humans the Anthari wanted to wipe them out entirely."

Kitlyn gasped. "They didn't, though... just wanted them to stop abusing magic?"

"Correct. You, more than most, should understand how the allure of power can change someone," said Paelirron. "The same way your father fell victim to his greed and paranoia, the humans waged war on the Anthari. This war lasted for eighty-seven years. Many died on both sides."

The towers... Kitlyn imagined Noru Sendral not as a ruin but a glowing beacon incinerating scores of human soldiers to ash.

"We regretted bestowing the gift of magic on humans, for they took to it with great fervor and far more quickly than we anticipated. What humanity lacked in power, they made up for in numbers. After years of war, the humans of Valendar became consumed with hatred toward any cultures other than their own. Anthari sundered the very land itself in hopes of protecting themselves from a scourge we dragons inadvertently set in motion. What had once been a simple river became the Churning Deep."

"By Lucen," whispered Oona, hand to her mouth. "*We* are the evil ones..."

"No." Kitlyn faced her. "Humans who lived a really long time ago were. Aodh almost repeated their mistake, but *we* are not evil." She pulled Oona into an embrace, whispering, "We know what it is like to be despised for being different. I would like to hope it is not in humanity's nature to destroy everything it finds strange."

Oona lifted her gaze off the floor, staring into her eyes. "It would be nice to think you are right. Perhaps it is not *human* nature as much as how, in large groups, we become brittle, fearful creatures. Individually, or in small numbers, we think and feel more clearly."

"Did humans wipe the Anthari out?" Expecting a horrifying answer, Kitlyn winced inside.

Paelirron offered a comforting smile. "They did not. The war ended because the Anthari could no longer tolerate witnessing such cruelty and death, and so, they retreated to a place where humans could not reach them."

"Anthari still exist?" asked Oona, eyebrows rising in hope.

"Yes, but not in this world. They left it behind, perhaps never to return. I am not able to see the future, only remember what has already come to pass." Paelirron gestured up at the bookshelves. "After the retreat of the Anthari, the denizens of Valendar no longer had a common, inhuman enemy to focus their hatred on, so their aggression turned inward against each other. Those who wielded magic formed various guilds, each controlling a portion of Valendar and fighting to expand their land, power, and influence. Some smaller guilds operated as mercenaries, fighting for whoever paid them the most. Many, many died in those days."

The soldiers, who had been largely silent, emitted quiet gasps, murmurs of disbelief, or whispers of astonishment.

"Horrible." Oona shuddered. "It is exactly what we fear the nobles would do should ill fate befall us."

"There are almost no mages left in Lucernia." Kitlyn looked up at the bookshelves. "Mages learned here long ago?"

"Yes. The strife between guilds lasted for centuries. Battles tended to be small, confined to less than twenty people on either side, though stray magic often destroyed whole cities. A ruler the humans referred to as the Grand Archmage led the guild that ultimately became victorious, conquering all of Valendar under one ruler. For 213 years, the Grand Archmage reigned as a cruel and paranoid king. He claimed the need to protect his kingdom from another terrible war justified whatever he did. Atrocities occurred during this time I cannot bring myself to describe, as to hear them would shatter your innocence. The worst of these crimes were committed by those working for the Grand Archmage against their own citizens."

Oona shivered from sorrow and anger.

"Why?" rasped Kitlyn. "What would make him torture people?"

"Fear. Kings gripped with fear are the weakest leaders. He believed he would be assassinated or other, defeated guilds would rebuild themselves to overthrow him. Anyone he suspected of being involved in plots to overthrow him died gruesomely. Whole family lines disappeared over little more than unsubstantiated rumors. Simply accusing someone would often be enough to ensure their death. People reported suspected traitors both out of sincere desire to uphold the law as well as malignant claims to dispose of those they disliked. Reporting potential traitors did not protect a person from suspicion. One scandalous whisper about them in the wrong ear, and it would be them screaming for mercy. It was a dark time indeed."

"There are no mentions of this history anywhere," whispered Oona. "We never knew."

"The Grand Archmage obviously fell." Kitlyn tapped her big toe on the floor, pondering what she'd heard. "His evil eventually drove someone to assassinate him, thus completing the foretelling he'd been so afraid of."

Paelirron chuckled. "Perhaps, though I do not know if any foretelling warned of his demise. A pair of powerful mages you know as Lucen and Navissa led a revolution. They wiped out the Grand Archmage and then proceeded to purge all seven houses of magic, the remnants of defeated guilds that joined the Archmage's empire."

Oona gawked. "You speak of Lucen such? And Navissa?"

"A moment." Paelirron raised a hand. "Lucen established a new kingdom and declared most forms of magic too dangerous for mortals to possess. He and Navissa exiled or purged anyone who used magic except for their students. Most of the common people saw magic as the cause of nearly a thousand years of endless misery and war, so they accepted this so-called cleansing without question. Few citizens understood Lucen and Navissa themselves were mages, believing they simply had great powers to protect everyone. So adored were they for bringing an end to the Grand Archmage and his black-robed inquisitors, the people began to revere them as gods."

Oona stood in shocked silence, her expression as horrified as if she'd found Evie dead.

"Lucen, Navissa, and their son Orien eventually became gods," said Paelirron. "Tenebrea was born after and has never known mortal life."

"You're saying…" Oona pointed at the ghost, her glare shouting 'how dare you,' but she kept her voice calm. "You're saying our gods aren't gods?"

"No, child. They are. I am telling you they were not always so… except for Tenebrea." Paelirron held his arms out to either side. "What is a god but a being of great power? By any human understanding of the concept, Lucen, Navissa, Orien, and Tenebrea are quite clearly gods."

The soldiers murmured rapidly back and forth, questioning if the apparition should be trusted or tried to trick them into blasphemy.

Kitlyn squeezed Oona's hand. The look in her eyes said she hadn't sensed any falsehood in the dragon's words. As the realization nothing truly had changed—the gods *were* gods, but perhaps not the supremely powerful beings holding dominion over the entire world she once thought them to be—dawned on her, the tension faded from her body.

"Is this why the Temple of Lucen punished anyone who had the 'wrong' magic for so long?" whispered Oona.

Paelirron nodded once. "An unfortunate aftereffect of the wars among mages. I suspect some writings detailed Lucen and Navissa's revolution against the Grand Archmage. In the way humans tend to do with history, it almost certainly evolved into an exaggerated story of them driving 'demons' out of the land."

Oona winced. "Did they? We hold it as true Lucen purged demons from the land... is *that* a lie, too?"

"It would be more accurate to say mortals serving Lucen after he'd become a god spent many years cleaning up demonic beings loosed into the world during the wars between guilds," said Paelirron. "Over time, the distinction between actual demons and anyone the early Lucen worshippers regarded as dangerous blurred. Only two types of magic are inherently evil—demonology and necromancy."

Oona scowled. "Yes. Lucen suffers neither maleficars nor necromancers in his kingdom."

"I question whether humans have the temperament to wield magic of *any* kind. However, only those two will intrinsically corrupt anyone due to their nature." Paelirron smiled at Tamsen. "There are some humans who I do believe can be responsible with magic."

"I'm sorry," said Tamsen. "When you disappeared, I was angry with you for leaving me alone. But I understand now. You're a ghost. So, sorry for being angry."

Kitlyn's heart sank. "Our people killed the Anthari... persecuted mages. Aodh stole the Heart and made war on Evermoor. Our kingdom has been evil while claiming to be virtuous for a thousand years."

"No!" Oona grabbed her arms, shaking her. "We are not

responsible for ancient wrongs. We—humans—can learn. Magic is not the source of evil. Good or evil is a choice coming from the person."

"Except for demonology and necromancy." Tamsen held up a finger. "Those are evil."

"I thought it might have been the Anthari... but... we obviously deserved it." Kitlyn faced the ghost. "Who cursed us? What must I do in order to make amends?"

"Can't be the Anthari." Oona shook her head. "Otherwise, it would have killed Lucen and Navissa."

"The curse is quite old, yes." Paelirron paced around them. "However, it did not exist before they became gods, and the Anthari left this world long before Lucen or Navissa were born."

"Can we end it or are we doomed?" whispered Kitlyn.

"It *is* possible to end." Paelirron stopped, turning to face them.

"Did the Grand Archmage cast the curse as he died out of spite?" asked Oona.

"No." Paelirron clasped his hands. "The curse came from my mate."

35

ONE FINAL REQUEST

OONA

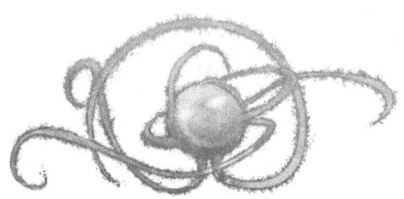

Chaotic thoughts regarding the gods swirling around Oona's mind jammed to a halt.

"What? Your mate?" She gawked. "Why?"

"A few decades after Lucen, Navissa, and Orien ascended to god-dom, humans from your kingdom decided to consider everything they believed might threaten them 'demonic.' Once again, humankind surrendered to the belief that all beings other than humans were inherently evil and needed to be destroyed. They convinced themselves dragons were sent by demons to corrupt them with promises of power and magic."

Oona folded her arms. "I'm not saying they are right, but if what you've told us is true… can you not see where the belief came from? The truth is dragons taught humans magic, which led to a thousand years of war and misery. It's *humans'* fault, but…"

"Humans always seek to blame someone other than themselves," said Paelirron.

Oona and Kitlyn sighed at the same time.

He resumed pacing. "Yes. I understand how a weak grasp of history allowed them to believe dragons responsible for their problems. We are, also, somewhat formidable in appearance at times.

An army from the kingdom recently renamed Lucernia came here to destroy me and all who studied here. Once again, they allowed their fear to fill their minds with untruths. The humans believed I trained an 'army of mages' intent on destroying Lucernia."

Oh, no! Sudden lightheadedness made her grab Kitlyn to stay upright. Not only had those who followed Lucen—yet again—done something horrible in his name, all those ashes in the entry corridor had to be from ancient Lucernians. Too horrified to speak, she whispered, "They killed everyone?"

"I managed to save a great many of my students, but doing so cost my life." Paelirron ceased walking, gazing up at the shelves surrounding the chamber. "I do not regret sacrificing this incarnation for their sake. My mate, Tyndris, already knew great fury with humans for their war against the Anthari. Upon my death, she cursed the kingdom responsible."

Kitlyn exhaled, tilting her head back to stare straight up at the open top of the chamber. Dark jags of stony thorn vines broke the sunlight up into hundreds of irregular shapes. "How can we possibly apologize enough to a dragon for your death?" She froze, then lowered her gaze back to him, jaw slightly agape. "Your mate is still alive? There's a real dragon out there?"

"She is." Paelirron smiled. "However, Tyndris goes to great lengths to avoid humans, so she isn't tempted to kill them."

"Do you think she will see reason? Humans... we don't really live very long compared to dragons." Oona wrung her hands. "No one alive in Lucernia now even knows a tenth of what you've told us. I fear even telling them Lucen, Navissa, and Orien may once have been mortal could incite people to madness or violence."

Paelirron rested a hand on her shoulder, though it had no substance beyond a faint chill. "It is not important for your people to know every detail about their gods. Not all secrets are bad to keep. The gods themselves appear to be noble enough... it is the people who serve them who misunderstand."

"Why wouldn't Lucen reveal this truth to his most dedicated servants?" asked Kitlyn.

"No matter how noble or well-intentioned a god is..." Paelirron smiled. "Becoming so powerful changes them. It is certainly possible Lucen does not remember ever being mortal, or chooses not to."

"So, you're saying there's a real live dragon somewhere?" Rakden stabbed two fingers toward the ghost. "How is it no one has ever seen such a creature?"

Tamsen pivoted to look at the soldiers, her blanket cloak swishing around. "Dragons invented magic. Are you really surprised they're good at hiding?"

Paelirron chuckled.

Rakden pursed his lips. "How many are there?"

"I am unsure, though Tyndris is the only one in Lucernia."

Oona gawked at the spirit. "There is a *dragon* in Lucernia? She's not here in the moor?"

"No, I am afraid she became quite angry at humans. Specifically, the ones in your kingdom. She relocated to watch her curse work."

"Has she become evil? Consumed with hate?" Kitlyn fidgeted. "Please tell me she won't try to kill us before talking."

Paelirron appeared close to laughing, but merely smiled. "No. She would much prefer to watch her curse do its work than resort to getting her claws dirty. I confess she may antagonize you verbally, perhaps make it quite difficult to reach her."

"How are we supposed to talk her out of a 2,500-year-old grudge?" Oona grabbed her head in both hands, feeling dizzy again.

"The answer is both simple and dangerous." Paelirron pointed at the floor. "I am certain you will be able to convince her to end the curse if you bring her my essence."

"Your essence...?" Kitlyn tilted her head.

"When a dragon dies, the energy comprising our being, something humans call a soul or spirit, coalesces into a solid gem. Bring this to her and she will almost certainly agree to your request to end the curse."

Oona nodded.

"What is the dangerous part?" Kitlyn folded her arms, eyes narrowed in suspicion. "Surviving meeting her long enough to say we brought the essence?"

"The essence is with my remains in the lower catacomb."

Paelirron gestured to the side. One of many decorative gold inlay circles in the floor around the perimeter of the main circle glowed bright green for a second before vanishing, leaving a hole three feet across. "There are stray magical energies below, as well as the unquiet remains of those who came here to destroy us. In my present form, I can do little to assist you other than disarming the glyphs."

Kitlyn pointed at the dragon skeleton. "These are not your remains?"

"Alas. Korlinth gave his life here, trying to defend the door. This chamber did not give him sufficient room to move. We are fearsome, but far less so when we cannot fly. I made my stand down in the catacombs."

The magic Lucen gives us is not greatly effective on creatures other than demons. Certainly, it would be a monumental task to slay a dragon this size. Oona looked over the bones. *They must have fought it using ordinary weapons. Grr. Fools. The instant they noticed their magic having a weak effect, they should have known dragons are not demons.* She bowed her head. *Or they lost his favor as Aodh did for heresy.*

"What are these glyphs?" Kitlyn approached the hole in the floor, peering down.

"Magical defenses. Certain death for any who are not skilled mages." Paelirron raised one hand. "You need not worry about them."

If we don't do this, the curse will take Kitlyn's life. A painful twinge gripped Oona's heart. *We could both be killed here. We've already come all this way.* "Kit?"

Kitlyn looked over, paused a second, then walked up to her. "Yes?"

"I will risk whatever dread lurks below with you if this is something you wish to do."

"You are afraid we will die." Kitlyn caressed Oona's cheek. The warmth of her hand sent tingles spreading throughout her body.

"Yes." She looked down. "It is not that I am afraid. This choice must be both of ours."

"We might die down there, yes. But if we do not attempt to recover this dragon's essence, we will definitely die to the curse. I loathe the fear of having a blade I cannot see to my throat, ready to strike at any moment."

Oona steeled herself. "Then let us go down into the catacomb."

"Tamsen is staying up here," said Kitlyn.

"Umm, might be a bad idea." The child raised a hand. "Pelar said there are creatures made of loose magic down there. Can either of you dispel arcane magic?"

They stared at her.

Tamsen flashed a less-than-confident smile. "I *am* scared, and I *would* rather stay where it's safe, but not if it means you're going to die." She approached and grasped Oona's hand. "You jumped in front of me, holding a dagger away from my face. Both of you almost died to save my life. I will help you even if it's scary."

"Aye, highness." Yerbin nodded. "This curse is going to kill you if you do nothing. After all you did for us, the people I mean, ending the war, making life a little bit nicer... we can't let some old curse take you away from us."

Beowyn drew his greatsword. "Whatever it takes to keep you safe."

"Many will suffer if Lucernia loses you." Rakden pulled his longsword. "We all swore an oath to the crown. Forgive me if what I am about to say is improper. Not until the two of you sat upon the throne, did I truly feel pride in my oath to defend the crown."

"Aye." Danos approached the hole. "We are with you, highnesses."

Oona waited for the lump in her throat to shrink. Hearing four men speak so highly of them felt undeserved. How could simply wanting to do what Lucen commanded, what she felt right, stir the hearts of her people so deeply? "Paelirron, what does your essence look like? How will we know it?"

"It is a sapphire gem in the shape of an egg."

"All right." She walked over to the hole, peering down a narrow set of spiral stairs leading into darkness. After summoning her light orb, she locked eyes with Paelirron's ghost. "We will take your essence to your mate."

Tamsen hurried over.

"We're really going to bring a child with us?" asked Kitlyn.

"Does being six years older than me make you adults?"

"Yes," said Oona and Kitlyn simultaneously.

"According to the law, at least," whispered Oona.

Tamsen whisper-giggled.

"We want you to be safe." Kitlyn squeezed the girl's shoulder.

"I'm your only means to dispel arcane magic." Tamsen set her hands on her hips. "A runaway scrap of magic could be simple for me to get rid of but kill all six of you because you have no way to destroy it."

Oona looked at Kitlyn. "I don't want her to be hurt. She's been through enough already with those fools."

"You have Orien's gift. If she is careful, we can protect her." Kitlyn pointed at Tamsen. "If something too dangerous is down there, you are to run. Do you understand?"

"Yes." Tamsen tapped her foot. "If you remember, I suggested we run away from the big root monster, but no one listened to the kid."

Rakden chuckled.

"All right. Be careful." Oona started for the stairs.

Beowyn moved in front of her.

She stopped short, gesturing for him to lead the way, waited for Rakden to go next, then followed them down the stairs, saturated in the comforting light radiating from her little orb. Its tiny eye spots appeared wider than ever before, as if saying 'please be careful.'

I fear no darkness; Lucen is my light. I fear no death; Tenebrea walks at my side. I fear no harm; Orien protects me... and I am with Kitlyn.

36

THE REMAINS OF WAR

KITLYN

Kitlyn descended the stairs behind Oona, arms out to the walls to steady herself.

Unable to see much past everyone ahead of her, she opened her senses to the Stone, searching for anything moving. Eight twists around the spiral later, she stepped out of the stairwell into an underground hallway inexplicably lit as bright as an ordinary room on an overcast day. Oona's orb created an area of more intense light closer to their group. Given the strange sourceless light down here, they didn't *require* the orb to see, but it also revealed falsehoods within its radiance.

Having only one way to go, Beowyn and Rakden proceeded forward.

Red marble tiles covered the lower half of the walls on either side like wainscoting in swooping arches between faux half-columns. It didn't take them long to discover evidence of a past battle in the form of smashed chairs, broken vases, and cracked tiles. An archway on the left opened to a study containing long tables and bookshelves in disarray.

Another study on the right also lay strewn with damaged furniture. Since neither chamber contained a dragon's skeleton, they ignored them and kept going straight to a four-way intersection, where Beowyn and Rakden paused, looked each way, and went right.

Dozens of doors at close intervals along the passage turned out to be small bedrooms.

"Students must have lived down here. This is not the right way," said Rakden.

They returned to the intersection and turned right again, going in the same direction as before.

A short distance from the intersection, they went through a smashed set of double doors, entering one end of a vast rectangular room lined with bookshelves, long tables, and numerous chairs. Most of the furniture bore battle scars, including acid burns, scorch marks, and arrows. The smell of moldy, wet paper tainted every breath.

At the opposite end of the room, a grand archway and double doors led deeper into the catacomb. The soldiers proceeded into the room, kicking charred books, broken bits of furniture, and the occasional metal helmet out of their way.

"It's scary down here," whispered Tamsen. "I haven't had bad dreams in almost two years. I might have one tonight." She paused. "If we're not all dead."

"That's reassuring," muttered Danos.

Metal scraped the floor when they neared the middle of the old library, far enough off to the left it clearly hadn't come from any one of them. Where seconds ago the room felt empty to Kitlyn's stone sense, the area around them came to life. Though the motion felt like numerous people pushing themselves upright from lying on the floor, but they didn't weigh enough to be alive.

"Skeletons!" yelled Kitlyn. "Undead! Be ready!"

Dry hissing and clacking broke the silence. The hollow rattle of metal helmets rolling on stone accompanied the unmistakable ring of swords being lifted from the floor. Dusty skeletons clad in the tattered remains of chain mail over white robes clawed their way upright, emerging from under tables, breaking through collapsed bookshelves, and pulling themselves out of debris piles. Broken hunks of wood clattered to the ground.

Only about forty of them... not as bad as the lich's cave.

Kitlyn projected a burst of magic into the ground, focusing on a skeleton in torn robes ambling toward her dragging a massive two-handed war mace as if too weak to lift it. A rocky spire thrust up from the floor at an angle, smash-impaling the undead, which collapsed into a scattering of loose bones. Its huge weapon thudded to the floor.

"Four corners," said Rakden. "Queens and child stay behind us."

The soldiers closed in, all turning their backs to Oona, Kitlyn, and Tamsen, forming as much of a circle around them as four people could. Oona threw a bolt of blue light at a skeleton, knocking it teetering for a second and sending a few ribs flying off over a table.

Tamsen waved her hands around, chanting, *"Na'ava sura kaz maranhi eht."* Her voice carried a faint tremble of fear, though it didn't match her determined expression. An unusually loud stream of fire roared from her outstretched palm, engulfing a skeleton coming at them from the rear. The undead disintegrated to ash in under a second, allowing the fire stream to hit a second skeleton behind it, destroying one arm and most of its left leg. Skeleton two tumbled to the floor fully engulfed, soon nothing more than a cloud of embers and ash.

Hissing skeletons hurled themselves into battle, attacking mindlessly from all sides without fear or any sense of self-preservation. Their maces, axes, and swords spat dust each time they crashed against the soldiers' blades. Kitlyn focused on the skeletons coming up behind them, summoning fist-sized rocks as fast as she could and hurling them into the skeletons. Each glow-shrouded meteor bashed through multiple skeletons, knocking off arms or pulverizing hips. Unfortunately, the broken pieces continued trying to attack. A skeleton reduced to just a skull, one arm, and bit of ribcage continued dragging itself at Yerbin.

He kicked the skull, smashing the jawbone and sending the rest of it sliding off under a table.

"What in Lucen's name are those?" shouted Beowyn.

"Skeletons," called Yerbin.

Beowyn growled. "No, not those. *Those!* Hey, kid!"

Kitlyn whirled around to look.

Three glowing smears of violet-pink light seeped out of the double doors at the end of the room, bright enough to tint the area around them the same color. Formless and clearly inhuman, the entities lacked anything approaching a humanoid shape. Their appearance resembled giant brush strokes of glowing paint smeared on reality, no two the same size or pattern. Lightning sparkles danced back and forth within each cloud, snapping louder than the clang of weapons and battle screams from the soldiers.

"*Auruun naeth milar!*" yelled Tamsen while thrusting her hands forward, both ring fingers bent down, the others splayed.

The center apparition flickered, dimmed, and burst into a puff of smoke a half-second before thin blue lightning arcs leapt out from the other two glowing squiggles, striking Beowyn and Yerbin. The *bang* of the electrical discharge inside a closed room struck Kitlyn like a punch to the head. Beowyn and Yerbin both flew backward off their feet. The seven or so skeletons they'd been holding off staggered from the concussion, but didn't seem at all stunned. Without the soldiers in the way, they'd rush right in.

Kitlyn didn't consider herself—or Oona—helpless in a swordfight, but eight-on-two wouldn't go well for her. A surge of protectiveness empowered her magic. Before the skeletons could recover from the blast and charge in at them, she raised a wall of stone from the floor to the ceiling where the two men had been standing.

The scent of roasting meat came out of nowhere.

Beowyn groaned.

"Ack! I can't see through stone." Tamsen darted to the right, crouching low to peer around the wall and reach one hand out. "*Auruun naeth milar!*"

Oona rushed left, two-handing her longsword as she crossed weapons with a mace-wielding skeleton. A second skeleton on the right side exploited Yerbin's absence to lunge in and swing an axe down on Tamsen from a blind angle the child didn't see coming.

"Get back!" shouted Kitlyn while thrusting her sword in the path of the strike.

Axe struck sword inches above Tamsen's head. At the *clank*, she yelped, scrambling for cover. Two more skeletons came around the end of the wall, grabbing her blanket cloak when she attempted to dart away and yanking her over backward. Before they could drag her off to her death, Kitlyn stomped on the blanket, stopping her slide.

Oona let out a heavy *oof* and staggered into Kitlyn, gasping for air.

The skeleton that hit her raised its mace and rushed after her.

Screaming, Tamsen rolled around, rapidly kicking both legs at the two undead attempting to pull her toward them while Kitlyn feverishly tried to keep the axe-wielding one from hitting either of them. Seeing Oona about to take a mace to the top of the head, she pivoted to parry, exposing her side to the axe.

"Highness!" yelled Danos, throwing himself in the way.

He deflected the axe swinging for her ribs with his broadsword at the same time she swatted the dusty mace away from Oona's head. Two other skeletons he'd been fending off stabbed him in the back and leg.

Rakden bellowed a noise part way between war cry and scream of frustration, furiously trying to defend himself as well as peel the two off Danos, who moaned and collapsed to one knee. Beowyn twitched, babbling nonsense, tiny sparks lapping over his face. Yerbin hadn't moved since the lightning hit him.

A glowing purple squiggle floated around the left side of the stone, lightning gathering at the center of its core.

Kitlyn roared in anger at the mace-wielding skeleton, summoning a column of rock up from beneath the bony horror and smashing it into the ceiling.

"*Auruun naeth milar!*" yelled Tamsen, thrusting her arms up over her head, still lying on her back and still kicking at skeletal hands grabbing for her legs.

The glowing arcane scrap burst into dull smoke, releasing a small lightning bolt off to the side, which nailed a skeleton in the face, having little effect beyond charring it. Down on one knee, Danos hacked his broadsword through the pelvis of the axe-wielding skeleton, destroying its ability to stand. Despite collapsing to the floor and being legless, it continued chopping at him.

Tamsen sat up, thrusting her arms forward. *"Na'ava ɔura kaz maranhi eht!"* She directed the fire spray over the two skeletons holding onto her blanket cloak as well as the half-skeleton chopping at Danos.

Oona struggled to her feet, swinging her sword up to defend Danos from the skeleton that hit him in the leg. Fighting in a longsword-and-dagger style, Rakden somehow held off six skeletons by himself, only two of which remained on their feet, but his frantic defenses left no time for retaliatory strikes. Every few seconds, he parried by kicking one skeleton into another, fouling both their attacks. Rapid clanging of weapons clashing drowned out the dry hissing.

Tamsen scrambled upright and backed away from the end of the summoned wall, flatting herself against the middle.

More skeletons spilled in from the rear, one heading for Oona, one Tamsen.

Kitlyn overextended herself, successfully swatting a flail aside so it didn't hit the child, but couldn't recover in time to avoid a wooden staff—or perhaps an axe handle—breaking over her head. Dazed, she staggered to the side, crashing into another skeleton. She reflexively grabbed its ribs for support. It hissed in her face, one dry tooth falling out.

Growling, Kitlyn shoved the surprisingly light monster off its feet, but the dizziness of being walloped over the head caused her to crash down on top of it. She liquefied the stone, pushed the fiend into the grey fluid up to its shoulders, then released the magic, making the floor solid again. The trapped skeleton flailed and kicked, still evidently able to see her despite its entire skull being encased in rock.

Beowyn rolled to his feet, swaying side to side as if he'd had far too much to drink. Though his balance faltered, he kept himself upright, teetering after each great, cleaving swing of his giant greatsword. Every skeleton he touched blasted apart into loose bones. Stray arms, partial torsos, and the occasional leg kept twitching and trying to kill someone.

Tamsen sprayed fire whenever she had a moment to do so, but mostly weaved around to keep someone alive between her and skeletons. Fortunately, the mindless undead lacked the ability to recognize magic as a greater threat and simply tried to kill the closest living person. Her flame spell reduced any undead she hit with more than a glancing spray to smoldering pebbles. Those she grazed ignited, but continued attacking.

I will see flaming skeletons trying to kill me in my dreams for as long as I live. Kitlyn smacked a sword going for her chest aside, then called a rock spire to smash the skeleton wielding it.

Thoonk!

Rakden howled.

Kitlyn twisted to look.

A dusty crossbow quarrel stuck out from the back of his left shoulder.

Tamsen threw fire at a skeleton reloading a crossbow by the end of a bookshelf twenty feet away. The ancient, dried-out undead vanished under the flames, ashed over in seconds.

Oona let out a scream of desperation. A shell of blue light appeared over her. All dozen or so skeletons still surrounding them smoldered and smoked. While no open flames appeared on them, the intense radiance of her magic forced the fiends to recoil away.

Between Beowyn's sword, Kitlyn hurling rocks, and Tamsen throwing fire, the remainder of the cowering skeletons perished in short order. Once the last of them fell, Oona ceased concentrating on the radiant light—and rushed to Yerbin's side.

As soon as she looked at him, she broke down into sobs.

Beowyn rested the tip of his sword on the ground, leaning on it.

Rakden gritted his teeth, breathing hard.

Danos eased himself down to sit on the floor, groaning.

"Oo?" Kitlyn crouched next to her.

Oona looked up at her.

At the sight of blood dribbling from her wife's mouth, Kitlyn gasped, grabbed her shoulders, and rasped, "You're hurt!"

"He's dead." Oona closed her eyes. "Yerbin is dead."

The realization of why she smelled roasting meat made Kitlyn sick to her stomach. She held in the urge to vomit, too worried about Oona.

"Highness," said Rakden in a slow, forced tone. "Any one of us is gladly willing to give our lives to protect the two of you. We swore an oath to defend the crown knowing we put our lives at risk. As I said before, I will lay down my life to defend the ruler of Lucernia, but I am *proud* to defend a monarch worthy of my loyalty."

"Absolutely," rasped Danos. "Our queens are all we have stopping the nobility from tearing Lucernia apart in a war for the crown. Soldiers can be replaced easily. *Good* leaders are much more difficult to find."

Oona fought back tears. "No. No person can be replaced. He's dead because we wanted to come here."

"We came here to break the curse." Kitlyn grasped Oona's face in both hands, forcing her to make eye contact. "If we don't break the curse, we die... eventually."

"You're bleeding, too." Oona reached up, touching a finger above Kitlyn's left eyebrow.

"Got hit over the head. Probably only a splinter in my scalp."

Oona rested her hands on Kitlyn's shoulders. Warm, golden light surrounded her.

Numbness spread over the top of Kitlyn's head—and the room became significantly less blurry. *Oof. I didn't realize how dizzy I was.*

Tamsen stood with her back to the defensive wall Kitlyn summoned, watching Oona attend to the soldiers. Poor Yerbin had already gone well past Orien's ability to help. Due to Beowyn's sheer size, the lightning had only stunned him—as well as left some burns. He waved Oona over to Danos first. She called upon Orien's gift to mend the two stab wounds and a few bruises he'd suffered. Rakden escaped the battle with only a crossbow quarrel stuck in him. His left arm would be a bit weak for a few days.

Oona held her hands out to Beowyn until the golden light faded. The only visible sign of anything happening came from his determined glower softening to a faint smile as the pain of various burns lessened. Finally, Oona asked Orien to take her own wounds away. A skeleton had walloped her in the stomach hard enough to knock the wind out of her. If not for her leather armor, she'd also have suffered a spike puncture.

Once Oona had done all she could for everyone, she crawled over to Yerbin and prayed to Tenebrea, asking her to guide him safely to her realm.

"I'll carry him out when we are finished here," said Beowyn.

Rakden clapped him on the shoulder. "How are you feeling?"

"Sore, but hardly the worst I've had. Your arm all right?"

"I'll hold up." Rakden helped Danos up. "Leg?"

"Just a little pain. Not as bad as eating anything Beowyn cooks." Danos gave a mirthless chuckle.

Beowyn pointed at him, eyebrows up in a playful threatening glance.

"The man's a fine cook." Rakden grimaced while rolling his left shoulder around to test it. "He's missed his calling. Ought to be running an inn."

"Bah. Ain't old enough to sit on my backside all day yet." Beowyn wiped dust off his greatsword.

"Thank you," whispered Oona before standing. "Tenebrea guides him. Let us be done with this place."

Tamsen scurried over to the double doors, whispering to herself and waving her hand at the knobs. "It's safe. Well... I mean the *doors* won't kill us."

Beowyn grasped a handful of the child's cloak, gently pulled her out of the way, and opened the doors. Sword high, he led the way into a plain stone corridor. A fair distance ahead, a large circle of magical symbols covered the floor, illuminating the corners of a four-way intersection in a faint lavender glow.

He stopped and pointed at it. "What is that?"

"A glyph," whispered Tamsen. "Don't go near it."

The luminous sigils abruptly darkened.

Paelirron's voice filled the passageway. "It is safe to proceed. The glyphs are silent."

37

MANY TALENTS

OONA

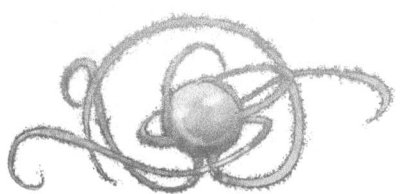

G rief stung Oona's heart, bothering her far more than the
physical bruises.

Her armor didn't help much against the impact of a
mace, though it had prevented the dull spike from tearing her open.
The skeleton hit her high on the stomach, right under the base of her
ribcage. Being unable to breathe for about twenty seconds had been
terrifying. Considering they'd been ambushed and surrounded by
thirty or forty skeletons, only one of their number dying should have
felt like victory... but didn't.

Sensing Tamsen trying to conceal fear, Oona approached and
took her hand. The girl jumped, looking up in confusion for a few
seconds before blushing faintly and squeezing her hand back.

*She hasn't been with anyone who truly cared about her since her
grandfather died.* A chill ran down Oona's back. Had they insisted the
girl wait for them upstairs to 'stay safe,' those apparitions would
likely have killed them all. *Even with her helping, we still might've failed.*
The soldiers held off the skeletons fairly well until Beowyn and
Yerbin both went down to lightning. Kitlyn's wall prevented a
second person's death. Because of it, the arcane scraps had to
reposition before they could throw lightning again. Tamsen could

only dispel them one at a time. Without the wall, one of the two remaining scraps would've killed someone while she dispelled the other. If it chose to attack the child, the third scrap would have been free to wipe them out.

Yerbin was somewhat small for a man, but still much bigger than Tamsen. She wouldn't have survived the lightning. Nor would I or Kitlyn. No one normal would have. Beowyn is huge.

"Argh. Here we go again. More," said Beowyn.

Oona snapped out of her mental wandering.

Another group of skeletons rushed toward them from the dark corridor ahead. A few wore tattered remains of Lucen temple armor. Robe scraps clung to the others, likely former students who died during the attack.

"Why are *both* sides undead?" asked Oona.

"Worry about that later, highness." Beowyn moved forward to block the passage.

Rakden stepped up beside him on the left, Danos a few paces behind them in the middle to block any skeletons making it past them.

"Leave me room for fire." Tamsen raised her arms.

These souls belong in my realm, whispered a female voice. *Send them to me.*

Oona bowed her head in reverence. *I shall do as you command.*

A mild mental nudge gave her the same sense she felt around Mary, Laura, and Rowan whenever they called her 'highness,' almost as if Tenebrea told her she didn't need to be quite so subservient when no one else could see them.

Beowyn and Rakden had the advantage of a corridor limiting them to facing off against three to five skeletons at once—rather than a large room in which they could be surrounded. However, the bottleneck began to collapse after they smashed a few skeletons apart. Legless undead attacking from the floor tried to stab them in the knees, forcing them to give ground as they could not parry so many weapons swinging at once.

Tamsen cast Drake's Fire, projecting the stream of flames between the men. Danos dove to the side away from the burning ray, yelping in shock. Due to the skeletons cramming themselves together in their mindless pursuit of blood, the three-second blast of fire ashed five skeletons and ignited a few more.

'Send them to Tenebrea' was a relatively vague instruction. When Oona desired to do so, she heeded the urge to raise her arm in the same manner as when casting beams of Lucen's light at a demon.

"Lady Tenebrea, spare these tortured souls their wretchedness," said Oona.

A shaft of pale grey light projected forward from her palm, widening into a cone. Every skeleton—some eighteen or twenty closest to the soldiers—struck by the light abruptly stopped moving and clattered loose to the floor, the nefarious forces holding their bones together gone.

A green comet flew from Kitlyn's hand, its dark stone core pulverizing the spine of a skeleton some thirty feet away, past the now-empty area. She didn't appear to have been aiming for one so far. "Oo? What in the name of—"

"Tenebrea is helping us."

No longer the least bit afraid of moving bones, Oona stepped forward, squeezing between Beowyn and Rakden, then raising her arms. She waited for the hissing skeletons to close the gap, then called upon Tenebrea's gift again. Her pale grey light filled the corridor in front of her, toppling the remaining skeletons into a heap of stray bones. The musty, dry scent of long-dead corpses filled the air, riding on the dust.

Oona turned around to face everyone.

Beowyn grinned back at her, though Rakden and Danos looked ever so slightly fearful—the same reaction most people had around Tenebrea's priests.

"You have no reason to be afraid. I am the same person I've always been. Tenebrea does not decide *when* a person dies. She guides them after death and protects their souls. As Lucen despises and protects us from demons, so, too, does she revile necromancy. Tenebrea is a guardian, not a destroyer."

Tamsen whistled. "I think that is all of them."

"Yes." Kitlyn closed her eyes. "I do not feel anything else moving around."

Beowyn kicked a skull. It rolled a short distance and wobbled to a stop. He watched it for a moment, then, satisfied it would not get back up, again took the lead, guiding the group down the long, plain stone hallway. They arrived minutes later at an archway where the corridor connected to another massive cylindrical library chamber, similar to the one in which they found Paelirron's ghost. This one, however, extended six stories down from where they entered and lacked sunlight.

Oona approached the edge of the circular walkway, peering over. A second dragon skeleton lay at the bottom. This one hadn't fallen apart, some unexplained force still held the bones together as they had been in life. Dark blue light glowed from within the ribcage, painting eerie shadows around the bottom of the chamber. The others also crept up to the edge to look. Kitlyn and Oona both grabbed Tamsen, worried she might fall.

Surprisingly, the girl didn't complain.

After a few minutes taking in the scenery, the group made their way around the circle, following a series of stairwells positioned at alternating opposite sides. Oona couldn't tell if they'd been placed to make the walk to the bottom as long as possible purely for annoyance or if it served some tactical defensive purpose. Tamsen whistled in awe at all the bookshelves, tables, sculptures of creatures, paintings, maps, and so forth tucked into the various rooms occupying the alcoves around the rings on the way down.

The closer they got to the bottom, the more obvious it became the dragon remains here were modestly larger than the first set of bones. Perhaps it only seemed bigger because it remained intact. A dried miasma of former guts coated the floor beneath the bones, having decayed to a black tar-like gunk. Light from Oona's orb flickered and glinted from thousands of metallic blue scales scattered around the remains, some no bigger than a human fingernail, others the size of shields.

A massive egg-shaped sapphire sat on the floor below the ribcage, giving off as strong, dark blue light. Tamsen paused to pick up a six-inch scale. She held it up to the light, tilting it back and forth. The soldiers stared in awe at the remains. Kitlyn watched the room around them, seemingly expecting another attack.

Guess I'll grab it.

Oona squeezed between two ribs, feeling like a bird in a giant cage. She crouched beside the head-sized gem and grasped it in both hands. The instant her skin made contact with the warm stone, insight flooded her thoughts. A brief vision of Paelirron's final moments played out in her mind, the great dragon desperately twisting around in the confined space of this library, clawing and biting at dozens of people in Lucen garb. The death blow came from a spear to the heart. At the instant of his death, a terrible magic storm burst outward from the dragon's collapsing body, melting the flesh from everyone in sight. The dragon's soul coalesced into the gem, trapped within the body until it decomposed.

The soul spoke to her of its purpose.

She knew beyond a doubt Tyndris would break her curse in trade for it.

"Dragons cannot truly die." Oona stood, holding the gem out at arms' length. "If we bring this to his mate, she will bear children, one of which will allow his spirit to return."

"It will resurrect him?" asked Kitlyn.

"No." Oona slipped out of the ribcage, carrying the huge gem. "His spirit energy will return, but he won't be Paelirron anymore. He'll be reborn as a new being."

Tamsen dropped the scale and ran over to gawk at the giant sapphire. "Wow. Every thief from here to Ondar would kill their own brothers to steal a gem this size."

Kitlyn and Oona stared at her.

"Not me." The child held her hands up in a gesture of innocence. "Only an idiot would steal a gem as big as a baby. I don't want to be murdered for it."

Kitlyn chuckled. "We are teasing. We don't think you will steal."

"Only food." Oona winked.

Tamsen grinned. "I can hide it if you put it in your satchel."

"I was planning to." Oona stuffed the massive egg-shaped gem into the satchel hanging on her hip, making the bag appear ponderously pregnant.

"*Sa'oro val norath iaani nurimah,*" chanted Tamsen while tracing complex hand symbols in the air. A brief shimmer of light circled the satchel. It promptly deflated, appearing empty. "There. Safe."

Oona nearly yelped in alarm, but noticed it hadn't become any lighter. She opened the flap to look inside, and *did* yelp at the sight of a completely empty bag. "What happened to my things—and the essence?"

"It's a handy spell called Imric's Bag." Tamsen clasped her hands behind her back, grinning. "It hides stuff to stop thieves. Everything is still there, but it's only 'there' when you want to take it out. The bag isn't really empty. If you try to put more stuff in it, it will rip."

"How do I take something out?" Oona blinked in astonishment at the heavy, yet seemingly empty satchel.

"Think of something in the bag and reach for it. After you take it out of the bag, it won't disappear again if you put it back in. The spell stops thieves because you have to know something is in there to be able to find it."

Oona closed the flap. "Interesting."

Tamsen shrugged. "There are many strange spells like this. Old mages must have been really *bored*. One of my books has a spell to enchant a book so the pages turn for you when you're reading it. Talk about lazy."

Rakden shook his head.

Kitlyn patted the satchel. "Amazing. This will definitely protect us from thieves on the way back to Lucernia. Quite handy."

Tamsen puffed out her chest, beaming. "I have many talents."

38

ARCANE REASONING

KITLYN

Eager to leave a dangerous place, Kitlyn walked over to the stairs.

She paused to pluck a few stuck dragon scales from her feet before going up. The others hurried after her, Tamsen somewhat dawdling to ogle all the books. She grumbled about having to find a spell to turn herself into an Anthari so she could live long enough to read *all* of them.

"Please bring my essence to Tyndris." Paelirron's voice echoed around them from no apparent source. "You will find her high in the Dawnspire Mountains at the western border of Lucernia."

Where she can look down on us all. Kitlyn slouched in frustration. She'd hoped the other dragon wouldn't be so far away.

Oona rested a hand on her shoulder. "This is our life."

"Yes. I know. The idea of such a long journey is draining. However, it is at least toward home."

"Then, let us be on our way to the Dawnspires."

Kitlyn stared into Oona's eyes, as blue as a sapphire gem and glimmering in the light from the little orb. *She is so beautiful, even covered in dirt and blood. I would walk to the ends of the world for her. Traveling to our kingdom's border is nothing.*

She resisted the urge to kiss her or hold hands, still too wary of attack. They'd have plenty of time for that after reaching the surface.

THE CRACKLING GLOW OF A FIRE WARMED THE DINING ROOM OF the inn at Kolbrin's Quay.

Kitlyn sat at a large table beside Oona, having a genuine meal for the first time in a few days. Imoa and Lliard reacted to the grim news of Yerbin's death much as she'd expected—initially somber, then complaining about being left behind, then moving on to telling stories about him.

This swamp town had little in the way of tailor's shops. Only one shopkeeper had clothing in Tamsen's size. Apparently, every child in the village wore the same drab grey style of peasant tunic and no shoes—because only one person made child-sized clothing here. Despite more than half of her faded red dress being missing, the garment still served well enough as a shirt when worn with breeches, so they decided to hold off on replacing her clothing until reaching a larger town. 'Looking shabby' did not amount to an emergency.

Yerbin's remains would spend the night in Beowyn's room. Tenebrea's magical gift to Oona also included the ability to preserve a body from decay until burial. They intended to bring him back to Lucernia for a proper funeral and honors.

While the soldiers drank ale and shared stories of the past, mostly involving their dead comrade, Oona conversed with Tamsen, trading random small bits of information like favorite foods or stories of happy times.

Kitlyn adored having an actual meal again as opposed to rations, but she still looked forward to finishing it so she could soak in a bath. She felt as if she wore half her bodyweight in swamp muck. It worried her the innkeeper asked 'what do you want a bath *for*,' but he did have a tub. *Oona should ask Lucen to purify the water first.*

"I think the gods are protecting us from the curse," said Oona out of nowhere.

"How did you go from talking about Tamsen's most beloved doll to our curse?" Kitlyn glanced over at her.

Oona put an arm around the child. "You missed us switching to discuss magic. It made me think the gods are so tremendously generous to me. To us... We've had so many opportunities to get killed, but have defied the curse. It has to be the gods."

"Might be." Kitlyn ate a bite of fish. She rather wanted chicken, but this village didn't have any. The innkeeper said something about them getting stuck in mud.

Oona stared at her plate. "Are we doing the right thing accepting magic? Is it really not evil?"

"You're afraid another Grand Archmage will happen in another hundred years if we don't continue purging mages from Lucernia?" asked Kitlyn.

"Somewhat."

Tamsen shook her head. "Paelirron said magic isn't evil. Only demonology and necromancy. You should treat magic like swords. Having it is fine, but using it wrong is not."

"Our soldiers carry swords to defend the kingdom from other people with swords." Kitlyn scooped some of the unknown vegetable stuff onto her fork. "We should not let ourselves become defenseless to mages, or they might take over. Instead of purging them, we should consider establishing some official group of mages to protect the kingdom from the bad ones."

"Like a guild?" Tamsen grinned.

"Not exactly. Part of the army. Like we have scouts, archers, soldiers, and so forth," said Kitlyn before eating the lump of beige goo—some manner of mashed root vegetable.

Oona nodded, her mood improving. "Yes. We should keep our original plan, not chasing mages away or forcing others to join the temples. Maybe we could assemble a council of mages—like our advisors—to act when someone abuses magic, if there are ever enough of them in Lucernia. We also might need them to help us handle magical beasts we haven't seen in thousands of years."

"Like those arcane fragments." Tamsen shivered. "Soldiers

couldn't ever kill one of those. Such strange beings. Extremely dangerous, but a simple first circle spell destroys them."

"Or the giant root monster." Oona cringed.

Tamsen held her fork up. "Magic doesn't turn anyone evil. It reveals those who already are. Some people don't like it because it allows physically weak people to protect themselves. A few weeks before Aztian found me, some bandits tried to kidnap me. I didn't have any money for them to steal, so they wanted to take me to their camp and make me cook, wash clothes, and stuff. They became quite angry with me for defending myself."

Oona stopped before eating a bite of fish to look at her. "How did you defend yourself?"

"I used Torin's Hand to throw them off a little bridge into the river." Tamsen examined her fingernails. "They crawled out of the water and chased me, so I got to try out Forbin's Fleastorm."

"Oh, I so would have *loved* to be able to do that to Fauhurst." Oona smiled.

"I am *so* ready for a bath." Kitlyn itched all over from the mere thought of magical fleas.

"As am I." Oona sighed. "We have a long ride ahead of us."

Kitlyn rushed chewing her last bite of fish. "Yes, but we are out of the swamp. I never thought I would miss ordinary dry land."

"What is Lucernia like?" asked Tamsen.

"In the interest of not being up all night, would you mind waiting until we ride tomorrow for me to answer you?" Oona nudged her.

"All right." The child sat in silence for a moment before looking up at them. "So… you don't need me to get into Isilien anymore, and, umm, you haven't tried to get rid of me."

Oona ruffled her hair. "We're not going to abandon you, Tamsen. You are not an orphan any longer. You have a home."

"It just so happens to be a bit of a castle." Kitlyn feigned a grimace as though telling her she'd have to sleep on a straw mat in the kitchen. "I hope you can tolerate such living conditions."

Tamsen teared up, chuckled, and leaned against Oona.

SAFETY AND SECURITY

OONA

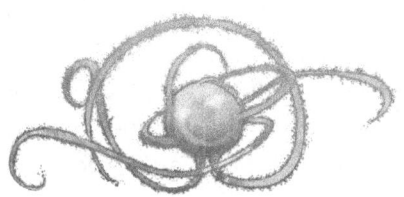

One day's ride west from Kolbrin's Quay brought them to the much larger town of Thiobel.

There, they purchased a few new outfits for Tamsen, clothing rugged enough to travel in due to having a long ride still ahead of them. For two days, they rode north over the plains, camping out in the grass at night. Oona filled much of the time telling Tamsen stories about Lucernia. Around noon on the third day of travel, they reached the Arch of the Ancients, crossing the massive bridge over the Churning Deep into Lucernia. While they wanted to spend some time visiting Kethaba, they preferred to do so once fear of the curse no longer haunted them.

Midway across the Arch, Tamsen finally appeared to accept the truth she wouldn't be abandoned. Joyful tears lasted for a little while, then she bounced back to her normal self... if somewhat noticeably happier.

They rode at a brisk pace along the road, arriving at Castle Cimril a couple hours after sunset two days later.

Entering the actual castle, seeing undeniable proof Oona and Kitlyn hadn't been teasing her, left Tamsen gawking. When Advisor Beredwyn and Lanon rushed over to welcome them back, the child fainted. Oona carried her upstairs while Kitlyn dealt with the advisors.

We could give her one of the guest rooms on the other wing as a permanent bedroom, but she might feel like we are keeping her separate from the family. Evie would definitely be willing to share my old room with her. It's big enough for twelve people. Oh, how wonderful would it have been to share a room with Kitlyn at her age? Oona sighed. They'd arrived home fairly late in the day. Despite the hour, she went to her little sister's bedchamber, formerly the one she'd used as 'princess,' intending to introduce them.

Tamsen woke before they made it halfway there, apologized for passing out, then passed out again once she realized she hadn't imagined being inside a huge castle. Oona jostled her awake, laughing and reassuring her she wasn't dreaming.

The gods have a sense of harmony. This child's life is so much like Kitlyn's... and mine. A peasant thrust into wealth. At least she doesn't have the responsibilities. Smiling, Oona led Tamsen by the hand into the bedroom and tried to nudge her little sister awake. Alas, Evie could sleep through a war. Deciding not to disturb the little one, Oona instead brought Tamsen to the royal bedchamber. She would spend the night with them and have a proper introduction to her new sister in the morning.

Piper and Meredith rushed in via the secret door shortcut leading to their private quarters, overjoyed to see her back in one piece. They briefly panicked over Kitlyn not being with her, but relaxed once told she'd remained downstairs to tell the advisors they'd have to wait for tomorrow to discuss anything requiring more than a few minutes. The handmaidens both doted over Tamsen while introducing themselves.

Kitlyn theatrically shoved the door open and marched across the room while discarding armor and clothing along the way. She stripped down to only her smallclothes, then fell face-first onto the bed.

"Does she do that often?" asked Tamsen.

Oona stifled a laugh. "I believe she's quite tired."

"Me too." Tamsen yawned.

"Ugh. Yawns are contagious." Oona lost the battle to resist. "I do believe we are going to retire early this evening."

THE NEXT MORNING, THEY INTRODUCED THE GIRLS.

Predictably, Evie took to Tamsen right away, thrilled at the idea of sharing the bedroom with her new sister—or technically, aunt. Neither Oona's sister nor an adopted daughter like Tamsen would have any claim to the throne. This reassured her for their safety, as any nobles who might threaten the children came from the same traditionalists who held to the sanctity of royal bloodlines. Those scoundrels wouldn't consider either child a threat—though might try to hurt them out of spite. Any 'legitimate' heir in their eyes would have to be born of Kitlyn, since Oona was a commoner by birth. Alas, it would be *quite* difficult for her to impregnate Kitlyn. Only a direct blood descendant of a Talomir would have any substantive claim to the throne.

If they died without a 'legitimate' heir, the noble families would almost certainly make war on each other in a mad, bloody scramble for power. Even if only Kitlyn died and Oona remained alive, the hard-liners might try to declare her ineligible to sit on the throne due to her common birth. She hated to think about the idea of Kitlyn being forced to have a child with one of the noble sons in order to protect the people from such a conflict. She also hated the very idea of royalty. One's birthright alone didn't make a person 'better' than anyone else. After all, no one could tell Kitlyn had been a 'true' royal for most of her life. It made the whole concept of being 'royal' sound like nonsense.

Hopefully, they could change the political climate enough before they died.

After breakfast, Evie practically dragged Tamsen out of the room to 'show her around'. Oona and Kitlyn remained at the table, discussing their plans to recover from the trip to Isilien by spending a few days at the castle. Even without a desire to rest, they had duties to attend to as well as making preparations for the second leg of the journey to the Dawnspire Mountains.

In the interest of not being foolishly young and racing off blind, they planned to have Spymaster Hinlor send an agent or two west in search of information regarding Tyndris or dragons in general, even if considered mythic folklore. Paelirron's only clue about his mate's location implied the approximate center of the mountain range, which could still translate to quite a bit of land. The more information they had prior to leaving the castle, the better.

She wondered why his ghost hadn't visited Tyndris or why the other dragon didn't go to Isilien herself to recover his essence. Perhaps the angry, grief-stricken dragon didn't realize it still existed. When she'd first touched the giant sapphire, it released a burst of information into her mind. She knew the essence could be drained via demonic or necromantic magic. When Paelirron claimed dragons could not be destroyed, he'd referred to ordinary death. Dark rituals and the work of demons could, in fact, consume him. Perhaps Tyndris feared the worst and had been too despondent to go there herself.

Once Kitlyn and Oona decided on a basic plan for their upcoming trip, they made their way to the grand hall to meet with the advisors. They sat through the usual updates on taxes, questions on legal clarifications, and a handful of appeal requests from citizens with relatives sentenced for crimes, asking for a lessening of punishments deemed unfair.

A break in the monotony came when Beredwyn produced a scroll. "We have received a response from Ulfaan. He intends to continue studying magic and assisting those he is able to. Our spy reports he did not fully trust the man. However, this could be due to the unsettling presence about him. I'm sure you both sensed it as well."

Yes, he did feel... different. Oona briefly wondered if such an intense aura of otherworldliness might mean he had the chance to eventually become a scourge like the Grand Archmage Paelirron told them about. Tamsen didn't radiate any strangeness. Such an unnatural presence would have made it impossible for her to remain undetected as a mage in Torjin. *It is Aodh's doing those simpletons tried to kill her. It is wrong to coerce people into the service of the gods. The gods speak for themselves to those whom they choose. It is not a mortal's place to decide who should serve the gods and when.*

"So, he intends to start a… school?" Kitlyn glanced at Oona. "We saw no trace of him at Isilien. It seems we can put to rest any doubts of his involvement."

"The place will be looted bare in days." Advisor Lanon chuckled.

"Hopefully not." Kitlyn tapped her fingers on the padded armrest of her throne. "Unless thieves can move an enormous stone door and a gigantic tangle of petrified roots."

Only a mage could unlock the door again… and they'd need a stonecaller to move the vines. Granted, many more difficult tasks existed than locating a stonecaller in Evermoor. Oona idly daydreamed about a grown-up Tamsen using the same 'teleportation' magic as Ulfaan to one day return there in search of knowledge.

Kitlyn told the advisors of their journey, strategically omitting the detail of the gods having once been mortal mages. That, she would save for a later, private, meeting with Balais and Alonna. She did briefly touch on the ancient history of the mage guilds and resulting wars, and Lucen inspiring a revolution.

They debated the legality of mages for some time, both Kitlyn and Oona preferring the course of permitting them but being vigilant for misuse.

"Concerning Ulfaan," said Oona. "Send him an invitation. I would like to speak to him regarding relocating his school here in Cimril, and perhaps assisting us as a court wizard."

If he is trustworthy, perhaps he can teach Tamsen as well.

The advisors expressed concern, Balais being the most resistant to the idea of involving a mage in the affairs of the crown. Oona clarified she did not mean to add him as an advisor, rather someone they might call on if needed to defend the kingdom from threats only a wizard could handle. Essentially, she intended to retain his services in exchange for—most likely—a grant of property in the city.

Murmuring and debate continued for several minutes before

Beredwyn silenced the advisors by raising both hands. "It may be wise to do so, provided, of course, the man is not deceptive."

"Of course, Beredwyn," said Oona. "I, and Balais, will know if he speaks truth."

"Only upon their approval." Kitlyn nodded at Balais. "Assuming his intentions are pure, we should endeavor to make an ally of this man rather than an enemy. The number and type of unusual creatures appearing in Lucernia is increasing. We may need his help or at least advice—after we have Lucen's confirmation he can be trusted."

This appeared to settle the advisors' worries.

"You intend to travel again so soon?" asked Advisor Alonna.

"In a few days. We've only recently returned." Kitlyn took a deep breath. "I realize the importance of breaking the curse, but I can still smell the swamp."

I must tell Balais what Paelirron said of the gods... "We also plan to attend the funerary services for the soldier, Yerbin."

Advisor Alonna and Balais both bowed their heads.

"I am tempted to insist only Oona and I travel west." Kitlyn's gaze hardened. "We will be able to move faster and more easily without disruption on our own. We aren't defenseless... and it is often easier to obtain information when we blend in."

"She adores being able to surprise people by revealing who she is after they think we're commoners," deadpans Oona.

The advisors, except for Beredwyn, chuckled. Worry deepened the wrinkles on the elder's face.

Kitlyn smirked. "You jest. I do not take pleasure in waving my title around... unless someone is woefully out of line. Then, I admit, it is somewhat amusing to see their reaction. In all seriousness, sometimes being inconspicuous offers the best security."

"You should not go alone." Beredwyn glided closer to the throne dais. "There is too much at risk with your lives, not the least of which is this poor old man's sentimental fondness."

"I understand your worry, but if we cannot travel within our own land and not fear for our lives... we are obviously failing in our duties to the citizenry." Kitlyn gestured at the empty court.

Advisor Alonna clasped her hands in front of herself. "You presently have the respect and admiration of most. It is a precious gift not to be squandered."

Kitlyn nodded once. "I have no intention to."

"Their openness shows their sincerity," said High Priest Balais. "Aodh carried a burden of guilt his daughter does not bear."

Oona grasped Kitlyn's hand. "You think of me. The guilt I suffered over Yerbin's death. You do not wish any more to die for us."

"You have goodwill among the common people. Guarded skepticism from the nobility." Beredwyn nervously stroked his long, white beard. "Do not allow yourself the false security of believing those who crave power will hesitate to take it even from the most kind and benevolent of leaders."

Kitlyn exhaled. "No... you are right. I am thinking purely of convenience and how it pained me to watch Oona's guilt. I must think of the citizens and the future of Lucernia as well."

"Yes. It is all right." Oona smiled. "I've come to understand. We are the same as Yerbin, or any soldier, willing to sacrifice ourselves to protect the people of Lucernia."

"We will not be foolish." Kitlyn nodded to Beredwyn. "When we set out for the Dawnspire Mountains, soldiers shall accompany us."

The elder relaxed visibly.

"What do you hope to find out there?" Advisor Lanon raised both eyebrows.

"A dragon," said Oona.

The advisors chuckled.

"In all seriousness." Kitlyn's determined expression silenced them the way Aodh's glower used to. "If our word is not sufficient, speak to any of the soldiers who traveled to the Ebon Mire with us. They all saw the bones of two dragons. There is at least one surviving dragon hiding high up in the Dawnspires."

"Lucen protect us," whispered Balais.

Oona smiled, gazing up at the ceiling. "Yes. May Lucen protect us."

40

OVERBROOK

KITLYN

A mere three days following their return to the castle, Kitlyn decided to set out for the Dawnspire Mountains.

She and Oona left Cimril accompanied by ten soldiers who'd volunteered, including Beowyn, Danos, Lliard, and Rakden. Imoa still had a minor limp, so Oona insisted she remain behind and rest despite the woman wanting to go. While the soldiers wore heavier chain armor this time since they wouldn't need to worry about marshes and bogs, the queens kept their scout's armor for its mobility. Also, it let them blend in among the soldiers. Unlike her father, she had no desire for pageantry. As ridiculous as it was to even imagine Aodh going anywhere himself to do anything, if he *had* left the castle, it would've entailed a procession of coaches, over a hundred soldiers, and fancy tents.

Despite wanting desperately to go with them—mostly to see the dragon—Tamsen obeyed their decision she stay at the castle and be safe. While she might have the magic of a novice mage, it didn't change the truth of her being ten years old. Far too small to run around the kingdom doing dangerous things. Bringing her to Isilien had been an exception of need they would endeavor not to repeat.

Kitlyn's original plan to rest for at least a week fell apart as

Paelirron's tale worsened her fears regarding the curse. It had been one thing to set aside when only her life hung in the balance, but the curse stalked Oona as well. She couldn't tolerate the worry. The past two nights, sleep proved difficult, her thoughts in a constant swirl. How long *would* they have before the curse affected them in some way? Had Aodh become obsessed with power and decided to steal the Eldritch Heart because of it, or did the greed occur naturally? She eventually decided Aodh had done that on his own. The curse came from the dragon, furious at the people of the kingdom for attacking Paelirron. It didn't feel right her curse would again cause Lucernia to make war on Evermoor. Perhaps it played some role in keeping her and Oona alive long enough to bring about Aodh's death, but with them now on the throne, the curse would certainly do the opposite of protecting them.

She couldn't blame the supposed wickedness of the Grand Archmage on Tyndris, as the dragon didn't enact the curse until after people claiming to follow Lucen killed her mate.

Kitlyn debated if magic not derived from natural sources or the gods *was* evil, or at least corruptive. It made sense for early followers of Lucen to hate arcane magic after centuries of rule by a despotic wizard. But for them to blame *all* mages for the crimes of one group struck her as wrong. It also bothered her somewhat to watch Tamsen running around the castle, playing with Evie and Pim like any ordinary—if somewhat overly mature—child of ten. A child capable of killing an adult rang all sorts of wrong notes, especially since they couldn't exactly take her weapon away. Even naked in a bathtub, not a dagger nor any deadly item in her possession, Tamsen could easily slay an armed soldier in full armor. Fortunately, she entirely lacked the temperament to do so. She'd known the Lucenites would likely kill her and didn't resort to lethal magic to defend herself against them.

One might say Oona and I are also children with deadly magic.

Kitlyn gazed off into the Mistral Wood on her left, annoyed at no one in particular. She hadn't wanted to be queen at all, much less so soon. As a child, she'd believed she'd been left at the castle for mysterious reasons, and often daydreamed about a noble on a black horse riding up to the gates to claim her as his daughter. She fantasized about watching Fauhurst and the others who'd been so cruel to her react in horror upon realizing she had status. Seeing the man's face when he realized he'd been tormenting the king's daughter almost made enduring the years of hard work and derision worth it.

While not the ideal life she imagined, Kitlyn accepted her position. Other than Oona dying, her greatest fear entailed the curse corrupting her into the same sort of tyrant her father had become. Her magic came from the Alderswood and would not grow weak or stop working entirely if she offended a god. If the curse drove her to madness, she could do a tremendous amount of damage.

At least having Tamsen with Evie is like a hidden bodyguard. Would she defend them against an assassin or kidnapper? The girl might have been able to protect herself from the Lucenites, but having lived among them for a while gave her hope she could talk her way out of punishment for being a mage. A complete stranger might not be so lucky—though she might try using the magical fleas first.

I hope the gods let her grow up a bit more before she's forced to kill a person.

They traveled west along the road, skirting the Mistral Wood all day. At dusk, they made camp south of Duskdawn Lake. In the morning, Rakden—once again the most senior soldier in the escort—informed them the night sentries spotted 'unusual creatures' approaching their camp. The men described spindly figures not quite four feet tall with glowing yellow eyes. Kitlyn and Oona both assumed them goblins, due mostly to their small size and evident cowardice.

Two days later, they arrived in the town of Shimmerbrook, relatively close to the southern end of the mountains. A dozen or so small villages dotted the rolling grasslands between there and the large city of Gwynaben far to the north. The Mistral Run flowed down out of the Dawnspire Mountains. Roughly one third of the mountain range lay to the north of the river's origin. Kitlyn planned to go village to village up the plains in search of information. Tyndris supposedly dwelled at the midpoint of Dawnspires, so if they reached the river, they'd gone too far north.

They could reach the center of the range in two days' ride assuming they traveled in a straight line at a relaxed pace. She hoped someone in a village on the way might be familiar with the various trails going up into the mountains, and possibly even knew the location of ruins, caves big enough for a dragon, or any such place where such a creature might hide. It didn't seem likely a dragon could exist in this area without there being at least a few strange rumors. Sadly, the spies hadn't found much.

They slipped unnoticed—insofar as being the queens—into Shimmerbrook, and spent the night at an inn. Oona had trouble falling asleep due to her worry she might not be able to pull the sapphire egg out of her satchel. If the magic failed or acted strange, they didn't have Tamsen there to help. Kitlyn held her close, rambling increasingly silly comments about how much she loved her in hopes of distracting her from worry. They fell asleep in each other's arms, stifling laughter.

Over the next few days, they rode north into the grasslands, traveling from tiny village to tiny village asking everyone they encountered if they had ever heard stories about unusual places or beings up in the mountains. Openly talking about dragons might make people laugh or think them crazy. Also, they doubted Tyndris would show herself to humans. Paelirron said she went to great lengths to avoid them. Most likely, her lair hid behind magical protection. Oona suggested such a defense might create an uneasy feeling in people much the way being near Ulfaan had.

No one offered any useful information, but many villagers spoke of observing unusual creatures. Some descriptions sounded like goblins. Two people claimed to have seen large white lizards. Several children told stories of seeing faeries out in the meadow. Many villagers described hearing or seeing things at night they believed not to be people, but hadn't seen more than a glowing eye or large shadow. One man even claimed to have observed a fire-breathing sheep.

He'd also been quite drunk.

Late afternoon on their third day in the grasslands, they arrived in the village of Overbrook, which straddled a small stream branching south from the Mistral Run. The place reeked of fish and salt. Every hut in sight had at least one wooden stand where fish covered in salt hung to dry out. Cloud tossed his white mane like a preening noble out in public.

Chickens, small dogs, and toddlers scattered out of their way as they rode along a strip of bare dirt shaped somewhat like a road. It didn't lead anywhere, each end disappearing back to meadow soon after extending beyond the village's borders. A short distance past a large dirt area serving as the town square, an arched stone bridge spanned the large stream dividing the town in half. One inn, one general goods store, and a tailor's shop appeared to be the only buildings in Overbrook other than small private homes.

Kitlyn went straight to the inn, figuring whoever ran it would have heard every crazy story in the area. She hopped down from her saddle, not bothering to tie the reins to the post—since Apples knew better than to wander off—and stepped into a long room saturated in the fragrance of savory soup. Every breath tasted like vegetables and some form of meat, eliciting a growl from her stomach. Oona entered behind her, looking around at twenty or so small tables, a little bar counter, and a doorway near the bar counter. Sounds of activity came from the door, but the outer room had no people in it other than them.

"Hello?" called Kitlyn.

"Greetings," called a thick male voice from the next room. "Allow me a moment to finish cutting these carrots."

The soldiers entered, making quite a bit more noise than Oona or Kitlyn had. Soon after the commotion started, a portly man in a brown tunic hurried out of the kitchen. A horseshoe of shoulder-length black hair wrapped around his otherwise bald head. Heavy jowls stretched into an overjoyed smile at the sight of twelve people in his dining room. Upon noticing Kitlyn and Oona, his expression showed a hint of confusion.

"Hello, strangers. Welcome to my inn. I'm Olban." He rubbed his hands together. "Might be a bit of a challenge boarding all of you, but I can certainly feed you."

They settled in for an early dinner, spread over three tables. Kitlyn requested 'whatever I'm smelling' for her meal. Olban brought her a bowl of thick soup—nearly a stew—containing at least three different kinds of meat plus various vegetables. The brownish substance resembled the glop she used to eat as a servant sometimes, but tasted worlds better. Tiny still-warm bread loaves made for the perfect addition.

In the midst of eating, they called Olban over to their table and asked him about rumors concerning strange goings-on in the mountains to the west, specifically if he knew of anyone who'd located odd ruins, caves, or places they'd felt a strange urge to flee from. Olban proved to be a smooth talker, getting Oona to admit they looked for a dragon after a few minutes of discussing the local folklore.

"Dragons hmm?" Olban scratched the side of his head. "Can't say I believe they exist. 'Course if they did, you'd need more than ten soldiers and a couple o' scouts to take one on."

"We're not interested in killing the dragon or even fighting her." Kitlyn dipped a hunk of bread into her soup. "Merely interested in speaking with her."

Olban hooked his thumbs in his belt, his hands vanishing beneath his rounded stomach. "If there's a person 'round here might know about such things, it'd be the ol' hermit witch. Hear tell she lives pretty high up in the mountains."

"Old hermit witch," said Oona in a flat tone. "Does not sound friendly."

"Eh, whether or not she's friendly or fierce depends on luck, I hear." Olban chuckled. "You two look old enough, shouldn't be in too much danger... but you might want to be extra careful just in case."

Kitlyn hesitated before biting her soup-coated bread. "Why would we be in danger?"

"Rumor says the ol' hermit witch sneaks into villages near the foothills every so often to snatch up young girls."

Oona gasped. "What?"

"Aye. She keeps 'em. Turns 'em inta witches or some such thing. Likely got a whole coven up there if ya believe the stories. The two of you are probably old enough not to be tempting. People say she takes younger children, small enough ta carry under one arm."

"Where would we find this 'old hermit witch' if we decided to look for her?" Oona carefully cut off a bite-sized piece of her steak.

Olban gestured at the wall. "Follow the river north out of town a ways. At the falls, you'll want to head west toward the Dawnspires. Should find the old mine road after a couple hours. Head on up that trail and you'll eventually see a bunch of witch stuff once ya get high enough into the mountains."

"Witch stuff…" Kitlyn dipped her bread again. "What, exactly, is 'witch stuff'?"

"Poles with feathers and fur and such. Dead animals. Never been up there myself, just what I hear people talking about." Olban grimaced. "If you do go up there, be on your guard. They say the ol' witch can make herself look like a raven or a young woman ta trick people. How dangerous she is depends on who's telling the story. Heard some say they saw her and she didn't do anything but watch them go by."

"All right. Thank you for the directions." Kitlyn eyed Oona tilting her head in a 'what do you think?' gesture.

"Yes. It's something out of the ordinary. We should look. It means at least going to the mountains where we're supposed to be looking anyway." She ate the bit of steak off her fork—probably meadow sprinter, as they hadn't seen many cows around.

Olban headed off to refill the soldiers' ale or water cups.

They discussed what the 'witch' might be over the rest of their food. Kitlyn doubted any truth to the rumors of the witch spiriting young girls off in the night. A person or creature making a habit of routinely stealing children generally resulted in angry mobs or pleas to the king for help. Not once had any such request been whispered about in the castle. Oona wondered if the forest witch might be a mage in hiding, using scary stories and putting up ominous totems to keep people away.

Soon after daylight weakened, people arrived at the inn. Some to eat, most to drink and relax after long hours of tending flocks or preparing for winter. At this time of year, most of the harvesting had to be finished. As was common for smaller villages, the citizens tended to have meals in groups to spread out the labor of cooking and lessen the amount of food going to waste. Oona suggested they move from their tables so the locals could eat.

Kitlyn took three silver crescent coins from her pouch and approached the innkeeper, who leaned on the doorjamb between the dining room and the kitchen. "For all twelve of us. The food was superb."

"Thank you, I—" Caught off guard by the few coins she dropped in his hand rather than the substantial fistful of low-denomination coins he expected, Olban glanced down and sputtered. "Girl, are you sure you've intended to give me this much?"

"I am." She smiled.

"These are silver crescents. Each one's a hundred tin crowns. The food and ale for your friends is only about... eh, forty-eight for the food, another twenty in ale..."

"It is fine. All the way out here, I'm sure you don't see as much business as innkeepers in larger towns."

Grinning, he bowed to her. "You are most generous. Lucen bless you!"

"And you." She bowed in farewell, then headed out the back door to join the others.

Rakden and two soldiers who hadn't been with them in Evermoor went to collect and feed the horses while the rest had set up a camp right behind the inn. Lliard got a small fire going for warmth and light. Since the inn only had two rooms—far short of what would be needed for their entire group—Oona and Kitlyn decided to sleep outside among the soldiers. They spent some time brushing and tending to Cloud and Apples, then sat around the small campfire, explaining what Olban told them about the 'hermit witch,' and the plan to go looking for her in the morning. Their conversation drifted to how no one they'd spoken with in any village thus far believed dragons to be real. It didn't surprise them, since up until meeting Paelirron, they wouldn't have considered the possibility either. Learning an actual dragon *did* exist and presently lived in Lucernia scared them.

Happy at the generous overpayment, Olban brought them a bowl of bread and cheese to snack on.

"How dangerous is this dragon?" whispered Kitlyn. "Could she destroy Lucernia if we say the wrong thing?"

Oona bit her lip. "I'm certain 2,500 years ago, the entire Lucernian army didn't go to Evermoor all at once. They managed to kill two of them with what... a hundred or so soldiers?"

"True." Kitlyn gave a somber sigh. "However, we're guessing at numbers because of skeletons. How many perished so brutally no bones remained?"

"I'd rather not think of such things."

Kitlyn pointed upward. "Also, a dragon up in the air would be far more dangerous than one stuck in a small room."

"Yes." Oona pulled her boots off before stretching out on her bedroll. "I still appreciate a proper bed, but I've become rather fond of sleeping under the stars on occasion."

Kitlyn also took her boots off. She'd worn them as she didn't expect to encounter much danger traversing Lucernia. She, too, crawled into her bedroll. "There is one small issue for us, camping near the soldiers."

"Oh? What?"

"Certain things I would otherwise be inclined to do, I cannot do."

Oona looked over at her, eyebrow raised. "Such as?"

"You must be truly nervous." Kitlyn reached out from under the blanket to take her hand, then whispered, "What do you imagine I might wish to do in your company we cannot do while ten soldiers sit nearby able to see us?"

Oona's face turned red.

Grinning to herself, Kitlyn gazed up at the stars. "No matter what is happening around us, I am happiest when you are with me."

"As am I." Oona squeezed her hand.

They lay in silence, stargazing for a little while.

"Even when Miss Harper paddled you?"

Kitlyn gave a sleepy chuckle. "That is the one time I can think of where it would have been better had you not been in the room. It pained me she forced you to watch."

"The witch—Miss Harper, not the actual witch in the mountains—knew how fond I was of you. She took great delight in making me suffer because she wasn't allowed to paddle me."

A tingle of discomfort spread across Kitlyn's backside. "I'm not entirely sure which one of us got the worse end of it."

"Do you think I'd have been less a terror if they hadn't gone to such trouble to keep us apart and allowed you to stay with me as a handmaiden?" whispered Oona. "If you say no, I will throw a wad of grass at you."

Chuckling, Kitlyn rolled onto her side. "Why ask if you don't want me to be honest?"

Oona gasped.

"I jest." Kitlyn leaned over and snuck a quick kiss. "If they'd not kept pulling me away to do chores, I do not believe you would have been as demanding, whiny, loud, unpleasable—"

A wad of grass hit her in the face.

"Whiny?" Oona whisper-gasped.

Kitlyn spat grass aside. "You were, but only a bit. And with good reason. He'd been overly indulgent trying to make up for the guilt he felt knowing you'd likely be killed by assassins."

"I cannot tell which to regard as worse. Hanging a peasant child up as a target or pretending you weren't his daughter."

"Oona?"

"Hmm?"

Kitlyn settled into her bedroll, trying to get comfortable. "Let us speak of more pleasant subjects than him."

"Oh. Yes," whispered Oona. "What else would you like to talk about?"

"I'm trying to think of a way to call your eyes beautiful, but the stars aren't up to the task of being compared to them."

Oona emitted a soft, embarrassed gasp.

41

SIBRI

OONA

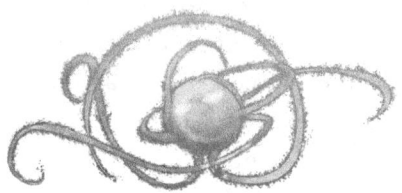

Oona awoke with a start, surprised at having fallen asleep.

The sun blued the sky in the east, perhaps ten minutes shy of being fully up. Already awake, Rakden and the other soldiers packed away their bedrolls while discussing if they should eat rations or wait for Olban to prepare breakfast.

"We may as well eat here and have proper food," said Oona in a sleepy half-whisper. "We needn't rush."

The soldiers murmured happily.

It occurred to Oona she hadn't been chilly at all, despite the relatively thin blanket—compared to her bedding at the castle. Kitlyn still held her hand, explaining the comforting warmth and the reason she'd been able to sleep at all. Spending the entire night in armor except for boots still bothered the 'princess' in her, but not enough to make a sour face.

Before long, the sun finished its climb into the sky, Kitlyn woke up, and everyone migrated to tables inside for breakfast. Though small, Overbrook had plenty of chickens. The soldiers who accompanied them in Evermoor cracked jokes about the people in Kolbrin's Quay thinking it normal to have fish or 'mud creepers'— strange bug like creatures possessing a hard shell, two pincers, and a long, flexible tail—for breakfast. For whatever reason, the locals insisted on seasoning mud creepers rather spicily.

Here, they could enjoy eggs and potatoes.

Minutes into the meal, a tall, blonde woman walked in, heading straight to the table Kitlyn and Oona shared with Beowyn and Rakden. Her unusual outfit—a ruffled dark blue thigh-length dress under a leather armor vest, knee-high boots, small sword, dagger, multiple pouches hanging from her belt, and a black, hooded cloak— made her look like a traveling theater performer who'd taken up highway banditry.

Oona studied the woman's face, drawn to her blue eyes. She found her attractive, but not too much so. The woman had the kind of looks she'd remember as having seen someone pretty without recalling much detail hours later, but not so shockingly beautiful as to be distracting. She seemed early thirties, old enough to be Oona's mother. The woman also had an unusual air of confidence about her, brazenness befitting of a person willing to attempt to singlehandedly rob a group of twelve soldiers.

Something about her unsettled Oona. A dress a little too frilly for a rogue, armor too authentic to be worn by a stage performer, sword a little too small to belong to a warrior. Women as tall as her didn't often come from Lucernia, suggesting she might be Ondari, which could also explain the odd clothing. Perhaps their female scouts preferred skirts to breeches, though it still seemed rather expensive a garment to wear into the wilderness, and offered no physical protection for her arms or legs beyond thin metal plates attached to the fronts of her tall boots. The Ondari military as well as their royal crest prominently featured the color blue, so perhaps she *was* a scout or tracker. A spy wouldn't wear something so obviously unusual. Her presence in Lucernia meant she'd either retired, gotten quite lost, or deserted.

"We do somethin' for you?" Beowyn sat up out of a slouch, looking the woman over.

"I overheard a pair of young ladies discussing an old mountain witch." The woman eyed Kitlyn and Oona, mostly Oona. "Perhaps I may be of assistance."

"You're no mountain witch." Beowyn chuckled.

"Not a hag at least," whispered Lliard.

The woman smiled faintly and drew her hood back. For some reason, Oona expected to see the pointed ears of an Anthari, but her ears were ordinary and human.

"My name is Sibri. I frequently travel into the mountains, guiding travelers back and forth between this kingdom and the Untamed Vale."

I wonder what it is like there... Oona knew little about the land west of the Dawnspire Mountains except for the general shape she'd seen on maps. Roughly a third the size of Lucernia, it had no known civilization. The land between Lucernia and the ocean, south of the Seven Kings River—which formed Ondar's southern border— couldn't possibly be empty. *Something* or someone had to be there, perhaps barbarian tribes or monsters. Hearing this woman say people went there for various reasons simultaneously thrilled and frightened her.

Of course, Oona didn't truly want to go to such a potentially dangerous land, merely enjoyed the idle romanticized notion of it... like something from a storybook.

"Why would anyone travel to the Untamed Vale?" asked Rakden, a bit of a chuckle in his voice.

"They mostly seek ancient ruins." Sibri offered a dismissive shrug. "Far more go there than return. I hear there is great wealth to be found for the lucky or fast. But we needn't go that far to find the witch, if, indeed, you are looking for her."

"We are." Oona leaned over to grab a chair from a nearby empty table, dragging it over. "Please, join us."

Sibri smiled graciously and accepted the offered seat. "I am curious why a pair of ladies so young would be willing to take such a chance for old stories."

"Chance?" Oona blinked. "Is this supposed witch dangerous?"

"According to the stories, she can be deadly to anyone who does not tread lightly." Sibri glanced occasionally at the soldiers or Kitlyn, though her attention kept drifting back to Oona. "I've never had any troubles from her. Nor have any whom I've escorted into the mountains."

"What's yer fee?" asked Beowyn. "Yer clearly fishin' for coin here."

Sibri held up a hand. "Whether or not I assist you is not dependent on coins, but your reasons for seeking the 'old witch.'"

Kitlyn nudged Oona. "She thinks I'm going to die if we don't find her."

"I don't think." Oona nudged her back. "I know. We will both die. If anything happens to you, I will beg Tenebrea to take me as well so we remain together."

"You will not!" Kitlyn glared at her. "If you love me, you will live as long as the gods see fit to give you, no matter what happens to me. I will happily wait for you."

Oona shuddered from imagined grief.

"Oo..." Kitlyn pulled her into an embrace. "Would you want me to send myself to Tenebrea if something happened to you?"

"No." She sniffled. "But you would anyway."

Kitlyn scowled. "Ignore my hypocrisy. You have different rules. You're not to end your life early if anything happens to me."

"Why not?" Oona glared.

"Because I will be heartbroken," said Kitlyn matter-of-factly while prodding a fork into her eggs.

Oona clutched both hands to her chest. "I will be heartbroken if you hurt yourself."

"Such cheery breakfast conversation," whispered Danos.

Both Oona and Kitlyn cracked up in muffled laughter.

"You seek the 'old witch' because you both expect to die if you do not find her?" asked Sibri, one eyebrow up.

"Yes." Kitlyn exhaled. "We are hoping she can help us."

Sibri studied them for a moment, then leaned back in her chair. "I am curious to see how this plays out. All right. I offer my services to you as a guide."

She is not lying. Surprising, but... welcome. "You mentioned you do not desire payment. Might I inquire as to your reasons for offering to help us?"

"Curiosity mostly. Assisting you is something to occupy my time, and there is something about you I find intriguing."

Again, truth.

Kitlyn glanced over. "Your armor is rather unusual. Are you from Ondar?"

"No." Sibri shook her head. "I have explored the lands to the north, but am not from there. A brother of mine settled in the Iron Peaks some years ago, but my home is here."

Oona vaguely recalled looking at a shadow in the distant sky from the window of a coach. Aodh took her to visit Ondar when she'd been twelve, presumably to arrange her marriage to Prince Lanwick. The Iron Peaks jutted out of the ground like a cluster of giant black daggers in the northern reaches of the kingdom, so tall they could be seen from as far away as the castle, if only as a dark spot on the horizon. Though she'd never seen them in person, what she'd read of the Iron Peaks described the region as frigid and largely inhospitable. The relatively short mountain range didn't comprise a border to another land, merely stood out in the middle of open plains like a fortress crafted by stone giants.

"An unusual place to live," said Oona.

"He is also an explorer and is quite fond of visiting places people are afraid to go." Sibri smiled. "My brother lacks my inclination to assist random travelers."

Oona mulled the situation over while eating a few bites. "Please pardon our caution. It is not often we have someone appear out of nowhere offering assistance."

"Understandable." Sibri bowed her head in acknowledgement. "You have been asking after strange legends in the area, stories few would consider anything more than folly. When you learned of the old witch and decided to seek her out rather than flee, I decided the two of you might be interesting."

This woman does not appear deceitful thus far. "Your intention is not to lead us to harm?"

"No. As I said, it is mostly curiosity."

Satisfied Lucen revealed the truth of Sibri's words, Oona smiled.

"We would appreciate your assistance. I am Oona. This is my wife, Kitlyn..." She introduced the rest of the soldiers.

"When are you planning to begin the trip?" asked Sibri.

"As soon as we finish our meal." Kitlyn stabbed a fork into her eggs. "This man is too skilled behind a stove to be so far out in the midst of nowhere."

Olban, presently carrying a stack of dirty plates past their table, paused to bow graciously at her before continuing into the kitchen.

"Very well." Sibri indicated Oona's breakfast. "I am able to leave as soon as you are ready. Would you mind if I had something to eat as well?"

"Please do." Oona scooted closer to Kitlyn, making a little more room on the table for another plate.

Sibri waved to get Olban's attention once he returned to the dining room, then pointed at the food. "You are adorable together. Your parents must be so proud."

The innkeeper nodded and ran off to fetch her a meal.

Oona cringed. "Not exactly."

"My father was quite proud, not necessarily of me. It does not matter, though. He is gone," said Kitlyn in a toneless voice.

"Forgive me." Sibri bowed her head. "Those who have never loved deeply cannot appreciate it in others. It is their loss."

"Thank you," whispered Oona.

"I'm sure my opinion matters little as you've only just met me, but if you do not die together, my suggestion would be that whoever meets their end first haunts the other, and the survivor patiently awaits a reunion naturally."

"Ach." Beowyn fake shivered. "Together all the time, even in death? If I had a wife, we'd be sick of each other by then."

The other soldiers chuckled.

"I am sad for you, dear Beowyn." Kitlyn scooped some potato onto her fork. "I'd live a thousand lifetimes with Oona at my side and still react to the sight of her every morning as if it is the best day of my life."

Sibri said 'aww' with a stare, before leaning back so Olban could set a plate of eggs and potatoes down in front of her. She handed him a few coins before he walked off.

Oona blushed again. "I think a thousand lifetimes would make me rather tired of everything… except you."

"This will wear off in a few years." Beowyn gestured at them. "They've not been married a year yet."

No, it won't wear off. Oona grinned at Kitlyn. "We should hurry along or we shall spend the entire day at this table."

42

A BALANCE OF FEARS

KITLYN

Grassland stretched to the limits of Kitlyn's sight in all directions except straight ahead.

The Dawnspire Mountains rose up from the rolling green like a curtain of grey capped in shimmering white. Ice, snow, or some unknown quality of the rock made the peaks painfully bright, the topmost points glowing as if they'd been dipped in sunlight. Depending on the season—longer in summer—the effect lasted for about an hour in either direction from midday.

The glare made riding toward the mountains somewhat vexing as looking straight ahead forced her to squint. After so many long hours dusting the shelves in the war room, she couldn't help but think tactically. Any battles staged in this part of Lucernia gave a strong advantage to the force coming from the west, attacking to the east. Though she didn't expect to run into a random army itching for a battle, it bothered her being on the disadvantaged side with limited visibility ahead.

Oona believed the mountains' glow came from Lucen, a sign of his presence—light—and promise to protect the kingdom from demons. Even if the peaks really only reflected sunlight, she believed Lucen made them do so. They'd learned almost too much history in a short time to process, and it called much into question. Fortunately, it did sound as though the gods *were* actual gods, despite having mortal origins. She hated to think about it, but her earlier dismissive attitude toward the Steelfather of Ondar—because they openly acknowledged he had been a mortal swordsmith at one point—now felt arrogant. The line between demon and mage, however, remained much less clear in terms of who Lucen made war on. Obviously, as Oona's magic destroyed demons with ease, it proved the gods hated them. She had not yet tried to use her magic to harm a mage; however, Tamsen clearly showed no aversion to basking in the light of her orb. In fact, the child had gazed upon the glow with adoration and hope in her eyes.

We will know the truth if Lucen's light is as effective on mages as it is on demons, though I do not believe it will be.

Ulfaan radiated an unsettling aura, though Kitlyn couldn't quite bring herself to call it evil. If the man accepted the invitation to meet, Oona would have her light orb out before entering the room with him. His reaction to the radiance would reveal much. Curiously, Sibri's horse put her on edge ever since they'd departed Overbrook. The pure white animal appeared ordinary—albeit gorgeous—in every respect, but it gave off a similar otherworldliness as Ulfaan. Ever since the animal appeared, Cloud acted obviously jealous, continually trying to maneuver Oona so she couldn't see the other white horse. Adding to the oddity, Sibri rode bareback, not even using reins. The horse simply appeared to know where she wanted to go.

And the animal gave Kitlyn weird stares.

Then again, horses frequently looked at her as if having thoughts deeper than an animal ought to have, likely due to their sensing the Alderswood energy in her. The great tree predated all human civilization in Evermoor, going back to the time of the Anthari. King Lanas and his spiritcallers certainly seemed to act in a way more akin to the ancient elves than humans. Most stories of the Anthari mentioned their unusual kinship with animals of all kinds, and sometimes, Kitlyn felt as though she might possess a portion of the same gift. Animals—except perhaps doom needle wasps—often behaved in abnormally friendly ways around her.

Explains Beowyn's protectiveness toward me. She grinned to herself.

They stopped for a brief rest and lunch in an area of open grass. Other than a stiff, cold breeze rolling down from the mountains, the day brought perfect weather. Having no cover other than tall grass for dealing with certain needs of nature made Kitlyn slightly jealous of Sibri's dress/skirt—at least until she lowered her breeches and the chill of autumn in a higher elevation made her gasp. Once all the soldiers and Oona had relieved themselves, they gathered in a cluster for a quick meal of rations, bread, and cheese.

"What do you know of this old hermetic witch?" asked Oona between nibbles of a ration.

Sibri gestured at the mountains. "An entity has made these mountains her home for quite some time. Most people who've seen her cannot seem to agree on what, exactly they've witnessed. Some describe an old hag, others a young woman, sometimes even girls younger than you."

"Olban told us she abducts children." Kitlyn bit off a hunk of bread.

"I cannot say for certain no children have gone missing in this region." Sibri leaned forward, elbows on her knees, her blonde hair fluttering off to the left on the wind. "The witch has no interest in stealing anyone else's children. Perhaps she once told someone she longed to have some, but could not. Rumors can start from the smallest things."

Kitlyn finished chewing a bit of cheese. "Does this witch have magical powers? There must be some reason everyone is frightened of her."

"She has some magic, yes." Sibri smiled. "People are often afraid of things they do not comprehend. The witch is quite old. I assume the stories of child abduction came about from attempts to explain how a 'hermit witch' continues to exist after hundreds of years. They believe she takes a girl, teaches her how to be a witch, and then the child grows into the next 'hermit witch.'"

"But it's not? Are you saying she's been the same woman for so long?" asked Oona, eyebrows up.

"Yes." Sibri broke a hunk of cheese off and ate it. "Not many know there are multiple trails into the mountains. I believe the Untamed Vale contains the ruins of an ancient civilization destroyed or abandoned thousands of years ago. They—or perhaps those who lived in Lucernia at the time—made several highways traversing the mountains. Most are in ruins, though one remains passable. The witch lives on a trail connected to this route."

"Does she attack anyone trying to cross the mountain?" asked Caslen, the youngest of the soldiers at twenty.

"No." Sibri shook her head. "She prefers to keep to herself unless she has good reason to do otherwise. What are you hoping to gain from meeting her?"

"This may sound strange and unbelievable." Oona squinted into the wind, gazing off at the mountains. "We are trying to find a dragon. Our interest in this witch is only to ask her if she's heard of one nearby."

Sibri regarded them in curious silence. "You sincerely believe such creatures as dragons exist?"

"Yes," said Kitlyn. "We think one dwells in the mountains here and need to speak with her."

"Hmm." Sibri appeared to be trying to conceal her laughter. "Perhaps you have heard too many legends. I know of a sizable cave up at the top of the highway, which may be the source of such rumors."

Kitlyn perked up. "A large cave? Big enough for a dragon to lair?"

Sibri chuckled. "I suppose, if such creatures are of a mind to 'lair' anywhere."

"Will you show us this cavern?" Oona's eyes widened in hopeful excitement.

"Hmm." Sibri regarded Oona for a long moment. "I expect you will be greatly disappointed. However, the cave is on the way to the witch's home."

"Grand." Oona beamed.

They continued discussing the hermit witch while finishing up the meal and resuming the trek into the foothills. As far as Sibri knew, the old woman lived alone in an isolated hut at the end of a long, treacherous trail no horse could navigate.

In the midst of their conversation, the soldiers' horses abruptly became agitated, balking. Caslen and one other younger man lost control of their mounts and went flying to the ground. Cloud emitted a shriek of a neigh, whipped around, and fled to the east, still with Oona on his back shouting futilely for him to stop. Apples stopped walking, flattening his ears in the most obvious expression of concern she'd ever seen from him. Sibri's horse showed no reaction to whatever had spooked all the other animals.

"Danger approaches!" Sibri pointed forward. "Be wary!"

Kitlyn struggled to see through the glare shining off the mountaintops. Nothing appeared obvious to her, but the concern in Sibri's voice sounded too genuine to disregard. She leapt down from her saddle and pressed a hand to the earth, opening herself to the Stone, green glow wisping up her arm to the shoulder. The tromping clawed footfalls of beasts charging toward them became known to her. A line of four creatures significantly heavier than horses approached, two head on, one each coming in from an angle on either side.

"Four large beasts." Kitlyn scrambled to take her boots off.

"How large?" asked Beowyn.

"Twice the length and weight of a horse."

A faint 'oof' came from Oona as she fell into the tall grass some distance away. "Silly horse!"

The soldiers all jumped down, their horses far too panicky for mounted fighting.

Kitlyn projected magic into the earth, calling stone up from below to form a foot-thick wall in the path of the charging beast on the left. An instant after the grey block sprouted from the grass, a heavy *thud* shook the ground, a white tail whipping briefly into view above it before flopping out of sight. Seconds later, three other reptilian creatures charged out of the meadow, their long bodies low to the ground on stubby legs. Each creature spanned about twelve feet from nose to tail, covered in white scales. A row of bright blue bony plates ran down the center of their backs, the same shade of cobalt as their claws. Though reptilian, they didn't look much like dragons, their heads being flatter and wider, the snoot rounding off rather than coming to a point. Frosty mist puffed into the air from between their teeth.

Despite never having seen creatures such as this, the soldiers all rushed to engage them. Deep groans and gurgling noises came from the fourth monster, which had run headfirst into the wall. It lay there motionless, dazed. Kitlyn summoned roots to entrap the lizard nearest the one she'd knocked senseless, dragging it down onto its belly—for a brief second before the bony plates along its back sliced them as easily as a huge sword.

Eep! They're just animals. I don't want to kill them if I can—

The rightmost lizard opened its mouth, roaring out a spray of luminous white fog at Danos. He dove aside in a partially successful attempt to avoid the blast, landing flat on his chest, his legs fused together in ice up to the thigh. Soldiers striking the other two creatures had difficulty dislodging their blades as their weapons appeared to freeze and stick on contact if they didn't bounce off the scales. Two lost hold of their weapons due to the creatures' thrashing about.

"Do not be close to them when they die," yelled Sibri.

"When they die?" Kitlyn summoned a rock spire beneath the one trying to encase Danos in ice, flipping the beast over onto its back. "Must we kill them?"

"They will not relent." Sibri opened a small case on her belt and withdrew a long, plain wooden rod. "We will either kill them or become their dinner."

A soldier named Raald stabbed Lizard Two in the side. Ice flowed out of the wound, rushing up the length of his blade, encasing his arm halfway to the elbow in a thick crystalline shroud. In response to pain, the beast whipped around, seizing both of the man's legs in its mouth.

Kitlyn hastily launched a small boulder at the monster before it could bite the man's legs off. The blurry-fast stone smacked the lizard in the gut with a hollow *whud*, launching the creature into the air, flipping it over sideways. Raald popped out of its jaws, yanked into a spin by his stuck arm before the ice fusing his hand to his sword shattered. He yowled, collapsed to the ground, and cradled his right wrist to his chest.

Sibri pointed her stick. A small orb of brilliant orange light formed at the tip an instant before a ray of fire blasted forth at the same lizard. Unlike Tamsen's spell, this firebolt remained a completely straight beam, rather than behaving like a flow of liquid. The creature shrieked an agonized wail as the fire melted through it —and exploded. A twenty-foot patch of meadow instantly froze into a layer of ice as thick as a person's arm.

Upon seeing that, the soldiers ceased attempting to kill the beasts using swords, resorting to distracting strikes and defensive maneuvering while Lliard and another soldier named Kybern ran to fetch crossbows from their saddles.

Apples stood mostly still, flicking his ears while the fight progressed. Sibri's horse remained where she'd left it, behaving as clueless and indifferent to the giant lizards as a statue. The other warhorses had scattered back about thirty yards, though Cloud ran so far away he'd become a tiny white dot on the grass.

Oona finally made it over to Kitlyn, somewhat out of breath from running. She stopped, watching the men swat at the beasts for a second or three before firing a beam of Lucen's light from her hand. The strike seemed to do little more than annoy the giant lizard, about as effective as Beowyn punching it in the head.

"Clear away from them!" shouted Kitlyn. "They explode."

A steady, if slow, series of crossbow bolts flew in from the meadow behind Kitlyn. Most hit the lizard attacking Beowyn, sticking into its side and tail as it whirled around after the big man.

Danos chipped at the ice around his legs, his sword not terribly effective at the job.

"Use your magic to slow and trap them." Sibri nudged Kitlyn. "The men aren't going to be able to gain distance. If I melt one with the men right next to it, the frost may kill them."

Kitlyn raised her hands, focusing on the creature presently

receiving a pummeling from Beowyn. He swatted its head back and forth using the flat of his greatsword, more trying to knock it out than kill it. Alas, the beast proved more stubborn than Aodh, raking claws and snapping at him. Caslen caught a tail whip across the chest, which flung him to the ground, rolling. Fortunately, he pushed himself up to all fours fast enough to scramble out of the way of an icy blast from its mouth. A long swath of ice appeared on the ground where it breathed, glinting in the sun.

Green magical energy gathered around Kitlyn's arms. She loosened the ground below the beast snapping at Beowyn, creating a patch of deep mud. Once the creature mired in it, she hardened the mud to solid stone, trapping the lizard's legs. Stuck, the beast roared, waving its head side to side while exhaling a blast of magical ice at Beowyn. He staggered away looking like a snowman brought to life, grumbling, evidently more annoyed than hurt.

As soon as no soldier remained close to the trapped beast, Sibri projected another firebolt from the stick. The lizard burned away to ashes in mere seconds, setting off another explosion of ice. Almost at the same instant, the lizard chasing Rakden and another soldier succumbed to a pair of crossbow bolts hitting it in the head. It flopped dead on its belly, then burst into a shower of glowing fog. Rakden and the other man froze in place, living statues trapped in a shroud of inches-thick ice. Living, at least, until they suffocated.

The dazed lizard by the wall finally collected itself enough to realize Raald lay wounded nearby. Kitlyn drew a melon-sized rock up from the ground, launching it at the monster. The stone nearly decapitated the beast on impact, detonating its skull in a shower of frozen gore. Its remaining body exploded, creating another large, round patch of thick ice.

Sibri waved her stick at the two fully encased soldiers. A faint cloud of fire appeared in the air around them, rapidly melting them free. Oona ran to Raald, crouching beside him to tend his broken wrist.

Apples glanced at Kitlyn almost as if to ask 'are you all right?'

She approached, patting him on the neck. "You're one brave horse. Maybe you could teach Cloud not to be such a chicken?"

Apples nickered.

"Interesting armor you've got there." Rakden tapped his sword at Beowyn's iced-over chest.

The big man laughed.

Kitlyn glanced over at him. A coating of ice, broken at the joints, looked almost like ridiculously thick plate armor.

"Ehh... it's too heavy to move in. This is slowing me down so much Rakden could hit me." Beowyn hammered the handle of his sword at the ice coating his right leg. "Though, I think it might stop a blade or two."

Rakden pointed at him. "We shall spar upon our return to the castle, and I will show you how slow I am."

Beowyn laughed.

Danos, still hacking at the ice on his legs, shook his head. "It's definitely going to stop a blade."

Sibri melted him free of ice, then thawed Beowyn.

"Praise Orien," said Raald once the golden light faded from Oona's hands.

She grimaced, looking at the bruise on his forearm. "You should not fight with this hand for a few days."

"I am still able to fire a crossbow." Raald stood. "Thank you, highness."

"Thank Orien. I am merely a messenger." Oona waved dismissively.

"I already did." Raald bowed.

Oona went around to check the men for injuries and offer healing magic.

"You seemed to recognize these beasts." Kitlyn approached Sibri. "What are they?"

"Rimefang. Elemental frost creatures."

Kitlyn set her fists against her hips, surveying the meadow. "Someone does not want us here."

"They hunt for food. Rimefang are no more sinister than hungry creatures." Sibri tucked the thin rod back in the case she took it from. "Hungry creatures so *stupid* they will not stop fighting until they kill whatever they've decided to make a meal of... or die."

"How did you make the stick throw fire?" Kitlyn gestured at the case. "What is it?"

"An enchanted wand. Something I found in one of the ruins across the mountains. Fire is the best way to kill these beasts."

Oona looked up from tending to Caslen's bruised chest. "These beasts proved quite difficult to deal with. If we did not have your wand and Kitlyn's magic, they would certainly have killed many."

"Aye." Rakden spat to the side. "They're more deadly dying than trying to bite."

Lliard and Kybern apologized to Rakden for killing the one so close to him.

"Didn't expect it to die so fast." Kybern pointed at one of the frozen patches. "The one tryin' ta eat Beowyn, we shot a dozen bolts into it and it kept going."

Beowyn laughed. "Crossbows kill better when ya hit the beastie in the head, not the arse."

Once finished healing everyone in need of it, Oona walked over to Kitlyn. "I think it is wise to reach out to Ulfaan. If more beasts such as these rimefang are to emerge in Lucernia, we will need magic to protect ourselves."

Embracing 'demon' magic so soon might not sit well with the people... especially nobility. "We should be cautious. Even if we need it, the people have all grown up believing all magic other than what the gods give us is evil."

"Tamsen." Oona sighed.

"Hmm?" Kitlyn glanced sideways at her. "What about her?"

"It is similar to her situation. She used her magic to help people and they still wanted to kill her."

Sibri frowned, shaking her head. "Fools."

Kitlyn wandered over to her boots and stepped into them. "The people may be more frightened of creatures than magic. Perhaps we are doing the right thing—if the man can be trusted."

"Oh..." Oona sighed. "I wish we could make decisions based on considerations nobler than what frightens people less."

"As do I." Kitlyn brushed a bit of frost from her arm.

"People are fearful creatures." Sibri shielded her eyes, gazing west. "A healthy amount of fear makes people cautious. Too much fear, caution becomes hate. Too much fear in the presence of ignorance, they become dangerous."

Who did she lose? Kitlyn peered out of the corner of her eyes at the tall blonde woman, struck by the note of sorrow in her voice. *Can anyone make a wand work or only mages?* Guilt settled in the pit of her stomach. Sibri's grief had been clear. *An innocent person she loved died for being a mage. My people have done so much harm in the name of fear.*

"The meadow is clear. We should make the mountains by dark," said Sibri, her voice confident.

She doesn't want to speak of it. All right. "That is good."

THE PRICE OF FOOLISHNESS

OONA

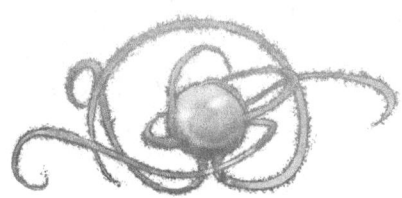

S ibri gazed off to the east. "Your horse is rather fast."

Kitlyn laughed.

Oona sighed, mildly embarrassed. "He's not the bravest creature, but he's beautiful."

"Like his mistress." Kitlyn winked.

A wave of heat washed over her face. "I'm not *as* frightened as I used to be."

"True. You haven't hidden under a blanket in a while."

Oona playfully shoved her. "I wasn't awake all the way. In the dark, he looked like a monster or ghost. And you fully understand how frightening the castle had been to me at night."

"Yes…"

Cloud looked up for no particular reason, faced toward them, and began trotting closer.

Odd… at least I don't have to chase him around again. She waited for him to approach her, patted him on the neck, comforting him while whispering soothing nonsense. Apples flattened his ears again as if insulted by the baby talk. Cloud seemed to like it.

"Rimefangs…" Oona hopped up into her saddle. "I don't

remember seeing anything like them in the book I have. What are they?"

As the group resumed riding to the west, Sibri pulled her horse alongside Kitlyn and Oona. "They are native to the elemental plane of water, specifically the frozen regions. Occasionally, they slip across into our world, living in cold climates such as up in the mountains. Rimefang have not been seen here in many hundreds of years."

"How do you know?" Oona brushed her hand at Cloud's snowy white mane.

"I may be a guide and tracker, but it doesn't mean I am unable to read." Sibri smiles.

"It would seem you are rather skilled." Kitlyn flashed a sly smile. "How difficult is it to make a 'wand' work?"

Sibri tilted her hand in a so-so gesture. "Old magic runs in my family, though I am no mage, if you are suspecting such."

Sensing truth, Oona nodded. "Wands... ice lizards... mages... it's as if an entire ancient world had fallen asleep and is only now waking up."

"This land used to be home to various creatures, most of which have been dormant for centuries." Sibri pointed ahead at the mountains. "Some migrated across the Dawnspires. Others were driven out. Most people believe them the 'demons' Lucen's followers banished."

Oona narrowed her eyes. "There *are* demons."

"Yes, of course," said Sibri. "However, people are quick to call everything they have never seen before and do not understand a 'demon.' True demons do not often appear in our world of their own doing. They are nearly always brought here by people playing with powers they should not disturb."

"They can also attack those of weak minds and weaker morals." Oona frowned, thinking back to the former Prior of Shimmerbrook. "Why are people so foolish?"

"A shiny enough prize can make even the wisest man fall prey to greed." Sibri's expression gave off a mix of annoyance and concern, like Beredwyn wanting to contradict Aodh but fearing the consequences too much to speak.

"Do you refer to the previous king?" asked Oona.

Sibri hesitated, then smiled. "Yes."

I sense truth yet somehow also deceit... not malicious deceit. Her words are true but my understanding of them is not what she intends. Oona opened her mouth to ask if she meant Aodh specifically or some other previous king, but Sibri spoke again before she could.

"Many, many years ago, people had little defense against certain magical beasts other than avoiding them. A creature such as a rimefang wandering into a village *could* be stopped and destroyed, but at the cost of numerous lives. While skilled archers could easily deal with the beasts from afar, no village in those days had more than one or two—if any. Once mages existed, they helped protect people from the more deadly beasts, allowing civilization to spread. Alas, the mages became greedy and allowed their power to control them rather than controlling it."

"Are these creatures returning because Lucen's followers purged the mages?" asked Kitlyn.

Sibri shrugged. "If the mere absence of mages is the only reason, they would have resurfaced long before now. A significant pulse of magical power came from the east some months ago. I believe it has shaken loose the enchantments responsible for banishing these creatures from Lucernia, much the same way a burst dam unleashes a flood that washes away bridges in its path."

Oona furrowed her brow. *Enchantments to keep creatures away? Paelirron claimed Lucen was a mortal mage at one point. A powerful one, too. Could he have made these enchantments? In later years after he became a god, his followers either misunderstood or exaggerated the history, claiming he drove all 'demons' out and made it so they couldn't return to Lucernia.* A ball of nausea swirled around in her stomach. It sounded possible, even if she disliked the implications. The story of a god banishing all demons permanently from the land gave her far more confidence than a legend about an ancient mage casting a defensive spell to repel beasts like rimefangs, goblins, wyrg, and whatever else has reappeared. She clung to her memories of destroying actual demons. Lucen's power *clearly* had great effect on genuine minions of the Pit. It had to be people making mistakes and twisting the story, not Lucen's intent.

"How much danger are we in from these creatures?" asked Kitlyn. "There aren't any mages left we know of except two. Of those two, one is a child, the other mysterious."

"I am not a mage." Sibri smiled at her. "I have, however read many books. If I had to offer an opinion, it would be to say the creatures will gather strength and numbers over time — if they even do. The chances of a sudden invasion destroying city after city is so low as to be impossible. If enchanted beasts are to become a significant, recurring threat, it won't be for years yet. The question to ask is if people will allow their own foolishness to kill them."

"Foolishness?" Oona raised both eyebrows.

Sibri's expression hardened into a glare directed at no one in particular. "Trying to destroy everything they cannot control. People can be incredibly stupid. They may allow their distrust of magic to rob them of their best defense against such creatures. Ironically, I doubt many will understand the mages they persecuted could have saved their lives when the beasts devour them."

"A path ahead!" yelled Rakden.

Oona looked forward.

They'd arrived in the foothills, the base of the mountains in sight a few miles away. Rakden pointed toward a paler grey spot, the mouth of a road weaving up along an ascending canyon. Though quite a distance off, it appeared wide enough to accommodate small wagons.

"I never knew such roads traversed the mountains." Oona stretched higher in the saddle, straining to look at the distant highway.

Sibri nodded. "Not many are aware of them. There is nothing out here so close to the mountains but wild goats and grass… and now perhaps rimefang. The people who live in the villages across this plain largely believe the land beyond the Dawnspires holds the demons Lucen banished and the shining light at the peaks serves as a fiery wall to hold them back. People fear being close to the mountains, much less crossing them."

"Didn't you say you guide people into the Untamed Vale?" Kitlyn nudged Apples to go a little faster.

"Yes, but those who seek my services as a guide do not live around here. They are mostly explorers and travelers from afar, looking for riches or history." Sibri peered skyward. "Most of the ones who venture off without me don't return. The ones who do come back didn't go far enough to find anything."

"Doesn't seem worth it to risk." Oona grimaced. "What kind of fool would gamble their life purely to gain power, wealth, or find some lost treasure?"

"The sort of fool who would tear the heart out of the Alderswood," muttered Kitlyn.

Oona suppressed a wince. "Perhaps... but he'd never have set foot in the Untamed Vale. The man makes Cloud seem brave."

Kitlyn cackled.

Apples nickered.

Cloud snorted, seeming offended.

By Lucen, I swear these horses seem to understand us.

44

TYNDRIS

KITLYN

*N*ight threatened to fall soon after they reached the base of the mountains.

Two crumbling obelisks flanked the entrance to the mountain road, mostly shrouded in moss. The growth filled in various cracks as well as the eroded remnants of carved writing in no language Kitlyn had ever seen before. She assumed the people who used to dwell in the Untamed Vale made them, or perhaps, whatever early civilization lived in this area prior to the Grand Archmage's era. Much could change in 2,500 years.

They set up camp in the field, intending to begin the trip into the mountains after sunrise. In the midst of the evening meal, Oona jumped as if startled, then hastily looked around.

"What?" asked Kitlyn.

"Tamsen?" Oona stood. "Where are you?"

"I hope she is where she is supposed to be." Kitlyn also scanned the area. "Evie has spoiled us as caretakers. We don't ever have to scold her."

Oona sank back into a seated position. "I could have sworn she just whispered in my ear, saying Evie misses us and they hope we are safe."

"Feeling guilty for leaving them behind?" Kitlyn rubbed Oona's shoulder.

"No, I—" She stared into space. "Again! She says she's safe in bed, don't worry about her, and you don't have to scold her."

Sibri looked up from a pouch of berries and nuts she'd been eating. "Is Tamsen a mage?"

"In a manner of speaking…" Oona fidgeted. "She's a child, but yes, she does have magic."

"A person does not need to be a powerful mage to send messages." Sibri grinned. "Nothing to worry about. She is merely talking to you from far away. The spell lets her hear what goes on around the person who receives the message for a short time."

The idea of sending a message instantly across Lucernia rather than waiting days for a fast rider to deliver a letter left Kitlyn's mouth hanging open. Mages communicating back and forth or even sending word to commanders could tremendously alter the flow of battles. Or even matters of civil law. If a person committed a serious crime in a large city, every magistrate in the kingdom could be told of their deed in mere minutes. Such a seemingly trivial bit of magic impressed her more than tearing a giant root monster in half.

Oona asked about the Untamed Vale while they ate. Sibri explained she hadn't found too many books detailing the history, but believed the entire society had been wiped out by a magical war. Rakden interrupted their discussion of theoretical history to discuss plans for night watch. Considering the rimefang sighting, he wanted two-person teams. They numbered thirteen, which left Sibri on her own. However, she had the fire wand and seemed highly knowledgeable about the area, so he accepted her being alone on one watch shift.

She also saw the rimefang despite the glare from the peaks. Kitlyn studied her, still not seeing or sensing anything unusual. *Maybe she felt the ground shaking or heard them.*

Kitlyn spent a little while brushing Apples and feeding him some actual apples. Oona did the same for Cloud while baby-talking to her horse. Apples stared at them, unimpressed.

"I know, but they both seem to like it," whispered Kitlyn.

He thwapped one ear.

THE NEXT MORNING, THEY PROCEEDED UP THE MOUNTAIN ROAD.
While wide enough for three horses abreast, they kept to pairs to avoid finding themselves too cramped in the event they needed to defend themselves should something attack. All the talk of dangerous hermetic witches had the hairs on the back of Kitlyn's neck on end — or maybe Sibri's horse put her on edge. Though it acted like any other horse barring its complete lack of fear, it still gave off the same sort of eerie energy as Ulfaan.

She didn't think the man had turned himself into a horse, hired Sibri to pretend to be his owner, and come here to spy on them. Though it *might* be possible the whole 'wand' story was a lie and the magic came from the horse. Sibri also had the poise and confidence of an experienced tracker, difficult to fake. Oona had not yet accused the woman of speaking false, which she surely would have done without hesitation. She did, however, give the woman a few suspicious glances in much the same way she often did when talking to barristers or mercantile guild representatives — people so used to dealing with Lucen priests ability to sense lies they'd mastered the art of saying one thing while meaning another: statements technically true while carrying a different meaning than the words themselves stated.

As Oona explained once weeks ago, such deceptions did not feel the same as outright lies, but she still sensed a mild intent to deceive. Oona almost always challenged the barristers to speak more clearly whenever she suspected such trickery. Her not doing the same to Sibri made Kitlyn think any deception too benign to worry about. Again, she wondered if the woman might be trying not to bring up painful history.

Sibri led the way, riding by herself at the front of the group. Unless she acted as a sacrificial decoy leading her enemies to an ambush, no one who meant them ill would expose their back to the entire group. She carried herself in total ease in spite of all her warnings about the danger in the area.

She either knows we are safe or has more than a fire wand up her sleeve. Kitlyn's mind spun in circles, searching for an explanation for how this woman could be so calm. *She didn't laugh at us when Oona mentioned dragons. Oh, by Lucen… could the 'hermit witch' be Tyndris, and Sibri knows it? Or is the witch a human the dragon has enchanted to be a servant? Is Sibri the dragon's servant? Knowing there really is a dragon here and being its minion would definitely explain how she's so fearless. Doesn't explain why her horse is creepy, though.* She blinked. *Could the horse be the dragon?*

Kitlyn pushed the debate aside so she could stay alert to her surroundings. The mountain road often had tall canyon walls on either side where even creatures as small as goblins could do a ton of damage simply by dropping rocks. As the highway weaved back and forth in response to the terrain, the walls also varied in height from several stories to nonexistent. Whenever they rounded a curve where the outside edge of the road dropped off as a cliff, Oona scurried all the way against the opposite wall so she couldn't see over the edge despite the breathtaking view.

The road followed a series of long back and forth zigzags, allowing it to ascend an impassably steep slope at a shallow enough angle for horses or wagons. It made the route twenty times longer than the actual distance they covered, but going in a straight line would be impossible without the ability to fly. Kitlyn felt like a mouse making her way up a human staircase. After a few hours, they reached a right turn leading to a long, straight ascent heading directly west over the spine of the mountain range. Snowy peaks towered over them, close on both sides. At this angle, the caps didn't reflect the sunlight enough to be blinding. The highest parts of the mountains appeared to be encased in smooth ice tinted metallic silver.

About two miles into the straightaway, the road leveled off. Feathers, fur, and some unrecognizable animal parts hung from a pair of rickety wooden poles on either side of the canyon, not far from the start of flat ground.

"The witch's totems?" asked Oona.

"So some say." Sibri rode past them. "If she did put them up, she likely meant only to scare away fools. It doesn't take much effort to frighten people sometimes."

Honestly… "True." *Some people are terrified at the idea of me loving Oona.*

Oona scowled. "Those fools were so afraid of a small girl, they refused to see Lucen's truth right in front of them."

"The cave I mentioned is not far now." Sibri pointed ahead.

They kept going for perhaps a quarter mile more. There, the road widened out into a huge crater-shaped bowl containing little more than plain dirt and a few scattered weeds before continuing through a notch in the canyon wall straight ahead across the open clearing. A hint of heavily forested land appeared in the space between mountain walls above the road, lush and green despite it being autumn.

"Wow," whispered Oona.

Kitlyn looked at her, then followed her wife's stare to the right, where a huge cave opening yawned into the darkness, big enough for a small inn to fit inside. Nervous tingles washed over her stomach.

If there is a dragon here, it's definitely going to live in a place like this.

Sibri dismounted. "This is the cave I mentioned. If you wish to go inside, I suggest leaving the horses out here." She pointed off to the left. "There's a little creek running along the far wall. They can drink."

Oona slid from her saddle, as always, she seemed to float to the ground like a giant faerie alighting on a branch.

She is so graceful… except when trying to climb trees. Grinning, Kitlyn jumped down. While she lacked her wife's almost elven grace doing so, she'd gotten enough practice riding in the past few months not to feel clumsy at it. At least, the soldiers stopped snickering whenever she dismounted, and she didn't feel as though she barely avoided landing on her face each time.

Sibri led them into the huge cave.

Rakden, Beowyn, Kybern and Danos accompanied them while the other soldiers remained with the horses. Sixty yards deep in the mountain, the titanic cave opened out to an oval-shaped grand hall— not a natural cavern. Four stories of walkways, rooms, and doors surrounded them, remarkably similar to the two main libraries at Isilien. Intricate patterns covered the floor, composed of tiles in varying shades of violet, blue, white, and black. A few open alcoves off the ground floor held furniture in human size. Some appeared to be sitting rooms, others dining halls.

Oona's awestruck whistle echoed over the chamber.

"I am sorry to disappoint at the lack of a dragon." Sibri chuckled.

"But she *has* to be here." Oona flailed her arms. "We were told a dragon is in the Dawnspire Mountains."

Sibri sighed. "Rumors of dragons are not completely accurate."

"In what way?" Kitlyn gazed up at the domed ceiling, also decorated in a tile mural simulating the night sky.

"Dragons are, for the most part, *not* giant monsters." Sibri paced around between them.

"Yes, we know." Kitlyn set her hands on her hips. *Are we to spend the next twenty years searching for Tyndris?* "Dragons are highly intelligent and not monstrous. Merely large."

Sibri laughed. "No, child. They are closer to what some people call demigods. The large, reptilian beings commonly thought of as dragons are simply a form they assume for battle. Most of the confusion stems from another type of creature called drakes. *Those* are fearsome, large beasts often mistaken for dragons. However, they are not much smarter than dogs."

"Hello?" called Oona. "Is anyone here?"

Her voice echoed back twice.

"It looks abandoned... for a long time." Kitlyn approached an open alcove decorated in the manner of a sitting room. Red velvet cushions on the chairs, rich tapestries on the walls, and polished wood made it look like a noble's home. "But there is no dust or evidence of neglect here. You would think such fine furniture sitting in a cave would rot."

"This has to be a library or school..." Oona grimaced. "Or was."

Kitlyn faced her. "I cannot help but feel like you know more than you are sharing with us. We need to find the dragon known as Tyndris. We have brought something important to give her."

"Oh?" Sibri raised an eyebrow. "What?"

"Yes." Oona nodded. "A large gemstone."

Sibri waved dismissively. "Treasure to a dragon is knowledge, not large quantities of shiny metal. Even if this dragon existed, she would have little interest in a bauble no matter how valuable people consider it. Dragons have no need of human wealth. It's a mystery to me where the rumors of vast piles of gold came from."

"But it's not just a gem!" Oona flailed her arms. "Paelirron asked us to bring it to his mate."

"What?" Sibri faced her, all mirth gone from her expression.

Oona held her hands out to approximate the size. "It's a sapphire egg."

Intense blue light flared in Sibri's eyes. She glared at Oona for a second before a dense cloud of smoky light welled up around her. The two glowing eye spots flew upward, drifted apart, and expanded to the size of doors. The empty space between them and the way out of the chamber took on a distinctly non-empty, supernatural—and massive—presence.

Kitlyn edged back.

"Uhh," whispered Rakden. He stepped in front of them, as did Danos, Kybern and Beowyn.

A long, mirror-silver dragon snout drifted out of the glowing smoke, three stories above the floor, gaze locked on Oona. Heavy, hot breath blasted from the nostrils, whipping Kitlyn and Oona's hair back. In an instant, the cavern went from chilly to comfortable —if a bit moist. A clawed hand, large enough to grab Beowyn like a child's doll stepped catlike out of the mist, the head continuing to glide closer.

Dark blue energy swirled within the giant almond-shaped eyes of a distinctly annoyed dragon.

Oona attempted an apologetic smile. "Oops."

45

THE ESSENCE OF DRAGONS
OONA

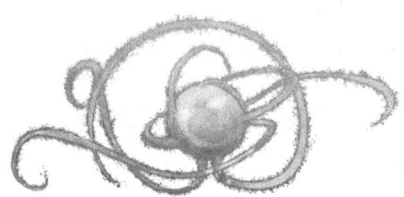

*O*ona hadn't felt so instantly afraid of the consequences of something she said since age nine.

She'd caught Aodh in a minor lie and, somewhat flippantly, pointed out Lucen saw his deceit. *Now*, she understood why he'd become so enraged over such a seemingly small thing. He'd panicked, wondering if she knew the truth of his crimes. She hadn't said anything antagonistic or stupid to the dragon to explain her instant anger.

She is still angry over Paelirron's death… merely speaking his name tore open the wound.

"I'm sorry," whispered Oona.

Kitlyn edged closer to her, whispering, "You may wish to hand over the egg now."

"Please don't be angry." Oona opened her satchel. "We're here because we want to give this to you."

Tyndris continued staring at them.

Oh, please let the magic still be working.

Shaking, Oona reached into the satchel, wanting to grab the dragon soul. A second after her hand disappeared under the flap, the bag swelled up as if she'd stuffed a whole chicken into it. She stopped trembling, exhaled in relief, and withdrew the sapphire essence. As soon as it came into view, great tears gathered at the corners of the dragon's eyes.

"Paelirron," whispered Tyndris in a voice simultaneously feminine yet tremendous.

"Let me by," whispered Oona, nudging the soldiers in front of her.

Reluctantly, Rakden and Beowyn shifted aside. Oona walked up beneath the dragon's head, holding the sapphire out in both hands as high as she could stretch her arms.

"This is his essence…" Tyndris took the sapphire egg, emitting a noise similar to a sniffle. "With this, we can have our brood. I thought he had been destroyed."

The sapphire flared bright, winking like a star before dissipating into a glowing mist the dragon inhaled. She closed her enormous eyes, head bowed. Kitlyn took Oona's hand, watching in silence. Blue energy radiated from Tyndris, shrouding her entire body in a soft dark blue glow. Minutes later, the glow faded and she opened her eyes, seeming somber and no longer furious.

"I didn't mean to upset you," said Oona.

"You did not upset me… I upset myself, expecting you to make demands in exchange for bringing Paelirron to me." Tyndris exhaled, the blast of air from her nostrils nearly taking Oona and Kitlyn off their feet.

Kitlyn caught her balance. "Is there really a hermit witch out here or… did people see your human form for the past few thousand years and make up stories?"

"There is no witch." Tyndris chuckled. "It is clear to me now why I felt drawn to you. I must have sensed Paelirron's essence nearby without recognizing it. Too much time has passed. Bringing this to me is a gift I cannot truly ever repay."

"There is something you might be able to help us with, if you are so inclined." Kitlyn walked up beside Oona. "Please understand we had every intention of bringing the essence to you without condition."

"So, I did sense desire in you after all, perhaps not in the cruel way I'd anticipated." Tyndris sat up in a cat's pose, curling her tail around her feet. "What is it you wish me to do?"

"Paelirron told us you placed a curse on Lucernia for what they did to him. Is there any way we might be able to convince you to break it?"

Oona clasped her hands in front of herself.

Tyndris let out a long, heavy sigh. "Admittedly, no humans alive now are responsible… but I do not expect them to be any less hateful today. I am surprised to see the two of you so open with your love for each other. Your kingdom's customs are so rigid, and the people adore destroying everything outside their view of what should be."

"Some things are beginning to change." Oona summoned her orb, creating thousands of tiny, glimmering points in reflection upon the dragon's shiny scales. "What Lucen wants and what people sometimes claim he wants are not the same. He made his feelings toward us known."

Kitlyn squeezed her hands into fists. "We will do everything we can to prevent anyone from abusing magic or surrendering to fear. The war showed us how someone can abuse the word of the gods to cause great harm. I admit we won't be able to prevent everyone from using magic for harmful reasons, but we can stop it from taking over again. Paelirron told us of the Grand Archmage and how our gods were once mortal."

"Child…" Tyndris leaned down, as close to eye-to-eye as she could get to them. "Why do you think *you* can do anything? What are two young girls going to be able to accomplish in an entire kingdom?"

Oona pursed her lips. "You have been living out in the middle of nowhere for quite a while."

"I am Kitlyn Talomir, and this is my wife Oona. We are presently the queens of Lucernia due to the death of Aodh Talomir."

"Ahh." Tyndris sat up again, smiling. "Now I understand. You are here to save yourselves. Easy enough. The curse will not affect you if you give up the crown."

Kitlyn held her arms out to either side. "If I knew beyond any doubt my replacement would be fair and just, I would. My only true desire is to be with Oona. I sit upon the throne of Lucernia out of duty to the people. Unlike Aodh, I do not measure my worth by how much power is at my fingertips. I am the last of my family line. Were we to abdicate the throne, it would plunge Lucernia into war all over again as the nobility clashed over the crown. Many would die for no reason other than my effort to preserve my own life."

"Yet if you remain queen, you will die young anyway… and a war of sovereignty would occur all the same." Tyndris widened one eye. "If the war is inevitable and your only desire is to be with your wife, why not preserve yourself?"

Oona bowed her head. "Because it is selfish and wrong."

"Yes. Abdicating the throne would be a choice to hurl my problems on the backs of innocent people." Kitlyn shook her head. "That is a choice I cannot make. Lucernia is still hurting from decades of pointless war. I cannot start another one and abandon our people only to protect my life."

Tears gathered at the corners of Oona's eyes.

Tyndris widened her right eye, narrowing the left. "Aodh Talomir. It is curious you do not refer to him as your father."

"He was my father only in the sense of siring me," said Kitlyn. "Due to the war and his fear of assassins, I was made to live as a common peasant girl, put to work as a castle servant when I became old enough. The truth of my identity remained unknown to me until this year."

"How… particularly cruel," said the dragon. "To show no affection for one's brood is unthinkable."

Oona resisted the urge to blurt, pushing emotion out of her mind. Since she didn't know to what extent the curse had been responsible for Aodh's crimes, she decided not to detail them, or the reason Kitlyn spoke of him at a distance.

"I did not ask to become queen." Kitlyn gestured at herself. "I wear the same armor as any of our soldiers. Power has never been my desire. Not too long ago, I believed the greatest feat my magic would ever accomplish would be to make a little boy laugh by levitating stones to fly around in the shape of a dragon."

"Yet you did not know we existed." Tyndris tilted her head. "Show me this stone dragon."

Kitlyn reached her arms out to either side, green light surrounding her fingers. A scattering of loose pebbles and stones came rolling or sliding across the room to her. Aglow in emerald light, they rose into the air and arranged themselves into the approximate shape of a dragon, the same trick she'd used over and over again to make Pim, and now Evie, laugh.

Oona rested a hand on her shoulder. "A bit easier to do that than raise Omun."

"A little." Kitlyn smiled.

"How did you learn of dragons to do this?" asked Tyndris, the sapphire-hued energy within her eyes flickering bright in amusement.

"Storybooks and drawings," said Oona. "We adored reading stories when we were younger. Many books tell of dragons, but they're all made-up."

Kitlyn directed the tiny faux dragon to glide around in lazy circles, flapping its wings.

"How has so much of the Alderswood's power come to be in a child of Lucernia?" asked Tyndris.

Kitlyn and Oona exchanged a pointed glance.

This is going to take a while.

They relayed an abbreviated version of how Aodh stole the Heart from the tree, bid his wife—Kitlyn's mother—to drink from it, and the resulting war which they'd recently brought to an end. Oona kept talking, telling of Solana's ghostly visit, their journey to Isilien, and meeting with Paelirron's ghost.

"I'm glad he is with you again in some way." Oona bowed her head, resigned to accept whatever fate the curse dictated for them. Kitlyn would never agree to abdicate the throne, and as much as she dreaded losing her, Oona also couldn't send the kingdom into chaos. She hoped the curse would take them both at once. It did not seem purposeful to make demands of a dragon. "I pray your children bring you some measure of peace. We do not mean to upset you any more than we already have. If anyone ever took Kitlyn away from me, I would feel the same as you did. It is time we return to our children. If you should reconsider, we would greatly appreciate it."

"Children?" Tyndris narrowed her eyes. "At your age?"

"Evie is my much younger sister and Tamsen is an orphan we have decided to add to our family." Oona smiled. "They are both likely worried about us being gone so long."

"Why would...?" Kitlyn looked up. "If a dragon's true form is not so different from humans... could Tamsen be a dragon?"

Oona squeaked.

Tyndris tilted her head. "What makes you ask?"

"Her eyes are two different colors, she acts a bit too brave and mature for a child of ten, and Paelirron's ghost visited her, gave her books, and taught her magic."

"Umm." Oona gave her side eye.

The dragon's chuckle sent a blast of warm air from her mouth, puffing everyone back half a step. "No. The child is human. The gift of arcane magic often lends an unusual peculiarity to a non-dragon who possesses it. In this girl's case, multicolored eyes. In another, such as Ulfaan Khera, it takes the form of a tangible air of power."

Oona breathed a sigh of relief.

"Wait... you know of him?" asked Kitlyn.

Eep! Oona stared. *Is he a dragon, too? Is that why he radiates power?*

"Yes. I sensed him soon after he returned to this kingdom." Tyndris tapped a claw on the floor, making a loud clicking.

"Should we be concerned about him?" Oona crept closer, her neck starting to hurt from making eye contact with such a large creature. "Is he a dragon?"

"No, not a dragon. As for being concerned...?" Tyndris pondered for a moment. "We do not have the ability to know what goes on in the minds of humans. However, my opinion is, if he wished to threaten your kingdom, it would have been far easier for him to do so while the war strained every resource."

"Oh, yes..." Oona relaxed. "True."

"Hmm. Why would Paelirron have sought Tamsen out and taught her, pretending to live down the street?" asked Kitlyn.

"I can only guess. His spirit would not have been able to travel too far from his essence. Perhaps he sensed a young person with the potential to become a mage and sought to give her knowledge in exchange for eventually asking her to carry his essence to me."

Or he saw the same thing the seer who mentioned the key did. Oona bit her lip. Alas, the dragon didn't sound too inclined to break the curse. After going so far across the land, Yerbin's death, and everything else, it broke her heart to simply walk away… but what else could she do? *It is as pointless to beg as it is to threaten a dragon.*

Oona hung her head. "Thank you for talking to us. I am happy you will be able to bear the children you so dearly wanted."

Kitlyn had the stubborn look in her eye she always got whenever she set herself on something, but also appeared to understand the futility of pushing a dragon. "We will cease bothering you. I wish only the best fate for you and your future offspring."

"A moment…" Tyndris stretched out on her belly, resting her chin on one forepaw. "I am curious. Tell me of your children."

Oona and Kitlyn recounted various stories of cute or funny things Evie had done, glossing over the reason she'd come to live at the castle. Kitlyn brought up how the girl looked exactly like a young version of Oona, claiming both were far too sweet and loving to be subjected to such a cruel world. Mortified and likely blushing, Oona recounted the story of meeting Tamsen, the idiots trying to execute her for being a mage, and her pivotal role in them being able to reach Paelirron.

Tyndris tapped her great claws on the floor, thinking.

Please, Lucen, let her change her mind.

"Hmm. I have lived for a—compared to you—long time. It is not often I meet humans who place the needs of others above their own so freely, or love so deeply. In my grief, perhaps my judgement of Lucernia had been overly harsh. I offer you an arrangement."

Oona clutched Kitlyn's arm, shivering with hope.

Kitlyn rested a hand on top of Oona's. "What are your terms?"

"State your agreement, as the monarchs of Lucernia, the kingdom will protect my offspring, and stand ready to fulfill a favor if some future need arises."

"As long as this favor does not require harm done to the innocent, your terms are agreeable to me," said Oona.

Tyndris nodded. "A favor I potentially may ask of you or your successor will not require harm to any person or creature undeserving of it."

"We will consider you and any dragon who does not make war on us an ally of the kingdom and subject to our protection." Kitlyn bowed. "You have my word."

"Then I shall rescind the curse. It does not escape me that you have no control over what your successors may do. However, ensure they know my curse can be reinstated in the event of betrayal."

Kitlyn clenched her jaw. "I understand."

Tyndris sat up on her rear legs, her great hands cupped in front of her nose as if about to drink. She breathed thin streams of black vapor into her hands, then drew them apart, dispersing the mist.

Kitlyn grunted at the same instant a jolt of searing heat rocked Oona's skeleton, there and gone too fast to make her cry out in pain.

"It is done," whispered Tyndris.

"I felt..." Oona glanced down at herself as if to make sure she still existed, then leapt to embrace Kitlyn, holding her tight. They didn't have to live in constant fear of death—at least from a curse they had no defense against. Overwhelming relief took the strength from her legs.

For once, Oona didn't cry first.

46

THE FAVOR OF DEATH

KITLYN

Soldiers waiting by the horses nearly fainted when Tyndris walked outside in her dragon form.

Because the people of Lucernia no longer believed such creatures existed, Tyndris decided to show herself in a most grand fashion, by flying Kitlyn and Oona back to Cimril. Kitlyn asked—though technically ordered even if she didn't phrase it as a command—the soldiers who escorted them to return to the castle without need to rush, while also escorting Apples and Cloud. While Apples could probably handle being carried by a dragon, Cloud's heart would explode from terror.

Tyndris used magic to levitate Kitlyn and Oona up onto her back, then leapt into the air. Oona yelped and held on to Kitlyn, trembling. Riding on Omun's shoulder had strained her fear of high places. Within thirty seconds of leaving the ground, they'd gone many times his height into the sky. It didn't help being in the mountains already put them at high altitude, making the ground in the distance all the lower.

Admittedly, Kitlyn spent the first fifteen or so minutes clinging to one of the silver spines along the dragon's back for dear life as well, but eventually calmed enough to take in the view. The land below them resembled the giant cloth map on the table in the war room.

This is unbelievable. Only the gods see Lucernia like this, from so far above.

"Look, Oona... the Churning Deep... and I think that's Eastmarch. The pine forest around Imric is still green. All the other woods are orange and brown." She twisted to look behind them at the Untamed Vale west of the mountains, the entire region covered in still-green forest. Beyond lay an endless swath of deep blue. "I've never seen the ocean before."

Oona squeaked.

"May I ask a silly question?" called Kitlyn.

"You may," said Tyndris.

"Why did your horse feel so strange?"

The dragon laughed. "I conjured it the morning we left Overbrook."

Not a real horse. Magic. No wonder it wasn't afraid of the rimefang. Kitlyn leaned up tall, wind in her face, and let out a nervous cheer. *I hope we are ready for how much things will change.*

Admittedly, they had been wandering north to south around the plains for several days, but the flight to Cimril felt as if it passed in mere moments. As they glided in over the Mistral Wood, Kitlyn finally got up the nerve to ask if dragons laid eggs.

Tyndris laughed. "Perhaps they do in your storybooks. It is not so different from humans for us."

Becoming pregnant by absorbing energy out of a giant sapphire is pretty different from humans. Kitlyn grinned. *I wish I could do something similar, just sniff a gem and solve my succession worries. Having a blood heir would greatly settle my fears for the future. Even if Oona and I live to ninety, we may not have enough time to convince the people to accept us trying to shift power to a council. Lucernia might be stuck as a monarchy, but we can try to make it a monarchy concerned for the people.*

Oona kept quiet the entire flight, but did manage to peek a few times.

Soon, they neared the walls of Cimril. Kitlyn prodded Oona into summoning a glowing Lucen symbol in the sky—so none of the archers opened fire. The first sounds of panic among the citizens petered out to stunned silence once the giant, glowing Lucen symbol appeared. When they landed in the street by the castle's front gate moments later, the entire city seemed to grind to a halt. A few hundred people stared in frightened shock at the huge silver dragon.

Tyndris crouched low enough for them to slide down to the street, then stood back to her full height, stretching her wings. She seemed about to leap into the air, but hesitated, tucking her wings while twisting her head sideways to peer at them.

"Kitlyn... Oona," whispered the dragon.

They leaned closer.

"I abandoned my sorrowful rage, and the curse, because I have never before encountered two humans who so fully knew love... for each other, for your citizens, even for my mate. I felt your sorrow at what happened to Paelirron, and for that, you have my gratitude and respect."

Kitlyn squeezed Oona's hand.

"Thank you," whispered Oona.

Tamsen came running out of the castle courtyard, Evie and Pim trailing behind her, squealing in delight. Upon seeing the dragon, Tamsen ran faster. Evie skidded to a stop, eyes wide as dinner plates. Pim slowed to a walk, his face stuck in an expression of 'whoa.'

"You found her!" Tamsen—looking entirely respectable and quite unlike a beggar in a nice white dress—stopped a few paces away from the dragon's leg, gazing up in awe.

"Hmm." Tyndris scooped the child up in one hand, lifting her close to one eye to get a better look at her. "Perhaps I shall have reason to visit again. For a small one, you are quite brave."

Tamsen grinned.

The dragon set the girl down, stretched her enormous wings, and leapt into the sky.

Everyone on the street turned in unison, watching her fly off to the west. A few people fainted.

Oona rested her head on Kitlyn's shoulder, sniffling.

Evie crashed into them. "You're back! Yay!" Giggling, she ran circles around them making happy noises.

"What?" Kitlyn patted her back. "This is not the time for tears."

Tamsen walked over to stand beside them.

"I'm emotional because she told the truth about ending the curse." Oona wiped her face.

Kitlyn leaned back to make eye contact. "I got the sense the curse ended when my bones zapped me."

"Yes, well… you aren't guaranteed to die early in a tragic way."

"I am not afraid." Kitlyn took her hand. "Tenebrea seems to like you. I am sure she will welcome us together whenever our time comes. Hopefully, not for quite a while yet."

Oona squeaked.

"What?" asked Kitlyn.

"Something Tyndris said… I just realized what she meant. 'A shiny enough prize can make even the wisest man fall prey to greed.'"

"Yes…?" Kitlyn raised an eyebrow. "She was talking about Aodh."

"No." Oona shook her head and whispered, "I think she meant Lucen. After he led the revolution against the Grand Archmage, he was, technically, the king of Valendar. That's why I felt as if she wasn't speaking the full truth when she said 'a previous king'. She knew I assumed she meant Aodh, and let me believe it."

Kitlyn pondered. "What do you think she meant?"

"Lucen forgive me…" Oona exhaled. "I believe she vented anger over Paelirron's death, the people twisting Lucen's war on mages into a desire to destroy everything not human. The shiny prize of becoming a god…"

"Oo…" Kitlyn kissed her. "What if she intended to tell us gods are not perfect, merely powerful? *Incredibly* powerful, but they still have all the emotions that make us human… including kindness and love. I believe Tenebrea considers you a friend."

Oona gasped, hand over her mouth. "We should not take their aid for granted."

"I know you will never do that. And so do they." Kitlyn smiled. "They also know it's okay to drop the formality in private, like we do with the staff."

"It does this old man's heart good to see the two of you back home unhurt." Beredwyn strolled up to them, gazing at the sky. "I imagine the two of you have *quite* the tale this time."

"Oh, yes." Kitlyn laughed. "We certainly do."

fin

ACKNOWLEDGMENTS

Thank you for reading The Sapphire Soul – Eldritch Heart #3!

I'd also like to thank Gwen for being the inspiration to take this series from a couple of jotted-down ideas to first one novel, then two... now three.

Thanks to Lee Sheridan for editing, Amalia Chitluescu for the amazing cover art, and Ricky Gunawan for the chapter illustrations.

ABOUT THE AUTHOR

Originally from South Amboy NJ, Matthew has been creating science fiction and fantasy worlds for most of his reasoning life. Since 1996, he has developed the "Divergent Fates" world, in which *Division Zero, Virtual Immortality, The Awakened Series, The Harmony Paradox, and the Daughter of Mars series* take place. Along with being an editor at Curiosity Quills press, he has worked in IT and technical support.

Matthew is an avid gamer, a recovered WoW addict, Gamemaster for two custom RPG systems, and a fan of anime, British humour, and intellectual science fiction that questions the nature of reality, life, and what happens after it.

He is also fond of cats.

Visit me online at:
    Facebook: https://www.facebook.com/MatthewSCoxAuthor
    Pinterest: https://www.pinterest.com/matthewcox10420/
    Goodreads: https://www.goodreads.com/author/show/7712730.Matthew_S_Cox
    Email: mcox2112@gmail.com

OTHER BOOKS BY MATTHEW S. COX

Divergent Fates Universe Novels

Division Zero series

- Division Zero
- Lex De Mortuis
- Thrall
- Guardian
- Harbinger
- The Shadow Fixer

The Awakened series

- Prophet of the Badlands
- Archon's Queen
- Grey Ronin
- Daughter of Ash
- Zero Rogue
- Angel Descended

Daughter of Mars series

- The Hand of Raziel
- Araphel
- Ghost Black

Virtual Immortality series

- Virtual Immortality
- The Harmony Paradox

Prophet of the Badlands Series

- Prophet's Journey

Divergent Fates Anthology

(Fiction Novels - Adult)

The Roadhouse Chronicles Series

- One More Run
- The Redeemed
- Dead Man's Number

Faded Skies series

- Heir Ascendant
- Ascendant Unrest
- Ascendant Revolution

Temporal Armistice Series

- Nascent Shadow
- The Shadow Collector
- The Gate to Oblivion
- The Queen of Discord

Vampire Innocent series

- A Nighttime of Forever
- A Beginner's Guide to Fangs
- The Artist of Ruin
- The Last Family Road Trip
- The Phantom Oracle
- How Not to Summon Demons
- Ordinary Problems of a College Vampire
- A Vampire's Guide to Surviving Holidays

- An Introduction to Paranormal Diplomacy
- A Vampire's Guide to Adulting
- How to Stop a Vampire War in Six Easy Steps
- Ancient Vampire Death Cults and Other Annoyances

Standalones

- Wayfarer: AV494
- Axillon99
- Chiaroscuro: The Mouse and the Candle
- The Spirits of Six Minstrel Run
- Sophie's Light
- The Far Side of Promise anthology
- Operation: Chimera (with Tony Healey)
- The Dysfunctional Conspiracy (with Christopher Veltmann)
- Of Myth and Shadow
- The Girl Who Found the Sun

Winter Solstice series (with J.R. Rain)

- Convergence
- Containment
- Catalyst
- Catacombs

Alexis Silver series (with J.R. Rain)

- Silver Light
- Deep Silver
- Silver Quarrel
- Silver Crucible

Samantha Moon Origins series (with J.R. Rain)

- New Moon Rising

- Moon Mourning
- Haunted Moon

Vampire For Hire series (with J.R. Rain)

- Moon Master
- Dead Moon
- Lost Moon
- Vampire Destiny
- Infinite Moon
- Vampire Empress

Maddy Wimsey series (with J.R. Rain)

- The Devil's Eye
- The Drifting Gloom
- Dark Mercy

Samantha Moon Case Files series (with J.R. Rain)

- Blood Moon

Immortal Operative (with J.R. Rain)

- Broken Ice

Four Elements series (with J.R. Rain)

- The Elementalist
- The Black Rose
- The Wakefield Curse

Young Adult Novels

The Eldritch Heart Series

- The Eldritch Heart
- The Cursed Crown
- The Sapphire Soul

Evergreen Series

- Evergreen
- The World That Remains
- The Lucky Ones
- Nuclear Summer
- The Nuclear Frontier

Progenitor Series

- Out of Sight
- Out of Mind

Diary of a Teenage Fey

(Short story series)

- Elder Horror
- The Hag of Barrow Falls
- Babysitter's Nightmare
- Lharakki
- Bauble for a Soul
- Simulacrum
- Amorphous
- Manticore

Standalones

- Caller 107
- The Summer the World Ended
- Nine Candles of Deepest Black
- The Forest Beyond the Earth

Middle Grade Novels

The Adventures of Ubergirl series

- My Dad is a Mad Scientist
- Aliens Ate My Homework
- The End of all Halloweens
- Dr. Infinity and the Soul Smasher

Tales of Widowswood series

- Emma and the Banderwigh
- Emma and the Silk Thieves
- Emma and the Silverbell Faeries
- Emma and the Elixir of Madness
- Emma and the Weeping Spirit

Standalones

- Citadel: The Concordant Sequence
- The Cursed Codex
- The Menagerie of Jenkins Bailey